BWB

(4)

50¢

THE FOREIGNER

D1714000

BY ZOE SAADIA

Beyond the Great River
The Foreigner
Troubled Waters
The Warpath
Echoes of the Past

Two Rivers
Across the Great Sparkling Water
The Great Law of Peace
The Peacekeeper

Shadow on the Sun
Royal Blood
Dark Before Dawn
Raven of the North

The Highlander
Crossing Worlds
The Emperor's Second Wife
Currents of War
The Fall of the Empire
The Sword
The Triple Alliance

Obsidian Puma
Field of Fire
Heart of the Battle
Warrior Beast
Morning Star
Valley of Shadows

THE FOREIGNER

People of the Longhouse, Book 2

ZOE SAADIA

Copyright © 2015 by Zoe Saadia

All rights reserved. This book or any portion thereof may not be reproduced,
transmitted or distributed in any form or by any means whatsoever, without prior
written permission from the copyright owner, unless by reviewers who wish to
quote brief passages.

For more information about this book, the author and her work, visit
www.zoesaadia.com

ISBN: 1539650901
ISBN-13: 978-1539650904

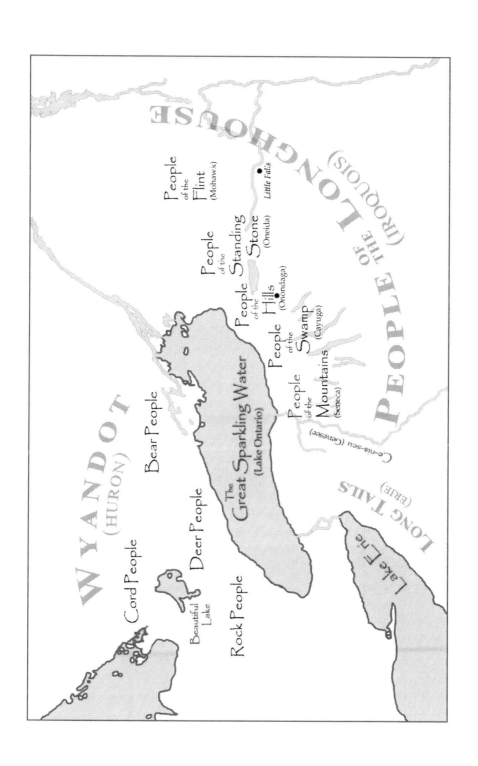

CHAPTER 1

The scream pierced the air, rolling down the hill, echoing between the trees. High-pitched and desperate, it made the men jump, not only the intensity of it, but the close proximity.

Abandoning their work, their hands dripping blood, clothes and faces smeared with the same, they froze, listening intently.

"What in the name—"

Another shriek made Ganayeda forget the half-carved carcass he had been working on since high morning, after hunting an impressive amount of both young and mature deer. Delighted with the quick turn their expedition was taking, having spent less than two days tracking the deer and less than half that time on trapping it, slaying enough perfectly good species to call their foray a success, he was a content man. They would finish here quickly and be back home no later than the next day or so, thank all the Sky Spirits.

Otherwise, they might have missed the return of the foreign delegation that was reported to descend upon High Springs, his hometown and the second largest settlement of their land, out of nowhere. Delegations from many large and small settlements of the Onondaga People were traveling to see the powerful War Chief, to ask for this wise, influential man's help and advice or representation, trusting him to solve problems and disputes. Often, messengers from other nations would come as well, relying on the prominent leader's judgment and his vast influence on this or that member of the Great Council.

Yet, all these petitioners belonged to the League of the Five Nations. While, this time, the visitors were complete foreigners from the far west. Long Tails People, or Raccoon People as they were sometimes called by their immediate neighbors, the members of the Great League, the Keepers of the Western Door, dwelling so far, far away toward the lands of the setting sun.

What these people wanted only the Great Spirits knew, but the Onondaga War Chief had agreed to receive them, against the advice of some leading men, adamant in his desire to hear what the foreigners had to say. He had taken them to Onondaga Town, where the Head of the Great Council resided, but they were supposed to come back toward the beginning of the Harvest Festival, something he, Ganayeda, had no intention of missing. A rising leader of his caliber, and the son of the mentioned War Chief, he was not about to be absent. Out of curiosity, yes, but out of loyalty as well. Father was inappropriately open-minded when it came to foreigners, and if these people meant trouble, then he wanted to be there to help. Although, now…

Charging uphill, his nerves taut, senses probing, hand clutching his bow tightly, his preferred weapon against forest dwellers and the human enemy alike, he still made sure that his knife was tucked safely in its sheath, though not cleaned off, dripping fat and meat juices, as his mind raced to determine what the trouble might be.

A raiding party assaulting some women? No, it was not possible.

Aside from no settlements being nearby—even Lone Hill, a large and fairly influential village spread at the distance of at least half a day's walk, was too far away to be the one suffering an attack—other suspicious noises reached his ears, grunting and growling, accompanied by panted breath. No human foe was promised by these. And so were the intensifying cries, now very close, belonging to another woman, with the screams of the first one turning into shrieks filled with pain. Not good.

Bursting upon a clearing, he already knew what he would find and so wasn't surprised. The bear was huge, grizzled and dirtied, standing on its hind legs, towering full length, roaring at two cowering women, who were obviously beyond the normal state of terror, unable to even scream. Its fur swaying wetly with the sudden movement, the pointed nose smeared with a mixture of mud and blood, the creature whirled toward the new danger, snarling in fury.

Bringing his bow up, fitting the arrow as he ran, Ganayeda felt his men close behind, following dutifully, ready to be of help. It reassured him. He wanted to believe he could face an enraged forest giant if need be—he had encountered and shot quite a few black bears, angered or not—but grizzled bears were a different matter, such dangerous beasts, ill-tempered, violent, strong, as fast as coyotes and as agile. To call a fight on such a dangerous spirit was a feat that demanded a sort of bravery not many could muster.

With a twinge of shame, he remembered Father's cherished necklace of claws. When very young, younger than the last of his sons, Father had slain a grizzled bear, alone and unaided, facing the beast in no less than a hand-to-hand, killing it with his knife. Mother never tired of telling them this tale, while Father would shake his head and grin in a conspiratorial manner. He had been courting her at that time, he had told them once, the unattainable, upright beauty that she was, so, of course, there was a need to do a few stupid things in order to make her look at him. This version of the events, she didn't like in the least, losing her smile and wearing a troubled frown whenever he said this. It had happened back in her people's lands, she would say, giving him a reproachful look, when the vicious bear had been the easiest of Father's challenges or troubles.

With his arrow swishing, sticking into the greasy pelt, he groped for another, not daring to take his eyes off the creature. It dropped onto all fours and charged with disheartening speed, but whirled again as one of the girls, silly thing that she was, probably blind with panic, rushed toward the creature instead of away from it. Stumbling on a clump of roots, she squeaked something inaudible and went sprawling straight into the bear's path, hardly five, six paces from the reach of the smudged paws.

More arrows swished, and as Ganayeda threw himself forward, aiming as he rolled, the foul smell enveloped him, and a powerful presence made his head reel. So much fury! He could feel it seeping through the panting nostrils, spilling out of the rumbling mouth together with the dark outpour, mixing with the stench of fresh blood and some other discharges.

His arrow had sailed straight into its eye, but seemingly not deterred, the beast charged anyway, sweeping the woman out of its way with one powerful push of the bedraggled paw. She went flying like a corn-husk doll, her limbs dangling, but Ganayeda had no time to watch the course of her flight.

Tearing at his quiver so viciously some of its decorations came off, he groped for the next arrow, rolling away, hurling himself into the nearest cluster of bushes. Not that such a meager cover would stop the enraged monster, but he had to settle for what was at hand.

The bear was pounding at the shrubs, right and left, wavering like a man who had gone into a state of talking to the spirits. It was impossible to aim in all the breaking mess, the stench and his fear overwhelming, making the world around him fade, disappear. All he could see was the foulness of the torn mouth, the putrid clouds coming out of it along with the vicious gurgling, desperate for only one thing: to rip off his flesh, to contaminate, to defile it.

Outside himself, as if in a dream, he watched his hands pulling at the bowstring until they shook, releasing the arrow, to dart through the entanglement of branches, then dive straight into the dreadful, heinous darkness.

The deafening thud was the next sound his mind managed to register. It shook the earth, and while his body was busy crashing through the surrounding shrubs, he wondered if the creature had decided to smash him instead of tearing him apart. Why else would he roll in the bushes this way, and why else was he, Ganayeda, struggling to break onto the open ground?

Back between the trees, the hubbub was overpowering. People were running all around, talking and yelling, and as he got to his feet, they surrounded him, making the pounding of his heart so much worse. He needed to understand, to appraise the situation. He needed to get a gulp of fresh air, too. If he did this, he knew, his mind may be able to start working again.

"Are you hurt?" As one of his fellow hunters caught his shoulder, squeezing it painfully but reassuringly even so, Ganayeda found it easier to get a grip of his senses.

"Yes, yes, I'm good," he mumbled, then swallowed to clear his voice. "Is it dead?"

"Oh, yes; now it is!" The man's face beamed at him, his pride spilling. "Your last arrow took the mighty giant away, at long last. What a marvelous shot it was!"

"Straight into his mouth!" another man cried out.

He remembered the roaring, the rancid depth, the powerful paws clawing at him, determined to take him away. So he wasn't wrong in thinking that his arrow had gone through.

"Let me pass." Pushing himself on, not sure that his limbs would have enough strength to take those necessary few paces, he nodded at people, trying to acknowledge or reassure, or maybe hide his inner turmoil, he didn't know for sure.

Kneeling beside the crumbled beast, he closed his eyes, welcoming the respite. While seeing the mighty forest giant off, asking for his forgiveness and understanding, he knew that his taut nerves would relax, enough to be able to face people, to sort it all out and make everything proceed as it should.

"What a marvelous face-to-face it was. A privilege to see!"

The murmurs reached him, as he rose back to his feet, ready to face them now, taking in the crying, a small, lonely sound. The girl, he remembered. Was she still alive?

A glance in that direction told him that it was not that simple. She was curled next to an inanimate form, wrapped around herself, clutching her pulled-up knees, shaking like a leaf in the storm, sobbing uncontrollably. Another girl was crying nearby, and a few of his fellow hunters knelt beside her, their grave silence telling it all.

He made his way toward them, surprised with the steadiness of his paces. His legs felt as though they were tied too loosely to his body, not strong enough to support him, not for real.

"How badly..." The question hung in the air, unnecessary to finish. He watched the woman's broken body, one leg folded strangely, in an unnatural way, her upper parts a bloodied mess, one side of her face the same. She was still breathing, gulping the air in a noisy, desperate way, her chest barely moving, not reflecting the efforts of her bleeding face and mouth.

"See her off." He motioned to one of his men quietly, not willing to squat and pray beside the dying woman himself. Hurt females were always a sight he could do without.

Turning his attention to the living girl, he narrowed his eyes. "What were you doing here all alone?"

The terrified gaze flew at him, registering no understanding. Then the renewed bout of hysterical sobbing took over. She was a pretty thing, he noticed, despite the mud and the bruises.

"We were … we were gathering berries," the second girl whispered. "Berries and nuts."

As though that explained it all. "So far away from your village?"

"Well, yes." She cleared her throat. "We, we wanted to get the best, the best fruits, you see. Nearby Lone Hill it's all been picked already. It's…" Her voice trailed off under the open doubt that his gaze must have been reflecting. Gulping, she glanced at the sobbing mess her friend presented, but it only made the wailing worse.

"One might think a herd of a thousand deer descended on their village," muttered one of the hunters. "You are almost halfway to Onondaga Town here. Who would pick all the berries and nuts so deep inland?"

But, of course, these women were in no condition to preach at them about prudency, or to catch them in possible lies, not with one of them scared and the other shaken too badly even to react, maybe wounded too, shattered by the terrible experience. He took a deep breath.

"Let us part our forces," he said, walking away briskly. "Osweda and Iheks will stay with me, help me skin the bear, while the rest of you go back and finish the carving. We should be ready to start back tomorrow with dawn, even with this delay." He narrowed his eyes, estimating the sunrays that managed to break through the thick foliage. No, they wouldn't have enough daylight to finish before nightfall. "Send word to our men upstream. I want them to come and camp with us tonight, whether they have hunted enough or not. As for the women," he eyed the pitiful group thoughtfully, "they'll stay with us until we finish. Then, some of us will escort them back to Lone Hill."

Their lack of enthusiasm poured from their frowns, expressed most clearly in the rolling eyes. He shared their feelings. Such an annoying detour, and just as everyone was eager to be back home in time for the beginning of the festivities.

"We can't let them go alone. Not in this condition, frightened and hurt. Not to mention the need to carry their dying companion."

The dusk was spreading fast, too fast. Ganayeda squinted against the disappearing light, knowing that they would have to cut the skinning of the bear short, despite the job only being half done in the best of his estimation.

The animal was too large and old and dirty, difficult to spread with no proper tools, its pelt vast and stiff, full of holes from the multitude of arrows that had pierced it, not easy to clean without causing more damage.

The padding of fat that lined it from the inside was so thick it would fill more than a few jars, and even back at the camp, they didn't have that many vessels with them, even if he decided to pour out all the water they carried. Not enough to collect half of what the old bear was yielding, in fact. A pity. Bear fat was useful, highly praised, good for everything, from cooking and making fire-arrows, to decorating and tending hair. There was always sunflower oil, if course, more readily available, as not many hunters managed to supply the animal fat, to kill a beast as vicious, as unstoppable as—

He pushed the memory away, ice filling his stomach, making his limbs weak, like it had several times through the skinning, every time he let his thoughts wander back to the terrible encounter – the heat, the stench, the viciousness of the bloodthirsty monster.

Wiping his brow with the back of his hand, although by this time it didn't matter, as all of him was slick and greasy, enough to make a fire arrow out of him, Ganayeda glanced at the darkening sky. No, no point in trying to work on. They wouldn't manage.

"Let us fold it as it is," he said, shrugging. "With paws and legs and all. We'll bury his head and his insides and be gone. No chance to finish before dark anyway, and the worst is still ahead of us. Scraping the fat and the rest of the meat will take us another morning, with the help of the rest of our people."

"If they have finished with the deer." Straightening up with a loud sigh, Iheks eased his shoulders. "Because if they did, we'll all be on that bear of yours, and this way, it'll go much faster."

"I don't believe they are done. There were many carcasses, much meat to deal with." Using a sturdy stick, he began to jab at the soft ground, pushing the chunks of it away. They didn't even have proper tools for digging. He wanted to curse.

"What about the women?" asked Osweda, picking up another stick to round up the scattered insides of the beast.

"What about them?"

"Do we take them back first thing in the morning?"

"Yes."

"Stupid foxes." Osweda's voice came out muffled, as he struggled to make the slimy pelt behave, almost buried beneath it. "People of Lone Hill are nothing but annoying villagers with no good sense. It's a wonder they have a representative in the Great Council. They shouldn't have, if you ask me. Such a small, stupid village."

Ganayeda blinked to make the sweat accumulating above his eyes go away. There was no point in wiping it with his limbs; it'd only make the grease spread more thickly. "Their representative is a good man. A wise, reasonable person. Someone worth listening to."

He remembered the man staying in their longhouse every time he would arrive from High Springs, usually on his way to the annual meeting of the Great Council. Father insisted on honoring this village's representative to such degree. Both were friends of many summers, their connection going back to the Great Peacemaker, or so the rumor had it. Before Lone Hill's Clans Council elected this man to replace the deceased representative, he had served under Father for many moons as this or that warriors' leader, always around and involved in organizing events and delegations, rather than raiding someone else's lands. Since the Great Peacemaker, there were no places to raid, no troublesome areas that wouldn't force the warriors walk or sail for half a moon and more just to reach their destination.

Unless they were willing to leave their native Onondaga towns and move eastward or westward, to live among the Keepers of either Western or Eastern Door of the confederacy, something his younger brother actually did, leaving close to an entire span of seasons ago, to disappear into the mists of the Great River of their father's former people.

Deepening the pit with the desperation of a person determined to get it done no matter how badly equipped, Ganayeda still couldn't fight the hint of a smile, wondering if the smaller party of hunters he had sent on a side mission had returned to their main camp as directed, with his unruly, high-spirited sibling among them.

They should have by now, he knew, and maybe tonight he would finally find the chance to have a good talk with his brother, something he had counted on since the beginning of this journey, as only a day before the planned expedition the young man had fallen upon the town, coming out of nowhere, sunburned and weathered, sporting new scars; changed, matured, full of purpose, with an exotic-looking girl of unknown origins in tow.

So much like the notorious troublemaker, thought Ganayeda, to do something like that, to fish a strange-looking creature out of the far east, dragging her all the way here, demanding the adoption ceremony and the full acceptance of his family and his town as though the girl had been a proper Longhouse People's woman.

Well, there had been nothing unlawful in such a demand, of course, still people just didn't do that. One could bring himself a woman from all sorts of places, from the east and from the west, from all over the Five Nations' lands. Even people from across the Great Sparkling Water were acceptable, enemies or not. After all, their own beloved mother was born a Crooked Tongue, coming out of these cold, misty lands, following their father, whom she fell in love with many moons and seasons ago. No one remembered her dubious origins these days. A Clan Mother of their longhouse and a leading member of their entire Clans Council, she was the most respectable woman, her accented way of speech notwithstanding. Crooked Tongues were still people, even if fierce enemies.

But the savages inhabiting the distant forests beyond the Great River of the Flint People? No, there was a limit to any acceptance.

Or should have been, he decided. And soon, if not tonight then tomorrow, he would have to find the opportunity to talk to the wild rascal, to find out what he was up to. Because this was the main reason he had insisted on the young man joining this hunt. A freshly returned warrior, Okwaho had protested, claiming his right to rest after his long journey, all the way from the Flint People's farthest settlement and only Great Spirits know where else. It must be tiring, indeed, to travel so far, but he, Ganayeda, the man's elder brother, deserved to hear all about the youngster's adventures, and before the entire land up to the Onondaga Lake had heard every possible detail. Hence, there he was, the young troublemaker, trudging along, making faces.

He tried to cover the newly blossoming grin, measuring the pit with his gaze.

"This will do. Shove it all in."

Osweda said nothing, doing as he was told. This was the best thing about his old friend, the ability to understand what needed to be done without spending one's strength on unnecessary talk. He watched Iheks struggling with the passable bundle he had made out of the unruly pelt.

"Now let us be off. We have earned a good meal and a thorough washing, haven't we?"

The light was almost gone, when the delicious aroma near their camp enveloped them, making their mouths water. Relatively clean after a quick washing, they hastened their step, not needing to coordinate their actions, even though their heavy burden was spread evenly between the three of them.

"How many carcasses were left for the cleaning tomorrow?" he asked those who came to greet them.

"Not many."

In the light of quite a few fires, the clearing looked friendly, accommodating, bursting with life, but in a cozy manner. The bloody scenery that had given it the appearance of a battlefield back at high noon was gone, the unnecessary parts of the game cleaned off, placed in the fork of a tree or buried with proper prayers and words of gratitude, not marring the peacefulness of the woods.

"Hungry?" They all peered at him, eyes glittering with mirth, baiting.

"What do you think?"

Their grins matched his.

"Where are the others? The second party?" He reached for the juicy cuts, not bothering to conceal his eagerness, squatting next to the larger fire, letting out a sigh of relief. "Did you send them a message, tell them to come here?"

"They sent word before that." Ahen, a hunter of his own age, as good and experienced, another old friend, pushed the flat bark that served them as a plate closer to the newcomers. "Said they had spotted a nice little herd. They are trying to trap it." A quick glance at the sky. "Maybe already did—if they were wise enough to do what we did, to track the deer along their drinking path."

"Ohneganos is leading them, and he is good." Ganayeda shrugged, reaching for more meat, picking the juiciest, less crispy slice. "I hope my brother gives him no trouble."

Iheks' grin spread to the widest possible. "The young beast would if he could. Although," fiddling with his pipe, a pretty, lovingly carved-out affair, the man chuckled, "maybe that particular buck has calmed down. Come to think of it, he looks different, that one. A span of seasons out there, in the lands of the rising sun, did him good. He looks matured."

"I hope so." Ganayeda grinned again. "I missed that wild spirit, although it was calmer at home without him getting bored every now and then, coming up with wild schemes, eager to fight someone, anyone. He would have declared war on Onondaga Town if he could. I swear I heard him saying how this town might have been taken, its perfectly steep hill and a double row of palisade or not. He was so eager to prove his worth as a warrior."

"Well, with such a father and older brother, one might understand the youngster's frustration. Not easy to keep up with this sort of competition."

Ganayeda shrugged. "There is no competition. Okwaho should live up to the standards of our people, not certain members of his family or the community."

But deep down, he knew his friend was right, and the knowledge of it warmed his heart. Yes, he was not easy to eclipse, thank all the Great Spirits for that. Father was way above everyone and everything in the merit and talent and brilliance of his ways, too perfect to even try to emulate. Not a single man in the lands of Five Nations would dare to dispute this claim. And yet, he, Ganayeda, the man's eldest son, hadn't done that badly. Successful, respected, fulfilling the promise he was claimed to display in his tender years. Oh, yes, his younger brother must have had a hard time, trying to live up to all of this, having too little diligence or patience and too much of an opinion and drive.

He shrugged again. "Fancy taking Flint People's names. Okwaho? What was wrong with our word for wolf?"

They rolled their eyes in unanimous agreement.

"I admit I won't refuse to hear all about his adventures," said one of the men from across the fire. "They say he brought an outlandish woman from beyond the Great River of the Flint People, from the places no one has even seen or heard of."

"Yes, he did." Wiping his mouth with the back of his hand, Ganayeda frowned. "I saw her only briefly as yet. Mother was busy making her feel at home, which means putting her to work, I suppose, doing all the women things. With the Harvest Festivities upon us, they have enough to do, all our women." He grinned. "Nevertheless, I'm sure our wives will have a detailed report on that fox by the time we come back."

"Can she speak our tongue?"

"Probably not. I wonder how he talks to her."

"He doesn't. Why would that young buck spend his time on an idle talk, eh?" Iheks' roaring laughter made the others around their fire chuckle as well. "Is she pretty?"

"No, she is not. The most outlandish thing you have ever seen." Grinning, Ganayeda reached for another cut. "But the lack of ability to talk must be of help. Yes, with women, maybe it's better this way. Sometimes I wish Jideah would speak in a tongue I didn't understand."

This drew more laughter. He picked another crispy piece, thinking of her, his wife of quite a few summers, a good woman, hard-working, ambitious, opinionated, with enough influence in her smallest clan of the town to help his own advancement along. Saucy and outspoken, prone to irritability and complaints, she was nevertheless a good wife and mother, a peer, a companion, a reasonable person. Unlike some of his peers, he had nothing to complain about. Still, like all wives, she was difficult to handle at times, capable of nagging, when not arguing, either forcefully or by pleading, getting her point across until he would give in and do what she required. Women!

The thought made him remember, and he looked around, noticing the small gathering on the edge of the clearing.

"Speaking of women, how do our guests behave?"

"Well enough. They have been quiet, so far. Relatively. Kept to themselves. Lots of crying and wailing, but nothing to give us trouble."

"Did someone talk to them? Give them food?"

"Of course." One of the men shook his head, while the others frowned, thrown out of their light mood. "They didn't want to eat, which is understandable, but they know it's here and offered. As for the talking, well, they have each other."

He nodded, recognizing the good sense of their ways, knowing that he would have to go and talk to these women, despite the assurances of his peers. Until delivered to their home village, they were his responsibility.

"Your fight against the old giant was a sight to behold." One of the men shook his head. "Not a vision one would forget in a hurry."

Ganayeda suppressed a shudder, conquering the new wave of fear with an effort, the mere memory of the charging beast making his feet tickle—the sinister foulness of the panting breath, the terrible roaring, the vicious determination to get him regardless of every arrow and wound, unstoppable, wicked.

"I shouldn't have drawn his attention to me, not before shooting all the arrows." Desperate to conceal his agitation, he studied the dripping piece of meat, as though not sure whether to devour it or not. His stomach was still rumbling, but his taste for the delicious food had suddenly faded. "It was stupid of me."

"Why did you?"

"That silly girl, she panicked and rushed straight into the path of the enraged monster. Stupid fox. She had no chance, unless someone took his attention away from her."

"How gallant of you," said Ahen with a chuckle. "And she is a pretty fox, too. Even with all the mud and the sobbing. They washed their faces after taking care of their friend's body," he added, as an afterthought.

"Did they find something elevated to put the body on?"

"No. I think they just spread it on a blanket we gave them."

He got to his feet resolutely, welcoming the distraction. Somehow, the cozy atmosphere of yet another hunting day, a good, successful foray, just wasn't there. Was it something about him? He didn't know, but the walk calmed his nerves, and upon nearing the mournful figures, he felt better.

"*Wipe your tears...*"

The words of the formal condoling ceremony came easily, but his gaze wandered, assessing the situation, taking in their pale, haunted faces that turned to him, wide-eyed and as though expectant. He eyed the inanimate figure wrapped in a blanket, looking surprisingly peaceful, unlike her living peers.

"She needn't touch the ground," he said, glancing at the surrounding trees. None offered a comfortable interweaving of branches. "We'll put some of the firewood to use. Make a platform down here."

"Her rites can't begin before we return ... before the faith-

keepers of our village … her clan." One of the girls was sti
over her words, her grief rocking her, making her voice sn.
"Her family … the faith-keepers of her clan …"

He waited patiently, respecting their grief. The temporary
platform he suggested had nothing to do with the rites. It took the
spirit up to nine days to leave, and there was no need to make it
difficult for it by keeping it down there on the ground, regardless
of the beginning of the ceremony.

"I'll bring you good branches," he said, when the flood of the
sobbing protests stopped. "You weave them together. Even if it is
only a small platform, it's better than nothing. Her spirit has
already begun seeking its Sky Path. It needs help, even if the
ceremony cannot begin as yet."

The first girl nodded, appreciating his reason, but the second
one remained staring, her eyes huge and unblinking, threatening
to drill holes in his skin. In the dancing light, her face looked
smooth and coppery, perfectly shaped, an exquisitely carved
figurine. Ahen was right. The silly fox *was* pretty.

"I'll bring you branches and twigs," he said, uncomfortable
with his thoughts, which lacked the respect the situation
demanded. This girl wasn't silly. She had panicked, and even
though it nearly cost him his life as well, it wasn't her fault.
Anyone could react in such an unreasonable way under such a
violent assault.

Their spare logs and branches were piled up at the edge of the
clearing, away from the fires and people's floating voices. A torch
would be of help, he knew, pulling at the long sprig, trying to
locate more appropriate material. This was their firewood, after
all, the opposite of what one needed to weave a platform from.

"Let me help."

The girl's voice shook the darkness, surer of itself than he
would have expected, no stammering or shaking in her words.

"Some light would be of help," he said, not looking up,
struggling with his find.

She dissolved back into the night without another word.
Wondering if she would be back, he located another pliant
enough piece of wood, then another.

By the time the small light neared, flickering weakly, he had enough suitable branches piled next to him, demanding more, but not by much. The dead woman was small and broken. She would fit into a tiny platform that would help to carry her back home as well.

"The light, does it help?" asked the girl hesitantly.

"Yes, thank you." He glanced at her, suddenly pleased. "It helps, very much so. Just hold it close. I'll go through that pile before it dies away."

She said nothing, but moved into a better position, her flame flickering wildly with the sharpness of her move, holding on. Aware of her presence, he pushed the logs away unceremoniously, enjoying none of the previous peacefulness.

"I suppose those will do."

Straightening up, he stumbled and almost dropped his uncomfortable cargo. She was staring at him as before, wide-eyed and unashamed, as though mesmerized, full of wonder.

"What?"

"I-I want to thank you … to thank you for saving me." Now it was her turn to stumble over her words, if not over her step. And still, her eyes did not leave him, clinging to his, as though begging for help. To be saved again?

"It's nothing," he said, greatly embarrassed. "Those things happen. I'm glad you didn't get hurt. Did you?" He remembered her flying in quite an arc.

"No, no, nothing that won't mend." At last, she dropped her eyes, her improvised torch burning away, flickering with the last of its light. "Just all those scratches and bruises. They hurt, but not badly. Not like Gayhi." This time, her voice broke for good.

"Gayhi?" he repeated, at a loss.

"Oh, Gayhi, the girl—the woman who was killed by … by the beast. She is all … wounded, broken. Hurt!"

"She is not hurting anymore." Shifting his spiky cargo, he took a deep breath. "She is beyond that. Her spirit is now seeking its path. You should think good thoughts, help her reach her Sky Path."

Oh, but those were such silly words. He wanted to curse

himself. Had she asked for his advice on how she should feel or think, or see her dead friend off?

Watching her sagging shoulders and the trembling of her palms that now covered her face, he felt useless. She needed his comfort, his encouragement, or probably just an attentive ear, and he was standing there, preaching on the right behavior.

"I'm sorry, sorry you feel so bad, sorry that you had to go through it. Sorry you almost died, too." The shrug proved the easiest gesture. What could one do with such an exquisite creature? "If I can do something to help, to ease your pain, tell me." So much awkwardness. But for her being so young or pretty, it might have been easier, actually. He would have known what to say. Yet, as it was, even an encouraging pat on her back seemed like something inappropriate.

She was sobbing openly now. "Can I … can I stay? Stay around? Please?"

"What do you mean?"

"Stay near you." Again, that gaze, so trustful, yet pleading now. "Near your fire. Sleep near. I can't there, with Gayhi, can't sleep. Please."

He felt like taking a step back, or dumping the branches and beating a hasty retreat. "You are safe there, with your friend. You aren't alone. We'll keep an eye on you both. Nothing will happen, nothing bad."

But she shook her head so vigorously, her braid jumped. "I can't. Please, please, let me stay near you." Her hands pressed against her chest, imploring. "Please!"

"Well," he shifted his cargo once again, trying to gain time, "let us go back to your companion now, make you two work on that thing." She refused to move, so he pushed himself past her. "Then we'll see. Later on. When everyone is tired and ready for sleep arrangements."

He could imagine the smirks of his friends, and the lifted eyebrows of the other hunters. Damn nuisance! But she was so miserable and afraid.

CHAPTER 2

The increasing breeze cooled her face, heralding the end of the climb. The incline was steep but not precarious; still, she didn't hasten her step as her impatience urged her to do, but proceeded at the same pace, careful to create no noise. These foreign woods were still a mystery, dangerous, alien, strange, and yet, they were meant become her home. Would they ever?

She sighed, then went on, pushing the troublesome questions away. He would be back from that hunting expedition soon—in a dawn or two, or maybe three more, he would return, and everything would be good again.

It was only without him that the urge to run away welled, growing too difficult to battle. With him sleeping beside her in that monstrously huge construction they called a house—or longhouse, to be precise—sharing a narrow bunk, instead of sleeping comfortably on the floor like normal people did, or walking around the enormously large town that spread upon the hill, with his broad-shouldered silhouette likely to appear out of this or that alley or pathway, oh, with him around, it was more bearable. With that readily flashing smile of his, or the warm twinkle of his eyes, or the way he always spoke, pronouncing words slowly, distinctly, for her sake, she knew, while his countryfolk talked in a streaming rush, not pausing for breath or bothering to make sure they were understood.

And no, they did not speak like the western foe her people knew. Oh, no! Apparently, there was more than one tongue spoken in the far west, more than one people inhabiting these lands of the setting sun. The warriors who were in the habit of invading her people were not his people, but they did belong in the same alliance, or so he claimed.

They were all the People of the Longhouse, he had explained to her again and again, while they had traveled westward, at leisure and alone, happy together, rowing in turns, because she insisted, as he was still recovering from the terrible wound and the brief illness that followed. He had turned hot and shivering on the first part of their journey, when they had left her village and sailed against the current with other warriors, eventually slipping into a mighty river that spread between high banks, so vast one could not always see the other side of it.

She remembered the stories about the Great River where the people of Skootuck lived, and it made her wonder if this one was as huge, or maybe even larger. It seemed impossible that such mighty streams existed, but here it was, rushing along the forested hills, splashing against the strokes of their paddles, carrying the people who claimed close ties to it on, guarding them. What spirits were watching over this land?

She didn't spend much time dwelling on these questions; she had been worried sick about him instead, but later on, she had wondered. Were these people so fierce, so determined and unstoppable, because of this river? Was its spirit aiding them, supporting and encouraging, making them strong?

The town they had arrived at first was large and bubbling with life, situated on a bank next to the set of roaring falls and with such an intricate labyrinth of palisade that one could lose one's way just trying to enter the settlement.

Cohoes Falls, they had called it, she learned, or the Place of Fallen Canoe. An appropriate name, as she would certainly not wish to be in such a canoe, swept by the vicious current and into the sharpest of rocks, glittering in the considerable distance below these cliffs. And yet, there was barely any water cascading down those stones, so maybe it might not be that difficult to avoid the fall.

She had shared her observations with him after wandering all around one day, but he had laughed and told her that in the spring, those cascades were as impressive as any, and that she should not wander about unescorted. They would be leaving soon, and she should be patient until then.

Well, this piece of news cheered her greatly. She didn't want to stay in that noisy settlement, with its people aloof and busy, gawking at her as though she were a rare animal, some strange creature out of the forest. Which, of course, she was. She understood their wonder and curiosity. Still, it was tiring, all those stares. Didn't they have anything better to do?

He had been recovering fast, gaining his previous strength, which was a wonderful thing, but it made him leave her often, wandering the town with other warriors, sitting around their fires, talking into the night. Something she understood too, but what was she to do in the meanwhile?

When they had finally left, she was on the verge of stealing a canoe and sailing back with the current, telling him nothing, missing home oh so badly. But it all changed the moment their dugout challenged the river's flow once again, only the two of them this time.

Oh, but those were the most thrilling days!

It had taken them close to a full moon to reach the end of their Great River and then to start navigating their way along the multitude of lakes and smaller streams, heading for the lands of his people and his hometown, a truly important settlement. He had told her proudly of the fact that it was one of the most influential towns in the entire confederacy of the Five Nations, because his people were the Keepers of the Central Fire, the ones to host, and often summon, the annual gathering of the Great Council, the ones entrusted with keeping an eye on the procedures, making sure no laws were bent, broken, or bypassed.

Fascinated and a little awed, she listened to his stories, enjoying them, but not as much as the journey itself. They had made such little progress each day, pausing on every abandoned shore in order to swim and fool around, not in a hurry to go on, hunting rabbits or trying to snare birds, cooking them clumsily, neither being especially good at that. And making love, plenty of love.

Oh, but it was the most incredible part of it, the lovemaking!

She never suspected that physical contact, something as simple as touching and kissing, could be that thrilling, that head-spinning, that full of wonder and fulfillment. Girls of her age were ever dreaming about young men and their love, she knew, silly Namaas or her other empty-headed cousins, but who would have thought it was all about the wonder of merging and melting and reaching the Sky World every time it happened? Why had no one ever told her?

He had laughed when she kept telling him how wonderful it all was, and why no one had ever spoken about that, and how girls had been missing the entire significance of it all.

Oh, yes, they did speak of it, all the time, he had claimed, smirking, looking too smug, pleased with himself. The men, that is. The men of all ages wanted to make love perpetually, to all sorts of women, not always the same one, if they could help it, he said, eyes glittering with challenge and mischief. And yes, they talked about all this, more times than not, every time they gathered together, preferably with no women around, or at least no authoritative Clans Mothers in sight.

As for the girls and women, he growled lazily, stretching like a mountain lion, mellow and greatly content, his naked skin glistening in the sun. Well, women didn't seem to be as occupied with this sort of thing, but he was glad she enjoyed it so much and didn't feel as though she had had enough. Because he was enjoying her as much, more than any other girl he had lain with, and it would be too bad if she had to say 'no' to him every once in a while.

"What other girls?" she had asked, resisting his arms that were trying to draw her closer again, the glitter in his eyes deepening, losing its lazy spark. To think of him doing such wonderful things with someone other than her hurt.

"None," he muttered. "Not anymore." And when his lips arrested her budding protests, she gave way to yet another wonderful sensation of loving him, and letting him love her with no restraints, but his words stuck, and later on, she had thought about it, and worried.

"How many girls you make love to?" she asked, when they

were through their previous meal's leftovers, too lazy to bother with putting on clothes in order to go and check their snares.

He made a face.

"Many?" she insisted, too perturbed to bother with the attempt to build a proper phrase. After the stay at Cohoes Fall and their journey, her grasp on the way his people spoke had improved, but not by much.

Some of the complacent amusement left his eyes. "Don't start turning all jealous, you wild thing. It has nothing to do with you and me now."

"If it has not, then why not tell me?" She felt like kicking at the pottery bowl they used for cooking, with its barely appealing contents still glittering at its bottom. "I just want, want to know. That's all."

"What for?" His frown deepened. "It'll give you no pleasure. Just troublesome thoughts." The mischievous glimmer returned suddenly, catching her unprepared. "Don't make me sorry for letting you practice with my bow, or promising to make you one. If you are a jealous little fox then I'm in for more trouble than I'm prepared to take."

Unable not to, she giggled. "I know how to shoot a bow. I knew before you show."

"But I did let you practice and hone your skill. It was a mistake!"

Throwing a piece of dried meat at him, hitting him square on the forehead, she felt better, ducking out of his reach when he pounced to grab her. It was the best thing about being with him, this unabashed messing around whenever they felt like it, swimming and climbing and wrestling or shooting his bow, or trying to best each other on finding the freshest footprints in order to place their traps. Such a great feeling, with no one to frown upon them or tell them not to. Sometimes she wished they would never reach his town at all.

Coming out of her reverie, she stopped, taken by the magnificent view that spread before her eyes. The valley sprawled ahead, wherever the gaze could reach, rustling calmly, the distant treetops far beneath her feet swaying with the fresh wind.

Trickling in the most pleasant of ways, some nearby spring hummed peacefully, out of sight but near, comforting. High Springs, she remembered. They called this town by such a name for a reason. The hill it was situated on did, indeed, abound with gushing springs, such pleasant diversity.

Watching the shadows moving lazily, spreading over the valley, heralding the nearing end of the day, she tensed, her senses warning her before her ears did. People were coming up the trail she had followed a short time ago, ascending it slowly, not in a hurry.

Darting into the thick foliage, she stopped breathing, terrified for a moment. *The enemies were coming!* Then she remembered and relaxed a little, staying where she was, but only because she didn't trust her legs to carry her now in a dignified manner. They shook too badly as yet.

Those people must be dwellers of High Springs, simple logic told her. They weren't enemies out to harm her. Maybe once, a moon ago or more, but now she was one of them. She had lived in their town for quite a few days, and even though she could barely speak and understand them—apparently, the tongue that she had boasted to know so well was painfully different from the one spoken in the lands of her people's immediate enemies—she was still a full-time denizen of this place. And yet, would these people know that? She was so new here, so foreign. What if they thought her to be a runaway captive and harmed her before she was able to explain?

Oh, but it was the stupidest idea, to sneak away like that. Stupid, stupid, stupid! And yet, without this breather, this much-needed respite, she would have gone mad, as simple as that.

To sort and peel cobs of maize from sunrise to way after high noon was the worst possible occupation she might have imagined. It made the day drag oh so very slowly, as though an entire moon and season had passed between each movement of Father Sun, who simply refused to progress, staying in the sky, motionless, indifferent, cold and aloof in a way the benevolent deity never behaved back in her lands.

Women rushed to and fro, authoritative elders and middle-

aged women, or just young girls as herself, all busy, swamped by
their apparent preparations for the nearing celebration. Of the
harvest, she presumed. It was the correct time, although no one
thought of informing her. It was no pleasure to talk to her, to try
to explain with slow words and signs or understand her disjointed
replies, so they didn't bother. Even the authoritative, very
pleasant-looking woman who seemed to be giving work to
everyone, never argued with or confronted, not even by men—his
mother of all things!—even she had been too busy to spend time
on idle talking. Not nasty or aloof, flashing a friendly smile and
some rapidly spoken words that sounded encouraging, the
woman had rushed off, tossing instructions at other girls who
were also set to sort enormously large piles of maize as she went.

Well, if those directions concerned her, the filthy foxes, every
one of them, did nothing but give her nasty glances, proceeding to
ignore her otherwise. Which was a mercy. She didn't want to
communicate with any of them as it was, girls or clan mothers.

Once upon a time, he had told her about Clans Mothers, but
she just laughed back then, finding it too bizarre to believe.
Women telling men what to do? She remembered him informing
her that she would make a good clan mother herself and how they
had both doubled over with laughter.

Well, it wasn't as funny anymore, as she had been left to face
all of this by herself, with him being out, hunting, having a good
time, most surely. Is this what she had left her people for? To sit
all day long, sorting ears of maize, peeling them into special
baskets, to be ground later on? If only it had at least been an early
harvest of the sweet, juicy corn that one could pop straight into
one's mouth, to make up for all the work. Back home, she had also
been forced to sort maize or grind it into flour. But never in such
quantity. The amount of corn this town produced could have fed
her village for quite a few spans of seasons, if not more.

The annoying foxes who were put to work alongside her did
not seem to be bothered by the boredom of it all. They chatted
away at the speed of agitated squirrels, sometimes getting up to
carry full baskets or to bring more kernels that needed attention,
sometimes going away for no apparent reason. They produced

snacks, tasty treats of cookies with berries, or handfuls of nuts, sharing their treasures with one another, while offering her nothing in the most obvious of manners.

When her basket filled at long last—oh, yes, she was slow and clumsy, not like the others, but they worked together, while she was struggling to fill her container all alone—she picked it up, welcoming the opportunity to stretch her legs at long last, to get away, at least for a little while, but a tall, saucy girl brushed past her, snatching her cargo in the rudest of manners.

"At long last," she said loudly, to the open merriment of the others. "And here we were thinking it would take you only until the darkness to finish this thing. You work fast!"

Understanding too well without the need to recognize some of the words, Kentika didn't spend her time on trying to talk. Grabbing the girl's upper arm, instead, she made her offender arrest her progress just as the filthy fox began turning away, about to take her, Kentika's, basket along, still talking, very pleased with herself. That stopped the torrent of words, and the girl's braids jumped in the silliest of ways as she wavered, just as Kentika's hands took hold of the basket, jerking it away with a force that made the stupid fox lose her balance and fall flat on her behind. She was still sitting there in the dust, stunned, amidst deafening silence, as Kentika went away, mighty pleased with herself, even if a little scared. They would take great pleasure in telling on her, she suspected, and then she would be in trouble.

Refusing to succumb to her growing dismay, she had delivered her cargo to the storage room of their longhouse, where some women with grinding facilities positioned themselves in relative comfort, but did not find enough courage to go back to more maize peeling. Who knew what the filthy foxes would do to avenge their assaulted friend? And anyway, she had had enough of sitting in one place for one day. To follow the twisted labyrinth of the palisade leading out of the town seemed like a better idea. It was that or go mad and do something even more stupid than pushing some stupid, malicious skunk off her feet.

Sighing, she made herself more comfortable in the relative safety of her hideaway, listening to the sounds of dragging footsteps, not really interested or needing to hide. Okwaho's mother, and maybe her fellow Clan Mothers, were sure to be furious with her by now, but the men who were now walking this hill had probably nothing to do with it.

There were two of them, she discovered, one tall and broadly built, the other short and middle-aged, both dignified, their voices carrying confidently in the wind. And yet, there was no calmness about them, no peacefulness. She could feel their agitation, coming in waves, marring the tranquility of the woods.

"It is not that I don't value our War Chief," one of the men was saying. "I do. I do respect this man. He is a great leader and an admirable man. He has led us for countless seasons, since the Great Peace was established. He is a good leader."

"And yet ..." The other man picked up a pinecone, eyeing it thoughtfully, as though curious to know what it was. "And yet, he has his faults, doesn't he? He may be a good leader with the best interests of our people in his heart, but in the matter of the Crooked Tongues, he keeps failing miserably. First, he does nothing for ten spans of seasons and more, letting the enemy grow stronger, sending tentative hints, trying to reach some sort of agreement. Then, when they start making trouble, he does send war parties, but not nearly often enough. And now, after meeting the foreigners, he speaks of talking peace again. Is it a just, proper behavior for a league as great as ours? We, who have enough might to punish the enemy; we, who have the power and will and courage to do that." The man paused, but mainly to draw in a breath as it seemed. "Before our Great Union, we warred on these people. We were courageous and determined back then. But we are not anymore. Today, we are nothing but would-be warriors, proud of our might, our spirit, our abilities, and our united prowess, but doing nothing to use this advantage, nothing at all." The pinecone went flying, crashing through the nearby foliage, hurled with much force. "And in the meanwhile, the Crooked Tongues grow stronger, again sending war parties, not afraid in the least. And why would they be, if all we do in return is kill their warriors who are caught on our side? No retaliation parties, no initiative of our own. Nothing! Our War Chief is nothing but a coward when it comes to the Crooked Tongues."

In the ensuing pause, Kentika held her breath. They were talking about his father, the War Chief. Unable to follow all of their rapidly rolling words, she understood that much. These people weren't happy with the man he admired the most. They even accused him of cowardice!

"This man is not a coward!" the other man cried out, obviously as appalled by the accusation. "He had seen hundreds of battles before the Great Peacemaker came, and he has led us to quite a few victories since that time as well. He may be many things, this particular leader, but a coward he isn't."

"I didn't say that." Another pinecone went flying, this time in a beautiful arch, to disappear behind the bushes adorning the edge. "I said that when it comes to the Crooked Tongues he acts cowardly. I know that he is fearless otherwise. And wise, yes. But not in this matter." Strolling toward the edge, the man halted at the vantage point where Kentika had stood earlier, admiring the view. "And the situation with the Crooked Tongues matters. It does! These people grew stronger over the long seasons that we did nothing to prevent it. The delegation of the foreigners that our War Chief received with such alacrity and against some prominent people's better judgment confirmed that. Didn't it?"

More silence. She tried to make sense of what they said. If only they had spoken more slowly. The tongue of these people was terrible, just terrible.

"It's good that he received them. If he didn't, we wouldn't have learned what we know now."

"If he had sent enough warriors' parties across the Great Lake through all those spans of seasons he chose to do nearly nothing instead – if we had been bringing in plenty of captives! – we would have learned all of it and more. We would have been able to stop them from uniting, maybe, eh? It's the long summers of quiet and lack of real war that allowed them to sit back and think, to try to emulate our Great Union. Imagine that!" The man's snort echoed between the trees. "How dare they? The Peacemaker did not come to their lands. He came to us, the People of the Longhouse, the only ones capable of accepting his message."

"The Peacemaker came from across the Great Sparkling Water, some claim," said the other man mildly, seemingly as immersed in admiring the view. "He has been to their lands, and they did not wish to receive his message."

"My point exactly!" The angry words shot out like hurled missiles. "The Crooked Tongues did not accept his message. We did! Our people received the Great Law of Peace. We sat under the Long-Leafed Tree of Peace, and we listened to the Messenger's words. And we accepted his every law, and so now, we live in peace among each other, and we are strong and united. But our War Chief," the word rang sharply, as though spat out, "oh, our War Chief thinks he knows it all. He takes it upon himself to interpret the Great Messenger's laws, and in the way that suits his views, of course, his course of action. He has been doing it for summers, yes, but now he has taken it too far." Another thundering pause. "Now he has the gall to speak of bringing foreigners to our union, outright foreigners! Who are those Long Tails People from the far west? Who ever heard of them?"

"He didn't propose to greet them into our Great League," said the other man mildly. "He just accepted their delegation. He listened to them and talked with them. That is all. It is not that simple to join our union, and no war chief or even the Great Council itself can decide on that without due deliberation and the agreement of every single representative of every nation. You fume over nothing, brother. The War Chief is not at fault."

"He shouldn't have received these people," repeated the man stubbornly. "And he shouldn't have opposed every suggestion to raid the other side of our Great Lake."

"There were a few raids over the past summers."

"Only a few, when we could have made the enemy's life a misery, silenced them once and for all. We do have the power behind us. We have the strength and determination. But not the leadership. And now the enemy is united. Two or even four nations, they said? In an alliance that might have resembled ours, of all things! The Left-Handed Twin must have guided these people, and he may have been guiding some of our leaders as well."

With the sun hurrying toward its resting place behind the western side of the valley, Kentika felt the chilliness of the dimming air enveloping her, pleasant and unsettling at the same time. The heat of the midday was gone, but the intensifying wind made her shiver, whether from cold or fear she didn't know.

These people talked war, and maybe treachery, too. She didn't need to understand all their words to gather that. His father had done things that made some people angry. He didn't go to war against someone, or maybe he talked to delegations he should not. Like Okwaho, he did things that he wasn't supposed to, going with his better judgment and against the convention. Well, they were father and son, after all.

She recalled the man's dignified, sunburned, weathered face, covered with so many scars they were spread like a war paint. It should have made the man look ugly—so many scars!—but it didn't. Instead, it made him stand out in the crowd, she had decided back then. Tall, broad-shouldered, handsome enough despite his age, *dignified*.

She remembered the large eyes resting on her, flickering with surprise and a question that had an almost playful quality; then another glance at his son, the eyebrows raised high, lips twisting in a suggestive grin. Okwaho was grinning back, perfectly at ease, not about to explain or justify anything, and so she relaxed, too. There was something about that man, mighty leader though he was, something calming. Prepared to be afraid, she had felt her own lips twitching as well, joining their grins.

"Welcome to our longhouse, River People girl," he had told her, talking slowly, making it easy to understand, his smile holding nothing but kindness. They were so much alike, she thought suddenly, physically and maybe otherwise, too. "You followed my son quite a long way. I hope you will find your new home here."

"She will," said Okwaho, standing by her side firmly, as he had since the first introductions, no matter whom they talked to. Quite a few people by now, because his father have not been around when they had arrived with the dusk of the previous day.

Like back home, *his* presence made her feel better, stronger and more secure, not like a cornered animal, like the dubious forest creature their open scrutiny made her feel like. With Okwaho by her side, it was more bearable. He would not let anyone harm or ridicule her.

The thought of him warmed her insides now in yet another deepening evening. He would be back soon, and she would tell him what she had heard. His father was too good of a man to let bad people say nasty things behind his back. If he had chosen not to war against someone, then it must have been the right thing to do. Okwaho had also made their people stop warring when no one thought it to be right or possible. Only this once, but he did it. And he had promised, when they had talked serious matters one day, not an often occurrence, that he would talk to his father and he would convince this great, outstanding man to make peace between his and her people, not as a temporary cease of hostilities like in her village, but a true peace. His father could do that, he promised. He was *that* powerful. He could make even the Great Council listen.

The gossiping men were still there, now squatting on the ground, comfortable and at ease, talking more quietly. She tried to listen, but the wind changed, carrying their words the other way.

Taking a good look, she memorized their features, or what she could make out in the deepening dusk, then began easing away, slipping through the bushes, blessing her ability to move as soundlessly as a real scout. These may not be her woods, but she still knew how to walk in the forest.

CHAPTER 3

Counting baskets full of shelled maize with her gaze, Seketa frowned, satisfied with their amount, but not with the towering piles of cobs that were yet to be taken care of.

So much work, and just as two of their longhouse girls had come down with sickness and the third one was too heavy with child to be of real use. And when the men returned from the hunting, surely before the beginning of the festivities, as no one in his right mind would wish to miss something like that, it would become even worse, with her charges growing more distracted, less likely to put forward a real effort.

"You did well, girls," she said, smiling encouragingly, tucking her frown away. "We worked hard through this last moon of harvest, if not before, and through these past few dawns you put in a tremendous effort. You deserve to be praised and commended, all of you! No other longhouse or clan could boast such dedication and skill."

They beamed at her, tired and sweaty, but encouraged, proud of her praise. She wasn't a person to say nice things for no reason. Her job was too demanding for that. A Clan Mother of one of the largest longhouses in High Springs, she could not afford to be pleasant when sternness was needed. Too many people and families were placed in her care, needing to be fed and taken care of, guided and coordinated, managed, assigned duties, kept happy and content. Over twenty families and two new young couples were due for expansion, extending their longhouse even farther, adding two more compartments to their already sprawling building.

The Clan Mothers, two more of her peers and the elder of their longhouse, their representative in the Town Council, had deliberated for a long time before agreeing. The building was monstrously long as it was, and the permission of the neighboring Beaver Clan longhouse needed to be obtained, as the new compartments would be nearly encroaching on their space. Plenty of meetings and discussions with all parties involved were held, yet, in the end, they all agreed it was permissible, these two additional compartments, and so here they were, about to grow bigger after the Cold Moons, when, with the coming of the Awakening Season, the bark peeling from the trees sent every settlement of the land into a building frenzy.

She sighed. So much to do yet, but after the Harvest Festival, they would be able to relax a little.

"Tomorrow we'll start earlier, before Father Sun comes to lighten our world." Their faces reflected elation and disappointment all at once. An immediate rest of today came at the price of more work for tomorrow. "Yes, I know. But we do need to finish grinding our corn before the festivities. Two more difficult days, and then we'll enjoy the celebration; we'll rest and dance and eat well, with the Great Spirits happy and our men and elders grateful and content, all thanks to you girls. Think about it."

"What would men do without us?" Onenha, a tall, merry, outspoken girl, one of those newly married couples due to rebuild, began scooping unfinished kernels into an empty basket. "They would shrivel and die of hunger, but not before they killed each other over this or that insult because they didn't know how to solve it otherwise."

Giggling, the other girls began getting up, picking their tools and containers, heading for the storage room of the nearest entrance.

"It might happen, yes." Hauling one of the full baskets on her shoulder, Seketa grinned, trying to make it look like easy work. Yet, it wasn't, not anymore, not like when she was young and full of strength. "They should thank the Right-Handed Twin every day for making them so lucky as to have us around and in good spirits."

"But we are not always in good spirits, are we?" Hayak, one of the elder women who was passing by, snickered, her grinding bowls and tools packed in a bag, tucked neatly one into another.

"Because of them. So it's still their fault." Done with the kernels in the speed and efficiency only she possessed, Onenha straightened up, then rushed toward Seketa. "Give me this, Honorable Mother. You should not carry such heavy things."

"I can manage, girl. I'm not that old." She pretended to fight for possession of the basket, but gave way gratefully. It was, indeed, heavy and cumbersome. "Do I look as though I have seen hundreds of summers?"

The girl smiled widely, unabashed.

"It might be that you have seen more than twenty summers, sister," said Hayak, sitting down with a sigh of relief, her back bent by the long summers of field work, child-rearing, and child-bearing, a respectable member of the community and Seketa's close friend of many summers. "You do look this way. But this young bird is right. We elected you to organize things, to make sure everything is functioning, to tell everyone what to do—something you are so good at. Not to run around, carry heavy baskets, and wave your braids in a playful manner."

"Oh, please!" It was too difficult to fight her grin now, their smiles beaming at her, making her happy despite the unfinished piles of kernels and ears. "I am around to direct, yes, but no one says I can't give a hand when needed. I'm not an elderly matron, not yet. When I am, I promise to sit comfortably, giving orders and doing little else." She grinned at them, challenging. "Then you will be complaining again, of me doing nothing to help this time." Their laughter was infectious. "Also, I didn't work with any of you today. So here you have your perfect matron."

"We saw you grinding corn on the other side of our building when the sun was still high, Honorable Mother," said one of the girls, laughing shyly. "Ehnida and I, we both saw you when we were on our way here."

"And yesterday you spent a whole afternoon with the girls at the fields," added Ehnida, her nod vigorous, making her braids jump.

"I can't get away with anything, can I?" Her attempt to keep up with the image of a respectable matron who was there only to direct and make sure the work was done lasted for no longer than two heartbeats, until her gaze spotted scattered husks and full-sized maize leafs that must have been blown out of their containers by the occasional breeze. Those were as precious as kernels themselves, needed in every aspect of life, from cooking to making mats, and so many other means. "The girls of the western field needed help. If we didn't finish picking the maize yesterday, we would not be so far ahead with the grinding today. All of us." Shrugging, she straightened up. "With Sqwak's broken arm and Gaawa being sick, the girls in the field could not manage."

"I hope Gaawa doesn't get sicker," muttered Ehnida. "She didn't look good this afternoon. She was all sweaty and hot, wandering the dream worlds, for the second day in a row now. I stopped by when I was on my way to pick up baskets from the other storage room," she added hastily, obviously not wishing to let her Clan Mothers, even someone as nice and approachable as Seketa, think that she was lazing around at such a pressing time.

"I asked the False Face Society medicine man to visit our longhouse tonight. They promised to do so. He will know what to do." Seketa suppressed her worry, for she liked both girls, Gaawa and her closest friend, Ehnida, very much, knowing them both, of course, since they were born. Of the same age as her youngest son, they used to follow him around, often playing together, if not getting into the same troubles. At some point, too late to catch it in time, poor Ehnida had developed inappropriate feelings for the boy. People of the same clan could never marry; still, the girl was heartbroken when Okwaho left.

The thought of her son brought another. "Where is the new girl?"

Indifferent shrugs were her answer.

"She has wandered off," said Onenha, not as cheerfully as before, returning to pick up remained baskets. "Some time ago."

"Wandered off where?"

"Only the Left-Handed Evil Twin knows, for she made trouble

before she disappeared."

"What trouble?" Their gazes refused to meet hers, too blank, full of too much innocence. "And why has no one kept an eye on her? I told you to do so, to make her feel at home, to help her around, didn't I?"

Now, even Onenha lost the last of her breeziness. Despite the friendliness and good humor, no one liked to make Seketa angry.

"She is difficult, Honorable Mother." There was a pleading tone to Ehnida's voice now. "You can't talk with her, not even by gesturing. She never smiles, and her ways are strange."

"She scares us," contributed another. "One never knows what she will do. She is violent and as unpredictable as a forest beast."

"She is not!"

Drawing a deep breath, Seketa tried to calm herself. The girl, indeed, was not the most likable creature, not pretty or charming, not even just cute like many girls of her age. What had made her son fall in love with this one, she didn't know, but it was not her place to ask that. If he bothered to drag the girl all the way from beyond the Flint People's Great River, from some distant lands no one had even seen or heard of, then he must love her, and she must be worthy of it. It was his life, and the girl deserved a warm welcome. Out of all people, she knew how it felt to be a foreigner, and no, not because of her personal experience. She shuddered at the mere memory.

"But she is! She is, Honorable Mother. She barely did any work, and when Onenha came to help her, she pushed her hard and made her fall. Then she ran off. Like a mad creature." Their eyes peered at her, pleading. "She is wild, a real savage."

Oh, but that was truly too much. The word savage! How long had it been since she heard that one?

"I don't have time to talk to you right now," she said sternly, squashing them with her gaze. "But I'm sure you did nothing to make that girl feel at home. Her behavior shows that you did just the opposite. And it is despicable, unacceptable, unworthy of people who respect themselves and others. You could be such a foreigner too one day, or maybe one of your children. Think about it! Alone, missing home, not even able to speak the local tongue, maybe. How friendly or sweet would any of you behave under such circumstances, receiving nothing but contemptuous glances, and maybe an open sneering, eh?" Their eyes were drilling holes in the ground by now. "Oh, you are the ones who behave like savages, like forest beasts!"

Turning around, she stalked off, her fury bubbling, marring the pureness of the early evening. Was it always the same, everywhere? Foreigners, true foreigners, not just people from neighboring nations, were thought to be little more than animals, wild beasts with no feelings?

Oh, but it had been so long; more than thirty summers had passed, but she still remembered her own hometown, so far away, across the Great Sparkling Water, before the Tidings of the Great Peace, before the Peacemaker, so long ago. She didn't miss it, not even her immediate family, not anyone, really, because she could never forgive any of them for how they had treated him, her husband of so many summers, now the powerful War Chief, back then nothing but the miserable captive, the wild youth, the despised foreigner from distant lands, the forest beast with no feelings, *the savage*.

Leaning against the wide maple tree—how did she get here, to the ceremonial grounds?—she heard her own breath coming in gasps, her teeth grinding against each other, such an ugly sound. Was it always the same, everywhere? So many summers had passed, happy, fulfilling summers, and still, she didn't forget, didn't forgive. The scars on his face wouldn't let her.

"Seketa?"

The voice startled her, making her heart jump.

"Are you well, sister?" The familiar face of the fellow Clan Mother from the neighboring Turtle Clan longhouse peered at her, concerned. "What is wrong?"

"Nothing," she said, gathering her senses hastily. "It's nothing."

"You look mighty upset."

"The girls." Waving in the general direction of their side of the town, she took a deep breath, shamed by her outburst. "You know how it is. Something the girls did made me angry. All those young ones, you can't leave them alone and trust them to do what they are asked. Can you?"

"No, you can't." Good-naturedly, the woman laughed, touching Seketa's arm in a reassuring gesture. "What were you thinking, a Clan Mother of your experience?" Another inquiring, mischievously glittering glance. "Will the Wolf Clan make us eat poorly through the first day of the ceremony?"

"No, it wasn't that." Seketa shook her head, smiling against her will. "They didn't finish peeling all the maize ears off as yet, let alone grinding the amount we will need, but that is something we can handle. We'll start earlier tomorrow, before Father Sun rises again. They know that they will have to put a real effort now."

"Well, it's the same in our longhouse. Our girls will have to work with no pause for breath as well, tomorrow and the day after that," confessed her companion, rolling her eyes. "The harvest was good this summer. Much corn, many kernels to grind. I suppose we have nothing to complain about, have we?"

"No, we don't. We can only thank the Great Spirits, which we will do. Aren't the harvest festivities all about thanksgiving?"

She remembered the three sacred dances that opened the ceremony, the speeches that followed, the fragrant tobacco smoke, sending the gratitude of people to the sky and the world of the spirits, letting them know. There would be no entertainment, no ceremonial games and lightness that would color the first opening day. Only the solemn addresses of the faith-keepers and the elder men and women of prominent positions, her husband being among the first to talk and dance. Oh, but she loved listening to him addressing either spirits or people. He spoke beautifully, never just orating for the sake of playing with flowery phrases, but always talking good sense in the best of the perfectly chosen words.

"That reminds me." The voice of her companion brought her temporarily wandering attention back. "The Peach Stone Game. It's time for us to decide upon the bets. What will the Wolf Clan be offering this year?"

Oh, yes, the game of the second day. Another thing to take care of. Seketa shook her head.

"We should meet tomorrow." She frowned. "No, the day after tomorrow, the moment we are all done with the other preparations. It'll leave us enough time to decide on the bets and the amount of participants. I'll talk to the Bear Clan Mothers this evening. I need to visit one of their longhouses, anyway." She thought about the sick girl, her stomach tightening. "I hope we will not have to make the Medicine Society people do more than their customary dance."

"Is someone in your longhouse sick in an alarming way?" asked the woman shrewdly.

"Yes, but we hope it is not the summer disease."

"Let me know if you need help. Many women of our clan know their way with herbs. I'm not that bad with making some medicine myself." Smiling smugly, the woman shrugged. "As for the game, I already talked to the Bear Clan Mothers, all three of them. We can squeeze a short meeting into our busy days tomorrow. Somewhere around mid-morning meal. Let the other two leaders of your clan know."

Seketa frowned. "Why can't it wait for the day after tomorrow? When we all should be less occupied with the most pressing matters."

"We need time to prepare all the items that would be offered."

"Do you have something unusual in mind?"

"Maybe, sister. Maybe." Her companion's grin returned. "If Turtle and Bear Clans raise their bets, would the Wolf Clan be afraid of a challenge?"

"No, we would not," said Seketa firmly, but in her inner heart, she groaned. Didn't she face enough challenges already, without the ambitious Turtles and Bears out to prove something, or to add spice to the traditional game.

Every year, it was the same: the Turtle and Bear Clans against the Wolf Clan in a throwing game that could last an entire day, with as many participants as hundreds, taking their turns, shaking the bowl with the marked and unmarked peach pits in it, hoping to make them fall on either of their sides, to let the thrower grab the beans collected by the rival. This was the tradition, the game that was not played for pleasure, but to honor the Sky Spirits, with every bet returned to their original owners at the end of the day. Unlike in regular throwing games.

"Yes, let us all meet tomorrow. If the items you are willing to offer have changed, then we need to know in advance."

For a while, they said nothing, immersed in the comfortable silence. The evening was pleasantly fresh, and it did much to cool off Seketa's anger. She had overreacted, hadn't she?

"It will be good to finish with the festivities already," she said, smiling. "We all need a good, thorough rest, all of us, clans' mothers and the girls, all the women of the town."

Her companion laughed outright. "Don't let them hear you speaking like that."

"I won't, but it is the truth. It is!" She frowned in mocking reproach. "Don't say you never wish to just rest and do nothing, walk along your longhouse's corridor without noticing what needs to be done, stroll around the town without paying attention to what was wrong or who has been neglecting their duties. Let others tell us what to do," she finished with a chuckle.

"Well, you take it a bit too far, sister." The woman's ample sides were trembling, her generous mouth twitching with mirth. "But yes, sometimes it might be nice to do nothing, let others fret and organize and make everyone do their duties. Still, I'm not certain I would manage to hold on to this state of affairs, not for longer than a day or two." The mirthful face beamed at her. "And neither would you."

"Oh, please." Watching a group of people who went past them, unhurried and at ease, their voices carrying with the wind, as did their laughter, she waved a buzzing fly away. "The foreigners. I hoped they would leave before the ceremony."

Her companion's face lost some of its good-natured beam as well. "Yes, they better go back to their distant lands and leave our men and leaders alone. They can't possibly try to suggest what has been whispered around the town. It would be too inconceivable."

Seketa felt the remnants of her well-being evaporating. "My husband thinks they might be allowed to state their case before the Great Council, when our respectable elders are due to meet again, after the Cold Moons." She watched the round, good-natured face closing up, turning blank, in too familiar of a fashion. She had seen it happening many times since the arrival of the accursed delegation. "There is no harm in foreigners speaking to our leaders. The laws of the Great Peacemaker provide for this opportunity, as much as for any other. Remember that *should a nation outside our union make known their disposition to obey the laws of the Great Peace, they may be invited to trace the roots to the Tree of Peace, and if their minds are clean, and they are obedient and—*"

"Yes, Seketa, I know the laws as well as you do. And yet," the woman shrugged, "our War Chief is an outstanding man, trusted and admired, a leader our people have been following for quite a long time. He is a good man, that husband of yours, a great leader, and yet, he has been insisting on listening to all sorts of foreigners for too long. There will be no peace with the Crooked Tongues. We all know it, and but for his insistence, we would have been better prepared, less surprised with the escalation of things." A rough, weathered palm came up, displaying the evidence of long summers of working the land. Partly successful, it managed to stop Seketa's indignant protests that were about to erupt. "Yes, I know, I know. We all know that when these people came over to raid our lands again, after so many summers of quiet, your husband did not hesitate in retaliating, doing so brilliantly, yes, punishing the enemy hard. And yet ..." The loud sigh was accompanied by another wave of large hands, this time palms up, relating gloomy doubt. "His heart is not in those raids, sister. One can see that. He still hopes to achieve peace with the enemy, somehow. And it's not a good state of affairs, not good at all. We need our War Chief aggressive, spoiling for a fight. We can't have him thinking of peace, planning for this possibility while organizing his raids. He needs to focus on how to humble the enemy, how to hurt them. Not how to make them talk peace as they did for some very short time, after the Messenger of the Great Spirits left our world all those long summers ago."

She wanted to close her ears, to push the words away, not to let them enter her mind, for she knew her companion was right. Brilliant in everything he ever did, from organizing the Great

Council's meetings to managing many smaller affairs of the entire union, he was just as good at making war. On the rare occasions he had authorized, and then organized the warriors' parties to head across the Great Lake, he did it well, like everything he undertook.

And yet, this woman was right. His heart was not in the warfare. The persistent hope to reach an agreement with the Crooked Tongues, her and the Peacemaker's original people, to have their representatives sitting under the shade of the Great Tree of Peace, taking a part in the greatest union, his most admired hero's creation, oh, but these hopes did color his deeds, did influence his decisions.

She wanted to shut her eyes, or maybe scream in frustration. He was loyal to the memory of a man who had been dead for many summers, gone, disappeared. He risked everything in order to save this man once, but in the long run, it brought him no good.

With no way to know for certain, he must have kept cherishing the hope of the Peacemaker still being alive, somewhere there across the Great Sparkling Water. Doing what? Only Great Spirits knew, and maybe not even them. The Divine Messenger, the Great Peacemaker, or maybe just a man with a special blessing, this legendary figure was gone, having completed his mission of bringing peace to this side of the Great Lake. He might have wished to do it for everyone, to bring all nations sitting comfortably under the long leaves of the Great Tree of Peace, sharing all those ideas with her husband, his most trusted partner and friend, and yet it was nothing but a legend now, events that had happened more than thirty summers ago, coated in a thick layer of mystery already, like everything concerning this man.

Knowing more than anyone, party to all her husband's deeds and most of his thoughts, remembering the legendary Peacemaker from her hometown, nothing but a discontent hunter and warrior, she still found herself believing the myth more and more with each passing summer. It was impossible to think of the Great Peacemaker otherwise, not in the light of everything he had achieved. The memories were fading, but the fruits of this man's vision and her husband's work were not.

She shook her head resolutely.

"My husband knows what he is doing. He has been our War Chief for long summers, more than some of us can remember, and he has never let us down, never disappointed our people. He was entrusted with the care of our nation, of all our towns and villages, and he does that in the best of ways; otherwise, he would have been replaced, like any representative who failed his people." She drew a deep breath, desperate to keep her temper under control, not to let it snap again. "People should accept his judgment instead of questioning his decisions every time it comes to foreigners. He has never done anything to warrant so much distrust."

Pursed lips and a shaking head were her answer, but in the depth of her companion's eyes she saw sadness, a well-hidden compassion. Oh, but this woman was right, wasn't she?

CHAPTER 4

The girl was watching him. Kneeling to inspect the old footprint, his entire attention on this new worrisome development, Ganayeda still felt her eyes, burning holes in his back. Just like they had through the night and the morning, and their independent afternoon journey as well.

As expected, nothing went according to the plan. With the bear and his new unasked-for charges—two living girls and one dead—they still hadn't managed to finish cutting all the deer before nightfall. Instead, the work spread well into the morning and high noon—cutting, skinning, and packing. He didn't wish to leave his people to do it by themselves, although, of course, they would have managed. Still, he was their leader, and it was his responsibility to finish the hunting properly, even if not to bring it all home by himself.

When everything was cleaned, packed, and ready, he decided, he would either send his people on, while he himself and a few of his fellow hunters would detour through Lone Hill, delivering this village's wandering women home safely, or he would charge someone else with doing this.

He was still deliberating when the rest of their party had appeared out of nowhere, answering yesterday's summons. With a few carcasses of their own, butchered, cut, and arranged in bags, their expedition had come to a relative success, as expected given little time and preparation, because these people separated from the main party on the spur of the moment, when Ganayeda agreed to split, having spotted the trail of a smaller herd that was too tempting to ignore.

Well, now they were back, successful and at the perfect timing, and when his eyes took in the wide-shouldered figure of his brother, strolling with his large leather bag that looked as though it had no weight in it, sunburned, impressively tall and so very pleased with himself, his tattoo glaring proudly and his eyes sparkling with amused challenge, he knew which of the two options he would be choosing. Let the young buck do some more work, carry the platform with the dead woman all the way to Lone Hill. Maybe it would make him lose some of this beaming air of well-being and proud self-assurance the wild thing had adopted since coming back home. It would also present the opportunity to travel leisurely on their way back, to have time to talk.

So even though the sun was already tilting toward to the trail behind their backs, they had set out, parting their ways with the rest of their people. Burdened with bags of meat, folded hides, and rolls of sinew, along with other useful parts they contained, the hunters disappeared quickly, more than happy to get started on their journey home. Iheks and Osweda had been smirking until out of sight, not hiding their baiting amusement, the pretty girl's insistent stares not lost on any of them.

The annoying girl. He had found himself watching her too, covertly, whenever her eyes would leave him. Tall and willowy, she had a beautiful grace to her stride, a dignity of movement that turned her into a very pleasant sight, even without the allure of the enormous doe-like eyes and the masses of flowing hair, not tied into a braid but swaying free, cascading down her back, so thick it could serve as a cloth had she lacked proper covering. The thought that would set his imagination on fire, in the most improper of ways. He was popular with his wife's clan and her longhouse, entrusted with all sorts of leading positions voted to him by the women of her clan's council, en route to true leadership.

Of course, important positions were to be reached in various ways, but the surest and shortest lay through the path of the Clans' Councils. A person of his aspirations could do the best following the accepted road, even though people like Father, people of true gift and destiny, did everything their own way. Still, such people were as rare as a snow-white rabbit in the summer forest, while most of the leaders arrived where they had doing everything the proper way, angering no influential women, fooling around with pretty girls being the surest way to do that. Troublemakers like his brother could do whatever they liked and still land on their feet, but then, this particular specimen did not aspire to anything, as it seemed, so did not need to watch his step the way he, Ganayeda, had to.

"What's wrong?" The girl's voice pulled him out of his reverie, back into the sunlit reality of the hilltop they stood upon. The trail they had been following twisted on, disappearing into the bushes, inviting to follow it, to enjoy the breeze and the shadow. Even though they had adjusted the platform in a way that made it comfortable to drag along whenever the terrain allowed it, the dead woman was still not an easy burden to carry for half a day. "Why do you—"

"Hush!" Okwaho's voice cut the girl off rudely, his gesturing reinforcing his words, demanding silence.

Raising his eyebrows, Ganayeda glanced at his brother, curious rather than put out with this sudden presumption to tell them what to do. Looking like a deer about to break into a heedless run, or a wolf on the trail of footprints, the young man poised on one leg, all alertness, leaning forward, rigid with attention, the annoyingly breezy confidence he had returned with gone. One good turn. He must have learned something through the whole span of seasons being out there and fighting, hopefully more than just spiriting away outlandish women.

"I'm going to check that thing," Okwaho's lips barely moved as he said this, his words just a breath of air, eyes indicating the footprint that disappeared into the foliage, showing a few broken branches but not much more than that.

Ganayeda just nodded. The young buck seemed to know what he was doing, although there was nothing especially alarming in those marks. Any hunter or other wandering local could have left those. They were in their homelands. Near the Great Sparkling Water, yes, with the enemy being in the habit of an occasional crossing, more scouting than raiding, usually small parties of warriors, easily manageable, a nuisance but not a full-scale war. It had been decades since the Crooked Tongues gave the Five Nations real trouble; before the Five Nations were Five Nations, come to think of it.

"Sit there and keep quiet." Glancing at the women, he indicated the platform with a curt nod. "Take a rest."

"No, please!" His pretty charge leapt toward him, not daring to touch him, but as though about to do so, her eyes sparkling with tears. "Please, don't leave." Her friend's silent stare reinforced the plea.

"Keep quiet!"

He listened to the rustling of the breeze, the insects and birds chirping peacefully, undisturbed. Nothing untoward there.

"Go and sit there with your friend," he said, avoiding her gaze and the temptation to steer her back. There would be no touching, not with this one. "I'm not going anywhere. Not yet."

"But what is wrong?" This time her voice was nothing but a whisper, and he appreciated that. Like Okwaho a few moments earlier, she was poised in that way of a deer about to spring into a wild race; in her case, a highly pleasing sight. She had the qualities of a long-legged creature about her, a certain grace of movements. He forced his eyes off her.

"That's what we are trying to find out. Now go there and keep quiet."

The look in her eyes deepened. The haunted expression gave way to a flicker of excitement, something feminine, disturbing. It set his nerves on edge.

Turning abruptly, he went back toward the prints, forcing his thoughts to concentrate, to probe with his senses, like Father had always taught him to do, like his brother had just done.

No, there were no eyes on them, hostile or otherwise. He could feel the forest surrounding him, calm, peaceful, concerned with nothing but its leisurely preparations for the night. Where had the young hothead gone? Did he think it was time to play around? If he didn't come back in a few heartbeats, he decided, they would set off without him. He, Ganayeda, had no time for this.

"We will reach your village before nightfall," he said, shrugging, readjusting the straps tied to the front branches of their makeshift means of transportation. The woman lying upon it was covered with a blanket, with only her face revealed, facing the clouded sky, calling upon it, her eyes open, faded and strange, an unsettling sight. The sooner the faith-keepers took care of her, the better, he knew, shivering against his will. His daughters were still young, eight and four summers old, pretty and bright, delightful in their playfulness and the lightness of their dispositions, nothing grave about either of them. Still in the care of their mother and other women of her longhouse, they were already old enough to receive chores that many times included wandering outside, gathering firewood or nuts and berries. What if they happened to cross the path of an angry beast?

He took a deep breath, desperate to banish such thoughts. It was not wise to think in this way, it was—

The sound of footsteps did not herald Okwaho's return, still he knew his brother was coming back. His own senses were not that bad, either.

The girls jumped but stifled their gasps as the young man's silhouette slid from behind the trees, his entire posture a study of alertness and concentration.

"What?" More gesturing than actually asking, Ganayeda made sure his bow was within easy reach, just in case.

"They are not many. Maybe five or six. Possibly as many as ten." Okwaho's gaze didn't focus, his senses evidently still wandering, still probing. "They camped not far away from here sometime during this morning. Then they went on, down that hill."

"What makes you think they weren't locals?"

"They made no fire."

"Oh."

Involuntarily, he followed his brother's gaze, scanning the rustling foliage in his turn. Could it actually be...

"We better hurry."

"Yes, honorable leader." Okwaho's eyebrows arched in an annoyingly suggestive manner. "Although they might be loitering right across our intended pathway."

"They still may be nothing but wandering locals." He jerked his thumb toward their charges. "Perhaps not hunters bothering with fire, but maybe women gathering things."

His brother's eyes went toward the girls, appraising them both with a certain amount of interest for the first time. Before that, he had been busy making faces, not especially pleased with the proposed detour, forced to take care of women he didn't know. The direfulness of his frowns related that he wanted to go home with the rest of the hunters. Eager to get back to his outlandish treasure? Probably. But Ganayeda had certain rights over this unruly sibling of his, and he was the leader of the mission.

"They were men," muttered Okwaho, eyes still on the women. "You both are from Lone Hill, aren't you?"

The girls nodded readily, although their gazes turned wary, and Gayeri, the prettier one, shot a worried glace at Ganayeda again, as though about to rush into his protection as had became her custom.

"Then you must know of another way, or ways, to reach your village without using the regular trail," Okwaho went on, oblivious to any of this, or maybe just indifferent. "Why would you wander so far away, getting into trouble, if you were not an adventurous pair of foxes who would know such things? You must know the trails around here."

Why hadn't he thought to ask them himself? Ganayeda narrowed his eyes. "Do you?"

"Well ..." Her frown was a pretty sight, the way her high forehead creased and her eyebrows met, looking like pointed arrows.

"Well?" Okwaho's voice was suggestive to the point of amusement, but his eyes were still on the trail, ears still pricked in too obvious of a way.

Ganayeda shot him a direful glance. "Tell me."

She pursed her lips. "When we descend this hill all the way toward the shores of the Great Lake, there is a creek. We can follow it, instead of the trail."

"Well, it's better than nothing." He thought about the walk still ahead of them. Too bad the girl didn't know of some truly good shortcut.

"No other way of going down there, bypassing this trail?" insisted Okwaho.

Now it was the turn of the second girl to shake her head.

"Not good."

"Well, this is how it is. So let us move on." Shrugging, Ganayeda picked up the protruding edge of their makeshift carrier. "We'll keep as quiet as we can."

"Not by dragging this thing all over these bushes." Okwaho's raised eyebrows kept making him angry.

"No, not by dragging this thing." The gaze he shot at his brother should have left a painful mark. "So bring your lazy carcass here and pick up your side. And if you continue with those smart remarks of yours, you will go for a swim in the Great Lake the moment we reach it."

"Oh, yes?"

But for the necessity to keep quiet, the wild buck would have burst out into a roaring laughter, realized Ganayeda, glaring against the flickering challenge reflected in the large eyes.

Another heartbeat of direful staring, and the generous lips twisted into the widest of smiles. "I could use a refreshing swim, true that." Shrugging, Okwaho, picked up the opposite edge of the platform with a showy lack of effort. "And so could you, oh-highly-esteemed leader of our expedition."

Ganayeda heard his own snort shaking the air. "Just keep your observations to yourself."

The girl's gaze was again warming his skin. She fell into his step easily, walking beside him in a natural fashion, like she had through this entire journey. Somehow he had come to expect her to do so.

Tearing his thoughts off her, he concentrated on their surroundings. The trail grew steeper, as though hurrying to leave the hill.

"About fifty paces from here." Okwaho's whisper hit his back. "You, take this thing."

He could hear the other girl halting, obviously startled by the request.

"Hurry!"

Their cargo shook, tilting dangerously with the young hothead abandoning his side. Ganayeda struggled to keep the body on it from slipping, welcoming Gayeri's propping shoulder and helpful hands. She was supporting the platform in the most helpful manner, in a no-nonsense way.

"I'll signal if there is trouble ahead." Okwaho's broad back was already fading into the darkening green.

"Why is he so concerned?" whispered the girl, shifting her shoulder, which the bundle of her few belongings was strapped to but seemed as though about to slip.

"The marks of the people roaming that hill might be that of an enemy." Unable to shrug, Ganayeda made a face. "He is good at scouting. I wouldn't have listened to him if he wasn't."

"Crooked Tongues?"

"Maybe." Detecting a fear in her voice, he smiled at her, trying to be encouraging. "We will be in your village before we meet them, so there is nothing to be afraid of. These marks that he saw were not from a raiding party." The platform shook once again, forcing him to fight for his balance anew. "Go back there and help your friend. Okwaho may be a good scout, but he was stupid to make her do the man's work."

"We'll manage." One more of her admiring gazes, and she was gone, swift and efficient, and so very graceful of step. He tried to hide his smile.

For a while they proceeded on, with both girls doing a good job supporting their burden in a way that made their progress easier. A hundred paces, then some more. No abandoned campsites, fireless or not, happened on their way, and no other indication. The forest was quiet, restful, settling for the night.

He wondered if his brother had come upon a chance to do his washing somewhere there down the hill, avoiding doing his duty in an elegant way he had made his own since the times immemorial. Oh, but the young troublemaker was incurable, and he would have to find a way to show him, to discipline that one, despite his recently gained glory.

The moisture in the air grew, carrying the message of the Great Lake being near, when the subject of his irritated musings materialized from behind the trees again, not marring their peacefulness but merging with it, moving like shadow. If his ears weren't pricked and his senses honed, Ganayeda knew, he would have been startled. As it was, the gasps of the women made him catch his breath. The danger was there, his brother's face told him, his eyes dark and sealed, with not a trace of the usual lighthearted mischief.

Without a word, the young man snatched the other edge of the platform, and together, they put it down carefully, making no sound. A curt nod signaled the women to stay where they were, before following the disappearing figure.

Deeper in the grove, the light dimmed, giving way to the premature dusk. Sensing the nearing evening, mosquitoes and other night insects came out in swarms, buzzing all around, eager to sample the uninvited intruders.

Where? he motioned, catching his brother's eye.

Down there, was his silent answer. An additional nod indicated the faint trickling of the brook somewhere beyond the entanglement of the branches.

He listened carefully, until his ears picked up an additional sound. Some branches creaked with no apparent reason. Not every rustling belonged to the woods and their natural inhabitants.

Three, Okwaho's extended palm told him. Then another two fingers came up. *Five*. Five men. Not hunters, nor local people. He regretted sending all his men back home.

Listening carefully, they went on, with Okwaho still in the lead, proceeding with a marked ease, turning to signal once in a while. What cheek! Had it not been for the need to keep absolutely quiet, he would have pushed his way past the presumptuous youngster, assuming the leadership that was rightfully his. They were not two brothers on a stroll around the town. And yet, to fight for a place while spying out a possible enemy was beneath a person of his status and dignity.

There!

This time, Okwaho went absolutely still, not even moving his head, but letting his eyes do the motioning. Slipping up beside him, Ganayeda peered through the colorful foliage, careful to not disturb a leaf, not even by breathing.

The men in the clearing seemed to be as alerted. Only two, as far as he could see; they merged with the brown of the tree trunks, their shirts long-sleeved and undecorated, of the same hue. The Crooked Tongues, most clearly. He didn't need to hear them speaking to arrive at this conclusions. Their clothes proclaimed their belonging, even if nothing else did.

The people from across the Great Lake were foreign, but only to a certain degree. The Great Peacemaker had come from beyond the enormous mass of water. He had spoken in the way the Crooked Tongues did, not coherently enough, understood, but with an effort; he needed people like Father and Hionhwatha, one of the original founders of the Great Peace and the High Springs representative in the Great Council, to speak for him, to be listened to.

Still, there were great similarities in the ways of both sides of the Great Lake, their customs, the tongues they had spoken, their clothing. Their attitude, most certainly. The Peacemaker wanted to unite them all, Father had claimed, striving to do the same against convention and much prejudice, angering many people.

And no, it had nothing to do with their mother, Ganayeda knew. She might have been born a Crooked Tongue as well, but she had been a perfect Longhouse People woman for more decades than any of them could remember. No, Father's desire to draw the notorious enemy into the great alliance had to do with the Peacemaker and his legacy alone. Nothing to do with Mother. Though both their parents made sure to teach their sons to speak like the enemy did, fluently enough, better than most of their countryfolk could.

From the corner of his eye, he could see Okwaho shifting his bow, pulling an arrow, disturbing not even the thin air in the process. Impressed, Ganayeda's fingers tightened around his knife, not daring to reach for the quiver behind his back. There was no chance of him doing it silently enough, drawing none of the invaders' attention.

He watched the enemies' unpainted faces, the alertness of their poses, the readiness of their weapons, nothing but knives and bows, light weaponry fit for sniffing around, with no heavy burden to hinder their progress. The enemy scouts. Did this mean that the Crooked Tongues were getting more organized? Of an old, these people would send an occasional raiding party, yes, but nothing as ominously prearranged as a group of scouts. What were they planning?

An abrupt movement near his moccasin made his heart leap in fright. Widening, his eyes caught the swift form of a rabbit, shooting past him, disappearing into the gap between two stones. It cost him an enormous effort not to move a limb; still, something changed. The people on the other side of the bushes tensed, looking around, gesturing briefly.

He could feel Okwaho cursing under his breath. When one of the enemies slipped forward, heading straight toward the trees they were using for cover, he knew there was no way back.

Okwaho's arrow hissed, tearing the silence, burying itself in the second man's chest. Still dazed from the speed of the happenings, Ganayeda watched the first man ripping his way through the shrubs, uttering a short cry as he did this. A warning?

He leapt aside in time to avoid the touch of a flying arrow, his senses warning him, forcing him into further movement. Another arrow swished, and he knew there were more people around, not just the two they had watched.

Okwaho was dealing with the first man, shooting again before pouncing, his arrow wounding the enemy but not rendering him useless. In a heartbeat, both were on the ground, struggling to pin one another into helplessness, both knives flashing in the last of the light.

He calculated fast. The man who was shooting must have been heading their way in a hurry, without a pause to take good aim. No more arrows flew, but he could hear branches cracking. More than one pair of feet. Not good.

Rushing toward the noise, he met the man halfway, readying as he watched this enemy jump over a pile of stones, his club raised high. So not everyone was armed with light weaponry!

He barely had time to avoid the smashing blow, crashing into a tree trunk and sliding alongside it, desperate to find some sort of cover, even if a temporary one. The rough bark tore at the skin of his exposed torso mercilessly, at the same time offering support, something to clench onto in order not to fall.

The man attacked again, viciously, skirting the obstacle with not a thought spared to his own safety, Ganayeda's lack of club clearly heartening his spirit. Clenching his knife tight, Ganayeda ducked again, then tried to feint an attack from the other side of the tree they were dancing around, desperate to throw the man out of balance, to force him into making the mistake of letting him closer. Or at least into pausing. The vicious blows kept bouncing off the bark, and he knew that one would land where it intended, eventually.

Leaving the support of his unsatisfactory first cover, he dashed toward another tree, tearing at his bow frantically, knowing he had no time to as much as bring it up, let alone to fit an arrow in. His rival was upon him again, and one more form sprang into his view, leaping above a cluster of bushes.

Throwing himself out of the range of yet another club, he rolled over the rustling ground, carpeted with a multitude of colorful leaves, his hands locking around some rotten log, desperate. It met the next onslaught with no chance of holding on, his newly acquired weapon lacking in durability, his hands not having the necessary support an upright position could offer.

The club was nearing, and he clenched his teeth, determined to hold on against hope, to stop the unseemly chasing around. The footsteps of another man were nearing too, but he paid them no attention, watching the club coming down with exaggerated clarity, as though in a dream. The sweaty face of its owner was twisted with strain, so very clear, expectant, exalted at the kill. When something collided with it and pushed it away, he was surprised. This was out of place, unwarranted, disrupting the ritual.

The sounds were back, and not knowing where the respite came from but welcoming it, he rolled frantically, snatching up his bow as he did, tearing the arrows out of his quiver, as many as his hand managed to grab, fitting them as he rose, shooting one after another, impaling his other attacker with too many feathered shafts.

For a moment, it grew eerily quiet, then his brother's blood-sprinkled face came into his view, beaming, the mischief back in place.

"No time to sprawl around, glorious hero. There are more of the filth eaters out there. I saw the signs." Another happy beam. "Stop lazing around."

"Shut up." Incredulous, he took in the slough that the small space between the trees had become, covered with blood and sprawling bodies, lying in strange positions, the man he had shot looking bizarre, with too many spikes sticking out of his chest all at once.

"You made a porcupine out of this one," commented Okwaho, bending to pull out the first arrow.

Placing one foot on the man's torso, he grabbed the feathered shaft with both hands, yet not before muttering the appropriate words of prayer. While he had been gathering his senses, Ganayeda realized, taken aback, his brother went from warrior to warrior, seeing their spirits off, quickly and efficiently, saying all the right words.

"Yes, I shouldn't have shot all the arrows," he muttered, blinking to make his head work. His eyes scanned the scenery anew. "You killed three men, Brother. How did you manage to do that? And so quickly."

"Oh, well, you know, we had no time to do it in a leisurely way." Wiping his brow, Okwaho tossed the released arrows at the ground before Ganayeda's feet, still chuckling. "Next time, we'll do it slower, for your pleasure."

"You annoying piece of meat, you didn't change." Picking up his returned weaponry, Ganayeda wiped the bloodied tips with a handful of grass. "You just learned how to fight, that's all. Don't feel too good about what I'm going to say, but you *are* good at that. Very good." He eyed the mess that stood in place of the head of one of their enemies. "That one was going to get me."

"Well, yes, but stones, they come in handy, sometimes."

"But you were busy fighting that other filth-eater with the knife."

"No, I was through with him by that time. The other one worried me, though; the one that you made into a porcupine. I didn't know you were going to do that, and he was very eager, spoiling for a fight." Another decisively provocative beam. "You get impressed easily, Brother. Go live with the Flint People for a while, sail their Great River. You will see sights worth seeing. Bored you will not be, I can promise you that. Not once you reach the River People's lands. Now there, you'll see enough fighting to make up for all the summers of boredom back home."

"Oh, yes? Well, it is not that boring here at home, apparently." Adjusting his quiver after fitting the arrows back in, Ganayeda picked up one of the offered clubs, impressed with his brother's efficiency almost against his will. He was still struggling to get a grip of his senses, while the young buck did everything, from picking up the weaponry to seeing the departing spirits off, enemy or not. "I don't need to go to the lands of the savages to learn how to fight."

But the beam was gone, replaced with a bleak gaze. "They are no savages."

"What?"

The good humor didn't come back. "The people whose lands our Flint People raid are called River People, and they are no savages." He saw the young face closing, before his brother turned to scan the clearing one more time. "I'll talk to Father about these people. We can have them in our Great League as allies and brothers. The sixth or the seventh nation. After the Crooked Tongues. Why wouldn't we?" The eyes came back, dark and narrow with challenge. "The Peacemaker's legacy allows it. His laws make it clear. Any nation that is of the right mind and willing to join can do so."

Ganayeda suppressed his snort. "I wish you well in this undertaking, Brother. Father didn't manage to make an alliance with the Crooked Tongues, and he worked to this end for longer than we both remember ourselves." He stood the darkening gaze, the sight of the pressed lips and the tight jaw making him pity the young man, but not enough to not tell him the truth. "Neither our people nor theirs are of a right mind or willing, although we have a long history of close ties. Just look at our family, or many others. The Great Peacemaker himself came from their lands, even though they weren't wise enough to listen to his message. Well, little brother, if a man of Father's caliber, the greatest and wisest man of them all, with all his wisdom, power, and influence, a person everyone in our Great League listens to, didn't manage to make them accept the Crooked Tongues, what are your chances to do that, to make anyone take you seriously, you and those strange, savage-looking River People of yours?"

Not to mention that if your woman can be considered as an indication, then even the word 'savages' may be too good for them, he thought, but was wise enough not to say it aloud, the blood-curdling glare of his younger sibling telling him that he had taken it far enough as it was.

Shrugging, he turned around. "Let us hurry back. In case—"

The piercing scream and the following noise was everything they needed to hear to break into a heedless run, panting uphill, their breath caught.

CHAPTER 5

"Where is that annoying she-moose?"

The girl by the fireplace stomped her foot, raising a small cloud of dust. From her cozy hideaway on the upper shelf near the ceiling, Kentika could not see them—even had she wanted to, which she didn't. The noise they made gave enough information for her imagination to follow.

"Honorable Clan Mother will be so angry," said another young voice, openly worried. "She will explode like a thunderbolt if we don't find her." A fretful pause. "I haven't seen her so openly enraged in a long while. She called us names!"

More perturbed silence.

"It's not our fault!" The whimpering voice began drawing away.

Heading down the corridor, Kentika surmised, to invade the privacy of the next compartment's dwellers, or the ones after them.

What a strange arrangement it was, to live all together, she thought again, for the thousandth time since arriving in this town. Not like a few closely tied families, like in her village, but the entire clan living side by side, sharing the same house. Longhouse! They even had a special name for their dwellings. Moreover, they named themselves after their houses; that's how proud they were of their strange living arrangement. The People of the Longhouse they called themselves, all those different nations. Four, five of them? She had lost count when he tried to explain. To understand these people seemed impossible, and she wasn't even sure that she wanted to. To huddle on the upper shelf and munch on the food supplies stored there seemed like a better pastime.

Wrinkling her nose, she took her time, picking between the rolls of cornbread, seeking one with the most berries in it. It was a delicious thing, those small buns of bread with berries. Dry maybe, yes, stored up here for a day or more, but still the tastiest treat. Better than regular bread, for sure, even if freshly made.

How had she not found this wonderful shelf before? she wondered, nibbling on the crumbling parts, not in a hurry to devour them. It was only this afternoon, when she had sneaked back into the town, tired and perturbed, mainly by the conversation she was forced to overhear, its meaning too obvious, even if she didn't manage to understand all the words, it was only then, after somehow managing to reach their longhouse undetected, that she discovered the wonders of the upper shelves.

Before that, it was always too crowded, too full of people, dwellers of this compartment, his immediate family, and their neighbors, all these inhabitants of the longhouse and their constant guests, too crowded to feel free to look around. But this time, even if afraid and in trouble, yet blissfully alone, she had dared to look up; to discover this treasure of easy-to-reach privacy in her temporary home.

And a temporary home it was, he was careful to explain. When she felt ready for the adoption process, she would have to pick a different clan, and move to one of their longhouses.

Why? she had asked him back then, terrified. His family longhouse was bad enough, but to switch it for another one, inhabited by total strangers? Oh, Benevolent Glooskap!

But he only laughed and told her to relax. They would be moving to her new longhouse together. He would be coming to live there with her, in her compartment, her longhouse. The men moved to live in their women's houses, he had told her, eyes twinkling, the mischief there, near the surface, sparkling challenge, tempting her to jump on him and try to make him fall, and tickle and laugh and tumble about. She would have done all that and more, but for them being surrounded by his family and only mighty spirits knew whom else, all those watchful eyes. Oh, how she wished they all would just disappear.

Well, two people of the same clan could not marry, he had gone on explaining, so she would need to be adopted into another clan. But there was no need to fret about any of it just yet, he had added, smiling and pulling her close, his touch so welcome, so reassuring. It would take time, and by then, she would be ready. Mother would see to it, he had said.

However, on the next day, he was off, joining that hunting expedition, and now his mother, the head of their entire longhouse and the member of their Clans Council was looking for her, angry beyond measure, so much so that even other girls, those who were sent to find her, were shaking in fear. Oh, all the great and small spirits!

Shuddering, she tried to push her fear away. What could they do to her? Punish her? Kill her? Could a Clan Mother do that?

After all, she did run away from her duties, and she did push one of the girls hard, making her fall. At the time, it seemed like an appropriate thing to do. The dirty snake gave her derisive glances all the time and then said nasty things. She deserved to be punched hard. In fact, the nasty fox got away lightly. But would their Clan Mother see it in the same way? No, most certainly she wouldn't, and apparently, she was already angry, furious even, so livid that the other girls grew frightened, those who were not guilty of anything at all.

Huddling closer to the bark wall, she regretted returning to the town. Maybe it would be safer, more prudent, to stay out there and wait for Okwaho to come back? The upper shelf of this compartment gave a measure of privacy, yes, but it was no place to hide. Everyone who bothered to look up could see her, an enraged Clan Mother, the mistress of this longhouse, sooner than anyone.

Through the roof opening, she could see the evening sky, glimmering darkly, studded with stars. But for a way of reaching that opening! To climb down the ladder and try to sneak away using the corridor would put her on the path of too many people, including the dirty foxes who were looking for her. But what choice did she have?

Judging by the voices ringing everywhere, most of the activity concentrated around one of the compartments, where someone was sick, she had gathered this morning. A girl, someone everyone liked and worried about.

Migisso would have known what to do, she decided with a stab of longing, making her way down the sturdy ladder—a very solid affair, probably carved out of single piece and not composed of poles and rungs like back at home. Her brother would have found how to make this sick girl feel better. He would have checked her forehead and then held her wrist, tapping gently with his fingers every now and then, listening to what it told him for a long time. And then, he would prepare a medicine, brew something smelly or bitter-tasting, burning tobacco and muttering prayers. And then, all would be well.

The tears were near, blurring her vision. Resolutely, she blinked them away. She wouldn't think about Migisso, not now. Maybe later, when it would be easier, when Okwaho was back and all was well again.

Pressing her lips tight, she headed in the direction opposite to the commotion, glad that their longhouses had two entrances, and that sometimes one was used more frequently than the other.

Successful at avoiding people and their questioning gazes, this time actually relieved that no one bothered trying to talk to her, ever, she dived into the vast storage room that separated the last living compartment from the entrance and the doorway that was rarely shut, gaping wide open, the bark sheet that was supposed to be used for this purpose slid aside, leaned against the wall, neglected.

The outside greeted her with a gust of cool air and the rustling of the autumn leaves. And voices. Those burst upon her, accompanied by silhouettes, blocking the doorway.

Hurriedly, she leapt aside, pressing against the wall, ready to fight if they tried to take a hold of her. She wouldn't be dragged, neither in nor out of the building. She wouldn't be going anywhere with them, Clan Mother or not!

Heart thumping, she watched them pouring in, passing through the dim, crowded space, paying her no attention. The elderly man in the lead held what looked like a rectangular wooden object, while those close behind carried bundles and drums.

Following their wide backs with her gaze as they proceeded down the corridor, Kentika let out a held breath, not daring to move yet. Who were these people?

Then her heart missed a beat, as more silhouettes blocked the flow of the breeze, and this time they belonged to women, with a tall figure in the lead, her way of walking familiar, brisk but graceful, as though in a dance.

Pressing deeper into the scattered tools and utensils, she tried to make herself invisible, but, of course, nothing escaped the watchful eye of a clan mother, the head of their longhouse more than anyone. Squinting against the semi-darkness, the woman slowed her step, motioning the others to proceed.

"Why are you here?" she asked quietly, not sounding angry or indignant, just very busy.

Kentika swallowed hard, part of her mind on the question, trying to find an appropriate answer, the rest contemplating her way out. It was still possible to just bolt for the opening and be gone.

"Listen..." As though reading her thoughts, the woman stepped closer, blocking her way. "I want to talk to you. Come with me and wait. It won't take long." The large eyes appraised Kentika sincerely, holding no reproach. "The False Face Society people will not need my presence. Until they are done, we'll have time to talk. Come."

The light nod and the wave of the long-fingered hand made Kentika follow, quite against her will. Oh, but this woman was used to obedience. She didn't even look back to see if she was being followed. Instead, she proceeded to catch up with the rest of her entourage, who, unlike her, were shooting curious glances despite the obvious gravity of the occasion. Whoever those people with masks were, they were evidently heading toward the sick girl's compartment. So it must have something to do with the healing. Or did it?

To take her thoughts off the troublesome topics—what would

her punishment be for today's transgressions; why was this woman so brisk and matter-of-fact, not looking angered in the least?—Kentika glanced at the crowded space, standing on her tiptoes to see better. Her height always gave her an advantage, but not among these people. Everyone seemed to be tall in this town, and sturdy, and well fed. She thought about the staggering amount of corn she was made to peel this morning, baskets piling one on top of another, threatening to spill, not about to end, with all this treasure belonging to only one longhouse of one clan. How much food this town produced and consumed!

The elderly man was chanting, busy above the nearest hearth, fiddling with the glowing embers until the tongues of flame produced the familiar, pleasant scent of burning tobacco, spreading along the bark walls, banishing the odor of sickness. When the elder knelt next to the huddled figure of the sick girl, whose mind seemed to wander, not registering the procedures, Kentika barely managed to stifle a gasp, as his face was covered by the most frightening mask she had ever seen, with a pair of bulging, unnaturally round eyes, the semblance of a broken nose, and a row of protruding teeth bared in what looked like a deadly grin.

A hand caught her elbow, pulling hard, making her heart nearly jump out of her chest in fright.

"Look away!" hissed an elderly woman she did not recognize. "Don't stare."

Now she noticed that the people around her dropped their heads, some drifting away, others joining the chanting. The soft drum of the rattles filled the air.

"I not know," she muttered, the glare of the woman still upon her, burning her skin. "I did not—"

"Just don't stare the way you did," repeated the old crone, uncompromising. "It is wrong, inappropriate. It will harm the healing." She dropped her voice to a mere whisper when others glanced at them, as direful and admonishing. "You should know at least that."

Alarmed by too many reproachful gazes, Kentika struggled to free her hand, now frightened for real. There were too many angry people and too little space, the corridor packed, blocking her way of escape, the chanting intensifying, fraying her nerves. She needed to breathe fresh air; not clouds of tobacco smoke. She would die if she didn't. Or maybe scream and faint.

There was a movement in the crowd, and another hand took hold of her shoulder. Not pressing or assaulting, it pulled her lightly, supporting, propelling her out. The bunks and bark walls disappeared gradually, and as she drew deep breaths, one after another, she felt her heart slowing down, falling back into its natural rhythm.

"Let us just stroll around," said the woman, straightening her own shoulders, as though also relieved to be outside. "Near tobacco plots, it might be quieter. We have less chance of being interrupted there."

This time, Kentika followed with no misgivings. Whatever this influential Clan Mother had in store for her, she seemed to be more reasonable, less unforgiving than the others.

"I not, not stare," she ventured when the chanting that was still heard most clearly even when outside began dying away, with their longhouse dissolving in the gathering darkness. "I not know, not hear that we not look. I didn't … I would not …"

"You meant no disrespect," concluded the woman, and this time there was a smile in her voice. "I know you didn't. I should have warned you, or better yet, I should have told you to wait out there." From the corner of her eye, she saw her companion turning her head, measuring her with a curious, or maybe even amused, glance. "The thing is, I wasn't sure you would wait. I suspected you might run away again. Wouldn't you?"

Kentika felt it safer to shrug and say nothing.

"But didn't you know about False Face Society's rites?" continued the woman as though not expecting the answer. "Who are the ones responsible for healing and the rites of the medicine men among your people?"

"Umm …" She tried to understand the question, not an easy feat with her companion talking too rapidly, as briskly as she moved. "I don't know."

"You can't not know that." The woman's laughter rang lightly, not holding offense. "But if you don't want to tell me, you don't have to. Let me tell you about our rites, instead." The darkness was thicker near the massive fence and the tobacco plots that dotted this part of the entrance into the settlement. "You see, once upon a time, when our creator, the Right-Handed Twin, filled our beautiful Turtle Island with life, he had strolled about, smiling, enjoying the sight of his creation, eyeing the plants and animals and people with satisfaction, pleased. It must have looked so different from the bare earth his grandmother, Sky Woman, had landed upon. Surely, it was the most beautiful sight."

Slowing her step, the woman beckoned Kentika to follow a smaller trail that twisted between the sprawling plots. As if she wouldn't have. By that time, she was afraid to breathe in case it would make her miss one single word. Her companion might have spoken differently, more difficult to understand than the others, but her voice was beautiful, mesmerizing, flowing like a calm current, telling of fascinating things.

"Well, as he was strolling about, he saw a man, walking in the distance. 'Who are you?' he asked the stranger as he neared. 'Oh, me? I'm just walking around, admiring my work, all these wonderful creations,' was the stranger's response."

Turning around, the woman peered at Kentika, as though making sure her audience was suitably surprised. Kentika tried to do her best, even though the foreign words kept whirling around her head, not easy to put together in a way that made sense. So there was this creator, a twin, like Glooskap, probably, and someone else was making him upset, interrupting his enjoyment of looking at the fruits of his work.

"'But you are wrong,' said our creator. 'It is I who created all this.' And so they began to argue, until the Right-Handed Twin suggested that they compare their powers, see who was stronger. 'There is this mountain,' he said, pointing at the high ridge that still, in these very days, adorns the beautiful lake at the heart of the Mountain People's lands. 'We will move it, and the one who pushes it farther will be the winner of this contest. He will be declared the creator.' And so it was." Again, a blissful, even if short, pause let Kentika attempt to make an order out of the pleasant flow of words, to try to compose it into the beautiful tale it must have been if understood properly. "'But we will be doing it with our backs turned to the mountain,' demanded the stranger. 'And we will not look back until each of us is done.' The creator agreed, and so it was. They turned away, and the stranger tried his powers first. When allowed to look back, the Right-Handed Twin was surprised to see that the mountain had indeed moved, even if only a little."

"But how," breathed Kentika, forgetting her previous wariness. "How he did, the stranger, how move? It's not …"

The woman's smile was wide, pleased with the effect. "Oh, no one knows that. The stranger, the one whom we know today as Ethisoda—our grandfather—had certain power as well, apparently. But back then, it was not known." Her smile growing more serious, the woman nodded, her hands coming up, fingers intertwined, as though channeling her words. "Well, our creator was impressed, but they went on with the contest, turning their backs to the mountain once again."

"And then what, what happen?" asked Kentika, unable to bear the ensuing pause.

"Oh, what do you think, young one? The noise was deafening, the roaring of the crushing rocks and falling stones. It startled the stranger into turning back before the time, and what happened next shaped the future False Face Society, you see."

"How?" Leaning forward, she tried to catch the words before they left her companion's generously curved lips.

"The stranger didn't know that our creator had moved the mountain so far, it now stood next to them, so close that his face smashed into it when he turned back toward it. It broke his nose and caved in one side of his face, so it looked crooked, twisted, deformed. For all times to come."

"Oh, but it's no good. Why do that? Why punish? He just ask—"

"No, no, girl, it wasn't on purpose." The interwoven fingers parted as the woman's hands waved in the air, pushing the accusation away. "He just turned around too soon, you see. It's not that he was punished for his presumption, although his original claim was arrogant enough, don't you think?" The smile was back, a cozy, conspiratorial smile. "No one likes his or her worked being claimed by others, eh? I hear that you can be pushed to violence if you think that someone might be claiming your basket that you worked to fill for a long morning. Can't you?"

"I-I did no wrong. I didn't mean…" The words refused to form, the accusation too sudden, uttered in a surprisingly friendly manner, but still an accusation.

Her companion's smile didn't waver, glimmering with a fair measure of playfulness still.

"Well, so did our creator. Think about it. He moved that mountain with maybe too much force, but he just wanted to prove a point. To create all the world and everything good in it is more work than to take care of forty, fifty cobs of maize." A friendly wink. "Anyway, back to our False Face Society, the mask you were staring at, don't you recognize it? The crooked side, the gaping eyes, the broken nose, eh? Oh, yes, this is Ethisoda, our grandfather, whom the Right-Handed Twin entrusted with healing people. He was impressed with his powers, you see. So he gave him very important work to do." Resuming her walk, the woman shook her head, as though awakening from a dream. "I'm surprised your people are not aware of Ethisoda's power. Too bad they don't use it, as surely all people created by the Right-Handed Twin could benefit from the healing rituals of the False Face Society."

The longing hit her again, more forcefully than before.

"My people, they heal, do healing. Our medicine man, he burn tobacco, and he pray, and he do medicine, prepare medicine. Not masks, yes, but he do other, other ceremony, and burn tobacco. And my brother," she swallowed hard, "he healer now, great healer. He saved Akweks, he treat rotten wound, that good he is! And Okwaho." The next gulp of air made a convulsing sound. "He save, he took the knife out, treat Okwaho, until he was good."

The yearning to see him, to feel his arms around her, welled, stronger than the previous longing for her village, even the wish to see her brother. They had never parted before, not since the terrible day when he had been stabbed, but it had been three dawns since she had seen him. No, four by now. Oh, Benevolent Glooskap, let him come back soon, and unharmed!

The woman in front of her tensed visibly. "What happened?" The large, beautifully spaced eyes peered at Kentika, blazing with tension. "What knife?"

Startled and a little frightened by the intensity in her converser's voice, Kentika hesitated. "The knife, when he wounded, when … before we go back here."

"Was Okwaho wounded badly?"

"Well, yes. It was all terrible, confuse. My people, and his people, and he try to stop. He talk and I talk in my tongue, tell what he said. And then, and then—" She pressed her lips tight, unable to admit the truth, shamed by it. Oh, but she would never forgive Father, never!

The warm palm locked around her wrist, tightening in a pleading manner, friendly, not threatening. "Tell me about it. Tell me exactly what happened. He tried to stop people from fighting. Why?"

"He try to save, save my village, save his people too. Many got killed, many warriors. Too many, he said. He said no point. Said need stop."

"Did he make them listen?" The woman's voice was no more than a breath of air, the lightest breeze.

"Yes, they listen. Not at first. At first not listen. The War Chief"—no, she wouldn't call this man father, not anymore; he was not her father—"talk bad, say bad things. But Okwaho did not stop. Not afraid. Face everyone. And talk, make his people listen. Then mine."

"And then what happened?" The wide-open eyes clung to her, burning, hanging on her words as though she, Kentika, were the most skillful storyteller.

"Well, then the knife, Father… the war chief… I tried to stop." Tired from the incessant search for words, she just gestured, showing the knife sticking into her ribs. "I hold, but he say no, go, talk to them, make them listen again, or all is for nothing. I didn't know what to do. But he say, insist." The mere memory made her shudder. "But my brother, he take care, he care for Okwaho, take the knife out, close wound, made medicine. Make all good again."

"He said nothing about it," muttered the woman, her gaze now upon the ground, immersed in her thoughts. "Not about the wound, nor about doing something as meaningful or as courageous as stopping a hopeless fight." The eyes came back up, puzzled, full of wonder. "His father will be so proud to hear that. So incredibly proud!"

"I think he no time," ventured Kentika. "His brother make go hunt. Okwaho make faces, but go."

Her companion's generous lips twisted into the hint of a mischievous grin that made the resemblance too great not to notice. Some of his looks and disposition obviously came from his mother.

"Ganayeda wanted him all for himself. This boy always needed to know first. I'm sure he has fished this story out of our young wolf in all its glorious details by now."

I hope not, thought Kentika, hugging her elbows against the cruel wind. *Not all of it. Not about Father, surely.* He wouldn't tell, would he? What would this scary-looking brother of his, such a formidable hunter and warrior, think? And his father and the other people of his family? And this woman, she wouldn't take it kindly that it was her, Kentika's, father who had been so treacherous, so false-hearted and crooked, wishing to kill her son in such a foul, despicable way. Oh, this woman would turn into an enemy, and just as she had come to discover how unexpectedly nice, kind, warm, and lighthearted company she was. Much like Okwaho, come it think of it. Probably a dangerous enemy, but a wonderful presence as a friend.

"I thank you for telling me all this," the woman was saying, her gaze resting on Kentika, a slight wonder in it obvious, as though questioning her companion's change of mood, but not bringing it into the open. "When we both have more time, after the ceremonies and the festivities are over, I would love to hear your entire story, if you wish to share it with me. This boy, he made us all wonder. The change in him is too glaring, too striking and deep to attribute it to a few seasons spent away, gaining fighting experience. He has seen close to twenty summers. He was not such a youth when he left." Turning away, the woman shook her head, still hesitating, as though deliberating if it was time to leave their relative privacy and take the narrow path leading back into the hubbub of the town. "No, it has to be something else that made him change so. Your story only proves my suspicion." The light nod invited Kentika to follow. "I wish I had more time, but even now, I had no right to run away like this. An unthinkable deed prior to the harvest festivities, to disappear for such a long time, telling no one." A soft chuckle wafted in the air. "So now we both are guilty of shrinking away from our duties, come to think of it. Two outlaws."

Pausing again, the woman turned back, her face alluring and youthful in the kind softness of the moonlight, hiding the signs of age. She must have been truly beautiful when young, reflected Kentika randomly, not feeling threatened, not anymore. Why was she afraid of this woman before? Why were the other girls?

"You know, I took you out here to talk about more urgent matters, about your place and your involvement in our longhouse's affairs. It is a temporary arrangement, yes—you will be adopted into another longhouse of another clan when the time comes—still, we need to make it work, you and us, the women of our corner of the Wolf Clan. There are quite a few moons of working and living together ahead of us." The smile flickered again. "But all we did was talk old stories and gossip this time. Yet, let me tell you something. What happened today, well, I don't blame it entirely on you. The girls complained of your being unfriendly, uncommunicative. Violent, yes. You did push one of the girls, made her fall, didn't you?" The smile was gone, and the stern gaze that replaced it reminded Kentika that this woman was a clan mother and the head of their longhouse for a reason. "Why did you do this?"

The wave of panic returned, but only a small ripple. The calm, unwavering gaze did not make her feel like a cornered animal, the way she had felt for the last few dawns, since he had left. There was a question there, a matter-of-fact inquiry. No accusation, no disgust or disdain.

"I'm sure our girls were as guilty of creating a problem as your lack of friendliness was," the woman continued, her eyes narrowing, turning thoughtful, as though weighing the problem. "So we will go about solving this differently. But you will have to help all you can, girl. No more violence, no more running away. If you have something to complain about, something you can't solve peacefully, you leave what you do and you come to me. Calmly. With no outburst of anger. You will trust me to solve the problems, won't you?"

Hoping that she caught the general gist correctly, Kentika just nodded, the beautiful eyes holding her gaze, willing her to trust their sincerity.

"You will work in a different place for the next few days, under my direct supervision if I can arrange that. And it means you will be made to work harder, more so than by doing the regular tasks the other girls of your age do. Do you understand that? There will be no special treatment, no easy way. You will contribute to this clan and its well-being, just like everyone else must do."

"Yes, I understand," whispered Kentika, judging that more nodding might show disrespect, somehow.

"Good. Then let us go back and try to make it all work." The gaze boring into her deepened. "It's not always easy to be a foreigner, a person of truly different past, a person from enemy lands. I know how prejudiced some people can be, how close-minded, how intolerant. Well, we won't let such people harm you. But we will not have you turning your back on them either; nor will you be allowed to harm them in return. We will have you changing their minds, instead. The people of our longhouse are good, well-meaning girls, women, and men. They are kind and straightforward. No nasty persons among them. They don't know who you are, so they are wary, afraid, some of them, and it will be up to you to change their minds, to show them what a nice person you are, worthy of acquaintance. You might make them think differently about your people even. You and me, we will help them change their minds, won't we?"

Mesmerized, she nodded again, unable to talk, staring at the warm brown depths, feeling the night enveloping her, pleasantly cool, calming, not cold and cutting, not anymore.

The wind rustled between the wide tobacco leaves, whispering softly, encouraging, as kind as the woman in front of her, and as wise. The local spirits, whoever they were and whatever they were called—maybe the Right-Handed Twin the woman had talked about earlier, or maybe this other healer-spirit Ethisoda, or even the Rainbow Goddess he had talked about when convincing her to come with him—they weren't enemies but friends, not hostile, not nasty or hateful. They did not hate foreigners like her. They may have been wary and careful, like the people they cared about were, but they would accept her and keep her safe, just like the woman promised.

CHAPTER 6

Complying with his brother's curt gesturing, Ganayeda froze, listening intently. Not a murmur disturbed the peacefulness of the near-dusk air, not a whisper. Even the regular forest sounds seemed to dim, with the day birds retiring to sleep and the nocturnal creatures not coming out as yet. Only the breeze remained, to rustle in the foliage, to make the smaller trees creak in a calming manner.

Okwaho knelt soundlessly, putting his face so close to the ground, he looked as though he was sniffing it. Was he?

Ganayeda studied the colorful carpet of leaves in his turn. No one seemed to have passed here, no one but the regular dwellers of the forest.

As though confirming his observations, Okwaho sprang to his feet. *They didn't follow us,* said the curt sway of his head. *Not through here.* Another bout of short gesturing. *But they are up there, waiting for us,* maintained the eyes, blank with concentration.

Appreciating this estimation, along with every other suggestion his brother had expressed so far, Ganayeda nodded, following again, as quietly as he could. Moving like a wolf on a trail, Okwaho seemed to be truly one with the woods, a part of it, not an intruder like he himself felt.

Held to be a good man, with enough gift and experience to be trusted with leading many expeditions, whether hunting or escorting dignitaries to this or that destination all over the Five Nations' sprawling lands, Ganayeda now felt curiously unsure of himself, like a young boy looking up to someone who knew what he was doing.

A sensation that irritated him greatly. Okwaho was his younger sibling, a youth of a mere twenty summers, a restless spirit whom not every leader wished to invite to his hunting party due to the youth's tendency to argue and do whatever he liked whenever he felt something should be done differently. An annoying type that one span of seasons spent away and fighting had evidently changed, but not in that aspect. Who did the young buck think he was to take the lead in this way?

And yet, but for his sniffing out the enemy before the unexpected intruders had spotted them strolling the woods as though inside the safety of their own town, but for his skillful fighting down there, they would have already been caught and killed, most surely at that. Were the lands of the savages so different, making one learn so much in so little time?

Shaking his head to get rid of irrelevant thoughts, he made sure not to hasten his steps, no matter how he wanted to. His charges up there, the girl and her friend, and their dead companion, must be in dire trouble, and somehow, he cared about it, enough to wish to expedite their pace, to fight again, this time better prepared.

Okwaho's hand came up suddenly, startling him, arresting his progress. The forest around them seemed to freeze. But for the urgent rustling somewhere up there behind the trees, it might seem that the entire world had gone absolutely still.

He counted his heartbeats, ten, twenty, then some more. Here, another broken branch. It couldn't be the wind or an animal.

Okwaho was easing into the nearby foliage, melting into it like a true spirit. Spellbound, he watched the space his brother had occupied only a moment ago. There was nothing there anymore but the wind.

Some more counting of his heartbeats passed. The silence was heavy, encompassing. No more whispering and no more creaking. To follow? If Okwaho was nearing the enemy, then of course he could use help, any help. And yet, if he, Ganayeda, moved now, he would ruin it all for the young man and whatever the enterprise he embarked upon this time. He could not move like a spirit, the way Okwaho did. He would alert the enemy, who was surely on the lookout, waiting for them.

Another ten heartbeats. Clutching his bow with too much force, he moved as quietly as he could, heading for the spot his brother had disappeared into.

The wind rustled with suddenness, startling him. And so did Okwaho's figure that materialized again out of nowhere, so suddenly he nearly bumped into it.

Narrowing his eyes in an expression that he hoped related to the presumptuous would-be leader what he thought about his spontaneous actions, he watched his brother's hand coming up quickly, holding out three fingers.

No women, related the shake of his head, his eyes troubled, forehead creased. The narrowed gaze held his, hesitating, asking for advice. To attack this trio or to sneak away in search of the rest of that party, and the stolen women?

Ganayeda hesitated for only a fraction of a heartbeat. Of course they had to use the opportunity to get rid of the enemy.

We circumvent, suggested a wave of his own head. Okwaho nodded readily. The spark of the large eyes was back, brief but unmistakable, provocative, mischievous, challenging. He was enjoying himself, the young hothead. Ganayeda fought the urge to stick his elbow into the muddied ribs of his sibling. The wild cub!

This time, their foray went much smoother. Unable to coordinate their actions better, exchanging nothing but glances and nods, Ganayeda agreed that Okwaho would be the one to sneak around while he would wait where they were, keeping an eye on the invaders until his brother attacked or signaled. The moment he heard a hoot of an owl, or any other similar sign Okwaho might choose to come up with, or maybe just the sound of the attack if his brother didn't manage to sneak upon them as soundlessly as he hoped to, he would shoot, swiftly and lethally, discharging all his arrows at once, hoping to take as many of them down as he could, all three preferably. He was renowned for the accuracy and swiftness of his shooting. Evidently something his brother suddenly remembered.

A peek through the twisted branches rewarded him with a glimpse of the clearing they had left before, gleaming peacefully in the gathering dusk. But for the warriors who crouched there, one behind an old log, the other leaning against a tree, it might have looked as though no one disturbed it at all. Even the makeshift platform was still in place, laid where they had left it, the body it was hosting untouched, wrapped in a blanket. He fought the urge to move closer in order to scan the entire place.

Where did they take Gayeri and her friend, the lowlifes that they were? Did they harm them? The thought made him angry. Both women did not deserve that, whether their wandering about was warranted or not. First the bear, and now the enemy. Oh, but it was too much, and she was just a girl.

If he dared, he would have ground his teeth, his anger sudden and not easy to suppress. How bold the enemy grew! To send a party as large as this, to wander about their shores in such an assured manner, scouting and fighting if need be, kidnapping women. The enemy was growing too bold. Was it not the time to show them, to display the power of the united Five Nations League, the might of it? It would be a good opportunity to test it as well, to see how responsive the members of the union were if called upon. The Crooked Tongues were mainly the Onondaga People's and their western neighbors' problem. And yet, would the eastern members of the confederacy, the guardians of the Eastern Door, come to join the united enterprise if asked to do so? And what about Father? Would he be ready to forget his dream of an alliance with the dwellers of the other side of the Great Lake, the people who clearly did not wish to maintain any peace?

A cry of an owl cut his musings short, making his bow come to life. As an obvious noise from the other side of the clearing made the enemy jump, dashing in that direction, he tore his arrows out of the quiver, all four of them, careless of the noise he himself made now that the intruders' attention was taken away.

With practiced ease, his fingers arranged the feathered shafts between them, spending barely a fraction of a heartbeat on that. Before the alerted enemy reached the trees of the other side, his first arrow flew, then the second and third, embedding themselves in the startled warriors, one for each, rendering them helpless, writhing upon the ground.

With the last arrow still pointed, he pushed his way through the twisted branches, bursting upon the clearing to find Okwaho already there, kneeling beside one of the fallen enemies, ready to use his knife. Another inanimate form lay beside them, with the feathers of Ganayeda's shaft fluttering out of his upper back, a perfect hit.

"Attend that one." Okwaho tossed out, motioning toward the third figure, a man impaled through his lower torso, crawling upon the ground, smearing it with much blood, evidently in great pain.

Shooting his brother a dark look, not happy to receive orders yet again, Ganayeda knelt beside the man, placing his hand on the straining back, relaying a message. Behind him, he could hear Okwaho talking, addressing his charge calmly, with a practiced ease.

"It's time, brother. Prepare for your journey. Calm down, and think good thoughts."

He could hear the enemy saying something, murmuring in response. His own charge was still struggling, trying to escape. He pressed his hand firmer.

"Stop fighting," he said, wishing his words would flow as calmly as those of Okwaho. The strident tone to them was annoying, not to mention its trembling. "You have to prepare for your journey."

The man growled, his words gurgling, spitting out, impossible to understand, his desperately jerking movements relaying his message better. He wasn't about to give up and do things in a proper way. Ganayeda fought the light wave of nausea down. In the background, Okwaho was talking again, receiving nothing but relatively calm whispering back. How did he make his charge listen?

"Calm down. You need to embark upon your journey with calm." He listened to the stridency of his voice, unconvinced himself. There was no calmness about his words. They said one thing, but their tone relayed an entirely different message. The same panic his fallen enemy was displaying? The man was clawing at the ground, tearing at it, howling in a hair-raising moan, muffled by the fresh earth that now pressed against his face but still heard, the desperation of it.

"Finish him!"

Okwaho's frown was as deep as the darkest of nights. His club came up swiftly, out of nowhere as it seemed, diving downwards as a bird of prey. In a moment, it became eerily quiet.

"There was no need to prolong his suffering."

"I was not prolonging it. I was trying to calm him down." Getting to his feet with a certain difficulty, Ganayeda wiped his forehead.

"Evidently, your calming didn't work." Kneeling briefly, the young man muttered a quick prayer, then jumped back to his feet, his brisk, efficient, inconsiderate self again. In another heartbeat, he was back next to his own victim, pressing the body with his foot, preparing to pull the arrow out. "But you can shoot, Brother. Three arrows, three dead or lethally wounded, and all this before I had a time to blink properly, let alone to swing my club. How do you do that?"

Ganayeda just shrugged, still incensed over his own inadequacies. Clutching the feathered shaft sticking out of the fallen man's back, he pulled slowly, careful not to damage the flint or let the arrowhead come off.

Okwaho was already through with his charge, heading toward their first fallen. "You robbed me of the opportunity to fight, Brother. Next time, leave me at least one enemy to face."

"Stop trying to make me feel good. I know you are a better warrior."

In the same breath he had spoken, he wanted to take the words back, aghast by their meaning. Was it true? No, it could not be. His little brother was barely a man, a young troublemaker who never did anything in a proper way. Careless, impulsive, with not a grain of patience; promising, yes, but all the inappropriate things, as opposed to his older sibling. Ganayeda was the one to do it all properly, to walk the path in the perfect pace, upright and determined, fulfilling all promises. How could a single span of seasons spent elsewhere change all that? Were those things one learned in an actual warfare, while on the raid and away from home? Could one not learn by listening to the stories and fighting on small occasions?

"A better warrior than you? Stop talking nonsense." Okwaho's voice rang lightly, full of amusement. "Since when do you think so lowly about yourself, Brother? Where is that haughty sibling of mine, so perfect in everything he does that it hurts; the one who always knew what to do and how, lecturing and worse, trying to make a decent person out of everyone, me included?"

"Would you stop talking and let me think?"

"Think about what? What a good warrior I make?" With the last arrow out, and only one of the flint tips damaged, the young man was back on his feet, squinting against the last of the light. "And now to Lone Hill. We can make it there before midnight. The moon will be favoring us, unless this wind will bring clouds."

"We won't be there by midnight." Pressing his lips, Ganayeda straightened up as well, angered more than before, this time by his own troublesome dilemmas.

"Why?" The amusement in Okwaho's voice was no more.

"We'll follow the rest of the filth-eaters, get the women back."

"That won't be wise." The young man's frown was deepening together with the night. "We don't know how many they are, or how well prepared. Not to mention that they are alerted now, expecting the worst. If I were them, I would be very much on guard. We were lucky to surprise them twice instead of one time. But it might not work again. Unless they are hopeless fools, and we both know those people are none of that." The narrowing eyes peered at him, suddenly penetrating. "Let those at Lone Hill take care of their women."

Immersed in the study of the damaged arrow's broken edge, Ganayeda grunted, glad that there was something he could put his attention to instead of facing his brother's searching gaze.

"Those are our people we are talking about, Okwaho. Not some foreigners, but good Onondaga women who have just been kidnapped, and by the despicable enemy of all things. Lone Hill or High Springs, it doesn't matter. Those are Onondaga People, *our people*. How can you play with the idea of avoiding your duties as a man and as a warrior? I don't understand you at all!"

The righteous anger helped. He was right, wasn't he? Good warrior or not, his brother lacked the sense of responsibility. In this aspect, he hadn't changed.

"I see." Okwaho's voice came out slowly, thoughtfully, as though he was choosing his words, tasting them on his tongue before rolling them out. "Yes, they are our people no matter what settlement they belong to. I admit you are right about that. Well, then, rushing to Lone Hill as fast as we can still looks like a good solution to me. We would help by informing them, by joining their searching party if any of us would wish to do that. But rushing pell-mell, hot on the trail of this scouting scum, looks like a bad idea to me, not helpful to anyone but the enemy, who would be only too happy to greet us now, two battered and tired, even if gallant, hunters against how many? We don't even know that!"

"We'll find out. You are good at scanning the earth. Well, go ahead. Tell me how many they were and where they have gone. Before the last of the light disappears."

A dark glance was his answer. "You are not my leader to force me into joining your lust-induced enterprise."

The cheeky skunk! For a heartbeat, they glared at each other, transported back in time, into High Springs and their longhouse, into so many similar situations. The annoying cub had never done as he was told, respecting none of his older sibling's authority, accepting none, impossible to intimidate or even beat into obedience. Such an irritating nuisance at times.

Ganayeda shook his head. "Go away if you wish it so. I should have asked one of the other hunters to join me in this. A person I could trust not to run away at the first sight of danger."

"Oh, please!" The force with which Okwaho kicked at a rotten log sent it literally flying, jumping into the air, bouncing off the nearest tree. "If you want me to join something wild and insane, just ask, instead of pulling faces or throwing around stupid accusations. I didn't say I will leave you alone in this. I told you before that I'll go with you to Lone Hill, and I fought with you this evening enough to make you start muttering things you will regret saying. Even though you were right, just to let you know. I *am* a better warrior." The defiantly narrowed eyes were accompanied by a tightening jaw. "And if you say again that I ran away at the first sight of danger, I swear I will hit you, and I don't care what you will do about it."

Suddenly, he wanted to laugh. "You should care about what I will do if you dare to as much as come close to me with such intentions. Oh, yes, for your personal safety, you should care about that."

The stony eyes didn't thaw. "Well, I don't."

"Well, you better." This time, he laughed outright. "What a hothead you are. You may have gained some battle experience, but you are still no match for me, little brother." Shrugging, he slipped the broken flint into a small leather pouch, then bent to clean the rest of his arrows. "Do whatever you like. I will not try to force you into joining this mission, and I will not accuse you of running away. It was an undeserved slur, I admit that. Therefore, go away with a clean conscience. And hurry, so you won't miss the ceremonies of Harvest Moon."

With the arrows tucked in the quiver, and the bow placed safely behind his back, he picked up one of the enemy's clubs, then straightened, the defiant gaze still upon him, still bubbling with fury.

"Stop staring at me as though you would rather have me killed. You can't, so get it out of your head. Maybe if you spent a hundred spans of seasons fighting every fierce people ever created upon our Turtle Island, maybe then. But I doubt that. I will always be too strong for you."

"That's what you think, you conceited piece of meat." But now Okwaho's eyes flickered, heralding the return of the good humor. "You always thought the world of yourself."

"With good reason."

"Oh, please!" Tossing his club to place it more comfortably in his hand, the young man cast a pensive glance around the clearing. "I'll find you the footprints of the culprits who dared to take your pretty charge away. Never fear."

CHAPTER 7

"Honorable Mother!"

The girl's panted breath burst into the dimness of the storage room where Seketa, along with three other leading Mothers of Beaver, Turtle, and Bear Clans stood deliberating, discussing the amount of already-ground maize each clan was to contribute to the three days of the ceremony.

"I still think we should change our procedures the way I proposed," she repeated, picking up one of the smaller pottery vessels, inspecting its contents. "To avoid repetition of what happened on the last day of the Green Corn Ceremony, we better make sure every clan knows not only the amount of ground maize it is expected to provide for their day, but also the amount of bowls and baskets the others are required to volunteer. This way, we will know beforehand if something was about to be amiss."

"I don't know if we can do that." The Beaver Clan's woman grimaced, scratching her chin dubiously. "We can't force our leading sisters into sharing this kind of information. They might be reluctant to do that."

"And why would they?" Frowning, Seketa eyed her companions, all prominent women, associates of many summers. "We are not asking them to tell us all about the entire food supplies their longhouses managed to harvest and proceed. All we would require is to share the amount of meat and ground maize about to be contributed to the three days of the ceremony. That is all. I don't think such a request would, or should, be greeted with suspicion." Shrugging, she put the vessel she held down. "We do not need to worry about inadequate supplies in the middle of the celebrations only because some longhouses were not as well organized or prepared as they should have been."

They nodded thoughtfully.

"Your suggestion might be agreed upon, but there is not enough time to call the meeting of the Clans Council, sister," said the Bear Clan matron, a heavyset, pleasantly round-faced, even-tempered woman.

"We can talk to everyone separately. To agree upon such a change of procedures temporarily, for the sake of the nearing ceremony. Then, if we wish to change it permanently, we could call the meeting of the Clans Council." She eyed them pensively, troubled, but not by this issue. "The four of us agree to try it, don't we?"

More deliberating frowns.

"Yes, I suppose." The neighboring Turtle Clan longhouse's woman was the first to back her up, as always. "We can try it this time and see if it works. Can't we, sisters?"

The remaining two women nodded, their frowns smoothing.

"But I wish you luck with convincing the Heron and Snipe Clans. The wild fox that is leading the Heron longhouse won't let you sniff around their food supplies, nor any other of their precious belongings. She is as possessive as a squirrel on the onset of a bad winter. And the neighboring Snipe is under her spell."

This made them all chuckle. "What is true is true."

"Well, they can argue, complain, or fume, but if we, the most heavily represented clans agree, then there is little they can do without looking unnecessarily obstinate and petty. So many longhouses against two or three? No, they won't risk that." Glancing around once again, Seketa took in the multitude of baskets, piling so high they threatened to topple over. "But your longhouse seems to be in too good of a form this span of seasons, Sister," she commented with a smile, secure in the knowledge that her own was in as good of a condition. "Careful, or your clan members will grow fat over the Cold Moons."

Satisfied with the compliment, their hostess smiled back. "Our girls worked hard through the past few days. We barely had time to close our eyes at night." The smile widened, becoming more genuine. "But why don't we retire inside? I suppose we deserve to enjoy a little snack with our corn drink. I'll tell one of the girls to boil water."

"Oh, no," protested Seketa, knowing that there was no way to escape the invitation that she would have enjoyed greatly but for the pressing matters that still waited to be attended before Father Sun rolled behind the western hills. "You may be that well organized, sister, but my longhouse, along with the others of our clan, still needs to put on much of an effort before the first day of the ceremony is upon us."

"Oh, please, you are one of the most organized—"

The silhouette of a girl blocked the little light that managed to pour into the crowded storage room.

"Honorable Mothers!"

They all turned around, startled. "Yes, little sister?"

"The Council members, they have sent for you, asked you to come."

"All of us?"

The girl swallowed. "Only Turtle, Bear, and the Wolf Clans, Honorable Mothers. They have gathered at the Bear Clan's longhouse, near the ceremonial grounds."

"The Peach Stone Game." The Turtle woman smiled knowingly. "They wish to discuss the bets."

"We better hurry, then."

Once outside, Seketa felt her spirits lifting. There was still so much to accomplish or make sure it had been done, but having just returned from Onondaga Town, her husband would be present at the meeting of the Town Council.

His return had been heralded this morning, even though she hadn't had the opportunity to greet him properly as yet. Which wasn't something out of the ordinary, with both of them being so busy, but she missed him all the same. It had been quite a few days since he had left, summoned to the capital of their nation upon the shores of Onondaga Lake in order to introduce the delegation of the troublesome foreigners, the Long Tails People, that came out of the far west, to give trouble, or such was her private conclusion.

Who had ever heard of this nation? Even the Mountain People, members of the Great League and the Keepers of the Western Door, reported nothing but rumors of another Great Lake and some people inhabiting it. Long Tails People or Raccoon People— apparently, that's what the foreigners called themselves—were determined to make themselves known to the League of the Five Nations all of a sudden, while unsettling a less than perfectly stable situation along the way. Had the foreigners realized that? Surely they didn't.

She shook her head, angered. It had been so peaceful, so good through the past few decades, so fulfilling. Was it too much to expect such peacefulness to last forever? The Great League of the Five Nations had grown and strengthened, become a true thing, an unshakable building and not a temporary structure like it had been in the beginning, when every gust of political wind or someone's ill-will or wrongdoing would make it shudder and waver, threatening to topple over. Five fierce, warlike nations, enemies for so long, suddenly made allies, friends, brothers, working together, living by the Great Peacemaker's set of laws. A wonderful achievement, a perfect solution to the years of warfare, but oh, Mighty Spirits, it wasn't easy in the beginning. Even after the Great Peacemaker had left, there were still troubles, upheavals, disagreements, quarrels between people and settlements sometimes, antagonism and near clashes. The past was still fresh, still memorable.

She sighed. There were times when the Great Peace looked like a hopeless cause; only one or two times, but she remembered them vividly, because it was only due to her husband and his willpower and determination, his ability to make everyone listen and sometimes bend to his will that the unheard-of union didn't fall apart. He was like the mightiest tree, the sturdiest beam in a complicated structure, standing rock-solid, holding it all together. Oh, but he was a man like no other, a truly great spirit. They all revered the Peacemaker, the founder, now a legendary person; they all admired the legend, while she admired the living man.

"We will take this opportunity to discuss the matter of the hunting grounds with our council members," the Bear woman was saying. "If they deigned to summon us, taking us away from our duties, they will have to listen to what we have to say, not only to what they want to listen to."

"Yes, oh, yes," agreed the Turtle woman happily. "It is time we address that matter before the Town Council. We cannot ignore the complaints of our brothers and sisters from the west. Not anymore."

"We were not ignoring them," said Seketa. "We received their messengers, and we talked to them. My husband has managed to settle some of their complaints already. But I don't think our, or even Onondaga Town's, leaders would be able to deal with the rest of it. I'm afraid this matter will have to be brought before the Great Council when it gathers next."

"Because of the Swamp People's involvement?"

"Yes."

They shrugged in unison.

"Well, our Town Council members could at least pretend to care and understand. So far, indeed, only the War Chief has paid attention. But your husband represents the entire nation, while the lack of interest from our settlement's dignitaries in this matter makes our town look bad, not involved, indifferent to the plight of the others. We are the second largest town in the land. We can't behave like a small village."

There was a truth to this statement. Thoughtfully, Seketa nodded. "Yes, sister. You are wise. We should speak to our council members about it."

As her companions hastened their step, she noticed that the girl who had come to summon them still trailed behind, anxious to catch her eye.

"Yes, little sister?"

The girl nearly jumped, startled. Amused, Seketa smiled. A kind, encouraging smile. The girl was young and sweet, and she had waited patiently, behaving correctly by expecting to be noticed instead of pushing ahead like many of her peers would have done. Seketa's vow not to turn into a foreboding, humorless, uncompromisingly stern Clan Mother was not difficult to keep with girls and women like that.

"You wanted to talk to me, didn't you?" Falling behind, she signaled her companions to go on.

"Oh, no, Honorable Mother, it is nothing of importance." The girl's eyes glimmered with excitement.

"What is this nothing of importance?" She tried to remember the girl's name, but her ties with the Heron Clan were not so close, the only longhouse of this clan situated on the other side of the town, less involved in the general management due to it being so small. No representative in the Town Council, and only one Clan Mother in the gathering of clans. Even after her elder son took a woman from this same longhouse and moved to live there, her ties with the Heron Clan did not become tighter.

"Our hunters came back shortly after the sun reached its zenith. They brought a considerable amount of meat. It was a good foray."

"Oh, good!" Seketa exclaimed. "Their timing could not be better." All this fresh meat would be a wonderful addition to the first and second days' feasts. "Do you know if all the hunting parties came back? Or only those who included the hunters of your clan?"

The girl frowned, puzzled. "Oh, well, I know only what women of our longhouse said. The large party led by your son, Honorable Mother, they came back, carrying plenty of meat, but my cousin's husband, your son, he didn't come himself, and she is troubled and very put out."

"He didn't come back with his own hunting party. How so?" Now it was Seketa's turn to frown. Her eldest son was the epitome of correct behavior. It was not like him to not carry his responsibilities to the end of each mission. He strove to be a perfect leader, always, taking every duty he was entrusted with very seriously, too seriously sometimes. "What do his fellow hunters say?"

"Oh, well, I don't know, Honorable Mother. Jideah sent us all out. She is with child again and very irritable."

"Oh, she is? I didn't know." Making a mental note to talk to her son's wife before Father Sun left their world tonight, Seketa nodded. "Thank you for telling me, little one. Now go about your business. I'm sure your longhouse has enough work left to do before the first day of the ceremony is upon us."

"Oh, yes, yes." The girl turned around, balancing on one foot, ready to sprint away. "We've been gathering berries and forest fruit for half a day, and our Clan Mother says we will grind maize until there is no light left." Another hesitation. "We gathered much of what was left down by the river, but the women of your longhouse had difficulties with the sav—the foreign girl out there on their way to the place of berries."

Not again!

"Wait." Her words stopped the prettily decorated moccasins in midair, as the girl's braid flew excitedly, thrown behind her back. "Were you there, gathering berries with our women? What happened?"

"Oh, no, we didn't work together, but we met the Wolf Clan women by the spring, where the trail starts."

"And what was the problem with the new girl?"

"She didn't want to go where they went. She said there was a better place somewhere uphill. As though she would know, a foreigner like her." Seketa's unexpected informer made a face. "She tried to argue, or maybe to explain, but it was difficult to understand her. She speaks so badly! She made the woman who was responsible for your gathering party so angry!" The girl flopped her hands in the air, as though trying to show how enraged they all were. "She was yelling at her, but the wild girl still didn't do what she was told."

Seketa's heart sank. After their conversation last night, she'd had a good feeling, sensing that she had managed to reach her difficult charge and make her listen. Though strange and foreign her son's imported wife might have been, full of different background and lacking in proper knowledge, the girl turned out to be a person, just like she had expected, fairly pleasant company even, so very young and vulnerable, defenseless deep inside, but ready to react with violence when threatened. More echoes of the past. Such foreigners made perfect candidates for the status of an outcast with a bad name.

She shook her head. It would have been wiser to stick to her resolution of keeping the girl by her side until she felt more comfortable, more like she belonged. It would have been wiser, but for her lack of spare time, but for all her mounting duties.

She had been so busy this morning, and when the girl confessed to having spent half of the previous day, after the trouble with the maize peeling, out there, wandering around, claiming that she wasn't afraid of getting lost because she was good at reading the earth, that she remembered every trail she passed, that she was better than a scout even, Seketa immediately knew what to do. If her difficult charge felt better out there, then to gather forest fruit she would go. There was a party of women she was about to send out, anyway. How was she to know this would lead to trouble as well?

"What happened in the end?"

"I don't know. She ran away, I think. When we left, they were still arguing as to what to do about her." The girl's excitement was barely contained, spilling out of her glimmering eyes, her limbs positively dancing. "It was so embarrassing. She is such a savage. Like the worst of—"

Seketa's freezing look cut the words off in midair. "You are gossiping now, girl, and it is not proper and not welcomed. Go and think about your behavior." She pursed her lips, not pitying the rounding eyes that were filling with tears, and fast. "Also, think how you would feel if forced to live in a place that is not the town and the longhouse of your people. Maybe you would do no better than the foreign girl." Angrily, she turned around, anxious to catch up with her companions, who must have reached the Bear Clan's longhouse by now and were probably waiting impatiently, wondering at the delay. "Go and think about it before you open your mouth to gossip again."

"The large scale, official game. At long last!"

Watching his animated face, she could not keep her own smile from showing. Where had the stern, powerful, thoughtful leader, the War Chief of the entire nation, gone?

His weathered, sunburned, impressively prominent features positively beamed, like that of a young boy at the prospect of joining a hunting party. Only, in this case, it was a famous leader more than fifty summers old, a person without whom the Great Peace would not have been born or survived, a person whose leadership followed the most important nation of the league and whose judgment trusted the entire alliance. Such a renowned leader, now excited and glowing with happiness at the prospect of a ballgame, the ceremonial contest to be held outside the town, with too many participants to count and the field as large as an average valley reserved for it.

"I suppose, if the faith-keepers approve, such a contest could be a good way of closing the festivities," she said, not hiding her smile. He was such a boy sometimes. "You pressed the Town Council members into agreeing quite forcefully, leaving them with not much choice but to back your proposition up."

He appeared as though fighting his smile too, losing this particular battle.

"We haven't had a true, large-scale game for, oh, summers, and this is as good an occasion as any. Our guests from the far west will play, and our visitors from Onondaga Town. And Lone Hill. I was glad to see their representative. He came to Onondaga Town in time for the meeting, answering my invitation with his usual promptness. He is a good man!" His smile widened. "He will be delighted to play. We'll send messengers to the surrounding settlements as well. It will be a good game, a memorable day. The Right-Handed Twin will be honored and pleased."

Thinking about the representative of Lone Hill made her smile. He was, indeed, a good man, a friend and acquaintance of many summers, with their personal history going deeper, into the days before the Great Peace, when she had left her people in order to find *him*, the man who was now her husband, her chosen mate. She had committed a terrible crime while doing this, aiding a captive warrior, now the respectable representative of his village, to escape. They had crossed the Great Sparkling Water together, aiding each other, arriving in time to participate in the struggle for the Great Peace. Oh, but what turbulent days those were!

She shook her head, fighting her smile no longer.

"Our Great Spirits were not about to be neglected as it was. Also, you are not fooling me, oh-great-leader of our people. The prospect of being allowed to run all over the valley, trapping the ball in your net while pitting your might and skill against the others, is what makes you shine with happiness. Nothing to do with the ceremonial side of the game."

He laughed outright. "No trust from the honorable Clan Mother. What a shame." Glancing around, he nodded at a group of people, answering someone's greeting. "I suppose you still have much work to do. No chance of us taking a stroll outside the town?"

"I wish I could." The thought of the late afternoon woods just outside the fence, a short walk up or down the nearest hill, made her stomach squeeze with longing. To stroll one of these whispering trails with him, side by side and alone, free to touch and to fool around, to make love and laugh, or maybe talk serious matters with no prying eyes or ears. "After the ceremonies are over. Then we'll roam the woods until the Cold Moons force us back into the town, or until we have no power left to walk." She let her gaze deepen. "Or to engage in other sorts of pleasant activities."

The depth of his wide, unreserved smile warmed her insides. "That we will do." Then he shook his head, sobering. "I better be going. Both of us should attend to our duties before the last of the light is gone."

"What are yours for the rest of the day?"

"I have called the meeting of our warriors' leaders and other relevant people. There are quite a few important matters to discuss. The meeting at Onondaga Town was intriguing, to say the least."

"I'll walk you to the fence and the tobacco plots," she said resolutely, knowing that any warriors' meeting would be held outside, away from the town and eavesdropping ears. Her duties were pressing, but she wasn't about to miss the opportunity to learn the goings-on in the influential Onondaga Town, the largest of their land.

He nodded, grinning with only one side of his mouth, the typical grin that told her that he had seen through her, that he had spread that trap intentionally, knowing that she would fall into it. She didn't mind. Out of all people, he was the only one allowed to best her, to see through her, to read her with clarity. It had been more than thirty summers since they had fallen in love, and he was the wisest man alive.

She didn't try to conceal her chuckle.

"What?"

"You are transparent, Husband." Following his lead, she dived into the narrow corridor two longhouses created. "You could have simply asked me to walk you out."

He just grinned. "Did the boys come back already?"

She frowned. "Actually, I don't know. I heard that the hunting party returned this noon, but that Ganayeda wasn't with the people he led out."

The side glance he shot at her held a measure of worry. "Why?"

"That's the thing, I don't know. I have yet to find all this out." She shrugged. "The girl, who had run the entire town to tell me, caught me on my way to the council's meeting. She was just a silly girl, a gossiper. So I've yet to hear the real news." The wind was strengthening, playing with her hair, making it flutter across her face. She tossed her braid backwards. "But wherever he detoured and whatever kept him occupied out there, he would be in time for the festivities, and for your much-awaited game. No one would miss the first day of the ceremony."

"It would be good to wield the playing stick again. It's been a long time." He eased his shoulders, and she watched the muscles of his arms shifting, bulging under the cover of his weathered skin. He might have been considered to be growing old by the count of summers, she thought, but he wasn't, not in her eyes. The handsome boy and then the young man of the turbulent days when there was no peace and no concord, he was still pleasing the eye with his height and width and his bearing, with the way he carried himself, confident and proud, radiating power, his figure not sagging, not covered with fat, his face not losing its sharp angles, its dominant glow, its good-natured smile. Only his warrior's lock had thinned, and the creases that furrowed his face seemed to be challenging the original pattern of scars in their intricacy.

"Okwaho will be happy to participate," he was saying, apparently unaware of her scrutinizing gaze. "The timing of his return could not have been better. Last time such an important contest was held, that boy was near killing someone or setting Onondaga Town on fire."

"What are you talking about? He was too young and not even allowed to think of participation."

His chuckle floated in the deepening dusk. "That's what I'm talking about. He was so frustrated."

"He wasn't. Why would he be? He knew the rules. Only the warriors and the renowned hunters. It never changes. He could not have possibly hoped to be allowed, a youth of sixteen, seventeen summers with no achievements behind him. He played in plenty of regular games, every time he could lay his hands on the playing stick and have a few more youngsters to contest for the ball."

"And this is why he was so frustrated." His smile was wandering, full of memories. "He knew he was good enough to participate in the real thing, but our laws were against him." The smile was gone, replaced by a thoughtful nod. "It would be good to play with this boy, to spend some time with him. He came back changed. Matured, yes, as expected, but there is more to it. He didn't merely grow up or gain battle experience. No, there is something different about him. He learned more than just how to fight."

She thought about her conversation with the girl. "His woman, she told me some things. I haven't had the opportunity to speak to her properly, but from the little she said… Well, Husband, I think your son will make you proud; some of his deeds seem to be out of the ordinary."

He halted abruptly. "What?"

Watching his narrowed eyes, reading the excitement, the expectation behind the attempt to conceal any of it, a habit of many summers of leading people, even though there was no need to pretend now, in their brief, stolen moments of privacy, she didn't try to hide the depth of her smile.

"Well, this girl is the testimony in itself that he has been acting with his heart and eyes opened, not about to let convention rule his mind. In that, he seems to be his father's offspring, more so than his brother is."

His grin was reluctant, like that of a child who has been complimented unexpectedly. "His mother is not such an ordinary creature herself." The smile won, blossomed, then disappeared, giving way to the matter-of-fact curiosity. "What did the girl say?"

"She said something about stopping an important fight, saving her village, saving his fellow warriors as well…" She swallowed. "Getting wounded while doing this." Greeting some passersby, as they passed through another longhouse, helped. It gave her a blissful moment to collect her senses. "She is difficult to understand in the best of times. Her accent is terrible. My former people would yield their title of being crooked tongued to her people with no struggle." She paused to nod at another passing group. "So we have yet to hear all about it from him, the why and the how. But he seemed to be brave enough to go against his leaders' flawed judgment, and in the middle of a battle too, making them listen. Something only you could have done, out of all people I know."

His gaze made her wish that the town around them would disappear for at least a few moments that she needed to spend in his arms.

"As always, you are too kind." His eyes reflected the same sentiment. "I wish we could forsake our duties for this one evening."

She reached for his arm, to brush her palm against it briefly, hoping it would relay what she felt, even if custom held them from expressing their feelings in public, prominent leaders that they were. "It will come soon enough."

For some time, they proceeded in silence.

"The meeting with the Long Tails People's delegation was interesting, to say the least," he related, when the long lines of tobacco plots spread to their left, rustling in the breeze, the poles of the fence towering next to them, casting soft shadows.

"Did they come to talk peace?"

"Well, they seem to be inclined that way, but, of course, we didn't get that far, not yet." He paused to admire the carving someone had made on one of the poles, a detailed image of an eagle spreading its wings. "They brought unsettling news from across the Great Sparkling Water."

As always, the way her heart increased in tempo whenever her former people were mentioned angered her. They were of no consequence to her, but she wished they would stop being such a constantly troublesome topic. It would have been better if they weren't mentioned at all, ever, neither for good nor for bad.

"What happens with the Crooked Tongues now?"

"They have allied among themselves."

This made her stop. "What? How? When?"

He shrugged, not slowing his step. "No one knows when and how, but they have stopped fighting amongst themselves, two, or maybe even all four nations." He snorted. "I still remember their names, would you believe it? Rock, Deer, and Cord People. And yours, of course. They are united now, and if it in any way resembles our union, then it can mean only one thing—"

"No, it doesn't." This time, she caught his arm, disregarding the appropriateness or the lack of it. "It's been more than thirty summers. It has nothing to do with the Peacemaker. It is not of his doing, even if he was somehow still alive, which he most surely isn't."

His set face and tightly pressed lips made her wish to shake him. He wasn't listening. When it came to the Peacemaker, his ears would go deaf, always.

"If he was alive, he would have let us know, somehow. Through all those long summers, he would have sent you word." Tugging at his arm forcefully, she made him face her, hoping against hope to make him listen, only this once. "Do you imagine him living happily somewhere out there, back in my town, or any other, forgetting all about us and about what he did here? No, of course it isn't possible. He went back there, yes, he wanted to organize my people for the sake of the Great Peace. But sadly, I don't think he managed. Whatever happened to him, he is not among the living. None of them are. The old founders, they are all dead—he and Hionhwatha. Atiron from Little Falls. Even Tadodaho. How happy we were when that old snake died, eh? You conducted his condolence ceremony; you made such a respectable event out of it, but how happy we all were that this man was gone, remember?" She squeezed his arm warmly. "They are all dead. That generation, they are a legend now; they are gone, but we are alive, and we keep the Peacemaker's legacy, his laws, his Great Law of Peace, such a wonderful creation."

He was listening, staring at her warily, with an open suspicion, but at least he was listening.

"Crooked Tongues have nothing to do with it, Husband. They have their paths to walk, their destination to reach. They do not wish to have anything to do with us. Evidently, even the Peacemaker failed in making them see the truth. Even you, his most loyal follower, the man who kept his creation alive, who sheltered it and didn't let it falter when it still was not stable enough to hold on its own, even you were not able to bring the Crooked Tongues under the shade of the Great Tree of Peace. They will not trace its roots in order to sit beside us. They will war on us, instead. Not a raid here and there, but a full-scale war, and we should be ready for such an event." His hand felt lifeless in hers, so she squeezed it harder. "I know it pains you to do that. I know you would rather make his dream come true in its entirety. But he left when he left for a reason. It was done back then. The Great Law of Peace had reached its limit. It could not contain more peoples. It was meant to exist as it was when he left."

The wind was growing, storming through the cracks in the poles, groaning beyond them, swishing in the corridor the outer row of palisade created.

"There is finality in your words," he said quietly, his eyes blank, fixed on her but not seeing, wandering unknown distances. "It sounds as though none of us, those who are still alive, are needed anymore."

She caught her breath, the sadness of his voice tearing at her, the apathy in it, so atypical for him. "No, that is not what I said!"

His eyes focused. "Then what do you say?"

She fought the urge to lick her lips, the challenge and the slight animosity in his gaze irritating, urging her to tell it all to him, with no soft coating.

"You keep loyalty to the dead man, to the man who was great and outstanding, yes, the legend that will be remembered for many generations to come, but the man who has left because he could not handle his own plans and dreams anymore. And while I applaud your devotion to his legacy, the legacy that made our people's children and their children's lives better, I do not think you should let the memory of the man himself or his plans that have never borne fruit color your decisions or deeds." She stood the blazing fire of his eyes. "There are times when you are more loyal to the memory of the dead man than you are heedful of your people and their well-being."

For a heartbeat, silence prevailed, a heavy, suffocating silence. His eyes were as dark as the deepest lake at night.

"That is a filthy accusation," he said finally, his voice low but steady, in full control. "And if you think the War Chief of our nation is so inadequate, then maybe you should bring this matter before the Clans' Council of High Springs and the rest of the settlements."

She gasped at the unfairness of his words. "How can you say that?"

His face was a stony mask, lips clasped, jaw jutting. "I think we better go about our business now."

"Wait!" She caught his arm as he turned away. "Don't leave in anger. Those were harsh words, but they needed to be said. The man from across the Great Sparkling Water is of no consequence to us anymore. Whatever he wanted to achieve in regard to my former people is not achievable. You strove to avoid war for thirty summers. Is that not enough for anyone to understand our peaceful intentions?" He pulled his hand away, and she had to struggle not to let it go. "I know you know all that and more. You are one of the wisest leaders we have. But sometimes, sometimes it's difficult to see the entire scenery when you are too close, and in it. And this is why I presume to give you unwanted advice. Because I'm not as close as you are, not as involved." Leaning forward, she tried to catch his gaze. "Maybe you should take a step back too, see if the people who think we can't have peace with the Crooked Tongues are right, or at least partially right. You are too close now to judge correctly."

His face was still closed, eyes narrowed, unreadable, not letting her see what they held. "Is that the official advice of our longhouse's Clan Mother? Is that what the Wolf Clan council thinks?"

Oh, but he was so unfair! She stepped away sharply. "If you wish to hear me only in an official capacity, I will hold my tongue now."

He drew a deep breath, visibly trying to calm down. Her heart went out to him. But she had spoken too harshly, hadn't she? Her accusation of neglecting their people's well-being was unfounded, farfetched. It's just that his continued loyalty to the wondrous man who had brought peace and concord to these lands was harming him, his stance among his people, his reputation, his peace of mind. There was no possibility of peaceful arrangement with her former people, the Crooked Tongues from across the Great Lake, especially now, when they were growing bolder and pushier, maybe organized into an alliance. Oh, Mighty Spirits!

"Let us each go our own way now," he was saying, his gaze not thawing. "Later on, when we are less angry, we'll talk."

Unable to speak, she just nodded, watching him going away in his long, forceful stride, his back straight, diving into the corridor of the fence, displaying no misgivings.

Her heart beat slowly, unevenly. The dimming air surrounded her, not supporting. If she could, she would have run after him, called him back.

People were coming in, a group of men. They gave her curious looks but didn't pause, respecting her obvious need of privacy.

When lonely footsteps burst upon her, she was turning away, forcing her legs into working. There was so much to do yet. To check on her own longhouse, to see how everyone was doing, if today's chores were going to be completed, and if not, then what could be done about it. She had spent nearly half a day away, consulting with other clans' representatives, then attending the meeting of the Town Council, discussing so many urgent matters, and then later on, going away with her husband, ruining his happy home-coming mood.

The stony fist was back, squeezing her insides. But he didn't deserve this, he out of all people—

"Oh!"

The exclamation startled her into turning back, to peer at the shapeless form that was staggering in through the opening, progressing in a somewhat unsteady pace.

Puzzled, Seketa blinked. The baskets were large, tightly woven, deep containers with no straps, and they hid the girl beneath them, leaving mainly her splattered skirt and muddied moccasins to explain their progress. It was as though the baskets were walking all by themselves.

"What in the name…" Rushing forward, Seketa grabbed one of the containers, the sweat-covered, dirt-smeared face behind it beaming at her with its strange, widely spaced eyes and sharply outlined cheekbones.

"I bring berries, a lot." Arching her back, the girl balanced the remaining two baskets, revealing that another vessel was strapped to her back, a large container of an impressive size, full to the brim with glittering fruit.

"Why are you alone? Why is no one helping you with those?" In her turn, Seketa found herself struggling, her newly acquired cargo lacking in straps, cumbersome, not a vessel meant to carry things, but rather to store and use around the house. "Where did you get all those baskets?"

"In house, longhouse," said the girl slowly, searching for words, a frown making her previous beam dim. "I found woods, forest, place with many fruit, so I come back, take basket, go pick again."

"Why not with the others?"

"Oh, others." Her converser's face clouded. "They go bad

place, less berries. I tell know better place, many fruit. Up hill, by the brook. They no listen." A shrug proved impossible under so many baskets, but the girl's shoulders twisted in an obvious way. "So I go alone."

"You ran all the way back to the town to get the baskets?"

The frown was deepening, making the girl look unattractive again. She was actually a nice little thing when smiling, realized Seketa, remembering the conversation of the previous evening. Not ugly or wild like the others thought. Just strange, different, unpredictable. But then, why shouldn't she be any of that? Coming from such distant lands, of course the girl knew or understood little. But she would learn.

"Tell me what happened between you and the other women this morning."

"Oh, I tell already. They no listen. They say no. Go their way. But I know better, better place, much berries. Far yes, but better. Up there, not down, no valley."

Bending under the heaviness of her cargo, Seketa found it difficult to make the point that it was not the girl's place to argue with women she had been sent to help and assist. Evidently, the girl's finds somewhere up there had, indeed, yielded more treasure.

"How did you know where to go?" she asked instead, not wishing to make her charge lose her spirit. The wild thing was so obviously tired, so dirty and sweat covered, and yet her happiness was spilling over, her pride and satisfaction unconcealed. The haunted creature of the previous evening was gone.

"Oh, I know, I know marks. You see? Land, it shows. When I walk around yesterday, when I was out there, when…" The voice died away for a moment, and even though they were walking now, too busy to look at each other, Seketa knew that the gloomy expression was back, darkening her companion's features, making her lose the attractive look again.

"So you found a grove full of berries," she prompted. "A grove our girls neglected to plunder. Is it far?"

"Yes far, but not bad. No hard walk. Up there, you see. Where the spring, uphill."

"Oh, I see."

She shifted her cargo and fought the temptation to signal some of the fellow passerby women, requesting help. It was a sensible thing to do but for the girl and her unexpected spell of confidence. The cheerful openness might be gone again should they be joined by others.

"You took the wrong baskets," she related, instead. "Those are for storing things, not for carrying. You should choose the smaller baskets, with straps."

"Oh." From the corner of her eye, she could see the pile of woven vessels moving, reflecting the girl's nod. But the little fox was strong. To carry so much, and such a long way. Why, even one container was now too heavy for her, and she, Seketa, was not one of the spoiled women, reluctant to engage in physical tasks. And yet, she was struggling now, while the foreigner had carried three such vessels, two balanced between her arms somehow, and the third strapped to her back. A true show of strength. How had the girl managed? Tall and sturdily built, with inappropriately wide shoulders and chest, and this masculine way of walking, with no nonsense to her movements and no feminine grace, she was just a young girl. Were all the foreigners of her lands like that?

The thought made her uncomfortable. It was as though she was betraying her charge in some way. The girl was nice and good-hearted, and that was the main thing. Also, she was not useless, not like the other women thought. It was just that her inclinations were not of the usual kind.

"You are good at reading the earth, at remembering the paths you walk?" she asked, curious.

"Oh, yes, yes. I read earth, like scout. Can better even. Better than men." The unconcealed pride made Seketa smile. But this one was so young yet.

"How old are you? How many summers have you seen?"

"Seventeen," said her companion readily. "Seventeen summers, almost. I born when leaves falling. Mother say when all beautiful, many colors."

Seketa smiled. "Yes, a beautiful season to be blessed with a baby." She tried to imagine those faraway lands, full of fierce, warring men and masculine, unfeminine women. Did they fight alongside their warriors, scouting, wielding clubs? It was easy to imagine this new member of her family dealing with weapons. "You used to do scouting back home? What work did you do?"

Again, the baskets next to her lifted as though their carrier shrugged. "I do work, regular work. Like everyone."

"Hunting?" She wanted to laugh at the ridiculousness of her own question, but with the foreigners, true foreigners, who knew?

"Hunt? No!" exclaimed the girl, slowing down in her turn. The broad face peeked at Seketa from behind their woven barrier, full of excited expectation. "Women hunt? Here women hunt? With bow?"

This time she didn't manage to hold the laughter in. "No, women here don't hunt. No bows, no arrows. And no clubs and spears, for that matter." The girl's disappointment was so obvious, she found it difficult to hold the rest of her laughter in. "I thought maybe they did so in your lands. With all these scouting skills of yours. I wouldn't be surprised if you could shoot a bow."

"I can, can shoot a bow." The girl gazed at her, not joining in the laughter. "I shoot when warriors, when warriors shot. I break oil. It was a real bow." A flicker of mischief came, reflecting in the strange eyes. "Okwaho teach, teach shoot good. Real bow. Promise make one, only mine, for me."

Oh, that boy! Seketa tried to suppress another outburst of mirth. By that time, they neared the first of the Wolf Clan longhouses, the façade with the sketchy engraving of the magnificent animal, a beautiful carving, wielding a walking stick between its outlined front legs. Not her longhouse as yet, it was still a family, therefore many women pounced on them, relieving them of their burden, or some of it in the girl's case. Her companion seemed to be reluctant to part with her lawful catch, noticed Seketa, amused again.

"Thank you, girls. Bring it to our longhouse, will you? Tell them I will be there shortly." She glanced at the girl, who was now again closed and on guard, looking around warily, aware of the gazes. Oh, yes, they all stared at Seketa's exotic company, their wonder barely concealed. "Come. We'll detour a little."

The longhouses spread left and right, crowded now, bursting with life at this time of the late afternoon. She remembered her intention to see her elder son's wife, a highly respectable woman, perfectly suitable, unlike the creature that was walking next to her, striding widely like a man would.

Why didn't he come back along with the hunting party he was responsible for? And did it mean that his brother wasn't back either? Her husband would love to have his sons' company, surely through the ceremonies and the following game. The thought of him made her heart sink. Why didn't she keep her mouth shut?

"I bring more berries tomorrow," the girl was saying quietly, obviously uncomfortable now, aware of the gazes that followed them. "And nuts. There many nuts. I see many trees. Black nuts, all ready." The broad forehead wrinkled in an attempt to find the right words. "Dark nuts. Many trees."

"You seem to have found a real treasure, didn't you?" Glad to take her thoughts off her husband and his troubles, Seketa frowned. "But it is truly too far. I can't send enough girls under your guidance. Not now, when we have so much to do. Maybe later, after the ceremonies." She tried to think of how to make them follow the foreign thing no one was prepared to accept or respect. "After the festivities, there will still be the need to gather much forest fruit and firewood and other supplies to make our Cold Moons into a pleasant pastime. Your discovery will come in handy then."

The girl swallowed, tensed visibly. "I go alone. Tomorrow I go alone. I can bring much. You see now, many baskets. I'll bring more if take good baskets, like you say. With ..." Another painful frown crossed the wide brow.

"Straps?" Seketa offered.

"Yes, yes, straps. I take good baskets, with straps. Can carry much. Can go two times, not one, like today. Can go fast. Run all the way."

Seketa halted her step. "You can't go alone. It is not safe."

Her companion's eyes were boring into her, anxious, insistent, having a pleading glint to them. "I safe, I know the way. Not afraid. I can help, be use, of use. I bring much berries and nuts. Like now, but more." The anxiousness of the girl's voice intensified.

Seketa sighed, understanding too well. The girl didn't want to work with the others, not after two unsuccessful attempts. How to solve that?

"Well, let me see what can be done about it." She smiled encouragingly, liking the wild thing in a genuine way. She was a challenge, that one, but it was a good challenge. So much strength and determination, physical as well as that of the spirit, channeled in a proper way, could bring blossoming fruits. The girl was different, yes, but why would they wish everyone to be alike?

CHAPTER 8

Pulling the decorated blanket over her head, Kentika cursed softly, in her people's tongue for a change. She was so tired! Yet, no matter how tightly she tried to shut her eyes, the sleep wouldn't come, her thoughts racing, ears unable to block out the sounds.

Truly late though it was, probably near midnight or worse, the people of their longhouse seemed as though they were not about to retire, even if much work was expecting its womenfolk with the break of the dawn that was to herald the last day before the beginning of the festivities.

So many preparations!

She had found herself wondering, partly afraid, partly expectant, remembering the rituals of her village—the Maple or Corn Ceremonies, the Deer Sacrifice Ritual, the feasts of the sacred dolls—cheerful, happy occasions, with the villagers congregating around the ceremonial grounds next to the huge maple tree, chanting or dancing, listening to the medicine man or the chiefs talking, addressing Glooskap or other Sky Dwellers, thanking them.

Such wonderful days, but those never required so many preparations, so much food and clothing and tools, so much coordination between clans and longhouses. Okwaho's mother—such a nice woman!—with other leading females, running all over the town, supervising and making it all work. Were the festivities to last for half a moon, or to host every dweller of these lands? And where was Okwaho? Why wasn't he back already? He had said it was a short hunting expedition, three, four dawns, but here, five dawns later and with the ceremonies upon them, there was still no sight of him, and just as she needed him the most.

Blinking away suspicious moisture, she turned around, staring into the high ceiling, defeated. The sleep wouldn't come just like he wouldn't come. Was she to live like that from now on, surrounded by too many people and yet more alone than ever, running away whenever she could, to enjoy at least a morsel of privacy, to escape their wondering, the derisiveness or indifference of their glances? Was that what she had left her people for?

Clenching her teeth, she studied the bark squares comprising the ceiling in an orderly, surprisingly comforting, manner. With no rain expected, some were wide open, letting in the blessed flow of air, but also the noises from the outside. As though various footsteps and floating conversations all over the building were not enough.

Tucking the blanket around her, to ward off the chill, she sat up, eyeing the mats that were spread all over the earthen floor, spilling into the corridor. It had not been as crowded here before, through her first few days of arrival. Back then, only she and Okwaho had occupied a pair of straw mats that he had dragged from the storage space beneath one of the lower banks. She didn't want to sleep away from the floor, on a sort of strange even if cozy-looking shelf, and evidently, Okwaho had no trouble with such an arrangement, whether sensing her uneasiness or just preferring that himself. Their hosts were the ones to curl comfortably between their pretty blankets and furs, or their hostess, for that matter. The War Chief had barely enough time to tell them his greetings before he had to depart, heading for some place that sounded even more influential than that sprawling settlement, a place they called Onondaga Town. But now he was back. He and the throng of additional people, either visitors or maybe just returning locals who weren't around when she had arrived, a multitude of men, elders and warriors who flooded the alleys of the town and the corridors of the longhouses, sitting and talking, smoking pipes, or sleeping all over the floor until it looked as though it was made of mats and not flattened, well-beaten earth.

Bored, she had counted the mats, three occupied, two empty, with more spreading out into the corridor.

"Having trouble sleeping, eh?"

The voice made her nearly jump, coming from her left. One of the men, lying next to the fireplace, rose on his elbow and was looking at her, his gaze glimmering playfully in the light of the dying embers.

Frightened, she just stared.

Sitting up, he folded his legs comfortably. "I can't sleep, either," he related, rubbing his face, then pushing his braid away—a long, decorated affair that started on the top of his head, sliding downwards along the shaved sides, like Okwaho's but thinner. "Do they never rest in this town?"

Even though spoken slowly, his words were difficult to understand. Like Okwaho's mother, he seemed to talk strangely, as though not bothering to finish one word before uttering another. Okwaho had not spoken in this way, and neither had the other people she had met in the town so far.

She blinked, trying to make her mind work. *Who was this man?*

"Are you sleeping with your eyes open?" he asked, now openly amused.

"I... No, no, I don't, don't know, who you—"

His eyes widened. "Oh, you are not a local girl?" The phrase that followed was long and impossible to understand, other than the hint that it ended with a questioning tone.

She shook her head again, feeling incredibly silly. "I no understand."

This time, his eyes actually narrowed. "Where are you from?"

"I..." After the completely different tongue, she didn't mind his accented way of speaking. "The Great River, beyond." She waved her hand, indicating the general direction. "Rising sun. My people far, far away."

"Oh, their Eastern Door Keepers, or whatever they call them these days."

Out of her depth, she just shrugged, glancing down the corridor, where a group of people conversed quietly, sitting next to the fireplace, its flames playing brightly, unlike their own fire, which was nothing but glowing embers by now.

Where were Okwaho's mother, and the War Chief? she wondered, not feeling threatened anymore, but just curious. This man wanted to talk, and he was obviously a guest here, in this compartment of the longhouse, a foreigner. More than she was, come to think of it.

He was still eyeing her, openly curious. "What are you doing at the Onondaga War Chief's compartment?"

"I live here," she said, suddenly pleased with herself. "And you, what you do here?"

"I'm visiting, obviously. Our delegation came from far, far away, farther than your eastern keepers live. The opposite direction, though. The setting sun, beyond their Keepers of the Western Door." He shook his head, his easy playfulness spilling out, but not disturbing, not anymore. "Our Great Lake is bigger than their Sparkling Water. And prettier, too."

Unable to follow the rapid flow of his words, she leaned forward. "Far? The setting sun?"

"Yes, Long Tails People. You must have heard about us."

She shook her head. At the far end, another group entered the corridor, this time women, their voices hushed, floating lightly.

"Your Flint People are not very much involved, then," he said curtly, as though offended. "I thought they were influential in that highly praised union of theirs, as much as the Onondagas."

"My people are no Flint. My River People."

One of his eyebrows was climbing up rapidly. "There is no river-anything in your union. We may live far away, but we know who belongs in your Longhouse League. Why try to fool me, war chief's girl?"

The sudden animosity in his voice made her uneasy. "I no Flint," she repeated, offended by his distrust. "You can ask, ask people here. They tell." She shrugged. "If Flint, people would be nice. But they don't like me, because no Flint, no Longhouse People."

His frown was deep, and puzzled. "You said the lands of the rising sun."

"Yes, far than Flint, far away. Great River ends, then another Great River." She watched his eyes widening. "Yes, very far."

"Who lives there?" he breathed.

"My people, River People."

He shook his head, his gaze studying her, holding none of its previous amusement. "Hard to believe." Another puzzled frown. "So they have been raiding far and wide, our Longhouse neighbors. An interesting tidbit. Our delegation should hear about this." Then his eyes refocused, and his grin spread anew, decidedly one-sided and crooked. "And you live here now, eh? Should it lead me to the conclusion that the Onondaga War Chief awarded himself with an exotic spoil, showing us that the Five Nations leaders do live well? No one in our lands can take more than one woman, you know. Not at the same time, that is."

As she stared at him, hoping that she didn't understand correctly, his laughter wafted in the semi-darkness, making one of the other sleeping men stir.

"He does have a thing for foreign women, that renowned leader of yours. The Crooked Tongues, and now you." His eyes held hers, provoking, challenging. "Is it not so?"

She pulled her blanket tighter before getting to her feet. "I not know what say, what you say. No make sense." Using Okwaho's favorite phrase helped. "You say strange things. I don't want to listen."

"Wait," he called out, his teasing smile still in place, still taunting in the same friendly, good-natured way. "You take offense too easily. There is no need to run away."

Picking her way between the spread mats, careful not to tread on those that were occupied, she snatched up her moccasins.

"Wait, foreign girl." His voice held a measure of puzzled bewilderment. "It wasn't meant to offend. It was just to tease, to pass time."

But even though she believed him, she didn't turn back.

The night was pleasantly cool, even cold, but wrapped in a protective blanket, she didn't mind the cutting wind.

It was good to be outside. Wandering the open grounds where the longhouses were not placed too densely, she looked around, delighted at the opportunity to study this town with no dubious eyes meeting her everywhere.

Such a large settlement! She tried to think how many people it could host. There must have been ten or more of those lengthy constructions here, their sizes varied. The longhouse she lived in was huge, the largest, its corridor spreading like an enormous snake, a legendary creature from wintertime stories of old.

During her first days here, she didn't dare to look around while maneuvering her way between the fireplaces of other families, feeling like a shameless intruder, imposing upon someone else's lives. But later on, when Okwaho had left, and especially after their Clan Mother turned out to be such a kind, friendly person, she had gathered the courage to glance up while proceeding in or out, counting the fires.

Eighteen was the number she came up with. Eighteen fireplaces, which meant eighteen families, each having up to six, seven members—usually couples of various ages with children, small or grownup, and an old grandmother or grandfather, or sometimes both. The adding up of all those brought her to the conclusion that up to a hundred people and more lived in this longhouse alone, all accountable to Okwaho's mother, only one of the Clan Mothers, as the Wolf Clan had more longhouses spread around the town.

So, nice person though she was, this woman wielded much power and influence, and liked and admired as she seemed to be, she was obeyed, always, even by the men of their dwelling.

Oh, but it was beyond one's understanding, a woman managing more than a hundred people and all their affairs, settling their disputes, making everyone work and contribute, her word being the last one, even when dealing with men. Impossible!

Shivering in the new gust of wind, Kentika pressed her blanket tighter, passing by a relatively short longhouse, with the image of a slender bird, probably a heron, engraved upon its facade. How many fireplaces were there in this one, she wondered? Five, six? How many families?

She slowed her step to study the engraving in the strengthening moonlight just as voices burst upon her with a woman storming out of the opening, her hair flowing wildly, dress askew, paces unsteady, a bowl clutched in her hands.

"Leave me alone!" she yelled toward the gaping opening. "Don't come after me. I don't want to—"

The rest of the phrase died in a loud hiccup, as the woman pressed her free palm to her mouth, struggling to keep her cargo from falling. Turning abruptly, she had probably intended to rush on, but ended up colliding full-length with Kentika.

This time, the bowl went flying. Frozen in surprise, Kentika watched its contents splashing upon the ground, something unappealing, foul-smelling. Vomit? To reinforce this conclusion, the woman doubled over next to her, retching wildly, bringing up more of the smelly substance.

Wishing nothing more than to run away into the freshness of the night, Kentika found herself catching the swaying figure, supporting her with both hands—a certain effort as the woman was small but not thin—taking some of her weight. Others had come out by now, surrounding them, while someone knelt to collect the bowl, then throw some earth over the spilled refuse.

"Go away, all of you," groaned the woman, clutching onto Kentika with both hands. "Can't a person get some privacy here?" She steadied herself with a visible effort, then looked up. "Who are you?"

The animosity of the question was startling, although there was no difference in this address than the one intended for the women from the building.

Kentika took a step back, hesitating, answering the narrowed gaze with her own. She felt her fists clenching. The woman was in no position to attack her, even if she looked as though she might like to do something violent, but her followers were still out there, gazing at the intruder now too, looking anything but friendly.

The woman coughed again.

"Go away and leave me alone," she repeated firmly, turning to her fellow longhouse dwellers, in control once again. "Give me that bowl!" The girl from whose hands it was snatched uttered a cry of surprise. "I can manage. I'm not disabled. And if I didn't listen to you about eating that porridge…"

More murderous glances. Even though unable to see it, Kentika was sure of that, watching the girls turning back hurriedly, all three of them, defeated.

"And you? Why are you still here? It's not a ceremony to watch. Go back where you belong." This time, the words were clearly meant for her. The angry gaze bored into her, defeating the night.

She took another step back, but her resentment kept welling, the unfairness of it making her wish to stay, out of spite, if for no other reason. She was allowed to go wherever she wanted. She was not a prisoner or a captive. The head of her longhouse appreciated her.

"I go where like," she informed the woman, crossing her arms to reinforce her words. "I go back when want go back. Now stay. Want stay."

The woman's eyes positively glowed, but her state of health was evidently not at its best as yet. Clutching her bowl with more force than required, she pressed her lips, then, giving Kentika what was surely supposed to be a squashing look, she stormed past her. Or tried to do that, as her paces were not steady enough for anything better than staggering. She wouldn't get far in this condition, a reflection that made an unwelcome wave of compassion come back.

"Where go?" she asked before able to stop herself.

"To dance at the ceremonial grounds," was the terse retort. "What do you think?"

"I not know," said Kentika, at a loss. The woman didn't look fit for dancing, ceremonially or otherwise, but with the strange people of the setting sun, one never knew. Maybe like the masked men of the healing society, the dwellers of this town did something ceremonial when suffering.

"That you do." Her companion's snort was as loud as her retching before. "I went out to wash this bowl and to drink clean water out of the spring, and not the muddy liquid our lazy girls filled our water vessels with. And to enjoy a bit of peace and quiet!"

The last statement was accompanied by a pointed glance as the woman halted again, turning her head and measuring her allegedly unwanted company with her eyes narrowed to slits.

Kentika searched for something sharp to say in response. This woman was the most foul-tempered thing she had met in a long time. Even her great-aunt, her grandmother's half sister and Namaas's adoptive mother, seemed more reasonable than this woman, who was not even of a respectable age, older than herself surely, but not by much. Not a leading woman of any kind. Or maybe she was. Who knew from what ages these women began to lead?

"Well, don't just stare. Take this bowl and come," said the woman, suddenly brisk and matter-of-fact.

Kentika pushed the offered utensil away. "I no come. No orders. You can't, can't tell what to do." The thought of Okwaho's mother made her wish to strengthen her claim. "Clan Mother, she tell what to do. I listen her. Not you. Or anyone."

All of a sudden, the woman's face cleared. The thin lips twisted into a hint of a grin. "Oh, yes, Seketa won't let you escape your duties. Good that you didn't think to try her patience, wild girl." Another measuring gaze. "Come along, anyway. It doesn't look as though you have something better to do."

For some reason, the invitation appealed. Falling into the woman's step, which was not a difficult feat, with her companion walking not as briskly as she had talked, Kentika proceeded along, making a point of not taking the bowl. She might have nothing better to do, but she wouldn't be ordered about.

"So you are living in the Wolf Clan's largest longhouse for now," said the woman, making it a statement. "So typical of that young buck to dump you on his mother and be gone, to have a good time with this equally inconsiderate brother of his."

"You ... you know Okwaho?" The longing seized her as suddenly as it always did when she thought of him, sneaking up on her at the mere mention of him. He didn't want to go on this hunt, he had said. But for the insistence of his brother, he would have stayed.

"Do I know that wild thing?" The woman laughed, evidently feeling better, her voice ringing with clarity that hadn't been there before. "Before he knew how to walk or talk properly, I remember him. It is difficult to miss such a troublemaker. But when Ganayeda moved to live in my longhouse, oh, then your handsome husband was at his worst, getting in trouble all around, such a restless spirit." A brief side glance made Kentika feel naked. "We should have expected him to do something as wild as this, to come home with something like you to challenge us with."

Before she could find something to say to that, preferably something sharp that would make this annoying woman regret her words, the trickling of the spring was upon them. Ebbing and bubbling, it looked more of a creek than a simple spring, a serious body of water unlike back in her village. Bordered by loosely placed stones at places, it flowed down the hill and away from the town, to disappear beyond the poles of the fence, to her estimation.

On the other side and toward another cluster of longhouses, fires were flickering, with people sitting around them, their voices interweaving with the crackling of the fire.

"The War Chief," related Kentika's companion, kneeling beside one of the stones heavily, as though afraid to make sharp movements. "Too many people waited for his return. I predict he won't get much sleep tonight."

"Why people wait war chief? Is war, war come?"

The woman's glance made her feel stupid. "You ask silly questions, strange girl. The War Chief of the entire nation doesn't deal with war. To make raids, we have all sorts of warriors' leaders. They can deal with any enemy." Cupping some water with her palms, she drank briefly, as though forcing herself, then splashed the rest of it over her face. "Give me that bowl."

Picking up the shallow vessel, Kentika knelt in her turn. It felt wrong not to help now that the woman didn't demand it. Despite her high, not to say mean, spirit, she was not well, that much was obvious.

"Wash it thoroughly," her companion said, not bothering with words of gratitude. "All this vomit, disgusting. I can't believe I'm that sick. It was never like that before."

"Why sick?" asked Kentika, not truly interested, but wishing to keep her companion talking. Would she tell her more about Okwaho?

"It's the child. Sometimes they make us very sick, especially in the beginning. Don't you know that?"

"Oh!"

"Yes, oh." The woman's smile was smug, full of unbearable superiority. "You will learn all about it, girl, if that wild buck of yours is as vigorous as his brother. Sometimes they make us more children than we are ready to deal with." Taking the bowl, the woman put it into the stream. "And sometimes we miss the right timing to solve this affair in a desirable way."

"His brother?" The childbearing challenges or the ways to deal with them were not as interesting as what the woman said first. "You woman brother? Brother's woman?"

Another superior smile flashed. "Yes, savage girl. We are a family now, come to think of it." Leaning against the nearest stone, the woman made herself comfortable by pulling her legs up, hugging her knees with one hand. The other brought up the bowl, as though contemplating if it was advisable to drink from it or not. "So I gather that our Wolf Clan's most prominent Mother is treating you well."

"She yes, treat well." It was encouraging to be able to understand, to follow the conversation with not too much of an effort. Her current company might not be the nicest, but this woman was definitely easier to understand then Okwaho's mother, who was the most pleasant, fascinating person to listen to but whose peculiar way of speaking made Kentika's head ache. "She kind, good, very good person."

Her companion's grunt held no ill feelings. "That she is. An exceptional woman. But don't try your luck with her if you are up to slacking at work. She won't have it. She is kind and good-hearted, but hard and implacable when it comes to doing your part of the work. Girls aren't eager to make her angry."

For a heartbeat, silence prevailed, interrupted by lively voices. Down there by the fire, men didn't seem to be getting sleepy or bored.

"I wonder what made her take you under her wing. She seems as though eager to protect you. Because of her son? I doubt that. The young hothead should be able to deal with the consequences of his own doings. She made sure to impress that upon both her sons."

That made Kentika wonder too. If not because of Okwaho, then why?

"Maybe it has something to do with her own foreign origins," went on the woman, musing, her face reflecting a genuine puzzlement. "But then, it was never hard for her, or so they say. The War Chief was not a person anyone dared to anger by treating his woman with any lack of respect, Crooked Tongues or not. He wouldn't have it, and she must have been as good back then, as quick and efficient, as she is now. You two have nothing in common, nothing at all."

Kentika pressed her lips. "You also no common," she relayed, too angered and offended to care about what she said. "She kind, you not. She look people's eyes, no judge. She different."

The hearty laughter was her answer. "Oh, but you do have spirit, foreign girl. You do. Maybe that's what she likes about you." Shifting into a better position, the woman peered at Kentika, her lips twisting into another challenging grin. "Why do you say I'm not kind? I didn't say anything bad or offensive. I'm just telling the truth, the truth you may not like to hear, but it changes nothing. You should hear what they tell about you out there, then you won't think *me* unkind." The smile disappeared. "Foreigners can do well, sometimes. Our towns are full of them. Well, were full of them, before the Great Peacemaker made our people into brother-nations. Then they ceased to be foreigners, but we still have enough Crooked Tongues who are not brothers or sisters of ours. Still, if those adoptees are nice and open, willing to adjust, then they can do well here. Just like our husbands' mother." The pointed eyebrows arched. "But you aren't her. You are wild and unfriendly. You are violent, or so they say. You can barely speak our tongue. You don't get along with the girls of your temporary clan, and you don't do your work well. None of this will bring you closer to acceptance, Okwaho's girl. He might be fond of you, may try to protect you, but it is not up to him to make you be accepted. That is something only the women of our town can do. Never a man." The narrowed eyes peered at her, gleaming again in a provoking way. "Do you understand what I say? Do you still think me to be unkind for telling you the truth as it is?"

Kentika shook her head, tired and spent, wishing nothing more now than to crawl into the darkest corner of her adoptive longhouse, to curl around herself on one of the upper shelves maybe, and sleep, just sleep, not to wake up for an eternity, until all the troubles sorted themselves out. Until Okwaho made it all work again. Like he always did. She hadn't been nearly as drained of strength while running all over the hills, crushed under the weight of too many baskets. It was different back then. To walk beside Okwaho's mother and talk to her was encouraging, even though she did not understand half of what the woman said. A foreigner herself? No, it could not be the truth. And if it wasn't, then what else had this sharp-tongued, mercilessly honest woman gotten wrong?

"Don't get that downcast, girl." The woman's voice was kinder now, warmer than ever before. "I told you it won't be easy, but it doesn't mean you won't make it. Somehow." A friendly wink. "With an active backing from our highly influential, mutual family member, it may be easier than you, or I for that matter, would imagine."

Getting to her feet with an obvious difficulty, the woman beckoned Kentika to follow. "Come. We have a busy day tomorrow and through the ceremonies. Our women work and work, and our men just enjoy the fruits of it, lazy carcasses that they are. How difficult is it to hunt a deer, eh? Nothing, not much sweat. But see them make the maize, the *Three Sisters*, grow, harvest in time for one of the biggest ceremonies, peel, grind, prepare all sorts of dishes and make it all go orderly and with no hitch. Eh? Do you think they would manage that, our glorious men?" The decorations of the woman's dress rustled as she laughed, her heavy breasts fluttering. "Never. Not even our War Chief, who is the most organized person among the entire League of the Five Nations, the masculine side of it that is. He organizes the meetings of the Great Council, and the way he does it, everything works well, without people losing their patience, all these hundreds of escorting warriors stuck together before Onondaga Town with nothing better to do but to wait for the dignitaries they brought there to deliberate and talk and smoke for days. Their meeting could go for half a moon, girl, would you imagine that? And yet it never ends with brawls and fights. A wonder, if you ask me, because men can be such a nuisance."

"The War Chief, he make meetings?" asked Kentika, all ears now. It was fascinating, even if outlandish. Didn't war chiefs make war?

"Oh, yes, he does, and not just meetings of a few battle-hungry leaders and chiefs. No, girl. The meetings of the Great Council are breathtaking events, with thousands of people flooding the valley near Onondaga Town, different people from all over the land. Five nations, speaking different tongues, having different pasts. We used to war, you see? War for, oh, generations. Such fierce fighting, or so the elders said. The Peacemaker came to our lands only three decades ago, think about it. Thirty summers. I was born shortly after the Great Peace prevailed. Not such a forgotten past, eh? And Ganayeda," the woman's voice lost its previously mocking, slightly arrogant tone, ringing with barely concealed excitement now, the pride in it obvious, spilling. "My husband was born into the Great Peace. He was but a baby on Seketa's breast, but he was present at the first meeting of the Great Council, and the Great Peacemaker himself paid him attention. Because our yet-to-be War Chief was his closest of helpers and greatest of friends." The broad face turned to her, beaming in the strengthening moonlight. "Would you believe it? It is all truth, no storytelling, no embellishments. It did happen."

The shadow of the shorter longhouse was upon them again, to Kentika's imminent disappointment. Warmed to her story, her companion was talking rapidly, using too many strange words or complicated sentences, and yet, she craved to hear more.

Okwaho's father helping that legendary peacemaker she had heard so much about since entering the lands of their Great River; his brother being looked upon by the divine messenger of the Great Spirits. Incredible!

"The Peacemaker, he see Okwaho too?" she asked, halting before the lower bark wall with the large heron engraved upon it.

"No, girl." Her companion's laughter broke the spell. "That wild thing is too young for that. The Messenger of the Great Spirits was gone for ten summers and more before your handsome lover was born. He had nothing to do with the Great Peace, and it's for the best, if you ask me. That one wanted to fight from the moment he could walk and talk, getting in trouble more times than not. He would jeopardize our Great Peace if it wasn't such a solid, unbreakable structure by now." The laughter grew. "He would lead a great war, not great peace, that one."

"He make peace, with my people," exclaimed Kentika, offended on Okwaho's behalf this time. "He great warrior, yes, but he stop fight, made everyone listen. He make peace. He great man."

The pointed eyebrows of her companion arched once again. "He made peace with your people?"

"Yes!"

A hearty laughter was her answer.

"He can't make peace with foreigners. Not a wild warrior of little summers that he is. He lied to you and your people, if he said that." The plump arm came up, arresting Kentika's heated protests. "Only representatives of the Great Council can bring up such matters, only they can deliberate and think of the advisability of peace with this or that neighboring nation. And if they decide it may be a good idea, then they would need to get everyone to agree on it. A mission that has proved impossible so far, as there would always be someone against or stalling." The woman shook her head. "Why, our War Chief tried to push the peace with the Crooked Tongues for decades, and he got nowhere so far. A man of his stature, eh? And you expect Okwaho to keep some silly promise to some strangers out there. Oh, please!"

"No, it's not like that!" Kentika fought the urge to bring her palms up, to press them against her burning cheeks. "He stop fight. They were to kill, everyone, his people and mine. But he made stop, made listen." She took a deep breath. "But yes, he say he talk to his father, and make peace, real peace, yes. He can do! He great man, and father great man!"

The motherly smile that stretched the thin lips made her wish to strike her companion.

"Oh, but you are in love, girl." The laughter rolled again, this time soft and delicate, and yet it held all the superiority, all the grownups' disdain. "Leave his father in peace, both of you. He has enough on his plate as it is, with those Long Tails coming from the west, determined to make it more difficult for him in his quest of peace with the Crooked Tongues. Some say they are Crooked Tongues themselves. Well, they certainly have the same accent." Smiling widely, the woman shook her head. "Well, enough politics for one night, girl. We have a long day ahead of us and a very short night now, thanks to our foray into history and peace treaties." The narrow eyes measured her, flickering in a friendly, slightly provoking, way. "You are fascinating company, foreign girl. I would never have expected it, in hundreds of summers, but..." The smile widened. "Feel free to seek me out any time you wish to be lectured on history and politics, or want to hear a more pragmatic version of events than your glorious hero relates to you. I like Okwaho, don't mistake me on that. His wildness and fierceness are delightful, and his light disposition even more so. He will make some sort of a warriors' leader, maybe. He won't go as far as his brother, but he will not make you ashamed."

A friendly wave of the plump hand, and the woman was gone, swallowed by the darkness of the storage room, leaving Kentika to stand in the wind, her thoughts rushing about, but her spirit warmed, curiously at peace, as though soothed, somehow.

Such a strange woman, she thought. Arrogant and annoying at times, then interesting and well meaning, fascinating with her tales of the past, then brutally honest, thinking Okwaho to be nothing but a young hothead.

Well, he was that too; of course he was. She had thought him to be that at first. But now she knew better. He was as great as his father, or even more so. He would make the arrogant union accept her people as allies and friends. He would manage, somehow.

CHAPTER 9

Ganayeda held his breath. The torches of the men upon the shore flickered faintly, almost friendly in the surrounding darkness.

There were many of them, too many, a group of highly alerted warriors congregating near the shore, and who knew how many more were prowling the woods, scanning them, searching for the locals who had managed to best their fellow raiders time after time.

Seven warriors, or scouts, *intruders*, he thought with satisfaction. Mainly Okwaho's victims, but a few of his own as well. Not a bad achievement for two men busy hunting. Not bad at all.

However, now they needed help. One look at the group that was dragging boats down the narrow strip of the shore was enough to take any ideas of a rescuing mission out of their heads. So far, they had managed against uneven forces, but their luck could not be pushed further than this. These people were highly alerted now, enraged by the unnecessary loss of quite a few of their fellow warriors, eager to find the culprits, not up to any more surprises. And yet …

Carefully, he slipped down the incline and into the cold of the cutting wind that came from the lakeside. It pounced upon him with unexpected viciousness, as though trying to stop him, to warn him, maybe.

He eyed the flickering lights. To wait for Okwaho was the right thing to do. They had both agreed on this course of action. He, Ganayeda, would watch them, keeping an eye on what havoc they were wreaking, while Okwaho would race all the way to the village and back, returning with reinforcements.

Not the most satisfactory solution, but they had no better one. Assuming that the raiders would not be willing to sail away before daybreak—the Great Sparkling Water was not the place to navigate in the darkness—they might have a fair chance of succeeding. Lone Hill was not that far away, and an unimportant village it was not. They would listen to Okwaho, and they would act at once.

Concentrating on his step, he made his way behind the still-satisfactory coverage of the trees, progressing one careful pace after another. But to be able to move as swiftly and as silently as Okwaho had up there on the hill!

He rolled his eyes, not daring to shake his head. That young buck, indeed, was a warrior now. But would he bring help in time?

The torches upon the shore flickered with urgency. He could feel their tension, carried with the wind. Oh, Mighty Spirits, but these people may sail in the dead of the night if feeling threatened. And if they did bother to go back, to find all those bodies of their fellow warriors but none of the locals who did the killing, then they would feel threatened, oh yes.

Slipping between the rocks adorning the shore, he strained his eyes, willing the moon to come out, yet also wishing it would stay clouded and concealed. To be able to see what was ahead would help, would show him how bad the situation was, maybe reveal the location of the girls, even. But to be illuminated, exposed, would not be a good turn for an intruder intent on sneaking around. He better wait for the reinforcements.

One of the torches drew nearer, coming into the open, its flames dancing wildly, indicating the strength of the wind out there at the shore. It must have been oiled, wrapped in cloth, not a simple burning stick, reflected Ganayeda. Those people were well prepared.

Shivering, he watched its progress, another flame joining it. The muddled shouts made his sense of urgency soar. Something wasn't right there, upon the shore. What?

Trusting the darkness, he left the protection of the rocks,

charging into the open space, running low, probing with his senses for obstacles and possible causes to trip. The sand was relatively clear, and as he dived behind yet another cluster of stones, he heard the shouts, more clearly now. People were milling around the silhouetted mound, probably piled-up boats, dark forms, rushing in the meager light then disappearing, clearly agitated.

One of the arrows was already clinging to his bowstring, out and prepared to pounce. A loud female sobbing left him with nothing to question. Even though he recognized it, he needed a better range before doing something stupid. The girl would have to fend for herself for a little bit longer.

When the silhouette of a fluttering skirt burst into his view, outlined brightly against the momentarily clear sky, he was about to charge through another open space, hoping for the best. The moonlight was the one to arrest his progress, but now it was aiding him, presenting a good view of the man who rushed after her. It was easy to shoot him cleanly, to make that one fall with not too much noise.

Leaping forward, he grabbed the girl, who struggled fiercely, kicking and scratching as though she were a wild cat, a mad coyote struck with sickness. It took him all his power not to let her twisting body go, his sides absorbing her blows, his mind fighting the idea to strike her into unconsciousness.

"Stop it," he breathed, falling back behind his previous cover, his bow again ready, staring into the darkness of the shore. The moon was gone again. How helpful!

The girl grew still all of a sudden, and he listened intently. The nearing footsteps were loud, bereft of care. More than one pair.

His hands shook with impatience, but he waited, fighting the temptation to shoot madly, with no aim, his nerves stretched worse than his bow. When more footsteps exploded behind his back, he darted to his feet, his senses screaming, demanding action, whether to run or shoot or just strike out with no aim or direction, *to do something.*

A flame neared, assaulting his nostrils with the stench of burning oil. Darting aside, he stumbled on the slippery stones, avoiding the thrust of a spear from behind by a miracle as it seemed. The light was blinding, making his eyes water, filling his vision with blots of orange, leaving him helpless. The woman, where was the woman?

The flame pounced at him again, as he threw himself over the stones that were blocking his way, tearing at his quiver. Blindness was the worst of it, but as his limbs hit the ragged surface, he felt his bow getting caught under his own weight.

The welling panic hit him with suddenness and viciousness as he struggled to free his only means of fighting back. The club, he should have kept the club from the clearing.

As though answering his thoughts, a familiar hiss made him roll away, tearing his skin against more of the jagged stone beneath him. The blow that was supposed to smash him into a pulp brushed against his upper leg, making him gasp with pain. Still, his arm clutching the bow was free, and it reassured him.

The glimmering blots that made him blind were receding, letting him catch a glimpse of his attackers, and the flicker of their torch. Oh, but he needed to make it extinguish, somehow. The darkness was on his side.

A silhouette darted toward him, and he heard his own arrow swishing, shot as though of its own accord. Evidently, it missed, as the man pressed on, with the tip of his spear cutting Ganayeda's shoulder, slipping against it, to scratch the surface of the nearest rock. It was evidently as hard for them to aim as it was for him.

Catching the choppy shaft with both hands, he pulled hard, making his attacker crash headlong into the stones beside him. For a moment, they thrashed about, clinging to the same weapon, both clumsy, uncomfortable, blind.

The torch was nearer, and as he felt its hostile, scorching presence, he remembered Okwaho and the clearing, and the stone his brother had thrown when unable to come to his, Ganayeda's, aid in time. Thinking with an unusual clarity, as though outside himself, he let the contested spear go, if only for a heartbeat, squirming free from his attacker's weight, groping for the sharpness of the jutting missiles. One such felt good in his palm, belonging, and he hurled it without getting up, aiming at the blazing spot, putting all his strength into the throw.

Still acting outside himself, as though he had time to do it all properly, deliberately, his hand, now free, tore at the knife that was miraculously still attached to his girdle, all the thrashing among the sharp rocks notwithstanding. Yet, the owner of the spear had enough presence of mind to recover as well, jumping to his feet with his weapon intact, his silhouette barely visible in the dimmed light, the torch, or the remnants of it, now flickering weakly upon the ground. Still, it gave the man enough illumination to aim.

The clarity of vision, the detachment, were gone. He saw the lethal shaft coming down again, diving like a bird of prey, determined, unerring. In desperation, he grabbed the edge of the shaft, the razor-sharp flint cutting his palms, slowing its plunge, but only a little. He was in no position to put enough power into it to resist the push.

Squirming, he tried to secure his elbows on the slippery stones that jutted against his limbs, to make them support him, give his arms enough strength to resist the advance of the lethal flint. His knife was still there in his right palm, hindering and not helping. It was of no use. Even with the last of the light gone, the spear was coming down, determined to take his life.

When another dark form collided with the one above him, he managed to twist a little, despite the rocks that were blocking his way. The flint was nicking his side, slipping away, cutting the skin and some muscle, hurting but not damaging badly, *not killing him*.

His rival was trying to pull it away, to attempt a better hit surely, but again, Ganayeda didn't let his side of the sturdy weapon go. Hands bleeding, eyes burning from all the sweat and mud and blood, his entire body screaming in pain, he yanked with all his might, but his attacker was ready, resisting the pull, not letting his advantage of the upright position go, not this time. Still, razor-sharp or not, Ganayeda didn't let his side of the shaft go; it felt safer to have the spear neutralized, even if momentarily.

Again, something took his attacker's attention away, and as he heard a strangled groan upon the ground—probably from the torch holder—a muffled curse came along with the cry of a woman, more of a squeak than an intelligible sound.

He hadn't spent his time listening to those. As he pulled sharply, managing to haul himself to his feet rather than making the spearman fall, with no time to waver, or fight for his balance, or try to appraise the situation, he threw himself at his rival, heedless and with not a care to his own safety, his knife alive, at long last, not as useless anymore.

It was over in another heartbeat, and while the presence of the girl was no more than a silhouette, he knew it wasn't *her*, as he grabbed her forcefully, using her relative steadiness to maintain an upright position.

"Keep close and make no trouble," he breathed, remembering her previous fight when he tried to take her away. They couldn't tell the enemy from the friend in such a deep darkness, but this moonless night was their only chance.

CHAPTER 10

The wall of the solid rock towered ahead, sporting plenty of dark openings.

Tucking her baskets in one of the lower niches, Kentika eyed her discovery, looking for a foothold. The cave she aimed to reach was not far away, gaping from the wetness of the wall, offering possibility. From there, the spring she wanted to see must be on full display, the wind blowing her way, promising hearing opportunities as well.

Why would she do it? she asked herself. Why would she try to spy on the War Chief?

The question alone made her shiver. If caught doing something like that, she would be done for. It was as sure as the rain of the next moon. The powerful War Chief, a good person or not, would not tolerate something like that, a foreign girl prying into his affairs. Clandestine affairs, at that! He would be furious, and not even Okwaho would be able to protect her against his wrath.

Biting her lower lip, she hesitated, then sank deeper behind the bushes adorning the wide shelf she had crouched upon. The trickling of the brook came from beneath, reminding her how delighted she had been yesterday, finding this place. It was so pleasant to wash in the shallow stream, the clearest water she had seen since arriving here. The spring that kept the town supplied with readily available water was a little muddy, not as transparent as this one.

The brook of the caves. Had she been right assuming that the man meant this place?

From her vantage point, she could see mostly the foliage of the trees adorning the closer bank, all yellow and red, dotted with the last of the green, the water flickering in the strong sun, washing lazily over the rocks, carrying leaves and broken branches. There must be more brooks with caves all around these woods. The man didn't necessarily mean that place. Or did he?

She remembered the night, the calm voices by the various fires, all men and warriors, with no females anywhere near. After her unexpected company disappeared into the depths of her longhouse, Kentika didn't feel like going back to sleep, not yet. It was so pleasant out there, cold but tranquil. It made her think of home. Even in the dead of the night, this huge, bubbling town held no resemblance to her village. Did these people ever pause? It didn't seem so. They were so busy, so full of purpose. They made her people look lazy.

Like this woman, Okwaho's brother's wife, of all people, plump and sharp-tongued, talkative, saucy, rude at times, well meaning at others, so busy and purposeful, walking in a hurried step, even though it was night and she was with child, and there was no need to rush anywhere. Still, the woman was a whirlwind of activity, if not doing her chores then talking, not pausing for breath. They were so busy, these people, men and women alike, their history so complicated, their politics impossible to understand. The Clan Mothers who told everyone what to do; the War Chief who dealt with peace.

She found herself wishing the woman had stayed and talked some more. She was so knowledgeable, so informed, ready to sound her mind, and in the most unrestrained of manners. Did she tell her husband, Okwaho's impressive brother, what to do? Was she the mother of her clan or longhouse? So different from the reserved, dignified, well-organized Seketa—was that the name of Okwaho's mother?—and yet somehow alike, as matter-of-fact, as businesslike, as well meaning, even if in her own slightly rude sort of a way.

Deep in her thoughts, she had neared the facade of the longhouse with the sketchy wolf's carving, only to nearly bump into the figure emerging out of it. One of the foreigners? The Long Tails People who made everyone agitated?

Unwilling to face the man who had talked to her back in the War Chief's compartment, in case it was him, she dived behind a tall bark partition that was leaned against the wall for some unknown purpose, probably a means to close the entrance to the house that seemed to be permanently opened at all times. Inclined in a sharp angle, it left enough space to sneak behind it, to cram oneself there and hope that the intruder would go away fast. It was truly uncomfortable, and if someone saw her doing this ...

The rustling of more footsteps made her heart race. The man who came out seemed to stay where he was, but more people were nearing, a whole group of them. Still, someone reached the poles of the facade ahead of the others, lonely but determined paces.

"Honorable Leader," whispered the guest, confirming her conclusion. Oh, yes, he was one of the foreigners, his way of saying even those two words unbearably twisted. Not her foreigner but another one. "A message, I carry a message—"

"Tomorrow, when the sun is at its highest." The War Chief's unmistakable voice brushed his guest off, not rudely but decisively. "The brook with the caves, the western hill."

The voices of the others were upon them, but what they said was lost on Kentika, her heart thundering too loudly, interfering with her ability to listen, the meaning of what she heard difficult to comprehend. The much-admired, all but revered War Chief doing something shabby, receiving clandestine messages from foreigners? Echoes of her father, oh, Benevolent Spirits. Her father was also an admired leader everyone respected and trusted...

And now, in the tranquility of the forested hill, surrounded by the radiant vividness of the mid-autumn colors, she felt her heart beginning to race again. Okwaho's father looked so reasonable, so wise and dignified, so patient and understanding. He would not do something shabby, not him. And yet ...

The sun had reached the top of the sky long since, staying there now, reminding her that she had promised to deliver two rounds of forest fruit, and not only one. That meant at least ten baskets full to the brim with berries and nuts, the goal she set for herself, desperate to impress her benefactress, to show her that the trust placed in her, Kentika, was justified, good for many more such missions.

And not that it was difficult, not at all, because she had set out truly early, before the first light, taking all those ten baskets of various sizes, intending to spend her day filling them all, then going back with half of her harvest, sparing time on dividing her work.

Until now, it worked well. This distant hill was full of treasures, untouched, yielding so much, so readily. Unlike the clearings the women of this town went to plunder on the day before. How silly. They spared an effort on walking but actually were made to work harder, competing with others for the same grounds and fruits to pick.

"Greetings."

The voice from beneath her hiding place made her jump. Holding her breath, she clutched the nearest branch, hoping she didn't make the surrounding shrubs rustle too badly. No figure appeared at her limited view of the stream beneath, but she could hear someone walking, treading on slippery stones. Lonely footsteps.

How long had the other person, the one the newcomer greeted, been there? Why didn't she hear him nearing?

"Greetings, Honorable Leader." The voice of the man from last night did not sound as calm as that of his converser, having an obviously strained tone to it.

"Whom is your message coming from?" The War Chief was clearly not about to spend his time on small preliminary talk.

"The other side of your Great Lake."

"What nation?"

"Oh …" The man hesitated. "The Bear People, Honorable War Chief. But it represents more nations. As our leaders have told you, the Wyandot people are united now. From one great water to another, or so they claim."

For a few heartbeats, a silence prevailed. She listened to the trickling of the brook, the rustling of the trees. There was no calmness in any of these anymore.

"In a union that resembles our Great League?" asked the war

leader after a while, his voice now a little too low to relay the perfect composure of before.

"No, I wouldn't say that. Their two leading nations seem to be allied by an agreement of mutual help and protection. With two more about to join." Another pause. "But they are not one people. Not like your people seem to be."

She could imagine the War Chief nodding thoughtfully, his face closed, the strong jaw tight.

"I see," he said after another spell of silence. "Who was the man who sent the message?"

"I don't know who the person who sent it was, as I was not the direct recipient of it. Neither was the man who asked me to talk to you." She could hear the messenger drawing a panted breath. "But they say it came from one of their leading persons, the man who was responsible for organizing their union."

"What nation does he belong to?"

"The Bear People. The people who dwell closest to the shores of your Sparkling Water."

More silence. Now she could hear the great leader drawing a breath of his own, quite loudly at that.

"What do you know about this man? What does he look like? Have you happened to meet him?"

The messenger hesitated again. "I have seen him once, yes. When our people went to visit our neighbors, the Rock People, the prospective members of their union that are residing closest to us. It was a few hunting seasons ago. Maybe two, or three. He had been visiting as well, with the delegation of his Bear People." A stone rolling over the wet rocks made Kentika imagine one of the men kicking at it. "He is tall and middle-aged, about the same age as you, Honorable Leader. He can speak your people's tongue, but with certain difficulty. We have conversed in this way for a little while. He was curious about your people and your union. Asked many question." Another pause. "About you in particular."

This time it seemed that the silence would last forever.

"Two hunting seasons ago, you say?" The war leader's voice picked up an additional tone, having achieved a stonier quality to it.

"Yes, Honorable Leader. They were united back then already, the Bear and the Cord People. Or about to do so."

More silence. She listened to the wind, perturbed by the strange rustling above her head, where the cliff overlooking the brook ended abruptly, adorned by raspberry bushes and shelves.

"What is the message you carry relay to me?"

The other man swallowed loudly. "We were to tell you that it was the time to start the talks. He said that if a delegation from the Five Nations came, it will be received and listened to. He said he would make sure of that. Personally."

Busy trying to understand, missing important keywords, she couldn't help but wonder about the cliff above, probing with her senses, her skin prickling. No more sounds came from up there, but her instincts told her that something was not quite right there, not as it should be. Was there someone up there? An animal? A person? There was a reason women went out in groups, she remembered. From enemies to forest beasts, it was not advisable to wander all alone. Why did she always forget this rule?

"Do you have a way of communicating a message back?" asked the War Chief, his voice returning to its previous quiet, unperturbed calmness.

"I can pass it on, yes. I can't promise it'll reach the person you wish to communicate to, but we will do all in our power to deliver your word."

"Impress it upon the people who sent it with you that it is important. Tell them to let this man, the Bear People's leader, know that after the Cold Moons, what he wishes may be possible to achieve. But not before. It will not happen before the Maple Ceremony, at the earliest." Another pebble made the shallow water splash. "He and his people must be patient. They didn't make it easy for us until now. If they are ready to talk, he must make sure they wait patiently. He must do everything in his power to prevent any further damage until we talk."

She could imagine the other man nodding, tense and foreboding.

"What would your people want out of it?" By the sound of his voice, the War Chief must have moved.

Preparing to leave? She strained her eyes in an attempt to catch at least a glimpse of them, but the patch of the stream she managed to see ebbed on, undisturbed.

"I do not represent the majority of my people. My leaders who urged me to contact you work hard to make our people listen. For now, they count on you to remember that it was our nations that did our best to assist, to bridge the gap and help the Five Nations and the Wyandot People talk."

"It will be remembered," said the War Chief gravely, assuming what sounded like a formal way of speech. "Your efforts in helping the Great Peacemaker's vision to expand will not be forgotten." The voice softened. "He went to see your people before he left our world. His wish to see your representatives alongside our Five Nations' dignitaries, sitting in the shade of the Great Tree of Peace, was strong." Another pause. "We will work to this end now that you showed your good will."

As they fell silent again, Kentika tried to wave away a fly without moving any of her limbs. The War Chief, if not his questionable emissary, were people of great experience. It was a wonder no one had detected her eavesdropping presence so far.

Another prickle of suspicion made her wish to glance up grow stronger. Something wasn't right up there as well. But for the need to keep absolutely still! How easy it would be for a long-legged predator to pounce on her from above, to kill and devour her before she had time to as much as cry out. Even if just a forest cat, not to mention a wolf, or maybe a mountain lion.

She clenched her teeth in order to stop the wave of wild fear. Why weren't the men below going away already? Hadn't they discussed everything they needed to?

Their voices, indeed, began to fade, and she let her breath out. Just to get down, snatch a few of her baskets and rush as fast as she could. But not on their heels. Oh, Benevolent Spirits, why did she get into any of this?

Trying to take her thoughts off the fear, she thought about what she had heard. So the War Chief, indeed, dealt with peace more than he dealt with war. Just like the woman by the spring said. But did the talkative wife of Okwaho's brother know that the fearless leader seemed to be sometimes including negotiations that weren't meant to reach his people's ears? Who was sending the powerful man clandestine messages, and why? And why through other foreigners, whose presence at the town was irritating enough as it was?

The natural silence of the forest prevailed. She counted another hundred heartbeats, then crawled to the edge of her shelf, relieved to see the brook below flowing calmly, abandoned again. Grabbing the protruding stone, about to climb down, anxious to reach the cave with the baskets now, she glanced at the towering wall briefly, mainly to reassure herself. Just to—

The cry that seemed to split the very air startled her even more before she realized that it was her who had cried out. The fear cascaded down her chest and into her stomach, wild, impossible to control. Her hands slipped, but her feet still made her stay where she was, clinging to the slippery stone with her entire body, although the fall was not a bad possibility, the height of her perch no more than that of two people standing on each other's shoulders.

The face that studied her looked slightly familiar, and it held an open surprise that was already mixing with amused curiosity, a playful question. She tried to slam her mind into working. To push away and just jump looked like the best of her options.

As she tore her eyes off him, she did just that, landing on her arms and knees, not especially gracefully. Her heart was pounding too wildly, not letting her do these things in a better way.

"Wait, don't run away!" he called as she jumped up, reeling a little, one of her knees hurting, palms on fire.

Whirling around, she broke into the wildest of flights, down the hill with no trail, pell-mell, oblivious to the slippery ground. One leap got her over the brook, but her knee burst in a spectacular show of pain, and she faltered, clutching the nearby branch to prevent the fall.

The man's panted breath reached her. Had he jumped down, too? He could not reach the ground that fast otherwise, could he?

Pushing her rickety support away, she rushed on, trying not to limp. Just to get away from here. Back in the town, she would be safe!

The slippery ground resisted her feet, trying to make her fall. Struggling to keep her pace, she didn't notice it turning rockier, and when the incline ended abruptly, with nothing but a cliff edge and a pretty view spreading below, she tried to halt, in panic, waving her hands, clutching onto the bushes, desperate to prevent the fall.

The prickly branches were thin, breaking one after another, but just as her feet lost the connection with the slippery earth, one of her hands managed to cling to a firmer sprig, and it gave her a pause, a blissful breathing space.

Freezing, she tried to appraise the situation, feeling enough steady surface under her chest and belly, but not lower than this. Her feet dangled free, from a height she could not estimate without turning back and thus losing the painfully gained respite in the fall.

Carefully, she tried to pull herself up, but her wobbly support wavered, bending unhelpfully, threatening to give way. In desperation, she tried to locate a better support with her free hand, moving it carefully, barely daring to breathe. The stones were so slippery.

When light rustling in the grass brought a pair of embroidered moccasins into her view, she was busy rejoicing in her success at planting her fingers into small cavities of the wall she was suspended from. Still, a sturdy palm locking around her wrist made her grateful, even though the pull was too abrupt, hauling her up in an inconsiderate manner. The sharp stones tore at her skin, but the benefit of standing on the firm ground again was well worth it.

Clinging to the supporting hands that didn't let her go right away, she tried to catch her breath.

"You are a wild thing."

The strange accent of the speaker made her feel better for some reason. She blinked forcefully, trying to make her mind work. But, for the foreign presence, she would have sat down, to let her racing heart slow its pace and her trembling limbs to rest a little.

Was she hurt? Her burning legs and arms told her that she was.

"Come," said her rescuer, touching her shoulders lightly, propelling her back uphill and away from the treacherous cliff. "You need to get back to that brook."

A soundly good idea. She followed his lead with no argument, too numb to think clearly.

The water was trickling, as peaceful as before, undisturbed, the sun still high. Nothing had changed there, save the absence of the War Chief and his questionable contact among the foreigners.

Taking her moccasins off and rolling her sleeves up, she dipped her aching limbs into the cool water, feeling better by the moment. But for her unwanted company, she would have stripped and washed most thoroughly, cleaning herself not only of the splattered mud, but of the bad feeling as well.

Why didn't the foreigner have good enough sense or manners to leave? Instead, the annoying man made himself comfortable upon one of the dry stones of the shore, watching her as though she were a throwing game or a ceremony, calm, openly amused, just like last night at the longhouse's compartment, when they both could not fall asleep. An annoying man!

Turning her back on him with what she hoped relayed her resentment, she sat on one of the glistening stones, rubbing her face clean of the splattered mud, dunking her entire head into the water. The coldness of it took her breath away, but the refreshing feeling was wonderful. Also, it kept her busy, too busy to turn back and address the object of one of her main problems.

"They will still know that you've been acting wildly." His voice reached her despite the pleasantly muffling barrier the water created. "You can't wash all those scratches and cuts off."

Straightening up, she kept her head bent forward, to let the water drain off her messed-up braids. She should have untied them, shouldn't she?

"I no act wild," she said, when the silence behind her back turned too uncomfortable. "I work, busy work. Then you scare."

"Work?" His laughter rolled across the stream, hushed and careful, but full of mirth. "Work by spying on the War Chief? Who gave you that important task to do?"

That made her wish to dive into the stream and be gone. He had seen her, of course he had. He had been up there all the time, the suspicious presence she had felt all along. Oh, Benevolent Spirits!

"Why did you?"

She squeezed her braids fiercely. "I no spy," she muttered. "I just work, gather things."

"What things?" His laughter subdued, but his voice still trembled with an unbearable, even if playful, superiority.

"Berries, nuts." The memory of her full baskets surfaced. "I almost finish. Then they come, surprise, interrupt work." More confident now, she turned to face him, tossing her braids back, trying to pay no attention to the unpleasant shower of drops the wideness of her gesture released. "I busy work. All women do. The ceremony, we are very busy. Clan Mother work day and night, make everyone work."

His eyes were flickering, measuring her with an open amusement, his eyebrows arching, lips twisting teasingly. In the daylight, he looked more imposing, sturdily built, his face broad, adorned with large eyes and a prominent nose and mouth, not as young as Okwaho, maybe five, maybe ten summers older, so very sure of himself.

"So you worked all morning, eh? And where, if it's so, are the fruits of your work, wild girl? Back in the town already, I presume."

"There, under that cliff." Attempting to walk as proudly as she could despite the limp, she gave him a steady glance, not trying to conceal her sense of victory. "Ten baskets. Ten! I work fast."

His eyebrows climbed higher. "Show me."

"I don't, no have to, to show." She tossed her head higher before turning to proceed up the incline. "You no Clan Mother. You guest, guest this town. But you here, why here, eh?" The thought hit her all of a sudden, making her stomach constrict. If she was spying on the War Chief, what was he doing here, if not the same thing? The flickers of fear were back, biting her insides. They were all alone out here, and he was a foreigner.

"I had a good reason to be here, girl. Better than your reason, I bet." His chuckle shook the crispness of the air. "Unless your baskets are not imaginary but real."

"My baskets real." Hastening her step, she scanned the towering wall with her eyes. "There. See?"

The genuine surprise transformed his face, banishing the baiting expression. In silence, he watched her fishing out her containers, the cranberries still glittering, delicious-looking, tempting; the late blueberries a bit limp but not in such a bad shape, either. The baskets with walnuts were heavier, but by this time, he recovered enough to help her pull them out.

"Have you been gathering those since before sunrise?" he asked, the admiration in his voice making her feel as yet more victorious.

"No sunrise. How can? It's long walk. At sunrise go out, out of town."

"Alone?" Asking for no permission, he reached into one of the glittering piles, helping himself to a treat of fresh berries.

About to protest, she hesitated, then decided to spoil herself as well. Her stomach was rumbling with hunger. But for this delay, she should have been back near High Springs by now, carrying half of her cargo, about to snatch something to eat before heading out to pick up the rest of her catch.

"It doesn't make sense," he was saying, devouring another handful, his hands and lips smeared with blackish juice. "No Clan Mother would have sent a young girl so far away, and alone at that, to gather forest fruit. The People of the Longhouse may be annoying creatures, but lacking in good sense they aren't."

Kentika pulled the basket closer and away from him. "My Clan Mother trust. She think I can. She believe when I promise."

He eyed her with an open doubt.

"I go now. Go back. Need hurry." Scanning her treasure with her gaze, she tried to decide what baskets should go with her and what to return to their hiding place for now. The nuts could wait, of course, but still, there were more containers with berries than she could carry.

"How were you planning to take all that treasure?" he asked, echoing her thoughts.

She picked up the nearest basket, seeking out its straps. "Take half, come back, take other half." His dubious expression did not make her angry, not this time. It was actually funny how one of his eyebrows was arching in proportion to the narrowing eye of the opposite side. It made him look young and not as foreboding, and he did save her from that fall back there by the cliff, even if it was he who made her run away in the first place. "If you want eat before go, yes. But berries, not nuts. Cranberry best. They easy, easy to collect. There is plenty. But no nuts. I work hard collect walnuts. Yes?"

His smile was spreading, as full of doubt and wonder as before. "You are generous. But I have a better idea. I'll come with you, help you bring your entire treasure back in one trip. Save you running all the way back. How about that?"

"I ... oh, yes, better idea, yes." Why didn't she think of that before? He was surely on his way back to the town as well, whatever made him wander about before. "I grateful help. Thank you."

His chuckle was her only answer, as he bent to pick up the baskets with nuts.

"No need to thank me, foreign girl. I'm not going with you just to help. I want to hear your story, you see? You made me curious." His smile widened as his gaze regained that taunting glitter again. "You may have worked here since sunrise or later, collecting those things. Doing your duties, yes, even though your Clan Mother must be insane to send a young girl out in such a way." The glitter intensified, turned openly challenging. "Unless she wants to get rid of you, eh? The foreign thing that you are, thrust upon her out of nowhere." He picked up another basket. "I made some inquiries, you see? Asked about you in the town this morning. You made me curious last night, so I asked. I didn't plan to run into you out here, I went out for another reason, but I did ask about you before I left."

The warmth of the early afternoon sun dimmed along with the evaporating sense of confidence she had gained only so recently. The fear was back. "Why ask? Why me?"

"I told you, you made me curious last night." He straightened up, his hands loaded with baskets, two on each arm. "Put that one with the straps on my back."

But she refused to move. "You follow me here?"

"No, I didn't. I told you that." Impatiently, he motioned toward the larger container. "Do you want to come back to the town before nightfall or not?"

Fastening the leather straps to his shoulders, she reflected how spoiled some men were. He wouldn't have needed her help with that had he only bothered to manage that larger basket first. The thought made her feel a little better, even though the sense of safety did not return. Why was he asking about her in the town? And what had he been told?

"So you came from so far away east, no one has even seen or heard of these lands before," he was saying quietly, as though answering her thoughts. "The War Chief's son must have been eager to prove his worth as a warrior. Who bothers bringing captives from such foreign places?" Moving his shoulders, evidently satisfied with the steadiness of his cargo, he straightened his gaze, studying her again, unashamedly at that. "Last night, I kept wondering what you were to the War Chief to warrant sleeping in his compartment of his longhouse. I admit my first assumption was wild."

The memory of what he said back then made her cheeks burn. "Yes, wild, you say wild things."

He waited patiently as she fiddled with her containers, not attempting to help the way she had helped him arranging his cargo. Arrogant beast.

"Well, yes. But the true story is not much more plausible. The War Chief's son acted wildly by bringing you here as a captive. He shouldn't have, if you ask me. It's not like exchanging adoptees between Five Nations, or even take one of our women to live among them, or the other way around."

Forgetting her baskets, she gaped at him. "I no captive!"

His eyebrows were climbing up again. "Forgive me for not believing you on that."

"Who say I captive? Who—"

The wave of his loaded hand and the motion of his head cut off her protests in midair. "Let us argue about that on our way. If you want me to spare you another trip here, we will go now."

The forested trail greeted them with a generous shade, unwelcome in this time of the seasons, with the rim of her dress and her sleeves still wet, clinging to her body unpleasantly. The sun would have dried those off.

"I no captive," she repeated, her mind unable to dwell on anything else.

"You can't be anything but that. You obviously have not gone through the adoption process as yet."

"Adoption?"

"Yes, that's when they make you one of them. That is if those arrogant grass-eaters will deign to do that for you. They don't accept just anyone."

"Yes, yes, I know adoption. I know what it is."

Oh, but how little this arrogant man knew. Okwaho told her all about it. He said they should wait until she felt completely at home. Then she would be able to pick the clan she wanted, to decide which one would suit her better. He said there was no hurry about it, as his family would host them both until it happened. But what if he was wrong? What if there was a need to hurry before his people decided that she was not good enough for them? This man was right about one thing. They *were* arrogant grass-eaters. She had learned all about it through the last few days since he had left, his mother and the few other good people she met notwithstanding.

She glanced at her companion, who was studying her openly, his curiosity unconcealed.

"Now you look upset," he commented. "For a non-captive girl, you lose your confidence easily."

She wished Okwaho was there. He would have shown this man.

"I no captive," she repeated tiredly. "I came live, came with Okwaho, he asked and I say yes. You can't know, know things about me. How know I not adoption already?"

"You wouldn't have lived with your captor's clan."

"He is not my captor!"

But her shout was greeted with unperturbed laughter. "Well, let us leave it for the moment, the technical side of your status. So you live in the War Chief's house, and in the absence of your man, you entertain yourself by spying on their great leader when he engages in less appropriate activities, meeting with all sorts of dubious messengers. Why? What do you hold against that prominent man?"

"I no spy on War Chief." It was getting silly, with him talking on and on and her only shouting back that she was not this and not that. She took a deep breath. "We talk, agree. The baskets, you see the baskets. I work. No spy."

He nodded, good-naturedly. "Yes, you work too, and very well at that. Impressive." There was a trace of appreciation in his voice, even though it still held too much amusement for her peace of mind. "Good speed. And you are strong, too. Just look how you walk, fast and with no effort, carrying all those baskets."

It was as though they were discussing someone else, gossiping about a person who wasn't present. She frowned at him, searching for something appropriately offensive to say.

"But all your merits aside, working girl," he went on, paying no attention to the direfulness of her glances, "you were eavesdropping on the War Chief—you were. I saw this wall, you see? The cave where you had hidden your cargo is down there. If caught unprepared, you would have hid in the grass, or this same cave with your baskets. It was a natural thing to do, even though you didn't have to hide at all if you had no quarrel with the War Chief and his family." Again, his hand came up, arresting her budding protests. "But say you panicked, dived into that cave with your treasures. An understandable behavior in a foreign girl, a stranger in the town, captive or not. But no, you hid your baskets, and you climbed up there, onto the shelf that you must have known existed beforehand, into a place that overlooked the spring, letting you hear better than I was able up there, on the top of that cliff. See? It wasn't a coincidence. You knew he would be coming, and you waited for him." His glance again held a measure of appreciation. "How did you know?"

She wished the journey back to High Springs wasn't that long.

Oh, but this man was unbearable. So haughty and presumptuous, so outspoken, so perceptive, full of such terribly wrong conclusions. How could she deal with this one without being able to even talk properly? And what if he told on her?

"I not know, and not spy and not want talk," she said decisively, hastening her step. "Also, how you know, eh? You say you eavesdrop, too. You say that!" She looked at him triumphantly. "How know where come?"

His laughter rolled between the surrounding trees. "I followed Anue. Was curious to see what he was up to." A shrug. "I knew he was up to no good. He and his people have been having talks with the Longhouse League for quite some time."

Startled at so much openness, Kentika peered at her companion, interested against her will.

"Who they? Who Anue and people?"

"Oh, that was the man your War Chief talked to. Fancy making shady agreements, or passing messages from the Wyandot." The man snorted, suddenly not amused. "Despicable."

"Wyandot?"

"Crooked Tongues, they call them Crooked Tongues." His eyes flashed dangerously, not playful or good-natured anymore. "The Longhouse People are arrogant, foreign girl. They think they are better than all the rest of the Turtle Island dwellers put together; they think no one can compare to them, neither in strength nor in wisdom. Before the Peacemaker, they didn't amount to much. Like anyone else, they were busy warring. But now, oh, now they are busy telling everyone what to do. Even that War Chief of yours. He more than anyone, with his 'let's draw everyone into our great league' attitude. On his and his people's terms, so you know. With no consideration to other people's customs or traditions, their will or the wisdom of their own leaders. The Great League's laws are sacred, word for word with what the Peacemaker declared. What a pile of rotten nonsense!"

But for the baskets, he would have waved his hands in the air, she thought, or maybe hit the nearest tree or rock, he was so angry. It felt safer not to walk too close to him.

"The Peacemaker wise, give good laws," she said mildly,

unable to resist the temptation to argue, to return him his own treatment of her. "Okwaho say great man, great laws. The Messenger from Great Spirits. Maybe should listen, maybe join, eh? War Chief wise man, knows what he do."

He whirled at her, losing his tempo and stumbling over an entanglement of roots.

"Oh, please! That's what they are telling you, girl. But you, of all people, should know. They are bloodthirsty beasts who war on everyone who won't accept their terms or their set of laws. And if you do show good will, they will deliberate for long spans of seasons, arguing in their Great Council, unable to decide if you are worthy. Because deep inside, they know you are not, but the people like their War Chief think it's advisable, for the sake of their league, to have us tamed and restricted." Hastening his step, he caught up with her, peering at her almost anxiously. "Do you understand what I'm saying?"

"Maybe," she said, shrugging. "Maybe understand. My people too far, can't say about Great League. I no politics, no care." The darkness of his gaze was unsettling, but not overly so. There was frustration in his eyes, a sort of helpless rage. "Why come then? You, why come with delegation, if hate so?"

He snorted and turned away, watching the trail that was turning steeper again.

"You ask too many questions for all those 'I no politics, no care' declarations." His shrug was a surprisingly light affair. "I had no choice but to come along. I speak their tongue too well. Our leaders insisted." The playfulness was back, lightening his features, a welcome change. "Also, I wanted to see for myself, to know if I erred in my feelings. Warriors' wisdom tells you to learn about your enemy, to know what you are standing up against, to find the enemy's strengths and weaknesses. So here I am, learning." His wink brought the man from the brook back. "About more than one peoples, apparently. The Longhouse Nations, but also the strange savages out of the lands of the rising sun. Now those I find truly fascinating."

"My people no savages," she stated, this time more pleased than offended. It was good to catch him in his own contradictions.

"You say Longhouse People arrogant, but you call my people savages. Who arrogant, eh? Who now?"

He frowned. "I didn't say it in this way. It was no arrogance." Narrowing his eyes at the loudness of her snort, he pressed his lips together. "It's not the same. You think too simply."

For a while, they proceeded in silence. Oh, but she got him there, she knew, greatly pleased. He and his people were as arrogant as the people they hated. But Okwaho's father was wise. His goals were surely good, even if he went about reaching them in unconventional ways sometimes, holding clandestine meetings with would-be friends or enemies, receiving or passing messages to more enemies or would-be allies out there. He wasn't arrogant, or haughty, or nasty in any way. But this man beside her was more complicated than this, and he wanted something from her.

"What want from me? Why make friends?"

He let out an exasperated breath. "You are something else, foreign girl. Why don't you act like a woman and not a man, sometimes?"

CHAPTER 11

"They still have Gayeri!"

His brother's presence was nothing but a shadow, impossible to see in the thickness of the night. He felt his nod rather than saw it, the graveness of it. There were other silhouettes all around. He counted more than ten men.

"Are you hurt?"

"Nothing dangerous."

He wasn't sure about that. The darkness made it impossible to inspect his various wounds, but he felt his shoulder still bleeding, pulsating with pain, the cut in his side burning, making his skin crawl with an unseemly fear. What if it was gaping, open and deep? He pushed the shameful waves of fear away.

"Stay here until we get back." Okwaho's palm brushed against his upper back, cold but reassuring.

"No." He shook the supporting hand off, then eyed the men his brother had brought, dark, silent forms. "You don't know the exact shore."

One of the newcomers snorted lightly. "We are locals, High Springs man. We can find our way around. Stop arguing, and let us go."

Some of the men began pushing their way past them.

"You are bleeding all over, Brother." This time Okwaho's voice held a hint of pleading. "Stay with the girl. We won't be long."

Ganayeda pressed his lips. Not spending his diminishing strength on any more words, he turned to follow the impatient locals. Just what did Okwaho think he was? A coward? A woman to stay behind? His wounds could not be that serious. If they were, he would have succumbed to the pain and exhaustion already, falling down somewhere along the way.

Instead, he had managed to take one of his rescued charges away, a sobbing, trembling mess, half carrying and half dragging her along. She might have been of help back upon the shore, interfering with the spearman, but her briefly gained courage had left her soon enough, as soon as they seemed to be out of danger, under the blissful coverage of the trees. There, the annoying fox deemed it a good time to break into outright hysterics, and he had to get them both away, stumbling in a near run, carrying the silly thing along. The temptation of striking her into unconsciousness was back, but by then, he was too exhausted to spend his fading strength on more than shushing her with a fierce whisper. Which, of course, didn't help. Females!

Back then, looking for a good hiding spot to place his unwanted charge, he didn't spend time thinking of Gayeri. He would be back soon, and hopefully Okwaho would return with reinforcements as well. They would rescue her, just like he managed to recapture her friend. She would have to wait just a little longer.

"Stop howling," he had hissed, when the ground turned muddier and more forested, with the sounds of the shore disappearing for good. "Listen to me!"

Shaking her hard helped, but it took away more of his strength, made him wish to slip to the ground and stay there the way she did. A luxury he could not afford. If he sat down, he would never be able to get up again.

Leaning on the trunk she had slipped against with his undamaged arm, he tried to catch his breath. His head ached, and his entire body hurt, as though dragged over sharp stones. Which it had been, actually, but his wounds were the ones to worry him. The throbbing in his side and along his shoulder, painful and wet, did not bode well for him. What if …

"Stay here for now," he had told her, pushing the wave of fear away. "You are safe, so just stay quiet. I have to go back, find Gayeri. I'll be back shortly."

Her noisily drawn breath was his answer. This and the way her body tensed. He didn't need to see or touch her to know how frightened she grew.

"I'll come back shortly. Also, your people will be here soon. My brother went to bring your men."

Her palm caught his arm, grabbing it firmly, with unexpected strength. It made him waver and curse with the surprise of it.

"Don't go," she whispered. "Please, don't go."

He fought to break free from her grasp.

"I have to. Your friend!" Successful at last, he took a step back, leaving the much-needed support of her tree. "She needs help. She needs to be taken away from the enemy before it's too late." His frustration began welling, turning into an impotent rage. "How can you be so selfish, so indifferent? You think only of yourself. You disgust me!"

He knew it was not fair. She was a girl with terrible adventures behind her—the bear, her dead friend, the journey, the captivity— and yet, how could she demand such an unreasonable thing from him? To forsake Gayeri?

"You are beneath words!"

She was sobbing again, protesting something inaudible, hiccupping so loudly he wanted to shut her mouth with his hands. They were not out of danger, not yet!

"Stop it!" Making a tremendous effort, he moderated his voice. Given a choice, he would have yelled at her now, among all other violent things one is not supposed to do to hysterical women. "Just listen!"

Somehow, it made the sobbing subdue.

"I'm going back there. Stay here. You are not in danger."

She seemed as though about to say something, but then the cry of an owl tore the darkness, one time, then another, and his heart leapt, first in fear, then in elation. Okwaho was coming back, and he wasn't coming alone. Two hoots warranted that.

And so now, here they were, with his brother and the other eager, battle-hungry men, ready to make the enemy pay for its crimes.

Desperate to conceal his panted breath, he tried to keep up with their pace, their paths seeming more difficult, full of too many obstacles, entangled roots and stones. Those jumped on him from everywhere, determined to make his walk torture. How was he not to trip, with this entire forest so eager to make it difficult, catching his feet with every step, the branches reaching out, flogging his limbs with no mercy?

Trying to protect his wounded side, he twisted again and again, wasting the last of his strength on those attempts, which made him stumble, drawing unwanted attention. If only the flimsy fog in his head would disperse. Was it near dawn already? The darkness suggested that it wasn't.

"Listen." Okwaho's arm caught him as he stumbled again, grabbing a nearby twig for support. Too thin to hold his weight, it bent readily, pushing him on, to crash down but for his brother's supporting arms. "We are going back. Don't argue about it. It won't help."

This time, the uncompromising tone was welcomed, rather than irritating. It reassured him, somehow, made the pain and the fear recede.

"They'll catch up with the lowlifes. Without us stumbling all over, their progress will be easier." After a brief conversation with some of his newfound comrades, the young man's voice rang more lightly. "Lean on me."

Even though their way spread once again uphill, he felt better, with no need to battle the unfriendly ground. Okwaho was such a reliable support. Sturdy and matter-of-fact, he didn't even sway, taking most of Ganayeda's weight as if his charge were not a man of considerable height and width, steering him easily, walking on briskly, as though there was nothing there to hinder his pace.

"They may not find the correct shore." Ganayeda stifled a groan as wet leaves brushed against his cut shoulder. Now that his mind was cleared of the necessity to concentrate on his every step, it drew back to the lake and Gayeri, at the hands of the vile enemy.

"I described it most clearly to them. They won't fail. It's their woman they are trying to save, so they will put forth an effort." A pause. "Her being the daughter of their most prominent dignitary will help them put out an extra effort."

"Whose daughter is she?" asked Ganayeda, mainly to take his thoughts off the rising fear. After another branch brushed against his wounded side, it now burned fiercer than before.

"The representative's. No more, no less."

"What are you talking about?"

"Well, Brother," Okwaho's voice gained this perpetually amused, mischievous tone again, "you bothered to save the daughters of Lone Hill's prominent men, one of them an offspring of the representative in our Great Council, from the bear, and then from the Crooked Tongues." His chuckle rolled lightly, disturbing no darkness. "Quite a feat. The influential men of this settlement will be ever so grateful."

"I didn't save the second one from the bear," said Ganayeda, suddenly incensed. "It was Gayeri who might have been slain by the beast, and I didn't manage to save her from the Crooked Tongues."

Okwaho's voice lost its amusement all at once. "They'll save her, Brother. They will. Don't fret about it." Steering their way across a large puddle, he made it look like an easy feat, even though he had to take his charge's entire weight with a suddenness of the attempted recourse.

"You make it look very easy." Trying to catch his breath, Ganayeda suppressed a groan, as the jerking movement made his side burst with a sharp pang of pain.

"What?"

"That wounded carrying thing. You look as though you have done it before."

"Do I now?" exclaimed Okwaho cheerfully, not bothering to keep quiet as they were obviously closer to the settlement, all signs pointing this way, even though the moon hid again. "You have no idea how it is to carry a bulky moose like that boy from Cohoes Falls." He felt his brother's head shaking mirthfully. "He wasn't of your height, but as broad, with such a padding of muscles one could break a fist trying to hit his stomach. Oh, he was worse than the carcass of a winter moose to carry!"

"What happened to him?" Trying to imagine Okwaho struggling with a wounded moose in his arms helped. It took his thoughts off the pain.

"Had his leg shot through. Such a clean shot, impaled his thigh for good, with the arrowhead sticking out a whole palm. They had to break it off before trying to pull the shaft out."

Ganayeda shook his head. "Not a good wound. It's a wonder he was alive to carry him anywhere."

"Oh, that fortunate piece of meat. He enjoyed the kindness of the Great Spirits much more than that later on. That incident of the shooting was nothing compared to what happened next."

"What?" He could hear the sounds of the near settlement enveloping them, even though the darkness did not let them see a thing. They were near, at long last.

"We were stuck on the shore, only the two of us—the others had already been killed by then. Or maybe not, not yet." The lightness of Okwaho's voice evaporated. "Yes, it happened before. We were washed onto that shore, and the rotten piece of forest rat who led us would not send someone to help." He paused again, as though collecting his thoughts, or maybe trying to control his temper. The latter, decided Ganayeda, knowing his younger sibling too well. "Anyway, we were stuck there for a few days, and by then, Akweks' leg began to rot."

Ganayeda let out a held breath. "Then he is dead now."

The dark mass of the fence was upon them, and as they both hastened their step, he could feel Okwaho scanning their surroundings, probing with his senses.

"We better let them know that we are not an enemy," he muttered. "Before they pounce or shoot at us from behind that fence."

A soundly good idea, thought Ganayeda. Oh, his brother was a true warrior. Shouldn't he have thought about it himself?

"Akweks didn't die." Okwaho's voice rang faintly, not concentrated on his story anymore. "He should have, yes, but he didn't. Kentika saved us both."

The ointment was sticky, unpleasantly warm, biting into his torn flesh, giving it no comfort. Clasping his teeth against the pain, Ganayeda took his eyes away.

The healer who was examining his wounds seemed to be indecently brief, in a hurry. Encouragingly, the old man dismissed the cut in his patient's side as unimportant, just a flesh wound, a lucky one, as a bit higher and deeper, and he may have started preparing for his Sky Journey after all.

Pleased with his own calmness in regard to this, Ganayeda just nodded, paying no attention to the painful cleaning and the thoroughness of the applied treatment. Curiously, the gap in his shoulder was the one to catch the medicine man's attention. It was deeper, oozing blood and another substance, something the healer didn't like.

"It needs to be stitched," he muttered, lines of worry furrowing his forehead, reflecting in the grimness of his eyes. "But it will have to wait for the morning, and by then, it may be too late for that."

"Why morning?" asked Okwaho impatiently.

"You can't operate without a proper light." The elder frowned, clearly put out with so much impudent questioning.

"Yes, we can. We can make fire. I can bring enough torches, make people hold them at the angle you need."

The healer's direful gaze froze the rest of the exclamation, made the young man quiet down, his own gaze shooting thunderbolts, but not daring to argue any longer. What he had said was terribly impolite as it was.

"A good healer can do wonders with as little as a small fire at night," muttered Okwaho, after the old man was gone, leaving more sticky salve on Ganayeda's shoulder to bit into his raw flesh, testing his willpower to its maximum extent. "If this wound gives you trouble, I'm going to kill that healer, member of False Face Society or not."

"Is he?" Again, it helped to address something meaningless and not connected. That talk of rotten wounds made his flesh crawl and his stomach tighten into a stony ball. Oh, what a terrible thing it was!

He had been very young when it happened, having seen maybe thirteen or fourteen summers back then. But he had never forgotten, never. That nasty fall, and the pain, the piercing, inhuman pain. He had tried to be brave, to choke the screams back, but then he saw it, that ragged edge of the whitish thing sticking out of his torn arm, and then there was no meaning to anything anymore, and he screamed in terror and fainted, to come back to the world of the living when all was relatively well because Mother had been there by that time, warm and brisk and matter-of-fact, the only person besides Father who knew how to make everything right. She had stopped the bleeding, if not the pain, and she had sent out everyone in sight to bring the first healer they spotted, no matter from what clan. No, she was not about to panic or do silly wailing like some women would. She was one of the leading women of their clan for a reason, elected to become their longhouse's Clan Mother later on.

And yet, she did grow frightened, did lose her composure and brisk efficiency when, a day or two later, the wound refused to dry, beginning to smell bad. Oh, did she panic back then! She had packed their longhouse with more healers and the False Face Society members, and she even sent a messenger to Father, who had been busy at the lands of the Mountain People, so far away from home, on an important mission by the request of the Great Council. Still, she had sent for him. Although, of course, by the time the message had found him, it was all over, with him, Ganayeda, still alive, surviving the operation when one of the False Face Society medicine men had enough courage and skill to cut the rotting flesh away, morsel by morsel, damaging his arm, but not badly. It was only beginning to rot, the man had explained. It might have been too late if they waited for one or two more days. Oh, Mighty Spirits!

With an effort, he brought himself back from the brink, the memories tucked away deeply, too terrible to be faced.

"I don't know," Okwaho was saying. "But he should have stitched your wound if he was any good." His snort was loud enough to attract the attention of passing men. "A lack of light, what a stupid excuse!" Where were they going? wondered

Ganayeda. To join the search party? But it would be too late by now, with the dawn almost upon them.

"How many men are out there?" he asked tiredly.

"What?"

"The villagers, how many did you bring?"

"Oh." Okwaho nodded lightly. "About twenty or more. They organized very quickly, with admirable readiness. I barely finished my tale and here they were, running around, collecting their weapons." A shrug. "They are good people."

"We should have stayed." He knew he wasn't being reasonable, of course he wasn't. And yet, the bad feeling was prevailing now that he had time to think about it. He had failed, failed miserably, failed her and himself. He had promised to bring her back to her village safely, but now she was in the hands of the enemy, and had been for quite a long time, the entire evening and night, and who knew what these people had done to her after he had managed to snatch the other girl. What if they sailed, not waiting for the first light? Gayeri would have no chance of coming back home then, no chance whatsoever.

He clenched his fists tight, welcoming the pain the effort brought to his battered body. He had failed!

"What?" Okwaho was asking, peering at him closely. "Your wounds, they hurt?"

"They won't bring the girl back."

His brother's face closed, and he hated the silence that prevailed.

"You think they will sail." It came out as a statement, an open challenge. He moderated his tone. "You don't believe they will find the Crooked Tongues, do you?"

A light motion of Okwaho's head stirred the darkness.

"We should have gone on with them!" He hit the wall he was leaning against with his fist and didn't care what pang of pain it sent through his battered torso. "We shouldn't have left."

"The way you stumbled all over the place, bleeding on me, we would have been nothing but a hindrance. They would have even less chances of stopping the enemy." Okwaho's voice rang quietly, with no passion in it. "You did all you could. You did more than many would have done. One can't make a miracle, unless you are the Great Peacemaker, which you are not."

"We still should have stayed. At least you. You are a good warrior. Why did you leave?"

"Oh, please!" The young man's snort tore the darkness. "Don't start that one again, Brother. I have no special feelings for that pretty fox. You may run all over and get wounded and nearly killed, but no lust dictates my deeds. Poor girl in need, huh! My brother was wounded, and he needed my help. It was no contest. No contest at all."

"You understand nothing." But for his wounds, he would have liked to catch the young man by his shoulders and shake him hard. "It has nothing to do with personal feelings, even if I had any for her. Which I didn't! I'm no young buck of your age; I'm not after young girls." Out of breath, he paused, so enraged he felt his hands shaking. "But what you should learn is responsibility, and it is more than just to help your family or friends. When someone, even a person you don't know, is entrusted into your care, a group of people or just a few, with or without planning beforehand, you take these people's safety as closely to your heart as that of your kin. If you want to lead, you must learn this."

For a brief while, they fell silent, listening to the voices of the stirring village, men and women, going about, speaking in hushed tones. The night was about to end.

"You talk well, Brother." Okwaho's voice held not a hint of recognition or deference. "But under all those pretty words about proper leadership and appropriate behavior lies the fact that you did fancy that girl, you did give her special treatment, you did try to save her, at almost the cost of your life even. The other one was your charge as well, and I don't say you neglected her, but you wouldn't be so upset if it had been the other way, if you had managed to snatch your pretty Gayeri, or whatever her name is, and the other one would have stayed in their captors' hands. You can deny it all you like, but I do have eyes, and my other senses. And we *are* brothers. I have known you for too long to be deceived by fine words."

The softness of his sibling's chuckle made Ganayeda's fury

soar. Had he any strength left, he would have flared at the insolent brat, squashing him with an appropriately sharp reprimand, if not something more violent. As it was, he just closed his eyes and cursed quietly. But for a chance to escape this bottomless exhaustion, and the pain. His head was throbbing more and more venomously, and every breath made his bruised ribs protest.

"You think you know it all, but you have much to learn yet."

He could imagine his brother's smile spreading, wide, unbearably cheeky, as always. In another spell of silence, they watched the darkness thinning, turning gray.

"What happened to your friend with the rotting wound? Why didn't he die?"

He could feel Okwaho's shrug, knowing that the young man's smile was turning genuine, losing its baiting quality.

"Her brother, he cut the wound, all the rotting parts. He is a great healer."

Ganayeda swallowed the knot tightening in his throat. "He must be very good. Most people don't live after this. Surely not with the rotting in places like upper leg." And how could they? Even when everything went well, the terror and pain alone... He clenched his teeth tight.

"It was his first time. He wasn't allowed to learn, or practice before." Okwaho's sigh was heavy, caressing the darkness. "He did it all alone, in the darkness, with only a small fire to light his way. We were useless, Kentika and I, good only for fetching things. But he did it all the same. And he was successful. Akweks didn't die. When I saw him last, he was in Cohoes Falls, hobbling already, not very well yet, but moving around." The young man shook his head, his sincerity filling the darkness. "He did the impossible. Like the old Thayuhini of the False Face Society, who was the only one with the courage to try to save your life back then, remember? But you see, he was helped and assisted, encouraged, believed in. He had so many summers of healing behind him. While her brother," this time the pause lasted for only a heartbeat, "her brother was alone and afraid, in the enemy's hands, with not a hope of help or recognition. Still, he did better than many medicine men would. He was a great man."

Again, his stomach tightened painfully. "Was he captured by our people?" The attempt to divert his thoughts from the path those were taking nibbled on his precious strength.

"Oh no, our people were dead by then. And the main forces, well, they hadn't arrived as yet. They were on their way, very near, but I didn't know it back then." Once again, the calmness of Okwaho's words helped. He clung to its warmth, the strange tranquility his brother's voice radiated. "I captured him when he tried to shoot me. And she, she made him help." With the young man's voice growing lower, the warmth in it intensifying, vibrating in a light, reassuring manner, Ganayeda opened his eyes, trying not to miss a word. "She was a gift, a personal gift from my guiding spirit. The Silvery Wolf, he sent her to me. I know one is not supposed to ask for something like that of one's guiding spirit, no direct help and no gifts, just guidance and advice. And yet..." He could hear the young man drawing a deep breath. "I did that. I asked when I was desperate, and the Silvery Wolf, he listened. He gave her to me, and I will always be grateful for his kindness."

The silence prevailed again, this time a comfortable, soft tranquility. So his brother did love his savage girl, did think her to be more than just a passing fancy. A gift of the spirits? A talisman? It was hard to imagine the strange, outlandish thing serving in this capacity. And yet, who was he to question someone else's interpretations and needs?

"She must be an outstanding woman," he said politely, not believing his own words.

"She is. Oh, yes, she is." An amused chuckle was back, warming the graying air. "She doesn't look or behave this way, but she is all of it and more, Brother. Believe me on that."

The raising noise from the direction of the palisade made them both look up. People were pouring in through the narrow opening, many people, their faces grim, tired, caked with mud.

Sweat-covered and stained, neither their skins nor their clothes displayed blood, old or fresh, not even a sprinkle of it. None. They had caught up with no enemy. Now he knew it for certain.

CHAPTER 12

"Today, we have gathered to thank our creators for the cycles of life and their continuation, for the wonderful gifts they bestow upon us. We have been given the duty to live in balance and harmony with each other and all living beings, the dwellers of our Turtle Island, those who surround us and give us their support. Today, we bring our minds together as one, and we give our greetings and thanks to our creators, those who sustain us and keep us safe. Our mind is one now."

Listening to the magic of these words, Seketa held her breath, watching him, her husband of so many summers, the powerful War Chief of Onondaga Nation, one of the most prominent men in the Great League, standing before the simmering fire, surrounded by clouds of fragrant tobacco smoke, spreading his arms upward, channeling his words, helping them reach the Sky World and its divine dwellers, letting them know how grateful their people were, how thankful and beholden.

"We are thankful to our Mother, the Earth, for she gives us all we need. She supports our feet as we walk upon her, and she sustains us and takes care of us, as she did since the times of our Grandmother, the Sky Woman. For the joy of life, we are grateful and thankful. To our Mother we now send our greetings and thanks. Our minds are one now!"

He paused, this time looking down, encircling his audience with his hands still spread and his eyes alight with a wonderful glow. He meant what he said, she knew, her chest tightening with pride. His words of thanks would reach the Sky World, would let the benevolent deities know.

Hundreds upon hundreds of people crowded the small valley between two hills, spread as evenly as they could around the elevated ground with the glimmering fire and the dancers in their colorful attire, ready to start, to reinforce the great leader's words. Oh, how avidly they listened, how earnestly, not about to miss one single word, even though the thanksgiving address rarely varied, repeating itself through every ceremony around the cycles of moons. Still, when the War Chief spoke, they all listened.

Oh, but he knew how to talk, this husband of hers, she reflected, blinking away tears of excitement. No matter what speech he gave, it was never dull or rehearsed. He knew how to make everything meaningful and alive, weaving his words like an elegant *wampum*, pitching his voice in the way that was reaching far and wide, heard even at the edge of the crowd.

"We give our thanks to the water for quenching our thirst, providing us with strength. Water of life. We know its power, and we are grateful, grateful to the waterfalls and rains, to the mists and streams, to great and small lakes, mighty rivers and creeks. Our minds are one now."

The lightest of breezes answered those words, and people murmured, enchanted. The spirits were listening, and they were of a good mind. They appreciated its people's gratitude.

The fish, the plants, edible and medicine herbs, were addressed next, thanked separately, profusely at that; animals and birds, Father Sun and Grandmother Moon and their fellow stars; Thunderers and Four Winds—they all received the Longhouse People's thanks and acknowledgment; they all heard the Turtle Island's dwellers and their gratitude.

"We gather our minds to greet and thank our creators, the Right-Handed Twin and his aides, the Sky Spirits, who have come to our help throughout endless summers. When we forget how to live in harmony, they remind us of the way we were instructed to live as people. We, of one mind, we send our greetings and thanks to our creators and guides."

The thanksgiving address was coming toward its natural end, and she listened to the drums and the rattles of the dancers, who were moving around the fire more vigorously now, surrounding it in a colorful wall, helping the sacred smoke reach higher, bringing the words of the people to the Sky World. The sacred smoke was the one to carry it up, but it could use the dancers' help.

Making her way toward the outskirts of the valley and the Clans Mothers gathering next to the fires that would be used for warming and serving food when the sun would leave its zenith and begin its journey toward the western hill, Seketa suppressed her smile, listening to the music, longing to join the dance. She had been a renowned dancer, allowed to participate in the most solemn of ceremonies for many, many summers, since before she came to live in these lands. She could have danced for an entire afternoon, not growing tired or thirsty, wearing as many as five and more rattles tied to her legs, a considerable weight but for someone with great endurance and experience. Oh, but how wonderful it had been, to flow with the magical rhythm, to let one's spirits soar, to connect with the other worlds.

She shrugged, shaking the longing off. She could have participated even now; she was not that old. For the duration of the opening Feather Dance, wearing only a few rattles or no rattles at all, she might have managed but for her duties as the Clan Mother. Those were what kept her from dancing.

"The food would be served after the second Thanksgiving Address and the Women Song," one of her fellow Wolf Clan Mothers was saying. "I suggest we start organizing it once they finish the Feather Dance." She was a stocky woman, good-natured and prone to laughter, unless pressed with work. Too anxious to get everything done, when too many matters attacked at once, this peer of hers was losing much of her good humor.

"It might be too early for that, sister," said another woman, the head of the third and the smaller Wolf longhouse of the town.

"It won't. We need time to make fires and spread the ware. Also to send for the missing items and foodstuff when we spot their lack. The girls would be useless, busy dancing or staring, so it'll leave us with less women to work and still hordes of hungry people to face. So many visitors this time. And the Long Tails foreigners!" The round face turned to Seketa, glaring with unhealthy red. "Tell her!"

"Calm down, sister." The arm she placed on her companion's shoulder was supposed to soften the amused quality of her smile. She was such a worrier, that peer of hers. "It is going to be well. I checked and rechecked all our supplies that were brought here, and they are enough. Didn't you see me counting all those people, then spending half the morning around our piles? There would be no missing items, no need to send reluctant girls in their festive attire. We have all we need here." The wink of the third woman made her smile widen. "We received the honor of hosting the first day of the ceremony, and we will not make the Wolf Clan look bad. Trust us on that."

A dubious head shake was her answer. "If you say so. But let us hope you are not mistaken. It would be embarrassing to run out of food or utensils. Our clan will be a laughingstock for many moons to come."

"It won't be."

Turning around, she watched the dancers and the fire, this vantage point even better than her previous one. The girls of the Wolf Clan were easy to pick out, the decorations of their festive attire different than those of the Turtle, Heron, or Bear Clans, or any of the others. Without noticing, her eyes checked their motions and regalia again, making sure all was done as it should be.

The people were crowding both slopes of the light incline, still fascinated, their attention not wandering. Another thanksgiving address by the Head of the Town Council this time, then the rituals of the faith-keepers, then Women Song—her mind was checking, point by point. Enough time to prepare everything, but they would have to start the preparations soon.

"In need of some help, girls?" The Turtle Clan's head woman neared with some of her fellow elderly friends in tow, all smiles. "Think we will be eating well this first day of the ceremony? Must impress the foreigners, mustn't we?"

"I think our guests are suitably impressed as it is," said Seketa, seeking her husband with her gaze, his tall, broad-shouldered figure easy to pick out and not because of the magnificent headdress he wore for the occasion.

Such an imposing man, even when surrounded by his fellow dignitaries and other prominent people of the town, faith-keepers and members of the council—a very colorful group, their headdresses and regalia shining brilliantly in the early afternoon light. Some of the foreigners were near him too, as expected, decidedly different and strange in their long-sleeved shirts, the fashion her former people followed these days, she had heard. Her former people!

She suppressed a grunt. He was heard speaking about the possibility of opening the negotiations again, claiming that it must be the time to do it now, when the Crooked Tongues were united and easier to communicate with. There had been a heated argument, she had been told, on the evening before. Not many people were prepared to go against him. Even if not all of them agreed with his summers-long obsession concerning the other side of the Great Sparkling Water, too many admired and respected him and his opinions. And yet, those who were not about to trust him as readily—maybe a few influential and less among the regular people, but there were such in High Springs and elsewhere—those were growing more vocal, gathering courage now that the foreign delegation brought unsettling news of the enemy's unification.

Her heart squeezing with worry, she didn't dare to ask him about it when they had retired to sleep on the night before, not wishing to bring up the subject she knew they would not agree upon. He had had enough as it was, without her turning against him as well.

So she had just hugged him and snuggled against him, instead, and when he enveloped her in his arms and whispered that he missed her and that if the accursed politics came between them once again, he would be terribly put out, she listened to the silence and the even breathing of their numerous guests, then let her hands wander, reassured. Lovemaking inside a longhouse was usually a quiet, careful affair, strangled under the furs and the blankets, unlike the beautiful playing around the couples engaged in out there in the woods. Even respectable Clan

Mothers. Or maybe not. Maybe it was only her. Living with such a man, how could she not?

"What is the meaning of that smile, sister?" The Turtle woman's voice brought her from her pleasant memories, made her aware of her twisting lips.

"I'm just enjoying the view. Such a large gathering. It's been a while since we had so many visitors for our festivities. I hope the Great Spirits will be pleased with the ceremony."

"Your husband opened the day with a remarkable speech," said the Heron Clan's leading woman. "He doesn't stick to the acceptable form of address, but his improvisations are always the most pleasant to listen to. I'm sure our creators enjoy them as much."

Seketa felt her smile spreading anew. "He speaks well, yes."

"Until it comes to certain topics no one wishes to listen to." The Heron woman's face was sealed, her gaze on the crowding people, wandering, assessing, as did the eyes of all of them, even though their mouths engaged in an idle talk. This event was their responsibility, the last festivity of the year. The next one, the Midwinter Ceremony, was scheduled for four full moons from now and was expected to be prepared and conducted by the leading men of the town, but the Harvest Ceremony was orchestrated by women alone.

"They should listen to his words, even if he says something they don't have the courage to face."

Those were harsh words, but they helped to banish the chill from her stomach, all this ice that seemed to be piling up. That last evening argument, it shouldn't have happened, not with the foreigners still in the town, surely. People were losing their patience, their subtlety; he more than anyone, as it seemed.

"He knows what he is talking about," she added, unable not to say it, their raised eyebrows making her angry. "Our people have followed his leadership for many summers, enjoying the Great Peace that might not have survived but for his efforts."

"We know all that, sister. And believe me, our community is appreciative, very much so. Your husband is highly admired and readily followed, as you know. And yet, you can't ask people to follow him blindly, can you? He may be mistaken from time to time, even such a greatly admired leader."

She tried to moderate the fury of her gaze. It was not the time, nor the place to start heated arguments, and yet this woman had crossed the line, or was dangerously close to crossing it. How dared she?

"I think we better leave politics for after-ceremony times, don't you think, girls?" said the Turtle Clan woman, her smile a little forced. "Why would we spend our efforts on the matters our Great Council should be dealing with? We have more important things to address as of now."

"Yes, we do." The other Wolf Clan women seemed to be breathing with relief. "I'll summon the boys to start making fires."

"And the girls who are not dancing. Let us round up all the loiterers." She was pleased to hear her voice cool and steady, despite the fact that her insides were still trembling with tension. "I'll supervise the food distribution. You two take care of the pots. Make sure the stew is warmed but not boiled. And the cornballs… Oh well, why am I distributing orders?" This time the smile came easier, her taut nerves relaxing. It was so much more pleasant to deal with matters as uncomplicated as the organization of an event, even if a large and important like this one. "You all know what to do."

Her smile made them feel appreciated, she knew, counting on exactly that effect. It made them feel that they were as important as she was. Even though that was not the case. She was the leading women of their entire clan, by virtue and by right. Her longhouse was the largest of the three, the longest and the most populated in the entire town, and her organization skills knew no peers. Yet, there was no need to rub their faces into any of it. It was easy to make them feel good, then do what she felt needed to be done. If only her husband had that female subtlety!

Their chuckles filled the air, and soon their corner of the valley was bubbling with life, full of comments and directions and helping hands; as busy as the center of the valley with all the prominent people of the settlement, and as important, maybe more so. An empty stomach was a sure way to ruin it all, prominent people and their speeches and politics or not.

Spotting Okwaho's girl, Seketa beckoned her briskly.

"Run back to the town and bring the largest pot, the one with painted patterns that is stored in the first storage room. Do you understand what I'm talking about? The painted pottery, the largest one."

The girl nodded eagerly, even though her face crinkled in a painful frown. "I find. Pottery? Storage room?"

"Yes. The large pot. The largest." The attempt to explain with her hands helped. "Tuck wooden plates and spoons in there, as much as you can find. Just pile them inside the pottery." She didn't hide her smile. "You are strong, strong enough to bring all of it at once. Just look at your exploits with yesterday's baskets of nuts and berries."

The troubled frown gave way to the brightest of smiles. "I can, yes. Very fast too. I bring right away."

"Good."

Watching the excited swirls of the undecorated skirt as the girl burst into the fastest of runs, disappearing quickly down the hill, Seketa shook her head, then made a mental note to take care of the wild thing's clothing. She would have expected the young woman to attend such a matter herself, either by making or at least by asking for a better dress this morning. But obviously her son's chosen mate was not about to spend her thoughts on such feminine concerns. This one should be wearing a loincloth and leggings, the way she was running or walking. Chuckling at the thought, Seketa headed back toward the commotion.

"We need more firewood, and more plates and spoons." Her fellow Wolf Clan leading woman was about to start crying as it seemed. "There is not enough, simply not enough. I counted and counted and—"

"Calm down, sister." Assessing the glimmering fires and the activity around them, she put a reassuring arm on her worried peer's shoulder. "It's all going to work out perfectly. We have enough fires for now, enough food already prepared, waiting to be distributed. When they finish with the last ritual, and come here, storming our side of the valley, we will be ready."

"But what if we run out of food, what if there will be not enough cornballs. The amount that we prepared was based on the count of less people, it was before—"

"If we run out of cornballs, they'll eat our delicious stew, instead. There won't be anyone complaining, sister. I sent one of the girls to fetch another pot and more plates from the town, so if need be, we'll put on more fires." Another reassuring pat and she headed off, toward the rest of the activity. "It will be all good."

Assigning tasks and duties, making sure everything was taken into account and prepared for, helped to calm her spirit, instead of upsetting it the way it did to some of her peers. Assuring that everyone knew of his or her role, she rushed between the centers of activities, directing, advising, encouraging. Many people were already drifting in their direction now that the drums grew fainter and the trill of the flutes stopped piercing the air in the most pleasant of manners.

"Put your pile of plates here and just hand them over," she told the women who seemed to be mulling around with no purpose, too close to the boiling pot, threatening to push someone into the fire. "You give her bowls, you pour the meal, you offer full plates to people."

Pausing briefly to demonstrate what she meant, she went on, satisfied. They were as ready as they could be for the colorful wave to descend on them, to reach their quiet corner of the valley and turn it into the hubbub of vibrancy and happy agitation. Many were ascending the hill by now, trickling in, in small groups, talking excitedly.

With a mixed curiosity, her eyes spotted the foreigners, walking up briskly, decidedly different, their regalia strange, sporting too many decorations, too many feathers and beads for her taste. Guests of honor, naturally they walked beside local dignitaries, her husband in their lead, but some of the outlandish clothing could be spotted elsewhere.

Puzzled, her eyes lingered on another group, a smaller gathering that was already approaching one of the fires, talking slowly, with no vividness that marked the conversations all around. Rather, their faces were too calm, too indifferent, with their eyes blank and wary, somehow. Hegweh, one of her husband's more vocal opponents of late, surrounded by some of his intimates and, surprisingly, two foreigners. But wasn't this man opposed to everything foreign? Wasn't this his main complaint about the War Chief's attitude? Why would he stroll in the company of the despised outlanders now?

Eyes on the stalls of food and the now-hectic activity they emanated, busy assessing, seeking where her help and advice might be needed, she drifted closer to that group nevertheless, hoping against hope to hear the general gist of their conversation. Why would they stroll about looking evasive, as though not aware of the celebrative mood all around?

To her astonishment, her ears picked up the sound of the long-forgotten words, the one she hadn't heard for tens of summers and more—her former people's tongue! Or something that sounded close to it. The two foreigners were conversing quietly, momentarily alone, pointing at the flat side of the valley, the wind bringing their words to her, but not all of them. She tried to shut the loudness of the surrounding clamor out.

"They would be playing there," one seemed to be saying, nodding once again toward the incline.

"It's too far away. Out of range." His companion was nearly mumbling, making the understanding truly difficult. She held her breath. "Too far."

"Here yes, but I'll send Aingahon to wander about again. This one is doing a lot of it, eh? Wandering all over, with no one asking him questions, challenging or otherwise." The other man talked most clearly, as though not afraid to be overheard. Did he think no one understood their tongue? Well, maybe. Not many could talk the way Crooked Tongues did, but enough people could, her and her boys for one, the War Chief for another. He had made sure to teach their children the possible enemies' or the prospected allies' way of speaking.

"Yesterday he was all around the town and even out there in the woods, would you believe it? He had an interesting adventure out there."

The nearing people made the foreigners fall silent, nodding

their greetings, their smiles polite and a little too forced. She ground her teeth at the interruption.

Oh, but they talked of something important, something she surely needed to know, along with her husband and the other influential people of the town. They weren't talking about ordinary things, and why was this person called Aingahon wandering all around? It's not that the foreigners could not go where they were pleased, being High Springs visitors and invited guests. But why did they put such importance on the wandering of one of their peers?

Smiling at feasting people, answering their greetings, receiving, of course, no invitations to join in—men and women did not sit together on an event such as this—she lingered, trying to hear more, but the foreigners fell silent, looking around, as though searching for their own peers. Which they probably were. Silly to hold clandestine conversations on such a crowded occasion, and yet...

"Why won't you just do as you are told?" The loudness of the outcry drew her attention to the nearest stall, where Hageha, one of the women from the neighboring Wolf Clan longhouse caught a plate a moment before it toppled over, balancing it in her large, weathered hand, saving it from spilling by a miracle as it seemed. "I told you to mind the empty plates. Not the full ones!"

Deftly, the woman brought the overflowing bowl forward, handing it over to a group of young men, not bothering to moderate her frown. The men snickered, exchanging knowing glances before heading off, to enjoy their meal in the shadows, among more of their companions upon the spread mats. By now many were seated, eating heartily, their chatter loud and happy, filling the afternoon air in the most pleasant of manners.

"I no trouble. I help."

She didn't need to turn back to verify that the trouble again involved her charge, the challenge Okwaho had bothered to present her with. That thought brought another. Where were both her sons? Why didn't they return in time for the opening of the ceremony? Did they stay in Lone Hill to enjoy this village's celebrations, their reported destination, according to their fellow hunters, those who did bother to return? No, of course not. Why would they?

"I take plates. You say I take," insisted the foreign girl, not about to be reprimanded with not a word of defense.

Oh, but what was one to do with such a high-spirited, independent thing? thought Seketa, turning to head in their direction. Tie her to one's skirt and make her follow around and away from trouble?

"She told you to take the empty plates!" cried out one of the younger girls, those who were helping with serving. "To think someone in her right mind would trust a clumsy bear like you to handle a full plate. Look what happened when you snatched one."

A healthy outburst of laughter followed that remark.

Hastening her step to get to the girl before it turned ugly—she did not expect the busy women responsible for the food to pay attention to the squabbles of the young girls; but for the involvement of the foreign thing, she would have paid it no attention herself—Seketa eyed the Long Tails she had been watching drifting aside, their hands loaded with edible goods, their gazes still wandering, still sliding over the abandoned valley and the opposite hill, all reddish golden with autumn foliage, a pretty view. Were they admiring it? She doubted that.

"I no fall, she take…" If not about to take founded or unfounded accusations from an elderly women, Okwaho's girl was evidently not prepared to go silent over the insults of her peers. "You bear, stupid and clumsy. No me."

"Girls, stop it, and make yourselves useful!" Hageha's voice rang out with an open displeasure, signaling the young ones to get back to work.

"You bear, stupid and clumsy." To the snickering merriment of the others, someone was mimicking the foreign girl's heavily accented speech quite well.

Seketa hesitated no longer. With the foreigners' backs drawing away, she turned around, regretting her inability to hear more. Even the decorations adorning their long-sleeved shirts related their tension. Those two were not discussing the beauty of the Harvest Ceremony. And yet, Okwaho's girl could use some help and encouragement, she knew. Before she did something silly, or maybe embarrassing.

"You not talk to me, you ugly piece—" The wild fox did not make Seketa wait to justify her misgivings. "I hit, hit hard—"

"I told you to keep your mouths closed and to be useful!" This time the woman in charge of the stall sounded truly enraged. "You! You bring nothing but trouble. Go away. Now!"

"Why do you yell at the girl, sister?" Still not near enough to stop the quarrel, Seketa saw the plump figure of Jideah, her elder son's wife, glimmering on the other side of the fire, difficult to see against the glow of the afternoon sun. "Why are you so impatient? Can't you handle a few plates and a few young girls for one small afternoon?"

Oh, that one was known for her sharp tongue and her readiness to pick quarrels. Seketa hastened her step.

"What?" The woman beside the bubbling pot seemed as though about to topple into it. "How dare you?"

"You know, you take your frustrations out on a young girl who did nothing wrong. Doesn't it mean you can't handle your responsibility and are in need of replacement? I'm only trying to help here. All those people, they are waiting for their meals while you are busy yelling." With a wide gesture of her pudgy arm, the small woman pointed at the smirking audience, all those waiting men, torn between impatience to get their food and amusement in watching the quarreling women, such an entertainment. "Do you want me to replace you while you take your well-deserved rest?" The sweetness of the last phrase was laden with derision, dripping poison.

The woman of the neighboring Wolf Clan longhouse was drawing such a long breath, Seketa feared she would faint.

"How dare you? Your clan is too small to handle anything for any amount of time, and here you come and tell me how to conduct a stall of food on the most important day of the most important ceremony? You are—"

"Stop it, girls. Both of you." As always, her voice was enough to make them all turn around. Seketa eyed them one after another, nodding politely toward the waiting crowd. "Let us get back to distributing food in an orderly manner. Hageha," she gazed at the woman at the stall sternly, but not unkindly, relaying the message. It was her fault the quarrel was threatening, no matter who started it. "Please, go on with your duties. You," a quick glance at one of the girls, the one she suspected of calling the foreigner a 'clumsy bear,' made the recipient of it wince, "run to the leading women of your longhouse and ask them to send someone to help. Someone mature, responsible, no quarrelsome young girls." That made the rest of them drop their gazes. All but Okwaho's treasure, who stared at her, wide-eyed. She let her eyes show a hint of a smile. "You, girl. Well, I suppose you better go back to your duties of running to town and bringing more missing items. It seems no one can do it as well or as fast as you do." That should show them! There were duties the foreign girl did better than many. She felt their astounded silence, even that of the listening men. "Go to the women of our longhouse and ask if they are missing any ware or items of food. And now, please, let us all go back to our duties. The Great Spirits deserve to enjoy our thanksgiving celebration without anger marring any of it. As do our people." A light notion at the surrounding men took the smirking off their faces, made them nod solemnly in return.

"That was a worthwhile speech," said Jideah, catching up with her as she turned away, to watch the once-again energetically swirling skirts of Okwaho's girl, disappearing in the direction of the fires and the commotion around them. "You made it all calm down in the way only you can."

"Why did you goad Hagaha?" Liking and disliking her elder son's woman at the same time, Seketa glanced at her company, taking in the flush of the round cheeks, gained probably as a result of the quarreling, as it began fading, making her companion look unhealthily pale.

"She was being nasty to the savage girl. It was annoying. I couldn't stand it." Jideah shrugged tiredly, slowing her pace, in order to lean against something supportive, suspected Seketa.

"Are you well?" Absently, she sought the Long Tails with her eyes again, but they were gone, wandering off or joining the rest of their people, maybe.

Another shrug was her answer. "The new baby makes me vomit too much. He makes me tired all the time. I can't tell you how irritating it is. I had no such troubles with my girls." The chuckle that wafted in the air was surprisingly light, full of warmth. "That's how I know it's going to be a son."

"I did not carry either of my boys differently." She eyed the haunted face with unusual sympathy. "Let us place you somewhere in the shade. Get you good food, and maybe a corn drink, eh? I'll make our girls boil it on the side, in a small pot." Listening to the voices all around, detecting no troublesome tones for now, she beckoned her companion to follow. "You are not a young girl anymore. That is why it's more difficult now to carry this child. But it will be over soon enough. By the time these trees will blossom again, you will be all energy, cradling your new baby, getting bossy around your clan's fields, complaining of my son's uselessness when it comes to family matters." She let the teasing quality of her smile show, noticing her companion's sudden flush of embarrassment. "I know what you've been saying around the town about his lack of devotion to family. And you may be right about that, too. Still, sometimes it's wiser to keep one's thoughts for oneself."

"Whoever said such nasty things about me—" Jideah began hotly, but Seketa halted the protests with a light wave of her hand.

"Don't take it hard. I said it mostly to tease. Just take care of yourself for now. Don't work too hard. The women of your longhouse will manage to prepare the harvested goods for the winter this span of seasons without you working yourself to exhaustion, directing them." She knew of this woman's ambition, no one better. A Clan Mother this one would be one day, no matter what. But how well would she turn out in such a capacity? Seketa had her misgivings. "Here is our high-spirited foreigner." Not fighting her smile, she watched Okwaho's girl coming back at a run, which seemed to be her usual way of moving, unless burdened with heavy cargo, or maybe even then. "What you did for that girl back there was actually kind. Why did you?"

Her companion's lips twisted into a one-sided grin.

"I don't know. I think I like her. She is something else, this one, so wild, so outlandish. And yet," a light chuckle related the woman's wonder, "I think I like her, as impossible as it may sound. I may wish to help her sometimes. The way you do, Seketa." The gaze that was shot at her had a piercing quality, searching, inquiring. "You took this one under your wing. You made it your business to help and encourage that girl. You go to certain lengths to assign special tasks to her, to try to keep her out of trouble, singling one out of many, and in a fashion that is not very typical to the type of the Clan Mother you are; you, the busiest, not to say the most influential, leading woman of our town. Why, oh Honorable Mother, why do you do that?"

Amused with the question, instead of turning uncomfortable, Seketa let the superiority of her smile show. This fox was smart and as sharp as a wasp, busy burrowing her way into their town's politics now that she was of the right age—a respectable woman in her late twenties, so very determined and fitting, married to the right man with a great future, her only lack being her membership in the wrong clan, too small of an extended family for the dominant fox's ambition. Well, this one may be used to having the upper hand with many men and women, but she was no match for Seketa. She was beyond being blackmailed or pressed into admitting secret agendas.

"I'm an old woman, girl. When you have seen as many summers as I have, you will understand better."

A polite nod accompanied with the sweetest of smiles and she was gone, beckoning the nearing foreign girl, ready to face the other challenge her sons bothered to present her with. Why couldn't one of them take a nice, ordinary woman?

CHAPTER 13

Even though expected to be back, Kentika didn't find it necessary to hurry. The temptation of the abandoned town, with its empty alleys and deserted longhouses, was too great to resist. Everyone who could walk was out there in the valley, enjoying the second, less formal part of the ceremony. Or so she had gathered, watching the people while trailing after Okwaho's mother, doing odd jobs of bringing missing items or delivering messages.

The frenzy around food stalls was frightening, but, of course, their Clan Mother made it all work, with minimum anger and yelling around. She was everywhere, this woman, as though sensing the spot where the trouble was likely to erupt, being there just as some turmoil was beginning to take place, just as a voice would start rising, solving everything with a few sensible comments and directions given in a pleasant way no one dared to argue with.

What a woman!

So nice and well meaning, and yet so stern, not a person to pick an argument with unless you have a good case; brilliantly organized, brisk and good looking, with her dress swaying softly, shading from the light beige of the perfectly tanned material to the deepest purple of rustling shells, spread all over it in intricate patterns, her girdle of the same hue, enhancing the curve of her waist, her hair graying but full, flowing freely, her figure too well shaped for a woman of so many summers, her walk like that of a dancer, a professional one. A vision of accomplishment that even men followed with their gazes and listened to, seeking her company, talking to her in the most respectful manner, listening to her words, nodding thoughtfully. Impossible but true.

"She is a tough old fox, that one," was Jideah's verdict. "Don't be fooled by her smiles and the friendliness, wild girl. She may like you, and may be willing to help. Whatever her reasons, she seems to be taking a fancy to you. But don't be tempted to take her goodwill for granted. There will be a price to pay. Never doubt that."

"Why price? What pay?" asked Kentika, unsettled, even though pleased with the unexpected friendliness and attention, welcoming it most eagerly. After the frenzy of the food distribution was over and some quick cleaning of the place where everyone ate done, with most of the celebrative crowds spilling back toward the circle of fires, she was again left to her own devices, welcoming the respite in work but not the lack of friendly company. It was tiring to always be on guard, to watch one's every step, to be ready to fend off yet another outburst of reprimanding or sneering.

Back home, it had not been much different. She never succumbed to the temptation of lying to herself. Still, her fellow villagers, while frowning at her inappropriate behavior and unfeminine ways, did not hate her or look at her as though she were a strange creature out of the woods. While these people, those enemies of not long ago, eyed her with such open doubt, their gazes aloof and questioning; when not outright hateful.

This was the thing that puzzled her most, a truly new experience, the acute hatred of some younger girls of their longhouse. Why did they hate her so? She wasn't even an enemy. Her people lived too far away from these lands to have a relative or a family member killed by them. Okwaho had reassured her on that matter. He promised there would be some suspicion to be overcome, yes, with her being a foreigner, but not something truly difficult. He claimed that his mother might have had a harder time when coming to live in Onondaga lands, following his father, because she had come from where the true enemies lived, a true foe with a considerable amount of local people's blood on their hands. However, it was not the case with Kentika's countryfolk, he had assured her. No one hated them in particular, because no one had ever heard of them, not in these lands.

But they will? she had asked him. They would hear of her people, and they would make peace with them, wouldn't they? And he laughed and said, yes, of course. They both would make it happen, somehow.

The longing was back, the intense yearning to see him, to run into his arms and hold him tight, to hide in his embrace from all the smirks and the raised eyebrows, to drag him into her favorite clearing with berries and the brook, or maybe even farther out, and stay there for days, playing around and making love, plenty of love. Oh, but she never thought she would miss him in that way too, physically, craving his touch and his kisses. It made the longing so much worse.

"What price?" Her companion's laughter helped. It pulled her back from the brink yet again. Blinking to clear her vision, Kentika concentrated on following the foreign words. "You know, the regular things. To be of use and obedient, to do your work, to make no trouble. An easy achievement for some girls, impossible for others." The amused side glance slid over her, challenging, teasing yet not offending, not like those of some others. "Not your strongest quality, I suspect. But Seketa is very strict. She won't be forgiving if you keep failing."

"I no fail," protested Kentika. "I do work. She like. I bring forest fruit yesterday, so many, more than others all together." She couldn't help but glow with pride. "She impressed. She say so, and I see."

"Good for you." Her companion's shrug held a measure of unexpected resentment. "If you make her happy, you are well set."

Slowing her step, Kentika peered at the closed-up face. "You no like? You not get along with Okwaho's mother?"

Her companion's chuckle shook the dusk, still lacking in mirth. "Yes, I do like, I do get along. She is no superior of mine. My clan has nothing to do with hers." In her turn, the woman slowed her step, her tired features darkening even more. "My clan may be small and not as important as hers, but we have our say in this town's affairs. We can't be brushed aside or bossed around, even though those Wolf and Turtle and Bear Clans' women would love to try and do that."

"Oh." She searched for something to say, understanding, if only partly. This woman's clan must be as small as her longhouse was, and probably as unimportant.

"Yes, oh." Her companion's face cleared of shadows. "Maybe you will be accepted into my clan when your time to find an appropriate family comes, eh? This way those spectacular Wolf Clan brothers would live together." Shaking her head, the woman resumed her walk toward the renewed dancing and clouds of fragrant tobacco smoke that enveloped the central fires. "You will have to choose carefully, wild girl. Once you get adopted, you can't switch your family anymore. This is a life-time commitment."

Kentika listened to the echoing of the drums, enjoying the deep, pleasantly monotonous sound. "Why can't stay in Wolf Clan longhouse? Why have choose?"

"Why ask silly questions?" But again, there was no offense in her companion's twisted grin. "You can't stay under Seketa's care, unless you are willing to give up on that handsome boy you managed to catch for a husband. Did you get tired of our Okwaho already? Did he prove too wild?" The thin eyebrows climbed high, in a suggestive manner. "Or maybe not adequate in lovemaking?"

She stared into the glittering eyes. "What?"

The last of the shadows cleared in the unrestrained outburst of laughter. "Oh, you should see yourself now, girl. Those huge, round plates they serve food on that you have now for eyes. A truly funny sight."

"Why say bad things about Okwaho?"

"Oh, I didn't. I merely told you that you can't stay in the Wolf Clan longhouse unless you want to give up on that boy." The fleshy hand came up, patting Kentika's arm in a surprisingly friendly manner. "Calm down, you wild thing. I was just teasing. He is a Wolf Clan man, and you have to be of another clan to be able to live and make children with him. That is all." Her companion's gaze lost some of its mirth. "Wasn't it the same in your people's lands?"

"I ... well, yes, but..." She tried to collect her thoughts. "Yes, it was. One no live with the same clan person."

"Then, there you have it. You won't stay under Seketa's care for much longer, but don't anger her anyway. She is highly influential, and one of the leading women of our Clans Council. Even though belonging to another clan, you'll still be better off having her sympathy on your side." A knowledgeable smile dawned. "You'll need it. You still have a long way to go toward the full acceptance. If ever."

She thought about these words. If ever, indeed.

"Why people hate? Why not just ..." Frustrated, she searched for a correct word, eyes again drifting to the intensifying music, the pleasant tempo enhanced by the rattles and the vibrating flutes. "Not nice, I understand. Foreign, different. But why hate? Why not just not nice, pay no attention?"

"Hate? I think you exaggerate about the hatred. Not many hate you in a genuine manner. Why would they?"

"Girls. Wolf longhouse and others, they hate. Why?"

"Oh, girls. Yes, of course they hate you. What did you expect?"

Startled by the unreserved confirmation of something she had hoped would be contradicted, Kentika halted abruptly. "But why?"

"Don't you guess?" Her companion halted before they reached the edge of the chanting crowd, where they would be forced to lean close to each other in order to keep talking. A glaring impoliteness. "You snatched up that handsome boy too many girls wanted and probably waited for. They all hoped to snare him one day, to have him come and live in their longhouses, such a spectacularly good-looking thing, all promise and strength, a great future, great family connections, all this bursting energy and skill. And what does he do?" The flickering gaze held hers, challenging again, prompting her to say something. "He comes back all weathered and changed, more handsome than ever, grown up, with plenty of achievements behind him. And with the strangest-looking fox in tow, the wildest thing anyone has ever seen." The cheerful smile kept widening. "What do you think all those would-be Okwaho's women should feel? Do you think they should have greeted you with smiles and loud cheers?"

She didn't take her gaze away, although she wanted to, the realization dawning. Oh, but this woman was so wise! And maybe well meaning too, but her way of telling truths was spiky, hurtful, even though she claimed she didn't mean it in this way. Well, it hurt what she said. It made Kentika feel as though she had taken something that belonged to someone else.

"Well, let us go and dance some, eh? The Great Spirits deserve our gratitude, and other people were expressing it for us for the entire afternoon." A short nod beckoned her to follow. "You are evidently not much of a dancer, and neither am I in my current condition, but we still can do something with all this wonderful music, can't we?"

"Wait!" She caught the sleeve of the decorated dress without thinking. "You say same clan no live together, make children, right?"

The woman peered at her, puzzled, her eyebrows climbing again. "Don't ruin my dress." But with the soft, embroidered material safely out of Kentika's hands, her companion did pause. "What are you asking?"

"If no people of the same clan, if can't take man of the same clan, why then Wolf longhouse girls, why nasty and hate?"

"Oh, this. Well, not all girls are wise, are they? Take Ehnida, for one. You can count on this one to hate you with all her heart, foreign girl. And a few others as well." A light wave of the slender arm indicated that there were plenty of those, female snakes one by one, ready to harm her if given their way. Kentika shivered. "Aren't you going to join in?"

"I, no. I stay, watch."

"As you wish." A quick know-it-all glance and her companion disappeared, swallowed by the colorful crowd, leaving Kentika at the mercy of the outside, and the wonderful music that now lost much of its magical qualities. The beating of the drums and the resonating singsong of the rattles, those vibrating in people's hands and those trilling on the legs of the dancers that made her spirit soar earlier now only irritated, the knowledge of all those underlying currents chilling her inner being, her foot not tapping to the beautiful rhythm anymore.

Eyes brushing past the celebration of colors, the dancers' attire wonderful, so much more beautiful and intricate than the ceremonial clothes worn back in her village, she began easing away, wishing to be anywhere but here. All those girls swirling in the inside and outside circles, serious and dedicated, or laughing and flirting carefully, flashing their eyes at the dancing or watching youths—in that aspect some dancers did not differ from her fellow villagers—all those sly foxes became rivals, or possible rivals, persons she hated as much as they hated her, malicious snakes out to take her love away from her. Filthy skunks!

The walk back to the town refreshed her, though, and now, strolling the deserted alleys, lit generously by the full, round moon, she felt better, less like a cornered animal fighting for its life, ready to strike hard whoever came close. He loved her and not those nasty snakes. He had brought her all the way here, and he made everyone know that she was his woman. These other girls may sport their pretty curves and well-fitting dresses, oh-so very perfect and well-behaved, but they would never have him the way she did. Or would they?

She cursed at the returning tide of doubts. She wasn't pretty or efficient, useful in the way women were. All those beauties dancing in the circle of fire back in the valley now, flowing with the music, swaying like graceful saplings in the gentlest of wind, or the others, moving not as prettily but laughing, sparkling with mirth, enticing, drawing the gazes of as many men. Would he be looking at those now if he was here? With her being so useless, not good in any of this.

She shifted her burden impatiently—bowls and plates piled in an empty pot that she was to dispose of in the storage room of their longhouse—longing to be rid of it. She was so tired! It was good to be able to do one's work well, to receive nothing but approval and appreciation from Okwaho's mother, who made use of her skills and abilities, ensuring that she, Kentika, did not have to work with other women or do the usual female tasks, the tasks she was so useless at, but it was tiring to run and carry things all day long.

The entrance of their longhouse gaped at her darkly, not inviting to come in. With the fireplaces of the long corridor barely glowing, spreading no light, it seemed dim and cold, distant, aloof, not a true home.

Making her way carefully in the cramped closeness of the storage room, she piled her cargo on the first available corner, then straightened up, startled. Voices floated along the corridor, quiet, comfortable voices. Obviously the building was not as deserted as it looked at first, with the glow of a distant fire flickering in its depths, banishing the darkness.

"... gorging on sweetmeats now..."

To lean forward didn't help. The words were coming from too far away to hear clearly, reaching from the farther side of the building, or maybe the central parts of it.

Against her will, she slunk into the corridor, bypassing the first compartment's fireplace, its embers barely glowing, lacking in life. Who would be here and not out there enjoying the celebration?

The voices were young and female. She ground her teeth.

"You should be out there, enjoying yourself." This voice was unfamiliar, low and strident, not a pleasant sound. It was as though the talker held things in her mouth, or maybe deep down in her throat.

A sick person? She remembered the healer with the mask. Oh, yes, there was an ailing girl on the other side of the building, the one who didn't get better on her own.

"There is nothing to enjoy there," said another voice, this one nicely melodious. "Boring ceremony, like every Falling Leaves Season. They did nothing but talk for the entire day."

"Oh, please, sister. There was a great feast too, and now they dance and enjoy themselves." The third talker seemed to be in a better mood, light and fill of mirth as opposed to the other two, the familiar ring to her voice making Kentika press her lips tighter. Onenha, the girl who was sneering at her when they were sorting corn, the one whom she, Kentika, had to push hard when the nasty fox had tried to take her basket away. "I'm going back soon. I will bring you two, lazy rodents that you are, plenty of sweet bread with berries upon my return."

"Lazy rodents?" cried out the second girl. "Gaawa is sick, and I'm staying with her so she won't be left all alone. There is no one in this entire longhouse to do that. I'm being a good friend, not a lazy rodent!" A thundering pause. "Don't say it, even as a joke."

But the outspoken part of the trio didn't seem to be impressed by her friend's reprimand.

"Gaawa is not sick anymore. She is recovering. And maybe she could use some sleep to do it better, but for your gossiping here all evening long, sister." A new outburst of provoking laughter preceded more of the indignant protests, from both other girls. "It's only you who think this celebration is boring, Ehnida; only you who used to dance with such zeal but stopped after the last Cold Moons."

"I did not! You are talking nonsense."

With all their yelling, it was unnecessary to come closer, but Kentika proceeded down the corridor anyway, unable not to do so. Ehnida! The girl Jideah had indicated most clearly, oh yes, the one who would give her some dark looks upon an occasion, although it was her friend, this same teasing Onenha who was truly nasty, truly unbearable. Well, she seemed to be this way with her friends, too. Not much of a consolation, but some.

"Yes, Onenha, stop talking this way." After some coughing and sounds of a cleared throat, the sick girl came to the aid of her friend. "It is bad and nasty. You are being cruel."

"I'm not. I was just teasing. Stop being so serious." The third girl, who had probably realized that she had been taking it too far, moderated her tone back to non-provocative lightness. "Both of you, relax and try to enjoy the evening. Even if you must spend it here and not out there."

In the ensuing pause, Kentika could hear the drums, still distinct despite the distance, rolling most pleasantly, calming. She wondered if everyone was dancing by now. Or had the celebrative crowd retired to enjoy the light snack that was laid out on mats; not the hot meals the people devoured so hungrily before, but a plethora of delicious cakes, cornbread sweetened with berries, a multitude of bowls and baskets offering nuts and dried and fresh forest fruit.

"They must be gorging on sweetmeats now." The exclamation echoed Kentika's thoughts. "I'll bring you some, if there are leftovers. You're sure you are not coming along?" This time, the pause filled with soft chuckling. "Don't miss the sight of the she-moose dancing. That must be a vision. In that torn dress of hers, and her hair sticking out everywhere. And that way she waves her hands when running. They would have to make a special space for her, like another circle."

A snort was her answer.

"She should join Feather Dance or Stomp Dance if she is so eager to show her gratitude to the spirits." The voice of the sick girl was hoarse but more lively now, full of excitement. "She is not a woman as it is, so why not admit her into the men's dances?"

"She is obviously woman enough to make Okwaho wish to keep her." Ehnida seemed to be less amused than her peers.

"Or maybe he doesn't like girls anymore, eh?" Their lively companion giggled. "That's why he picked some strange creature that doesn't look like a woman. Maybe he'll start looking at hunters and warriors next."

"He will not!" breathed Ehnida, appalled. "Don't say such things."

"Yes," contributed the sick girl. "There is no need to badmouth him; he is a good boy. It's just … well …"

"It's just what?" The aggressive thing was not about to let her companions get away with non-committal mumbling. "It's just that he committed too many crimes, first by making some of you think inappropriate thoughts concerning your own family members, then by tossing that outlandish creature upon our longhouse, forcing us to deal with her. He should have taken her along on their hunting mission, I say, the way she looks and behaves." This time, the pause was filled with more genuine anger than provocation. "Although our Clan Mother doesn't seem to mind, actually, eh? Demanding us all to be nice to that she-moose, giving her special tasks fitting for boys and not respectable women. Gather firewood, of all things, and alone! Do you think she is enjoying the challenge of taming the beast, or just trying to be a good mother to her spoiled brat of a son?"

The brief silence that prevailed did not fill with laughter as the speaker might have expected. Instead, the sick girl burst out in a fit of coughing.

The commotion it brought jerked Kentika back to life. As the shadows fell across the corridor, she tried to make her mind work, her teeth clenched too tightly to part, her entire body trembling with so much rage, she was afraid she would explode. How dared they? She was not a moose, and he did not love her because she was like a man, and he was not a brat and his mother...

The silhouette of the tall girl blocked the light of the fireplace. Coming back to her senses, Kentika glanced at the nearest compartment, contemplating diving into the relative privacy its lower banks and the wooden screen that parted them from the neighboring ones provided. Eavesdropping was as bad as gossiping, and it didn't matter that the others were guilty of the second crime. She was the one to listen in secret.

Still paralyzed, she watched Onenha straightening abruptly, turning to stare at her, eyes wide and openly perturbed, even frightened. But for the chance to turn invisible!

Clenching her fists, she glared back, not about to run away, not now. Yes, she was being horribly impolite by listening to the conversation she wasn't supposed to, but the filthy lies of the malicious skunk were just too much. She was not an ugly moose who pushed into the dancing circle and didn't let anyone perform properly—what filthy lies these were! And she was not a man to participate in men's dances.

"You!" breathed her rival in the end, evidently gathering her senses enough to mount an attack. "You were eavesdropping."

"I no, no eavesdropping. I come to fetch, fetch things." Suddenly unsettled, Kentika took a step back, her eyes taking in Ehnida's lithe figure appearing behind her friend, as wide-eyed and appalled.

"What things?" The tall girl was regaining her composure as fast as Kentika was losing hers. "There is nothing to fetch here. You were just sneaking around, listening to people's conversations. I wonder what our Clan Mother would say to that." Tossing her head high, Onenha stepped forward, clearly heartened by her companion, who kept close behind. "She won't be pleased, you know? She may be nice to you, but she is not a person to anger with improper behavior, wild girl. Did you know that? Or was this a proper thing to do in your savage lands, to eavesdrop on people? I suppose it was."

Her feet felt the border stones of the next fireplace, pressing against her heels, blocking her way. To bypass it, she would have to take her eyes off her rival, who was bearing down on her, frighteningly sure of herself, with the other girl close behind.

Kentika clenched her fists tighter.

"So tell us," her tormentor continued, lips twisting in the most unpleasant of smiles. "What will you do to convince me not to tell on you, eh? What would you do to prevent me from going straight to Seketa and telling her how badly you were behaving?"

She tried to gather the last of her courage, to bring the rage back. That wave of panic was frightening. Was it that unspeakable what she did? But she didn't mean to. She just came here to bring things, to put them in the storage room, to—

"Have you swallowed your tongue, savage girl?" Onenha's face was positively glowing now, not a bad-looking face, pleasantly round, adorned with prominent features. And yet it was so ugly, with the large eyes narrowed into slits and the generous lips barely a thin line, their corners turned downward, trembling with triumph. "You were all a show of aggression before. Tough enough to push me that day, eh? But now all quivering and afraid. Is that all you are capable of? Brave in daylight, with many people around, yet nothing but a forest mouse when alone? Is that what Okwaho likes in you, the timid little creature inside the clumsy bear? What a strange thing to like. Who would have suspected that boy to have such peculiar inclinations?"

The mention of his name helped. While Ehnida's giggle dissolved in the semidarkness, Kentika felt the life flowing back into her limbs. They were such vile creatures, those filthy foxes, with such filthy mouths. They had no right to talk about him, or about her.

With the tall girl stepping yet closer, her grin flickering in the nastiest of ways, eyes glowing with victory, she didn't need to move in order to close the distance. Her fist coming from below, the way one of the boys taught her back home, it smashed into her unsuspecting opponent's face, while her knee crushed into the softness of the belly, making the ugly fox double over in the silliest of ways, letting the air out—such a ridiculous sound, yet music to Kentika's ears. A push of the muddied moccasin completed the job, sending the stupid fowl rolling into the dust of the floor, to mar her pretty dress and maybe even ruin it for good.

Leaping forward in order to apply another kick, as her rival was struggling to her feet, with her fighting spirit seemingly intact, she felt more than saw the other girl gasping, bringing her arms forward in a half-pleading, half-demanding manner.

"Don't!" It rang with such desperation, Kentika's foot stopped in midair. "What did you—"

The exclamation was cut short, as Ehnida, already on her knees, was pushed aside by none other than her friend, waving her hands in order not to lose her balance.

"You filthy rat!"

On her feet again, Onenha, muddied and disheveled, the side of her face glaring red, lashed forward, her hands claws, eyes blazing.

"You dirty, sickness-stricken coyote—"

Avoiding the grasp of the tearing fingers aimed for her hair, or maybe her eyes, Kentika smashed her elbow into the unprotected ribs, marveling at the silliness of her opponent. Who would charge blindly in such a situation? No one but a stupid fox who thought the world of herself, having such a poison-dripping tongue in her mouth, but who knew not a thing about fighting. Another expertly applied punch sent the annoying skunk sprawling again.

"Stop it!"

This time, the timid Ehnida was reinforced by the sick girl, barely standing on her feet, a vision of protruding bones and unhealthy pallor.

"I no start, she fight," said Kentika, now in her element and the calmest of those present. She stared at her fallen rival, who was curled upon the ground and groaning. "You sickness skunk, you ugly moose. You men dance. Not me!"

They said nothing, Ehnida again on the floor, trying to minister to her friend, with the sick girl clutching onto the nearest pole on which the partition between this compartment and the next one was fixed. Her eyes were huge in the thinness of her colorless face, ringed and glittering, staring at Kentika in dismay mixed with an open fear, obviously afraid to make a move, as though mesmerized. It made Kentika feel bad.

"I no hurt," she said, not daring to move as well. If she did, the girl might try to flee, leaving her much-needed support, fainting right away, maybe. "No afraid, I no hurt."

"You only beat Onenha into bleeding. No hurt, indeed," hissed Ehnida from the floor, gathering courage she clearly lacked before.

"She hit first."

"She did not!" On her feet in her turn, the smaller girl glared at Kentika, curiously not afraid. "You hit her hard, and first. She was just talking to you, and you punched her and kicked. And then, when she tried to get back at you, you made her bleed, that badly you beat her, you beast." Lips pressed, eyes blazing, she stood her ground, not daring to come closer, but not about to give up, either. "Will you hit me too now? And Gaawa?"

This time, it was Kentika's turn to fight the urge to take a step back. "I no hit. She, she said bad things, very bad. She nasty, and she wanted hit, tried to … I'm not…" Frustrated with this mounting misunderstanding, her inability to explain, she brought her arms up. "She say bad things. I no want to hit. I … just…"

Something close to a puzzled frown crossed Ehnida's narrow face. For a heartbeat, she hesitated, then pressed her lips tight.

"You better go away," she said, turning back to her friend, her words ringing stonily, seeping through her clenched teeth.

The sick girl coughed and swayed, but Kentika knew better than to come closer in order to support her. Her help would not be accepted, not here.

The wind howled outside, bringing along flocks of clouds,

shadowing the moon, making its silvery light dim. It tore at her as she emerged from the protection of the wooden screen, cold and unfriendly. The night spirits were not about to show her kindness, any more than the human beings were.

Numb, she listened to the drums, the throbbing of the rattles reaching the town now more clearly, brought here by the fury of the wind. Were people still dancing and feasting, thanking their great spirits, this Right-Handed Twin he had told her about and the other Sky Deities? Heno the Thunderer, whom their thanksgiving speeches mentioned more than once during this afternoon? The Rainbow Goddess?

She swallowed the knot in her throat. He had told her she was as beautiful as this colorful deity when she smiled, but now he was away, for so long, close to seven dawns. They had never spent so much time apart, and he had said it was a short hunting trip only. He didn't plan to be away for so long. He promised to be back for the ceremony. She had heard him saying this to his mother when they talked about some game or ritual that was to be held. Peach Stone Game it was called, she remembered, having no idea what it was. Well, he had planned to participate in this game, but the first day of the ceremony was over, and there was no sight of Okwaho. What if something happened to him?

Her stomach heavy, chest tight, she rushed along the passageway the double row of palisade created, never comfortable in the closeness of this labyrinth-like construction. Too easy to get trapped in such a place.

Trapped by whom? She didn't know.

Okwaho told her it was a great means of defense. Back when the trouble in her village was at its highest, he had talked about that way of building the fence, laughing at her village's pitiful row of poles, telling her how the attackers had a harder time storming such a labyrinth.

Her stomach squeezed harder. Where was he? Why wasn't he coming back?

Outside the wind was stronger, whipping the clouds across the sky, letting the moonlight free, then hiding it again. She pitted her face against the fierce gusts. What now?

To go back to the celebration, try to find Okwaho's mother, and then what? Try to explain what happened? There was no good explanation for this, no excuse. She had hit a girl, had beaten her thoroughly enough to make her bleed, an unforgivable thing to do, here as surely as it was back home. Physical violence in girls was not permitted, not condoned. And why did she do it, anyway? She didn't know, couldn't remember. Yes, they said nasty things, and that Onenha had been threatening, oh yes. She did it, didn't she? But the other girl was right. Nasty as she was, the filthy fox did not touch her at all, even though she looked like she might. No. It was her, Kentika, who did the beating, and with real force, didn't she? She did it and no one else. Oh, Mighty Glooskap!

The flickering of the fires was near, and the silhouettes of the dancing people, the chatter of the onlookers and their laughter intermingling with the forceful rolling of the drums, the vibrating of the rattles, the trill of the flutes.

Against her will, she paused to watch, the moon pouring down in force now, illuminating the dancers, making it easy to pick out details from her remote vantage point upon a slope. Why didn't she stay here, away from trouble? Why did she go back to the deserted town? Okwaho's mother had sent her, yes, but she could have just finished her errand and rushed back. There was no need to stay and listen to the filthy things the malicious rats were saying about her, and about Okwaho. Ugly moose! But they were much worse than that, poisonous snakes, jealous skunks, all of them.

"Whom do you hide here from?"

The words made her jump, coming from behind, out of the darkness. She hadn't heard anyone nearing, no footsteps, no rustling of the earth, no change in the air, she who was always so good with her senses, whether reading the earth or listening to its messages. What was wrong with her?

Her heart thumping, she whirled around, to encounter none other than the foreigner's glittering gaze, full of the same playful challenge he displayed on their previous encounters. But of course; she should have guessed. His accented way of speech was too pronounced to miss, difficult to understand, like that of Okwaho's mother, but more prominent.

"Why aren't you down there, enjoying yourself?" he repeated, his smile glimmering with mirth, but his eyes measuring, trying to see through her.

"I-I enjoy before. Now tired," she said, on guard and not wishing to talk to anyone, but at the same time welcoming his friendly attention. There was so little of it around here. They hated her so, and now even Okwaho's mother might stop being kind, when she heard—

Oh, all the small and great spirits, what if the kind woman grew angry, or frustrated? What if she stopped being nice to her? The chilling wave was back, freezing her insides.

"Tired?" His laughter rolled down the incline, pulling her back from the brink of panic. "You were not in the dancing circle, not for one single heartbeat. I was there all the time. You were running here and there, but you didn't dance."

"I no say I dance, I... I do work. Clan Mother, she give work, all girls Wolf Clan work today."

The wave splashed again, reaching inside her stomach, making it tighten painfully. The girls of their clan, their longhouse, the Clan Mother. Oh, Mighty Spirits, she would be so furious when she heard. What would she say or do? Oh, but she wouldn't be able to face that woman, anyone but her. All the kindness, all smiles and interesting talk, the patience, the goodwill, the attempts to help, all these repaid in an ungrateful outburst of violence, in a stupid loss of temper and self-control. Oh, but she was incurable, the worst of savages, indeed.

"What's wrong?" The man's voice reached her, again uninvited but welcomed, somehow. It rang differently now, with no thread of amusement, puzzled, maybe even concerned.

"Nothing." She didn't manage to even understand her own words, the way it came out, broken. Clenching her teeth tight, she peered at the flickering valley as the lonely flute peaked, overcoming the drumming. Less dancers whirled around the central fire now, with the main crowd moving away, watching and chanting, tapping with their feet.

The graceful figure in the purple-adorned dress fastened with a wide purple girdle was impossible to miss, or not to recognize. Moving with her typical elegance, obvious even in the way she walked, Okwaho's mother swayed with the music as though she was an accomplished dancer half her age, so graceful and trim, so lithe of movement. Was there anything this woman did badly?

"Tell me what happened."

His words rang firmly, demanding but warm, an order from a friend. Okwaho would have talked to her in this way now, she knew. He had no patience for playing around, for extracting information in an intricate way. He would demand to know what happened, but his request, while firm and unwavering, would not awaken the urge to argue.

"I did bad... I..." Again, her breaking voice forced her into clenching her teeth tight, preventing more words from coming out.

"What did you do?"

She could feel his gaze, boring into her, the dancers down the hill forgotten.

"I hit girl, made her fall, made her bleed." This came out as a mere whisper. It was a wonder he managed to hear. But maybe he didn't. She glanced at him hopefully.

He was frowning, openly puzzled, the previous light superiority and mischief gone. "Where? Down there?"

"No. Back. Town."

"Oh." He nodded thoughtfully, as though the location explained it all. "What happened exactly? Why did you do this?"

She shrugged, suddenly feeling a little bit better, not as dreadfully alone as before.

"Come." Turning away from the intensifying music—the dancers' circle was growing again, joined by the more eager elements in the crowd—he beckoned her to follow.

For some time, they proceeded in silence.

"Let me guess," he said as the night enveloped them, his words again laced with amusement. "The silly foxes were not nice to you, not friendly."

"Well, yes." She skipped over a rotten log before kicking it away, feeling better by the moment. "They talk bad, real bad. Not just not nice."

"And you hit them?"

"Well, yes." She hesitated, not liking the way it sounded. "One, only one. And she was nasty. True nasty, not good. She say very bad things."

He was watching her, not attempting to conceal his scrutiny. "You are something out of this world, foreign girl. Did you fall from up there, like the Sky Woman did, through the hole in the sky?"

She glanced at him, puzzled, but his expression was back to its regular playfulness, his eyes on the silvery moon, perfectly round and again plainly seen, with the wind wiping the clouds away.

"A good night for the opening ceremonies," he commented, shaking his head, as though disapproving but not in a resentful way. "The spirits favor these people too much."

"You go back town?" she asked, recognizing the path they were ascending.

He shrugged, non-committal. Listening to the drums as they peaked again, she contemplated her moves, calmer now and more in control. To go back to the deserted town was out of the question. Even when it'd be full of people and life, she might be better off avoiding the largest Wolf Clan's longhouse, at least for a while, until she made some amends or at least tried to explain herself to Okwaho's mother. Would the busy woman listen?

She shuddered, her briefly gained confidence gone once again.

"You aren't eager to go back now, I gather," he said softly, as though talking to himself. "Not until this day's celebration is over."

Now it was her turn to shrug.

"Afraid of your Clan Mother, aren't you?" This time his lightness and amusement came out a little forced, and his gaze that brushed past her was openly deliberating. It was as though he was assessing her.

"I no afraid," she said, peering at him. The lack of focus in his eyes was unsettling, his concentration elsewhere. "She good, no mean, no nasty."

"No Clan Mother would condone violence among the members of her clan, let alone girls. You should be afraid, foreign girl. The law is in their hands, even had you been already adopted and a full member. As it is, you have no rights here, no one to shield you from clans mothers' wrath, even if people wanted to do that. Which, of course, they do not, with you being not very well liked to begin with."

She felt the chill coming back, trickling down her stomach, turning her insides into icicles.

"What she do?" she whispered, barely hearing her own voice.

He shrugged again. "Only Great Spirits know, or maybe not even them."

"Okwaho, he won't let..." She cleared her throat. "He will not—"

"The War Chief's son? He won't be able to do much. Not enough weight in the town's affairs, not in a young hothead of little years." He slowed his step and was peering at her again, eyes blank but again measuring. "But maybe there is a way to help you, to put a good word in for you, eh? The leaders of our delegation do converse with influential people, after all." He shook his head thoughtfully. "And not only the War Chief and his following. There are other people in this nation, people who might like to see certain changes. Maybe they will be able to help you, if asked nicely." The narrowed eyes measured her again. "I'll see what I can do."

She stared at him, wide-eyed. "Why help, why me?"

His grin flickered strangely, holding none of its usual mirth. "I don't know, wild girl. Maybe it's silly of me, but somehow I believe it is not." He shook his head as though awakening from a dream. "For now, go back and behave as though nothing happened. Avoid your Clan Mother if you can. If she stays as busy as she has been today, it won't be difficult to do that. Did you hear that a ballgame is to be held on the day after the next one?" Again, his eyes turned indifferent in a somewhat exaggerated way. "While sleeping in the War Chief's compartment and running all around, find out what side of the field the renowned leader will be playing on."

"I ... what?" She tried to understand it all, the furious Clan Mother, the people who wanted something from her or the War Chief or anyone, a game that should keep Okwaho's mother busy, too busy to pay attention to her, Kentika's, crimes. Or was it something else? "I no understand," she repeated. "What field?"

"Don't you know the rules of the sacred game?"

Bewildered, she just shook her head.

He drew an impatient breath. "Well, ask around. You'll have a whole morning to learn all about the ballgame. When the sun is high, meet me near the fence, next to the tobacco plots. By then, you should know if the War Chief will be playing with the defense near the gates, running all over the midfield, or busy scoring near the opposite team's marks." He frowned, peering at her, eyes dark with anxiety. "Will you remember all that?"

"I ... yes."

Unsettled, she tried to understand. Something was wrong with this entire thing, something was missing. The seemingly innocent remark had somehow become important, as though her personal trouble was somehow connected to the place the War Chief was supposed to take in some game. How? It didn't make much sense.

"I ask, yes."

He measured her with a piercing gaze. "Be careful about it. Don't let your interest show."

CHAPTER 14

With everyone's eyes fixed on the man holding the flat bowl of six peach pits adorning its bottom, Ganayeda watched his father. As spectacular as always, the War Chief sat with his back straight and his face immaculate, waiting for his turn to receive the flat-bottomed vessel.

The players of his team and the rivaling one squatted on the spread mats, with the multitude of onlookers crowding all around, pushing forward or standing on their toes to see better. The Peach Stone game was an important part of the ceremony, held on the second, or sometimes the third day of the festivities, the way to entertain the people and their creators alike. The Great Spirits, both Right-Handed and Left-Handed Twins, were reported to engage in the Peach Game when contesting for ascendancy over the world of their creation.

Tiredly, Ganayeda rubbed his eyes, careful not to disturb the crusts that adorned the left side of his face, all those freshly closed cuts and bruises. His right shoulder was still giving him trouble, harming his ability to lift his arm properly, and the cut in his side was throbbing again, protesting against all the strain, the rest prescribed by the Lone Hill's healer nowhere in sight. They had tried to make him stay for a day or two, to let his wounds heal properly. They argued, with Okwaho taking their side.

The young hothead did not mean to stay, of course. He had wanted to head home and let them know, while his elder brother rested and healed. But Ganayeda wouldn't have it. He was the leader of their original hunting party after all, and it was bad enough that he had to send his men home by themselves, enough that he found himself fighting Crooked Tongues in all sorts of encounters, none of them of his choosing. He did not manage to remain in control of the situation, to conduct this spontaneous enterprise in a way fitting a leader. He had lost the initiative, and while his brother did everything the right way, saving as much of the situation as he could, he, Ganayeda, had run all over the place, like a silly youth in a fit of rage, striking everywhere, making a fool of himself.

He had lost to the filthy enemy, he knew, had lost on the private score. And it didn't matter how many times Okwaho had repeated himself, stating various aspects of their relative success. Yes, they did manage to foil the enemy's scouting mission; yes, they did send the filthy invaders back home, with quite a few of their men missing, left behind, dead. Seven warriors, claimed Okwaho. Seven warriors out of a possible twenty was a respectable achievement for two unprepared men. They had killed those and harmed more, sent the stinking enemy back home, saved one of the girls, a daughter of a prominent man. What else could be counted as a victory if not this?

Ganayeda would just grunt in reply. What was there to say? They had lost only one girl, a woman he barely knew after one night and one day of traveling, a girl he had saved from the bear. She might have been dead long before the Crooked Tongues entered the scene, but now she was lost anyway, kidnapped and taken away, on the other side of the Great Lake surely, afraid and alone, maybe hurt, forlorn and frightened. And it was his fault, his failure, his wrongdoing. She had trusted him to keep her safe, and he had failed, failed miserably.

The familiar black wave was back, threatening to take him, to cast him into the depths of despondency. Through their last journey, it attacked him several times, making him wish to lash out, to scream or hit and kick, or maybe bang his head hard against the nearest rocks or trees. He was so useless! She was stupid to put her trust in him. She should have stuck to his brother, instead. With Okwaho, she would have been safe, still among her people, unharmed. But what was she if not a silly girl, too young and too pretty, probably spoiled on account of it, not understanding life at all. He might have saved her from that bear, but against the more sophisticated human enemy he was useless, not the man and the leader he held himself to be.

Grinding his teeth, he focused back on the game, in time to see Father receiving the bowl, nodding to the cheering people, a good-natured smile stretching his lips, lifting the scars that crossed them in some places. Father's scars were a legend, an object of many speculations and musings. The man must have seen hundreds of battles, people had whispered, before the Great Peace was born. He must have been a fearsome warrior back in his days. Such a great leader!

"Now let us see what the Turtle Clan can do with those stones."

Holding the bowl high, in a showy manner, the War Chief presented it to the crowds, tilting it lightly to each side, displaying its contents: six peach pits blackened on one side, unpainted on the other.

In spite of himself, Ganayeda grinned. The trick of trying to place the stones in a favorable way before the bowl was to be tossed and placed down was an old one, and Father's cargo definitely slanted a little as he passed it before the observers.

"Shaa," cried out voices from among the Wolf Clan watchers, not many and not as eager as they should. The exclamation was supposed to bring the bad luck to the player, but the War Chief was admired and liked universally. Also, while belonging to the Turtle Clan, he lived in the Wolf Clan's most prominent longhouse, having its most influential woman for a wife. A difficult position for the ardent supporters of the opposite team. And it didn't matter that the ceremonial aspect of the game obligated its participants to return all the won or lost items to their rightful owners. The passion that ruled games of luck was on, no matter what.

"Ga-hoo-da," yelled the Turtle Clan supporters, as the bowl landed on the ground with a bang, placed there forcefully, making the painted pits inside it jump. This cry said "make all one color," and as two men responsible for counting, one from each team, leaned simultaneously, their heads blocking the view, the crowd held its breath.

"One point," said one of the men loudly, straightening up. The people began breathing again.

"One bean to be passed from the Wolf Clan's possession," declared one of the elders.

The War Chief's smile widened. All six pits of the same color would win him the entire round, enriching his team by five beans, putting his rival out of the game, to be replaced with the next player from the opposite team. Still, only five pits was not such a bad achievement. It left the player in charge of the bowl, entitled for another try, and it gave his team one more bean to add to their growing pile. Too many times by now, the bowl had passed back and forth, with no results at all, as any amount less than five gave the player nothing, no beans and no additional round, which was the most common outcome, for both sides. The Peach Stone game could last for an entire day.

"This span of seasons, the Turtle Clan will show you," cried out someone, to the loud merriment or protests of the others.

"Why don't you join your clan's team?" Iheks's voice brought Ganayeda back to reality, in a welcome manner.

Glancing at his father, just as the War Chief took hold of the bowl once again, he turned to his friend. "Want to pit me against my own father?"

The man's grin beamed at him. "Why not? Not everyone wants the turtles winning, our renowned leader or not."

"They are leading but by five, maybe six points. It's not much. It can change in a matter of heartbeats." Shrugging with his unharmed shoulder, Ganayeda turned back to the game, in time to see the bowl passing into the hands of Father's opponent. The stones didn't favor the great leader this time. "One lucky throw and they owe the same amount of beans again."

"We don't know how many beans the turtles are leading by. Their holder covers their winnings well." Indeed, the man in charge of the cup that held the beans of the Turtle and Bear Clans pressed his vessel tight to his chest, covering its opening with both hands. As did the man who represented the opposing clan.

"If one follows the game and keeps count, one doesn't need to peek into their vessels." He watched Father grinning, saying something that made the men around him, even his opponent, laugh. How could he be so calm, so unperturbed, as though interested in the game and nothing else? wondered Ganayeda. Didn't he worry about what happened?

Their arrival early in the morning had created quite a stir, as they had entered the town just as the people were heading out, to resume the ceremonial activities—this time the faith-keepers' thanksgiving speeches and a few mandatory dances—before the game, the main part of the second day's festivities, was to take place. No one expected a band of Lone Hill's dwellers to descend upon the town. Hadn't they a Harvest Festival of their own to conduct? Many visitors were expected to arrive at High Springs, yes, but with the dawn of the next day, in time for the ballgame. Not before.

Well, one look at Ganayeda made many rush off, returning with every influential person who still lingered inside the fence, a few elders and two members of the Town Council, with some Clans Mothers in tow, those who were not responsible for the refreshments of the day. The War Chief was in the valley, a part of the ceremony, and by the time he came back, the story was out, making many eyes flash and many hands rise in agitated gesturing. To think of the enemy roaming the shores of their side of the Great Lake with such impunity, making it unsafe for the hunters to travel or women to wander about, and in such proximity to their own villages, was infuriating. Oh, all the great and small spirits, but the enemy was growing too bold!

By the time Father arrived with his throng of the town's dignitaries, already knowing some of the details—a messenger must have been dispatched to let him know—the newcomers were seated and fed, with only Okwaho gone. Indifferent to the implications of the incident, the young hothead must have been anxious to be reunited with his outlandish thing of a wife, but Ganayeda was in a different mood. Father might be reluctant to declare an outright war on their unpopular neighbors from the other side, might have cherished ideas of peace with these people, but this time, these same Crooked Tongues had taken it too far.

The gall!

He smashed a fly that was trying to land on one of his wounds. These people were nothing but dirty enemies, with no decency and no shame. There was no place for such lowly creatures in the League of the Five Nations. Father was wrong about that. These people must be hurt, they must be made sorry for their crimes. Father needed to be made to understand that. He must organize a strong fighting force, to be sent across the Great Sparkling Water. A large force, many warriors. There was no choice but to do that, whatever his personal preferences were. The enemy did not want peace. They wanted war, and they had declared themselves clearly enough.

He ground his teeth, disregarding the outburst of more cheers and heated exclamations all around. Who cared for the meaningless game when all he could think of was the size of the future expedition, the destination of it? Oh, but he would be joining this one, no matter in what capacity. He would be a part of this first serious offense against the old enemy, and he would make sure to bring Gayeri back, somehow. He would dedicate all his efforts to this end.

"You are sleeping with your eyes open, aren't you, brother?" Iheks's elbow nudged him lightly, careful not to touch the blood-stained piece of cloth that encircled his ribs. "Your father nearly takes his opponent out of the game, and all you do is stare ahead when the entire town goes wild with excitement."

"How many beans are left in this round?" asked Ganayeda, narrowing his eyes to see the players, curious against his will. He wasn't interested in any of that, and yet Father was there, representing his clan in the important ceremonial game. It was imperative that he won this round. In the light of the new unfavorable developments, it was good for the people to see that the Great Spirits favored their War Chief, however unpopular some of his ideas and notions were.

"The War Chief has three beans. Two more and his opponent is out and your Wolf Clan remains with a little less dignity than it had before."

"Good!" Genuinely pleased, even though the man who played

against Father was, indeed, a member of his own clan and the dweller of the neighboring longhouse, Ganayeda sighed. The moment the round was over, he would be off. Where to? He didn't know. Away from the multitude of happy, unconcerned people to be sure.

"You are not well, brother. One can see that." His friend peered at him, his frown light, concerned. "How about I take you to your longhouse, into the care of your womenfolk?"

"When this round is over." A shrug proved a painful business. "I will be off then."

"I still can't believe you managed to run into so many troubles while taking the wild foxes home." This time, Iheks's voice rang as gloomily as Ganayeda's thoughts. "Who would have thought? It wasn't wise to send all of us back home. Only you and that youngster troublemaker who calls himself your brother were clearly not enough." A shrug. "Was he any good while warring?"

"Okwaho?" Ganayeda felt his grin spreading against his will. "That young buck is so good, one can send him all alone across the Great Sparkling Water. The filthy Crooked Tongues wouldn't know what fell upon them." He shook his head. "He didn't spend his time in vain out there beyond the Flint People's Great River. He is an outstanding warrior now, better than many I know of."

"Oh!" The thickset man nodded, openly surprised. "That is good news. The War Chief must be pleased." Another perturbed scrutiny. "And yet, we shouldn't have split. It was not a wise decision to take the women back home all alone."

A sudden tension in the air forced Ganayeda's eyes back to the players, although his stomach twisted with already-familiar wave of irritation. Everything he had done since that accursed afternoon with the bear seemed to be wrong, criticized, looked upon dubiously, didn't it?

"We are not living in the days before the Great Peace," he muttered angrily. "There is no danger in journeying through our woods in small numbers. What happened near Lone Hill was exceptional. It—"

The War Chief shook the bowl once again, dropping it with a resounding bang. As the people leaned forward, Ganayeda caught a glimpse of his wife, making her way through the crowds on the opposite side of the ceremonial ground.

He hadn't had a chance of greeting her yet, with all the commotion, the ceremonies and the agitated discussions surrounding his return. No time to make a quick detour through the Heron Clan's longhouse and the cozy compartment at its far edge, next to the storage room. She must be busy and away with the ceremonial activities her clan would be expected to contribute, he had reasoned, when for a brief moment, on his way to watch the game, he contemplated detouring after all. On the second day of the ceremony, it was customary to make the smaller clans provide the food, while the Turtle, Bear, and Wolf Clans were responsible for the entertainment, being the traditional opponents of the Peach Stone game.

The silence was sudden and encompassing. Along with the rest of the surrounding people, he watched both counters kneeling to inspect the bowl.

"One more bean to the Turtle Clan!"

People let out a held breath. The cheers filled the air, louder, more uninhibited than before. No matter what clan each observer wanted to win, so many favorable throws in such a short period of time, with no luck at all for the other side, were a rare thing. The spirits favored the renowned leader, as they always had.

"One more bean and they'll have to look for another player," said someone.

"And in the meanwhile, we get our well-deserved refreshments." Iheks's voice was back to his usual lightness. "I'm starving."

"Don't count on the feast of yesterday," someone said with a laugh.

"Why not?"

"Wolf Clan is busy losing the game. They won't be organizing our meals today."

"So what? Others can do that as well."

"Not as well as the Wolves." The man next to Ganayeda beamed at him. "You should have been here yesterday, brother, instead of running all over, picking fights with our disgusting neighbors from across the lake. What a feast it was, and what dances! No one wished to retire to sleep, not one single person, not even our exotic guests."

"Oh, the Long Tails? They are still here?" Encircling the crowds with his gaze, he suddenly realized that he had forgotten all about this troublesome delegation. What became of them?

"Oh, yes, they are." This time it was Iheks again, shifting his weight from one foot to another, waving away a fly. "They will be participating in the ballgame, or so I hear. If our Onondaga Town's opponents will arrive in time, that is."

"Only four stones!" cried out one of their neighbors.

At the center of the contest, the bowl passed back to the Wolf Clan man, to many outcries of disappointment.

"No one can get five stones time after time," stated Ganayeda, as disappointed as the rest of them.

"Unless you are favored by the Great Spirits themselves."

"Well, the War Chief is favored. He won four rounds in no time. But then, it was only expected." Iheks's chuckle floated in the pleasantly sunny air. "I can't recall a time when our leader failed, whether organizing, campaigning, or engaging in throwing games."

Another bang of the bowl. Ganayeda shifted his eyes to the people crowding the other side. Jideah was standing among those in the forefront, looking pale and unwell. Was she ill?

Catching her gaze, he nodded amiably enough. Or so he hoped. Somehow he didn't wish to interact with his wife, not now. Maybe later, when he wasn't as angry over what happened near Lone Hill, when he had stopped thinking about Gayeri in the hands of the filthy enemy.

The wave of rage was back, washing his insides in perfect accord with the collective gasp that escaped many throats, rising like a tide. His mind snapped back to the present.

"What…"

One arm protecting his wounded side, he moved forward together with the shifting crowd, his attention again on the players. Father's back was as straight as an arrow, while his rival leaned forward, examining the contents of the bowl with his eyes

so wide they turned round. The counters from both clans froze as
well, bent above the object of the staring, as motionless as a pair of
rocks. The silence was brief but encompassing.

"Could it be?" breathed someone, and then the crowds erupted
into yells and cheers, while the counting man of the Wolf Clan
straightened up slowly, lifting the bowl, afraid to breathe on it, let
alone shake it.

"Six unmarked stones," he said, offering it to the closest of the
observers. "All stones are displaying their painted side." Clearing
his throat, he encircled his spellbound audience with a wide-eyed
gaze, repeating loudly, in an echoing voice. "The lucky throw!"

This time, the crowd erupted in a huge, deafening cheer. It was
difficult enough to get five stones out of six to display their either
marked or unmarked sides. But all six? It was one of the rarest
occurrences, making the lucky player the winner of the entire
round, his team getting all five beans, his rival out of the game,
replaced by the next player.

Elated along with the rest of the observers—a lucky throw was
a good sign, especially on the ceremonial game—Ganayeda felt
his insides twisting nevertheless, watching Father congratulating
the Wolf man warmly, marveling at the rare sign of luck along
with the rest of the pressing people. Oh, but he had been so close
to winning. Why should the lucky throw happen now, of all
times? The game was proceeding for some time, and it was to
continue for the remnants of the day and maybe into the night
even. Why couldn't it be someone else losing all the gained beans,
the bets and the place in the game?

"Well, the spirits do not favor the War Chief as eagerly as
before," murmured someone, while the beans were removed into
the Wolf Clan holder's cup and the players were getting up, the
limbs of the winning man trembling. "Maybe they are displeased
with some recent developments concerning foreigners."

"What do you mean?" asked Ganayeda, paying no attention to
the pain as he turned sharply, causing both of his wounds to
protest.

But the man just shrugged, refusing to meet his gaze.

"Well, this is a ceremonial game," said Iheks lightly, even if a bit hurriedly. "The spirits will be pleased no matter who wins. A lucky throw is always a good thing."

"Yes, it is." Still glaring at the other man, Ganayeda nodded to his friend. "The Great Spirits are pleased with us recreating their original game, and whoever wins or loses matters not to them."

People were drifting away, toward the mats spread in the shade of the huge maple tree, the refreshments upon it inviting, trays of cornbread in all forms and shapes, baked or roasted, sweetened or dotted with berries, bowls of nuts and other forest fruit, large pots boiling with corn drink, offered in elegant pottery cups. The break in the game seemed to be welcomed most eagerly.

"We better take ourselves over there in a hurry, before the best of the food is gone."

Following Iheks and the others, Ganayeda ground his teeth, hating the tiredness, and that constant feeling of fury, that wish to lash out at everyone and everything. What was wrong with him?

"Who cares to bet against the outcome of the entire game?" asked one of the men merrily, when a mat laden with snacks was occupied by more of Ganayeda and Iheks's peers, with them all squatting happily, devouring the food.

"What do you offer?" demanded a younger hunter. "It depends on your bets."

"He offers his torn quiver with no decorations and an old loincloth," cried out Iheks, waving his cup in the air. "He is that generous. What are you going to match that with?"

Amidst the loud outburst of laughter, Ganayeda tried to force at least a semblance of a mirthful smile. But for the past few days, he would have been the first to join the teasing, to goad the younger among their peers, or his fellow hunters, never above messing around. Studying his father's ways most thoroughly, in a conscious effort to imitate the great man, he always made sure to keep no distance between him and the people he was often required to lead, hunting if not warring. Yet, now all he could think of were Crooked Tongues, who must have landed already, traveling their filthy rivers and streams, in a hurry to reach home, carrying their spoil along. Disgusting lowlifes that they were!

"I was so sure that the War Chief was to win that round and a few more. The spirits have never abandoned him in the games of luck, have they?"

He fought the urge to get up, if for no other reason than to see where Father was. Among the groups of the prominent people surely, eating as heartily as any of them, conversing with his peers, indifferent to the loss of the game. At least on the surface. It was a bad sign, that it happened now. Was Father truly beginning to lose the benevolence of the Great Spirits? Were they angered with him for his insistence to include the Crooked Tongues, and maybe those other foreigners from the west, in the sacredness of the Great Peacemaker's creation?

"Yes. It was most strange and glaring. The timing of this last throw that overturned the entire round," someone else was saying. "Before what happened, I would have bet on the Turtle Clan taking the game. But now, now I'm not so sure."

"If he was allowed to play in another round, I would bet on the Turtle Clan still." He heard his own voice saying those words, and it surprised him, the calmness of it.

"It would be against the rules," said someone after a pause.

"Yes, but if it wasn't, I would bet on the Turtle Clan winning the game."

For a short while, they lost themselves in eating, surrounded by the clamor, eyes following the girls and women who were running around, refilling the bowls.

"Game rules or not, will you tell us about your wild adventures out there?" demanded one of the hunters, his smile light, free of shadows. "The rumors are running everywhere. No one knows what story to believe, from enraged grizzled bears to pretty girls in need of rescue, to hordes of enemies on the loose, we have heard it all by now, while you sit among us as though nothing happened."

Ganayeda shrugged. "It was wild, yes. Out of the storytellers' tales, some of it."

"Did you really slay the grizzled bear?" Now all eyes were upon him

"Well, yes. But I wasn't alone in this. They all were running and shooting." Indicating Iheks and the men beside him with a curt nod, Ganayeda picked out a warm roll studded with berries, not hungry in the least. "That bear was old. And mad with anger. A terrible creature."

"He did face it all alone," protested Iheks. "I was right there, and I saw it all. That girl, she was on the path of the beast, and our gallant rescuer rushed to challenge the enraged forest giant instead of shooting it from a safe distance. Too much bravery, if you ask me. But the girl was mighty pretty, I must mention that."

Among the amused loudness of their remarks, he felt his insides shrinking again. She was pretty yes, and sweet, and courageous, and now in the enemies' hands. Oh, but he wouldn't rest, he wouldn't...

"And the Crooked Tongues, what happened with those would-be invaders?"

He made an effort to show none of the strain getting to his feet involved. The damn wounds!

"I'll tell you all about it later. When I come back." Nodding toward the worst of the hubbub, he tried to sound as light as he could. "Going to get the corn drink they are offering out there. Need to warm my old bones."

The silence behind his back held a measure of wonder. They weren't convinced by his pretended lightness, he knew, clenching his teeth against a new wave of resentment. Did he owe them an explanation?

Next to one of the boiling pots, women of his longhouse were sweating, finding it hard to keep up with the growing demand. The warm drink was so very welcome in the chilliness of the strong wind. Evidently, the Heron Clan was responsible for this aspect of the ceremony. He sought out Jideah with his gaze. It wasn't like her not to be in the thickest of it.

"Father!" The small thing, nothing more than a mess of decorated leather and too much hair, collided with him, nearly pushing him off his feet. "You are back!"

He picked her up, paying little attention to the painful protest from his wounded side.

"Oh, yes, I am." Holding his daughter on his outstretched arm, he studied her with a pointed gaze, his entire being awash with warmth. She was such a perfect creature. "What have you been up to?"

She beamed at him, so round and fresh, all soft and plump and sweet-smelling. "I help, help all around. Mother says that I do a good work. Like a grown up person, she says. That good I am!"

He felt his grin spreading on its own, without being forced, for the first time through this day.

"Of course you are. Without you, they wouldn't manage at all." Ruffling her already disheveled braids, he marveled at the thought that something so small could contain so much sweetness. "Where is your mother? And your sister?"

"There," she waved her hand, non-committal, wrinkling her nose as she did this. "You smell bad."

"Do I?

She giggled, then pressed her face against his, inhaling loudly, in a showy way. "Yes, oh yes! And you are covered with dirty clothes. Why?"

"I've been hunting, you know. It makes people dirty."

"You should have washed and changed for the ceremony."

This time, he didn't manage to hold the laughter in. "You will make a perfect Clan Mother one day."

Her little face puckered in a frown. "Like Mother?"

"Your mother is not the Clan Mother. Not yet. Maybe one day she will be."

The thought of his wife and her ambitions made him frown. Jideah would want to hear all about his adventures, and she wouldn't take kindly to some of it, all this talk about him saving pretty girls that, thanks to Iheks, was now circulating around the town. He drew a deep breath. No, he wouldn't think about *her* being out there, in the enemy's hands.

"You hunted huge, scary bear," the girl was saying, nestling in the curve of his arm. "Ahen said it. This morning. He was scaring us, making awful noises. He said the bear was huge and that you killed it with your knife." Her wriggling made it more difficult for his wounded shoulder, but he didn't want to put her down, sensing her fear among this bubbling stream of words. "Just like that. Stabbed it right into its chest."

He shifted her into his other arm. "I did not kill it with my knife. One can't do that to a huge grizzled bear. Ahen doesn't know what he is talking about. He is a silly boy. You shouldn't listen to him."

"But you did kill the bear, yes?" She was turning whichever way, positively dancing inside his arms, now eyeing the people gushing all around them from her newly conquered height, then turning to peer at him, shining with happiness.

"Yes, I did. But with an arrow. Quite a few arrows, actually."

"And we will have a beautiful fur to sleep on?"

"Yes. When your mother makes it ready. Maybe we'll put it on your and your sister's bunk, eh? Sometimes, when it's truly cold."

"Yes, oh, yes!" Her new leap up his torso made him groan with pain. "Only mine and my sister's, yes. The baby brother will not sleep on it?"

In the process of bending to put her down, he froze. "What baby brother?"

She hopped all around, unable to keep still. "The new fuzziest fur anyone ever saw! Ahen will be so jealous!"

He caught her shoulders in an attempt to keep her still. "What baby brother, little one?"

"Oh, oh, the baby." Her eyes went toward the commotion that seemed to develop somewhere around the mats, not in their immediate proximity but not far away. "Mother has a baby in her belly, she says. He makes her sick. Like she ate something bad. A bad meat, you see? Or maybe a bad herb, eh? She does…"

He straightened up abruptly, causing the wound around his ribs to protest vigorously. Was Jideah with child? Again? Did she want it? And did he? A child, another perfect creation like this little thing. But at such a time, with all the troubles and with them being not especially friendly with each other, too busy, too far apart? And after what happened on the road to Lone Hill…

"You will let me sleep on this pelt whenever I ask, yes?" she was saying, hopping all around again. "I mean, even if I want to sleep all alone?"

"Yes," he said absently, listening to the people arguing somewhere around one of the pots. "But now run along, little one.

Go and help our women. They won't manage without you, as you know."

Thoughtfully, he watched her braids swaying in wide circles, while she ran as though all the bad spirits of the evil Left-Handed Twin were after her. What a spirited little thing, so easily excited, so full of wonder and love. How to keep her safe, from bears and from enemies?

He shook his head, then headed toward the worst of the commotion.

So they all had heard about the bear already, and Jideah was with child, and she expected a son this time. Well, a boy could be a welcome development. It would be a pleasure to have a son, to play with and teach. And yet...

Beside one of the fires, a group of the town's prominent men stood at ease, conversing idly, with Father in their midst, listening to someone, nodding thoughtfully, his smile calm. Neither his pose nor his bearing disclosed discomfort. If he felt disappointed with what happened at the game only a short time ago, he hadn't shown any of it. But that was the man, reflected Ganayeda, his pride welling.

Answering the greetings of the people around him, he hesitated, not sure that he wanted to face his father, not yet. What he had to say was probably better to be uttered in private. Or maybe not at all.

Oh, but he never felt the urge to question the great man's wishes and policies, not until now. The peaceful agreement with the Crooked Tongues was not in the forefront of his thoughts, yet he had never opposed the idea. If Father thought it was better that the fierce neighbors from across the Great Sparkling Water were included in the League of the Five Nations, then it was the best course of action. Father was too wise and farsighted to question his plans and ideas, especially the one that he felt so passionately about. Too many people felt the same, wavering, undecided, trusting the War Chief's judgment, not doubting his reasoning. But now...

"Quite a day, isn't it?"

He forced his mind to focus, staring into his new companion's face, the stringy young man from another clan, now a dweller of his former longhouse, a fellow hunter and a partner of many mutual expeditions.

"I wanted to tear my hair out when the War Chief was winning. He plays well. I wish he represented our clan."

"Oh, yes." Concentrating, his eyes took on more of his fellow Wolf Clan members crowding this side of the festivities, people he had grown up among, people he lived with until marrying Jideah and moving to her longhouse, as was the custom. "But our clan won this round after all."

"Oh, well, yes, but no dweller of our longhouse wanted the War Chief to lose. He may belong to the Turtle Clan, but he is our longhouse's member. He is our man more than he is theirs."

"That he is." Forcing a smile, Ganayeda shrugged. "It's just a game. And a ceremonial one at that. The winners don't even get to keep the bets."

But the man's mouth twisted in a troubled manner. "Too many things are happening all at once. The news from the Crooked Tongues, your trouble with them. And now the sacred game. Maybe the Great Spirits are displeased in some way."

"They are not!" He narrowed his eyes at his companion, suddenly perturbed. "Who was going around speaking that nonsense?"

"No one."

He held the blank gaze, not letting it sneak away. "Someone was saying it. And for some time. Who?"

The man licked his lips, then glanced away. "You know very well who. Not everyone is happy with your father's way of doing things."

"In Onondaga Town, yes, there are some who still remember his quarrel with the First Head of the Great Council. But they are few and far between."

"Well, there are people who feel the same here. They are also not many, but their weight in the community is not to be taken lightly."

"Hegweh!" He didn't care how loudly he had said it, remembering that member of the Town Council, a ruddy, calm-looking, seemingly content man, but only on the outside. They all knew how he felt about the War Chief and the vastness of the renowned leader's influence. "He has been speaking about the spirits and their displeasure, hasn't he?"

"Oh, you two!" The loudness of the exclamation made them both nearly jump, as the girl's voice broke into their tension. "Why so gloomy and with no food in your hands? I can't believe we have such bleak faces on our Harvest Ceremony. Shame on you."

Onenha's round face beamed at them, the plate in her hand overflowing with goods.

"Here, have this, and stop looking so glum."

Ganayeda forced a smile, liking her, knowing this object of limitless energy and mischief well, since the day his younger brother was born, on the same moon as this girl. Their longhouse was full of babies' wailing on that cold season.

"Yes, you are right, sister." Receiving the plate, he measured her with his gaze, taking in the pleasant roundness of her face, now marred with a swelling on her right cheek, which was bluish and slightly scratched. "What happened to you?"

Her face darkened. "I wish everyone would stop asking that. Nothing happened to me. I'm good."

He raised his eyebrows. "You look as though you were in a fight, a warrior girl that you are."

His companion smirked, but was quick to cover his grin, as she shot him a direful look. His status in the Wolf Clan's largest longhouse was not very well established, not yet, having moved there relatively recently, taking one of the local girls to be his woman. No, this man was in no position to anger the local foxes, but Ganayeda was a Wolf Clan man and in no need to pacify his extended family's womenfolk. It was different in the Heron Clan longhouse for him.

"Don't turn all red on me, warrior girl," he went on, now greatly amused. "I'm sure your rival sports even worse injuries."

She looked like a thundercloud about to burst. "You talk too much nonsense. You and your brother think too highly of yourselves. I wish he hadn't come back to live in our longhouse against every law and tradition. I wish he would live with you, until that dirty little savage of his finds an appropriate clan to be adopted into. Which, of course, may take moons, if not summers, as no respectable clan would wish to have such a stupid, useless girl, the ugliest of skunks."

He stared at her, puzzled, but only for a heartbeat. "Oh!"

Her eyes burned holes in his face, but before he could burst into more merciless laughter, making matters worse, Okwaho's unmistakably wide shoulders broke into his view, heading from the direction of their side of the town, bearing on them in a manner that promised no good.

Further amused, Ganayeda just started.

"Where is she?" demanded the young man, halting before Onenha so abruptly, his moccasins brought up clouds of dust, his eyes dark with anger, turning almost black.

"How should I know?" retorted the girl, whirling at her new adversary quite willingly, her eyes flashing with matched fury. "The dirty rat you forced on our longhouse does whatever she pleases, consulting no one, not even the women she should."

Okwaho seemed as though about to explode into too many little pieces. "If there is anything dirty or ratty around here, it's you, you stinking piece of excrement," he roared. "You lied to my mother. I know you did. Kentika did not attack you with no reason. I know her as well as I know you. You are a treacherous snake, always ready with your lies. Especially when you are afraid to get caught. Then you lie truly artfully, the filthy skunk that you are!"

Aware of the unwanted attention they drew, Ganayeda stepped forward, placing his arm on his brother's shoulder. It was neither the time nor the place to quarrel like this, to curse one's family member, a woman at that, with such viciousness and in the middle of the festivities, too.

"Listen—"

"Get off me!" His hand was shaken off violently, as the young man's blazing eyes kept boring into the object of his bottomless fury. "You are a dirty snake and a liar, and you deserve to be punished, you and not her!"

Onenha's face was taking the color of the strawberry drink, and it took her so long to draw in a breath, Ganayeda suspected she might faint.

"How dare you?" she cried out at long last, her hands, still holding the plate, shaking. "She beat me hard enough to have marks all over me, and you say I'm at fault. A liar? Me? How dare you!" Glaring at her offender, the enraged girl drew a hissing breath. "I don't know what she told you, but she is the liar, not me. She is the one who does not bother to do her work properly, or does everything wrong, clumsy, picking quarrels and turning violent, unable to get along with anyone. And it's your fault. You brought that ugly savage into our home. You made us live and work in her revolting presence. You are despicable for doing this to us, and you will pay for your insolence. Our Clan Mothers won't let you go around, cursing and blaming me!"

She was yelling at the top of her voice now too, enraged beyond reason, but Okwaho was in a similar sort of state, indifferent to the attention they drew, oblivious of the people who were drifting closer, some puzzled, some amused, many displeased, mainly the elderly among those.

"You are a lair, Onenha. You lied about this whole thing, I know you did! I asked Ehnida. It was not like you said it was. You lied to cover your own nastiness. And I swear, you will pay for this." His sudden advance caused the girl to take a step back, her eyes losing some of their previous spark, making her forehead crease in a frown. "If you ever speak to her nastily again, if you ever come close to her even, I swear—"

"Stop that!" The authoritative voice belonged to one of the elderly women, not of their longhouse but the neighboring one. "Stop talking like that, and stop yelling, both of you. Have you no manners, no respect for the Great Spirits, no appreciation for your people who are thanking them? You are shaming your clan, your town, your entire nation. Get away from each other, and stop defiling the sacredness of the ceremony."

That seemed to cool both antagonists. But while Okwaho, who never paid any particular heed to appropriate behavior, indifferent to reprimands, which he was used to receiving often enough to the best of Ganayeda's recollection, said nothing, Onenha turned to the their mutual accuser with her eyes huge and glittering.

"I did not defile the ceremony, Honorable Mother," she cried out, bringing her free arm up. "Okwaho did. He came to me, and he accused me of bad things. He was yelling and cursing; he called me terrible names!"

"Oh, please!" flared Okwaho, his nostrils widening dangerously, eyes still on the object of his fury. "She is going to play it innocent now, all hurt and tearful. What a show!" His gaze filled with fire again. "But I warn you, Onenha, you filthy snake. If you ever play that game with me or mine again, you will regret it for real. You will—"

"Cease speaking. Heed the words of your elders, young man!" This time it came from one of the elders, a prominent man of the Beaver Clan. "You will say no more to that matter now. Not a word."

Okwaho's tightly pressed lips bode no good, yet he managed to stifle words that seemed to be standing on the tip of his tongue, his eyes speaking for him, telling them all how truly enraged he was.

Ganayeda put his hand on his brother's shoulder once again, firmly this time. "Come with me."

But as Okwaho hesitated, drawing a deep breath through his clenched teeth, there was a movement in the gathering crowd, and a tall man burst from behind it, pushing people out of his way.

"Get away from her!"

He didn't need to shield his eyes to recognize Onenha's man, a young hunter of the Beaver Clan, who had moved to live with her in her family's compartment only a few moons ago, awaiting permission to build an apartment of their own with the coming of springtime.

Face livid with rage, hands stretched out, one still clutching a painted pottery cup with a corn drink he must have been enjoying, the young man halted his progress with difficulty, waving his hands, the drink in his cup splashing out in a multitude of hot drops.

"What do you want?" grunted Okwaho, not impressed. He didn't move a pace, eyeing his new rival with puzzled suspicion.

"You threatened my wife, you dirty piece of rotten meat!" cried the man, as unperturbed by the lack of fright in his rival.

"Onenha?" Okwaho made a face that caused some of the onlookers snicker. "You took her to be your woman?" The suggestively arching eyebrows made even Ganayeda, now worried and ready to stop the fight, wish to chuckle. *You must be desperate, brother,* Okwaho's twisted smile said.

"Yes, I did! And if you won't leave her alone, I will make you regret you ever dared to speak to her in this way."

But Okwaho was losing his briefly gained sense of amusement fast. "You can't make me regret anything, so don't even try." The air hissed out, drawn forcefully through the widening nostrils of his eagle-like nose. "Either make your woman behave as a person by leaving other people in peace, or let her bear the consequences. She has been nasty to my woman, and I have a right to talk to her about it."

"Not in the middle of the ceremony," said one of the elders, his voice cold and uncompromising, but not stony. "You can talk about it later, or better yet, you should bring this matter before the Wolf Clan's Mothers, ask for their council."

"I will surely do that," muttered Okwaho, but very quietly. One didn't argue with displeased elders, not in such a dignified gathering as this. Nor anywhere else for that matter.

"I did bring this matter before our Clan Mother and for her consideration," said Onenha, all innocence. "And I will be certain to inform her about this incident, as well."

Her eyes demurely upon the ground, she didn't glance at Okwaho, but his brother received the message as intended, of that Ganayeda was sure. The young hothead had no chance with the authorities against the canny fox and the smoothness of her tongue, close blood ties to the Clan Mother of their longhouse or not.

He pressed his brother's shoulder, signaling him to cease, to curse and yell at the filthy fox later if he must do that, but not now, not at such a public event.

Okwaho freed his shoulder in a sharp, irritated movement. "Just to think of all the lies our Clan Mother will have to listen to, as though she didn't hear enough of it until now." The words came out loudly, surprisingly calm. Ganayeda fought the urge to slap the young hothead hard. Would he never learn?

"Our Honorable Clan Mother will hear nothing but truth from me." Onenha's tone matched that of her accuser in its clearness and sincerity. A wonderfully upright member of the community. "The People of the Longhouse are always honest, always telling the truth. It is the way of our lives; it is something foreigners would not understand."

Okwaho's teeth made a screeching sound. "You are the dirtiest skunk anyone here ever saw!"

But that didn't go well with the girl's man. Before anyone understood what happened, his arm shot up, grabbing his woman's offender's shoulder, pulling hard.

Caught off guard, Okwaho wavered, waving his hands in the air, trying not to lose his balance. In a stunned silence, they watched his body arching, avoiding the fall by a miracle as it seemed. In the next heartbeat, his fist planted itself in his opponent's belly, making the man double over. Accompanied by a vicious kick to the head, it sent Onenha's man onto the ground, to lay there motionless, in a heap of limbs.

The collective gasp brought Ganayeda back to his senses. His instincts deciding for him, he leapt forward, grabbing his brother forcefully, with both hands. It made his wounded shoulder protest with a burst of sharp pain, but he paid it no attention, concentrating on the powerful body clutched in his hands, struggling with it. Did Okwaho intend to kick his fallen rival some more? He didn't know, but in case he did, it must be prevented. What had happened here was bad enough as it was.

"Let go of me!"

People were talking loudly, all at once, some kneeling beside the crumbled form, some just staring, at a loss. Onenha was screaming in an exaggeratedly high, irritating voice. Putting all his strength into the effort of preventing the rock-hard shoulders from slipping out of his grip, Ganayeda tried to slam his mind into working. Was Onenha's man dead?

"I will let you go when you calm down."

"I'm calm, calm enough. Get your hands off me." Breaking free at long last, Okwaho knelt beside the fallen man, pushing himself through the surrounding people with little ceremony. When he reached for his victim, someone began protesting, and Onenha, by now kneeling beside her unconscious man as well, uttered a funny sound before trying to grab the assaulting hand.

"Shut up," grunted Okwaho. "I want to make sure he is alive." His fingers were light on the man's throat, feeling it out. He was looking for the injured's heartbeat, realized Ganayeda. A good way, better than putting one's ear to the person's mouth.

"He is alive," said someone. "I heard his heartbeat already."

The people nodded solemnly. Okwaho rose once again.

"Go to your longhouse, young man," said one of the elders, exchanging quick glances with his peers. "Stay there until you are summoned."

Okwaho's eyes flashed.

"I'll take him with me." Stepping forward, Ganayeda held the rebellious gaze. "He will be in my longhouse until you send for him."

Their solemn nods conveyed their consent to the projected change of destination.

CHAPTER 15

Rushing along the alley the two towering longhouses belonging to the neighboring clans created, Seketa tried to catch her breath before the next incline was upon her. Her building, being the largest and most influential, enjoyed its position of the elevated ground, but sometimes it was a hindrance. Especially when one needed to reach it in a hurry, and after a long day of activity.

Granted, it was not as hectic, as pressing and demanding as on the day before, when the opening ceremony and everything about it was dependent on her ability to organize, prepare, and make it proceed without a hitch. Still, today was tiring enough, with all the small things mounting, piling one upon another. Her fellow Clan Mothers of the Heron, Snipe, and Beaver Clans asked for her advice enough times to indicate that her help was needed, until she had found herself supervising the distribution of the food that was to be served in the pauses between the game. Not as difficult a task as the need to feed the entire town with a warm meal her clan was required to provide on the previous day, but still enough running around, and just as she intended to rest and enjoy the festivities. *Like on the previous night.*

She felt her lips quivering, fighting a smile. Oh, but it was good to dance, just dance, to merge with the night and the music and let her inner being float, connect with the spirits, weightless and unconcerned. Last night was a revelation. It had been quite a few summers since she did this, forgot her duties and obligations and joined the social, and then even a few ceremonial dances.

Hadn't she been an accomplished dancer once upon a time, when still a young girl and living among her own people? The

Great Spirits made her go another way. They had put her on the path she never regretted taking, a wonderful trail of rewarding challenges, fulfilling work and achievements, surrounded by good people, with her immediate family so warm, so satisfying, her man magnificent and a great leader, her sons spectacular in ways no mother could complain about. The ceremonial dancing was the only thing missing, she realized now, and it had taken her only thirty-odd summers to find that out.

So last night she had let herself go, having even demanded to have rattles tied to her legs. Only three pairs, as her body needed to grow accustomed to their weight anew, but it was still the ceremonial dancing.

And oh, Mighty Spirits, how good it felt. To connect with the spirits in this way, and also to feel *his* eyes upon her, full of wonder and admiration; and love and desire, like back in the old days, when they were young and innocent, and he used to watch her dancing, getting in trouble with other boys on account of it, because many were the ones to watch her dancing. So many bittersweet memories. When it was time for everyone to join in, he had made his way into the inner circle, and letting the drums direct their feet, they had dreamed into each other's eyes, remembering it all, the good and not the bad.

And then, later on, when more refreshments were served, this time the women of their clan managing to feed everyone without her involvement, they had sneaked away and into the darkness of the forest, to make love until Father Sun was about to come up again. Like two silly youths in heat, he had said while laughing at some point, happy and unconcerned, holding her close, beaming into her eyes.

But oh no, she had told him. They were no silly youths, but two people who loved each other through so many summers, not ready to give up on their love, like Heno the Thunderer and his Rainbow Goddess. And when his eyes took that additional glint, the deep glow they always drew when he talked about his love to her, and his admiration, she knew he remembered it all, and her happiness soared to heights even the dancing did not manage to take her to.

However, with the darkness dispersing and Father Sun coming up to lighten their world again, promising yet another warm day with no cold and no rain, they had to go back and face their duties and responsibilities.

More trouble in her case, as she was quick to discover. Out of all places, her own longhouse was in turmoil, with two families, particularly the girls, waiting for her impatiently, ready to burst out with the tale of a quarrel, and even a physical fight. Of all things!

The foreign girl, she had guessed, her stomach heaving with a bad feeling. Who else? She knew it would be her even before the words 'savage' and 'wild' had been uttered. Ehnida and Gaawa were crying, subdued, muttering their stories, as though reluctant to talk. So she had to hear it all from Onenha, appalled to see the girl's face scratched and swollen, with her ribs displaying more bruises, readily presented. How could it have come to this?

The foreign girl was missing, nowhere to be found. But even had she been right there, talking in her halting, simplified manner, what could she possibly say to justify her deeds, wondered Seketa, disheartened. According to the girls, the foreigner had tried to overhear their conversation at night, when everyone was out and dancing. Confronted, the wild thing had hit Onenha hard, beat her and kicked until she could not get up, and then she had run away. Truly an animal and not a human being at all.

She had tried to think of mitigating circumstances, of something the girls were not telling her. Okwaho's foreigner was strange, yes, a wild thing, but she wasn't mean or bad-tempered. She didn't strike Seketa as a person who would do something sly, would wait for the opportunity to harm; or to kick a harmless person already on the floor, for that matter. If anything, she would expect the opposite to be true. The foreign girl was all impulses and spontaneous deeds, needing no more than a bit of kindness to turn tractable and be of help. And yet, the girl of her longhouse was bruised and hurt, with her family indignant, demanding justice. What was one to do with such accusations and with the main offender missing, nowhere to be found? Why didn't the girl stay to tell her side of the story? The heedless flight proclaimed guilt.

And now…

Pausing for breath, she frowned at her company, two girls she had chosen to follow, when many people came running to let her know of the new trouble, all flustered with agitation. So much contradictory information!

"Tell me again what happened," she repeated, trying to gain time, to give herself at least a little breather. It was unusually hot, and she hadn't had the time to eat or drink properly as yet.

One of the girls, a pretty, willowy thing, dropped her gaze, flustered.

"Like we told you, Honorable Mother." Her companion was apparently more spirited. "There was a fight, and … and one of the men of your longhouse got hurt. They took him to his home, and well, he came back to his senses, somehow, just as we were told to fetch you."

"And my son was the one to hit him." She made it a statement, having heard already about it, enough to comprise the picture she hoped was not true.

Now the second girl dropped her eyes as well.

"Do you know what they quarreled about?"

Both shook their heads vigorously, their braids jumping.

"We were not close. We were by the pots of the corn drink, with our friends," whispered the first girl. "We came to look only when we heard yelling and screaming."

"Was there much of it?"

"Oh, yes!"

She stifled a sigh, then resumed her walk, anxious to reach her longhouse, to find out the real extent of the new trouble. As though the morning worries weren't enough, with Okwaho's girl still missing, but with Okwaho himself already back, unsettled and angry, demanding to know what happened to his wife, not willing to hear any of the accusations.

And this aside from the rest of it, from Ganayeda, her firstborn, coming back as well, covered with wounds, bringing along the story of attacking Crooked Tongues, more grim than she had seen him in summers, if ever, determined to do… what? To demand the revenge on the intolerable dwellers of the other side of the Great Lake, she suspected. Ready to go against his own father's policies, and his mother's former people?

She hoped it wasn't the case, but in her inner heart, she knew it was. As though her husband did not face enough opposition already! Opposition that now was to be strengthened, somehow, by his loss of the game. The War Chief was always lucky, in the games of chance as much as in anything else, she had heard people whispering, their eyes clouded, wondering as to the nature of this change.

"Thank you for letting me know." By the gaping entrance, she looked at her escorts, her smile kind. "Go back to the festivities, girls."

They murmured their greetings, and she dived into the storage room, still wondering. Why had so many troubles befallen her family in one day? What were the spirits trying to tell them?

The dimly lit corridor swept along, deserted but for the obvious presence on the other side of the long structure. She made her way briskly, her head high, not surprised with all the faces turning to her, relieved and expectant, as though everything would be well now that she was there. A regular occurrence.

"Honorable Mother!" In addition to old bruises, Onenha's face was now puffy, smeared with a mixture of dust and tears. "Why does it keep happening?"

Embracing the girl who nearly hurled herself onto her, Seketa patted the trembling back, liking this particular dweller of her longhouse, troublesome tendency or not. Much like her youngest son, Onenha was always sparkling with life, always up to something, good or mischievous deeds, highly efficient and with a knack of getting things done.

The others, Onenha's mother, two more elderly women, and a few of her husband's friends stood near the bunk, where the young man slumped, pale and smeared with mud, looking very much alive. So maybe they were exaggerating? Her hope began welling again.

Onenha's mother gave Seketa a gloomy look, picked up a bowl full of foul-smelling contents and proceeded to squeeze herself through the crowding visitors, shaking her head as she went.

"Tell me what happened."

"Well, you see…" One of the young men shifted his weight from one foot to another, licking his lips when no one ventured a word in response, with Onenha still sobbing in Seketa's arms. "We were out there, enjoying the refreshments. It was the break in the game, you see, Honorable Mother, so everyone was on the ceremonial grounds near the fence. Eating." Another lick of his lips, a futile gaze toward the rest of the company, with no help forthcoming. One of the elderly women picked up a bowl with water, offering it to the injured man, who had taken it with lack of eagerness, not thirsty but probably happy to have something to fiddle with. "Well, there was an argument. Okwaho was accusing Onenha of things, and well, naturally Sgawah, he went to see what was happening. Because of all the yelling."

"He was accusing me of terrible things," wailed Onenha, not daring to leave the safety of her new hideaway, was Seketa's private conclusion. "He said I was lying to you. I, who would never … even if my life depended on it…"

"About what happened last night?"

A vigorous nodding was her answer.

"Listen, little one. Calm down. Please try to calm down. We will solve all these troubles, but I need you to tell me what happened. Now, and maybe last night, too. In case you remembered something you forgot to tell me before." With no response but the intensified sobbing, Seketa looked back at her best source of information. "Go on, please. What you say is very helpful. So Okwaho and Onenha were yelling at each other."

"Yes, and then—" Halting abruptly, the young man swallowed his words, and she felt the girl tensing in her arms. "Well, it was not so much of yelling, you see, Onenha was not—"

Cutting the rest of his words off, Seketa extended one arm, in a commanding gesture. "Now please, only the truth, we agreed on that already, didn't we?" She let her voice harden, while steering the girl back toward the lower bunk. No more tearful embraces and comfortable hideaways. She would hear none of their hastily concocted stories, not where her son was involved.

Where was he?? she wondered briefly. One of the people who had come to call for her, told her that he had been ordered to stay in his longhouse until called by the authorities, but if it was so, there was no sight of the young man anywhere around.

Pushing the girl gently toward the vacant space beside her man, she encircled them with her gaze.

"I have heard many versions of this trouble already, as many people came to summon me. Some of the accounts are contradicting. Not everyone was around to witness personally what happened. Therefore, I came here to ask you, Onenha, and you, Sgawah, people who are involved. I will question my son and those who were near as well, before I attend the meeting of our leading men and women, those who are concerned with this matter. So now, please, let us talk about what happened briefly and truthfully, with no attempts to minimize the involvement of either side."

"Will this matter be dealt with by our clan alone?" asked one of the elder women, nodding thoughtfully, clearly impressed. "Or will the Council of the Clans be involved?"

"We'll see." Against her will, Seketa sighed. What if the matter was handed to the Town Council's judgment, because it had happened during the ceremony, even if not through any sacred procedures? What if those who would rather see her husband humbled tried to use it against him, somehow?

She pushed the troublesome thoughts away. "Now tell me what happened, and do it quickly."

The injured youth cleared his throat. "You see, Honorable Mother, we all grew very angry. Okwaho and Onenha, and me too, of course. One doesn't enjoy hearing his wife being yelled at, even by her own family member." His voice rang gruffly, as if after a long vomiting, which probably was the case, reflected Seketa, liking this young man, despite what happened.

"And then what happened?"

"Well, he called her 'dirty skunk' and other cursing words, and well ..." His gaze dropped. "I did grab him at this point. I don't think I wanted to start a fight, but, well, some may say I started it."

She stifled a sigh. "I appreciate your honesty."

"But he didn't hit him, Honorable Mother," the girl burst in, in a frantic rush. "He didn't. He just caught his arm, or shoulder, I think. It wasn't a fight. Sgawah did not do anything to make Okwaho think he would hit him."

"Yes, I did," said the youth gruffly. "I pulled him. I think I just wanted him to face me and not her. But well, he almost fell because of it."

"Oh, please!" Regaining her usual fighting spirit, Onenha jumped to her feet, frowning at her husband. "It was not like you say at all. He wasn't about to fall. You see, Honorable Mother," the gaze turned to Seketa held the remnants of the anger, even though the girl made an obvious attempt to soften it with her previous sincerity, "he just caught Okwaho's arm. He was not attacking him. Okwaho was the one who looked as though ready to attack. Me, I suppose. Not Sgawah. But when Sgawah touched him, he went mad with anger." The girl's face twisted, now in genuine fear as it seemed. "He was like a mountain lion. His fists were so quick. One moment they were still up, facing each other. The next Sgawah was on the ground, breathless, his mind wandering another world, and no one even saw what happened." Drawing a noisy breath, Onenha blinked the new tears away. "He hit him so hard, and he kicked him in his head."

"He did this?" gasped Seketa, appalled.

Her youngest son might have been wild at times, yes, good at fighting, especially now, coming from the moons of warring in those distant lands of the rising sun. But to be so out of control, to kick a man lying on the ground, and in his head. No, it was not possible! Okwaho wouldn't do that.

"He did, Seketa," said one of the elderly women. "I was there. It happened so incredibly fast. No one understood what was going on before this young man was lying down there, his mind wandering other worlds." A mirthless grin accompanied a shrug. "He is very good at fighting, this boy of yours. He turned into a splendid warrior. I suppose he would do better finding another war, and in a hurry."

"He will do that, if he wishes to do so," she said coldly, getting to her feet, aware that she should hurry out there and see what the leading men of the town thought about this matter. If such interpretations circulated, there was no telling how it would go for Okwaho now. "He won't be sent away on account of what happened."

"No, of course not." The woman lifted both her hands, palms up. "I didn't mean it this way." The frown made her converser's face wrinkle. "He did not behave dishonorably, if you worry about that. His loss of temper was not a desirable thing, not in a youth of his age—the way he yelled at this girl was bad, inappropriate—but he did not disgrace himself. Don't let anyone tell you this. I was there, and I saw it all."

"To kick a man in his head, a man already lying on the ground, is not an honorable thing to do," muttered Seketa, refusing to meet the well-meaning gaze. "No person who respects himself would go on beating a fallen rival."

"But he didn't beat Sgawah after he fell." This time it was the other woman, her hands stretching out, imploring.

"But you said…" She couldn't help but look at them now, her heart filling with hope. "You said he kicked him in his head."

"Yes, he did. But when Sgawah was still standing. That's what made him fall, the kick."

The young man was studying the blanket that covered his legs, pressing his lips tight. Ashamed, Seketa knew. It was not proper to discuss him in this way, as though he was not present. Men were different when it came to such matters. This youth's pride should be spared, shouldn't it?

"He was standing, yes, but he was doubled over with pain from the previous blow," protested Onenha, forgetting the proper address while bursting into her elders' conversation. "It's not like he was ready for that fight or awaiting this blow. Okwaho should have stopped by then. What he did was the same as attacking a fallen man. It was not honorable."

Seketa pursed her lips in her turn.

"You forget your place, young one," she said coldly, her dislike of the girl growing, for the first time since she became the Clan Mother of this longhouse. "You tell different stories, not the ones that match the words of other people, also present and involved. You make me doubt your other story as well. I have not yet been able to make inquiries into what happened here last night, into yet another violent incident that involved you, but I will. Well, for your own good, I do hope that you were sincere, telling me truthfully what happened and not only your version of it. For your good, I hope my son's original accusations were unfounded."

It was easy to detect the fear that flickered briefly, to disappear into the depths of the defiant expression, to dissolve there. She kept her satisfaction well hidden.

"I did not lie to you, Honorable Mother. Not now, not before. Not ever," the girl was saying. "I would never lie to you. Okwaho has no basis for his accusations other than his desire to find me at fault, and so did that violent, unruly woman of his. He was not being fair about it. I don't deserve your anger on account of it."

"I didn't say I was angry with you." Sighing, Seketa turned to go. "Take care of your man for now, and you all have my gratitude. Your words enlightened me greatly."

Heading down the corridor and back into the world of the soft autumn sun refreshed her, made her head clear. It was time to find Okwaho, to hear what he had to say for himself, and then the possible meeting of the Clans Council, or at least some of its members. To catch her husband alone for a private, if quick conversation was not a possibility. The War Chief was too preoccupied, needed elsewhere, at the game and at the ceremonies that would follow, required to give yet another thanksgiving speech, to light yet another sacred fire.

Oh, Mighty Spirits, please guide him; please give him strength; please keep him safe, safe from the enemies and from those who envy him; and from his own stubbornness in regard to some matters.

Narrowing her eyes, she saw Onenha's mother coming back, carrying a bowl full of fresh water. Behind her, but at a considerable distance, another figure hurried, that of a young girl. Seketa's stomach twisted. Running young ones, girls or boys, meant only one thing, being the most handy messengers when a person needed to be fetched in a hurry.

"What do you think, Seketa?" The other woman's voice startled her, jerking her back from the concentrated effort to see if the messenger was heading their way. She was! "Do you think she is lying? It's so not like her to get into so much trouble. Onenha was always a good girl. Spirited, yes, lively more than one might desire, but not a mean person, not a nasty thing to get into all this violence and fights."

She forced her thoughts to the predicament of her peer. A worried mother, she knew exactly what this woman, an associate if not the closest of friends, was going through. No one better.

"I think she might have been carried away quarreling this time, sister. But you know how young people are. She seems to be having trouble accepting Okwaho's girl, but it will pass. They both will forget all about it with the passing of moons. Girls always do."

The older woman's face twisted. "Thankfully, the foreign girl will not stay in our longhouse, if your son is so determined to keep her. This will solve the major part of the problem."

Seketa pushed the familiar wave of anger away. "You are not being just toward the new girl. She is not as bad as people assume she is. Different, yes, not as tractable as one might wish her to be, but she is a good girl nevertheless. Onenha should have been busy helping her to learn, to fit in, instead of making it difficult for her by constant needling and provoking." She brought her hand up, arresting her companion's protests. "She has been doing this. I know she has. Do not believe everything she says. Talk to her, instead. Try to calm her down; try to make her understand. It will do your daughter good in the long run. Foreigners are no bad spirits with poison in their claws. They are people like us, sister. We would all do better realizing that."

Her converser's face was setting into a familiar, stubbornly resentful mold, but before she could say anything else, the panting messenger was upon them, her little face flushed, mouth wide open, gasping for breath.

"Honorable Mother, please come."

"Where to, little one?"

"The Town Council members, they are gathering on another

ceremonial ground, behind the Heron Clan's longhouse." The girl straightened up, her face assuming the expression of comical importance. "They required your presence, Honorable Mother. Other Clan Mothers are already there."

A meeting of the Town and Clans Councils called in a hurry? Seketa's heart fell. Such a gathering promised no good. And her son better be available as directed, ready to testify, or he would be in grave trouble.

CHAPTER 16

Kentika held her breath. Afraid to make a sound or to move a limb, she crouched in her small, unsatisfactory hideaway, her body cramped, head spinning with fatigue.

It had been such an exhausting night, physically and emotionally. What possessed her to eavesdrop on the filthy foxes of Okwaho's longhouse, to get into a fight with them? The question kept haunting her, even though the night was already gone and the sun was shining strongly, having reached its highest point in the sky.

No drumming came from the valley where the celebration had been held yesterday, and she wondered about it briefly. What was happening in the town now? Did they go on with the ceremonies or did they stop them for good? Because of what she did?

The chilling wave was back, washing her insides, filling them with ice. Was she going to be punished severely for her crime? She didn't dare to come back to the town, even though the Long Tails man told her to do so. He was nice and understanding, supportive even, not approving of her deeds, surely, but not judging her either, offering neither admonition nor reprimanding. Much like Okwaho, he seemed to be amused by her words or deeds rather than taken aback. A strange reaction, but an encouraging one. He was not an enemy. And yet ...

Waiting for the people she was watching now to resume their conversation, she thought about her last encounter with that man. What was his name, anyway? He was amusing and friendly, helpful at times, not derisive or hostile, but his interest in the War Chief was disturbing. Even unhealthy. Why would the foreigner wish to know all about the prominent leader and his movements, even as far as to learn on what side of the field he played in some important game? What was he up to? The mischievous spark, the idle amusement so typical to her other interactions with this man, would vanish with no trace when the War Chief's name or title were brought up. A puzzling reaction.

Not that it was any of her business. The foreigner could feel however he liked about these people or their leaders—his sentiment seemed not to even be shared by his fellow visitors— but whatever his reasons were, she didn't wish to have anything to do with it. The War Chief was a good man, and he was Okwaho's father, the husband of their longhouse's Clan Mother, the nicest woman she had met here so far. If someone wished him harm, she didn't want to help this person along.

"We should go back. It is not wise to be absent on such a day."

The voice of the man behind her cliff brought her back to the present, ringing out, too close to her hideaway, making her heart lurch in fright. He must have been walking now, maybe pacing back and forth, anxious and fidgety. She didn't know whom these people were waiting for, but it was clear that they were growing impatient. They had been here since the high morning after all, since she had spotted them while wandering about, not knowing what to do with herself.

Her resolve not to return to the town until Okwaho was back wavered again and again, along with her growing tiredness and hunger. Maybe his mother was not as angry as she imagined her to be; maybe she would again listen and understand. By running away, she, Kentika, was giving the filthy fox she had beaten the opportunity to badmouth her, to make her deeds look worse than they were. Although, how much worse? She had done the unspeakable as it was. No matter how badly she tried to twist it in her head, the details of the night's fight kept surfacing, the feel of her fist against the softness of her rival's cheek, or how her moccasin brushed by something that was clearly a hard part. A rib? A cheekbone? Oh, Mighty Glooskap! But she must have hurt that girl for real, left clear marks or true damage. How spiteful and unworthy. She was truly a bad person; the people who hated her, who suspected her of savagery, were right.

The tears were back, blurring her vision, making it difficult to breathe through her nose. Okwaho's mother had promised they would allay people's suspicions, would fight their distrust, would show how good and worthy she was, no matter where she came from. She had promised they would do it together, but now, oh, now she would turn away, as disgusted as they were. She would never understand, never forgive.

"We will, in due time."

This time it was another man speaking, his voice carrying from farther away, from the place she had seen them squatting around before. There were three of them huddled on the small clearing next to the steep cliff, not far away from the brook she had come to regard as her own. Two men, fidgety and uneasy, and the third one, her foreigner, whom she had spotted heading here earlier, when the sun was still only starting to warm the earth. Wandering with no purpose, she had seen him from far away, walking hurriedly, glancing around every now and then. The benefit of the elevated ground and the open space he was crossing allowed her to follow him with her gaze for quite some time, to guess his destination easily. The brook! If the War Chief was scheduling his clandestine meeting there, then why not the foreigner who was spying on the renowned warrior and leader, too?

Not daring to try to follow such a person up close—this one would sense her sniffing around most surely—she had made her way down the hill nevertheless, spotting his footprints with no trouble, proud of herself, her worries and anxiety receding, if only a little. This man! He seemed to cross her path over and over again, and he was not hostile, not angry with her, maybe not even now, even though she did not come to meet him by the opening in the fence as he wanted her to do, bringing the information he required.

Encouraged, she proceeded to follow the footsteps, losing them sometimes, but always finding the new prints farther down the incline. Speaking of good scouting. The smile was back, to be fought by the frown. Her spying around would not help her but bring her more trouble. Didn't her last bout with eavesdropping bring her the worst of predicaments already?

And yet, what else was she to do with herself now that she could not return to the town? The despondency was back, accompanied by violent constricting in her stomach. How was she to face any of them, even Okwaho himself? What if he got angry or frustrated with her as well? Was he to stay home forever, keeping an eye on her as one keeps an eye on a child? Oh, but she will surely disappoint him.

The voices of the men grew louder, carrying with the wind that was blowing in her direction. They were arguing, talking quietly but forcefully. Had she been on the other side of the cliff, she wouldn't have heard them at all.

Nearing as close as she dared, she had caught her breath, recognizing one of the men, a person of this very town, a dignified elder she had heard saying bad things about the War Chief on her first time venturing out—only a few days ago, but a lifetime as it seemed to her now. The other two she didn't know, but listening to them talking to the newcomer, she gathered that one was a local man, the other a visitor, another person of the foreign delegation.

"What took you so long?" the waiting visitor complained, addressing her foreigner, who made a face and proceeded to talk to the dignified man.

"They are engaged in the game, like you said they would be," he was saying hurriedly, in a rush. "All the dignitaries and other leaders, and the townsfolk—everyone. They will not gather to discuss matters of importance, not before the festivities are over. Or so your people told me."

"And not even then," the local dignitary said with a grunt. "Because then, they will be busy with the ceremonial game that our glorious leader is so eager to participate in. He behaves as though he is a young warrior, that man—all showing off and spectacular displays of power and personal skill. He has no shame!"

The pause that followed made Kentika imagine the sparkling eyes of the foreigner clouding. "What about the game? The shooting exercise can be done the moment I know what part of the field he will be playing this time." Another brief pause. "Defense, or midfielder? The attacking part of it, probably, eh? I may have this information today."

"This one in the defense? Oh, please!" The local man waved his hand in dismissal. "I can tell you beforehand where our glorious leader will be playing. But it won't do us any good. The game is not to be commenced before the day after tomorrow, and even this is not a certainty. If our Onondaga Town guests, the players and their multitude of supporters would not come in time, and they *are* in the habit of making everyone wait, stressing their pretended superiority and importance, then the game would commence after your people are safely on their way back. There is no use in your scheme."

In the angry silence that followed, Kentika took a tiny step back, then another, not daring to so much as breathe. The memory of how easily he had caught her back when they had both been eavesdropping on the War Chief made her skin crawl. This man was not the person to spy on, he was too alert and fast, too aware of his surroundings. There must be a way to escape his vicinity safely.

"I should go back now. There is no use in spending the entire day here," the local dignitary was saying, while she slipped back into the bushes, her heartbeat calming. "I urge you to do the same. The opportunity may present itself before your delegation takes its leave, but," not seeing any of them anymore, she could still imagine the man shrugging, "I would not hold your expectations high. This man won't be brought down, not him. His Crooked Tongues will be pulled into talks again and again, whether any of us, or you and your people, like it or not. But I swear that they will not be made a part of our union, not as long as I live. And our people will know about the War Chief's unauthorized dealings with the enemy."

"If you have an opportunity, do this. As long as I'm here and can testify…"

Feeling the solid stone of the cliff behind her back, she hesitated, frightened momentarily. But it was not as though she had been chased, she reasoned, trying to calm the renewed racing of her heart. There was enough time to find the way around it, or even to climb up.

"You heard him with your own ears, didn't you?"

"Yes, I did. He was receiving messages from one Wyandot leader, a Bear People's man. It was delivered by a person who came along with our delegation. It was clearly an agreed-upon procedure. The War Chief wasn't surprised, and it seemed that he was the one to summon the man to the meeting place not far away from here." The foreigner hesitated. "There is a girl in this town, a wild thing from the far east. She listened to this conversation as well. She is in trouble with the entire town as it seems. She may be useful. What if she testifies together with me?"

"The little savage the War Chief's son brought along?" the man cried out, surprised. "It can't be."

"It is. I caught her eavesdropping on him. She didn't admit her reasons, but she must have something against the man to endanger herself in this way." Another pause. "She may be made tractable, if approached in a correct way."

The man's footsteps were making rustling sounds, with no attempt to conceal his advance.

"The testifying is of no use to us, unless presented in the right moment, as though unintentionally. Still, you better come back with me and see what you can do." The voice came from farther away now, muffled by the thick foliage. "Maybe your other scheme will be possible to execute, somehow. With this man alive, there is always a good possibility of him wriggling out of any charges, no matter how grave or incriminating. He is too well-known, too admired, to be removed from his position or lose at least some of his influence over our town's dignitaries, or even the Great Council. But if removed …"

Their voices were drawing too far away, leaving her straining her ears in an attempt to hear more. Where those people plotting, *actually plotting*, against Okwaho's father? Even with no worthwhile command of their tongue, she knew she understood more than she wanted to.

Aware of the other two people who must still be lingering upon the clearing, she slid down her stony support, to squat upon the warmness of the earth and think. The sensible thing to do was to run back to town and try to talk to Okwaho's father, to make the man listen. Easier said than done. The War Chief was busy with the ceremonies, and she was nothing but a troublesome foreigner herself. Why would he stop to listen to her?

The Long Tails man was back. She could hear his voice again, talking to the remaining people, curt and matter-of-fact, his words muffled. Did the wind change? She wondered about it briefly.

Shutting her eyes, she went through her options again. To stay and listen, to find out what they actually planned? She was so tired. The rays of the friendly sun reached into her small hideaway, warming her skin. It was so pleasant here, no worries, no troublesome dilemmas. Just the sun and the wind, and this lolling sensation of drifting along.

When she opened her eyes abruptly, it was colder, and the sun did not sneak into her improvised den anymore. The wind had strengthened. It was sweeping the fallen leaves, murmuring in the treetops, unsettling in its intensity.

Her heart beating fast, she listened to its voice, blinking to make her mind work. Had she fallen asleep? It seemed so; otherwise, why would the sun disappear? It was still out there, lighting the world, but its angle was different, lower and less intense. The dusk was nearing.

Getting to her feet, she listened again, sensing the presence of others. They were quiet now, barely talking. Had the Long Tails man left?

The chance to find that out came quicker than she expected. As she moved along the rocky wall, intending to circumvent their clearing maybe, to come up from a different direction, she heard hurried footsteps. Someone was running down the hill, hastily at that, not attempting to conceal their steps at all.

Holding her breath, she listened intently. Was the messenger heading for the clearing and the conspirators upon it? Of course he was. Why would someone run anywhere else?

Her steps light, she left the supportive solidness behind her back, sneaking into the bushes, trusting her ability to move like a forest creature. These weren't her woods, but she was still better than many men, and even some scouts.

Upon the clearing, the men jumped to their feet too, the Long Tails man not among them. Peering in the direction of the running footsteps, they froze, all ears. She didn't dare to move any more. Instead, she listened as they did.

The bushes adorning the clearing parted, as did the ones behind her back. Terrified, she turned around in time to see someone, a broad face, peering at her with a measure of surprise.

She didn't spend her time on studying its features. Bolting for the opposite shrubs, she put her entire strength into leaping through the momentary opening, oblivious of the way they tore at her skin.

Her pursuer's cry of surprise echoing in her ears, she sprinted uphill, desperate to avoid the clearing that opened vacantly to her left. They must have seen her running, but she didn't care. The safety lay somewhere there in the woods, behind the hill maybe, or anywhere where these people were not present.

More breaking bushes exploded to her left. Darting back toward her previous hiding place, she tripped over a cluster of roots, but catching a nearby branch, managed not to fall. The cliff had plenty of footholds, she remembered. Upon climbing it, she would be out of their reach for a little while, enough time to race away, putting a respectable distance between her and these awful people, enough to reach the safety of the town, even if she had to run all the way without stopping to catch a breath.

The plan that might have worked but for another pursuer joining the chase. She could hear their footsteps everywhere now, breaking more branches, careless of the noise they made. But why should they keep quiet? They were the chasers, not the hunted prey.

In desperation, she threw herself into the thickest of the bushes, clawing her way toward the other side, scratching her skin, only to be pulled to her feet by someone's fierce yank.

Pushing and kicking, she fought the gripping hands wildly, but her captor held onto her with the firmness of a stone, hurling her toward the nearest tree, sending her crashing against it. Stifling a cry, she kicked at his legs, then drew her elbow into his temptingly exposed ribs. It went in with enough force to make him groan and momentarily relax his grip.

Frantically, she twisted, trying to slip along the wide trunk or around it, kicking at the man again as she did this. He was back, trying to recapture her, but she was faster, her push fierce enough to make him waver.

The freedom flickered for a heartbeat, and she dashed for it, only to smash sideways into the broadness of someone's chest. This time, she was held more expertly, over her shoulders and across her chest.

"Stop fighting," he was saying. "Stop it! I don't want to hurt you."

She wriggled madly for another heartbeat, then the familiarity of his voice struck her. The Long Tails man! Her relief was so sudden and overwhelming, it made her dizzy, and the firmness of his grip turned into a welcomed thing. She might have fallen if he let her go, her legs weak, trembling badly.

"Let go," she muttered, pushing him without much spirit.

He didn't even move. "Not so fast, wild girl. First, promise you won't fight or try to get away."

Stubbornly, she said nothing, hearing the others gathering around. Two more men, her ears reported. The foreigners? she wondered, refusing to look up. Their rapid speech in the tongue she didn't recognize confirmed this conclusion.

"Will you behave?" Again, the way he talked reassured her, his voice changing when addressing her, in some imperceptible way.

"Yes." It came more as a grunt, or maybe a childish pout.

He turned her around gently but firmly, fastening his grip on her wrists as he did.

"So you were eavesdropping again." It came out as a statement, a light confirmation, not overly concerned.

"I no listen," she said, struggling mildly in an attempt to free her hands. "I just walk around."

"Of course." He sounded as though about to burst into laughter, while his companions' scowls deepened. "Well, first of all, tell us what you heard while walking around."

"Nothing," she said, feeling silly. It was difficult to look at him while held from behind; still, she twisted her body, wishing to see what his face held. "I no part, your scheme, I no help."

That wiped the flickering amusement from his face, causing his eyebrows to climb high. "What exactly will you not do? What help do you mean?"

"No help," she repeated, feeling better now that he was not amused anymore. She might have been caught in an awkward situation, but he was acting as embarrassingly by plotting against the War Chief and letting strangers like her hear about it. "No say where War Chief play, what side of field."

"Oh, that," he said, shrugging with an open contempt. "Your help is not vital, or even needed. We can do without you."

"And testify," she said, angered by his disdainful dismissal. "No testify like you say."

That made his eyes darken with rage and his hands tighten painfully around her wrists. "You know that you are likely to be killed here and now?" he said in a low, growling voice. "You can't be that stupid as to not be aware of this possibility."

The stab of the icy fear in her stomach was piercing, making her urge to break free more urgent. Why did she feel safe to play games with this man, as though they were back in the town or the ceremonial grounds, the man whom she heard openly suggesting murdering the leader of the people they came visiting with peaceful intentions? Oh, Mighty Glooskap!

"I no care," she said, gathering the remnants of her courage, hoping that her fear wasn't showing.

He pushed her back toward the clearing, not as gently as before, but not too roughly, either. The phrases spoken rapidly in the foreign tongue made her regret her words even more. Were they discussing this? How to execute her?

Back upon the clearing, the man who had come running here earlier had managed to catch his breath and was peering at them with open curiosity.

"What is this all about?" he demanded, more puzzled than irritated.

"Nothing," said her captor curtly. "What is your news?"

"The Honorable Elder sent me. You must come back to the

town with me, and you must hurry."

"Why?"

She could feel the Long Tails man tensing.

The newcomer's eyes remained blank. "The councils are holding a meeting, the town's and the clans' councils."

"Oh." The foreigner's fingers were still pressed against her wrists, holding them in an uncompromising grip. "I see that Hegweh is a resourceful man."

"Oh, well, one doesn't need to be resourceful, not when the spirits send one a perfect opportunity." The townsman's chuckle was soft, caressing the afternoon air. "The wild hothead of the War Chief's youngest son made it easy for everyone by beating someone senseless, and in the middle of the ceremonies, too. The councils are gathering to discuss the incident, as they should. That is all."

She felt the air escaping her chest all at once, as though she had been hit in her stomach. It had happened to her, long ago, when she had still been very young, falling out of that tree she and some boys were competing on climbing. A wide branch had slowed her fall, had saved her from breaking limbs or harming herself in more serious ways, but the way it crushed against her stomach was so vicious, so merciless, she could never forget the sensation of the all-encompassing terror, of the terrible panic when she had realized that she could not draw a breath, not even a little. And now, the sensation was back, causing her chest empty of air, its muscles paralyzed, refusing to fill it with a new supply of the vital flow.

"The spirits, indeed, favor this man's enemies." The Long Tails man's voice came from far, far away, muffled. "I suppose we better hurry back." Pulling her lightly, he turned to face her, his eyes bright but frowning rapidly. "What's wrong?"

She was still struggling to catch her breath, her thoughts in spectacular disarray. Okwaho was back, and he was in trouble. But how and when? It had been only half a day…

"Are you feeling well?" He was still securing her wrists with one hand, but the other was now encircling her shoulders, supporting. "Better sit down and rest." Propelling her toward the sprawling roots one of the men had squatted upon before, he looked at one of his companions. "Stay here and keep an eye on her until I come back."

"Please, I go with you. Please." It came out weakly, no more than a whisper. "Please, I make no trouble. I no tell."

His frown deepened. "You can't." A curt nod made one of the men come forward. "Give me your shirt. I need something to tie her with." Pressing his lips, he scowled against his companion's protests. "I'll replace it with another if it gets damaged. I would have used mine, but I need it now, to impress their Town Council." A mirthless grin flashed, to disappear quickly. His eyes were on her again. "Don't make any trouble. Just wait patiently."

"Please." She heard her own voice trembling, breaking. "Please come, I come, with you. I do anything." The idea sparked. "I testify. Like you want, remember, want I testify. I will. Please."

His eyes were as narrow as a pair of slits. "No, you stay here, wild girl. It is safer this way." The creases lining his forehead cleared. "You don't have to worry about your safety. You will not be harmed. I will make sure of that." For a fraction of a heartbeat, his gaze took an additional glint, a strange glow that made her feel better. Safer, indeed. "You just wait patiently and make no trouble." He drew a deep breath, then straightened up resolutely. "Keep an eye on her, and make sure she is not harmed," he tossed to his remaining companion, then turned back to the townsman. "Let us hurry."

"Wait!" she screamed, but they didn't even turn their heads, disappearing quickly in the colorful foliage.

"You sit and no yell," said the remaining man curtly, his accent dreadful, impossible to understand. His push was firm, even if not aggressive, making her plop into the offered seat of the tree's roots. "Aingahon say no harm, yes, but you no trouble. Or I harm."

If she had any energy left, she might have glared at him, or even said something. As it was, she pulled her legs to her chest, daunted, spent. Oh, Mighty Glooskap, why didn't she wait patiently? Why didn't she just return to the town before, when it was still possible?

CHAPTER 17

"The reason for the quarrel is immaterial. To yell and shout and defile the ceremony with violence is a crime that is unforgivable in itself."

The man of the Town Council raised his voice, which already had a thundering quality to it. For the benefit of all those who were listening avidly, reflected Ganayeda, all the curious townsfolk crowding the open space near tobacco plots, not permitted to participate in the meeting but not asked to move out of hearing range, either. Usually, the meetings of the Town Council enjoyed the respectable privacy they demanded.

"What are our benevolent spirits, the Right-Handed Twin, the Three Sisters, the Thunderers, to think now, hearing anger and curse words instead of the thanksgiving speeches, instead of the fragrant tobacco smoke, along with the good will our elders and leaders were sending them through the words of gratitude and dances?" The man's piercing gaze encircled his audience, the members of the council, the Clans Mothers, the various leading warriors. "What are they to make out of it?"

From his vantage point, not far away from the squatting or standing circle, waiting to be summoned to testify, as he knew he would be, Ganayeda sought out his father's face, rewarded with only a glimpse of it, the view of the half-turned profile, with its proud aquiline nose and the prominent cheekbones, the pattern of scars that had always been a part of it entwining in an intricate manner, like war paint. He remembered himself studying this pattern as a child, fascinated, attracted to touch, to trace the sharp lines with his finger, never daring to do that. Well, now all he

wanted was to know what Father's face held. What was he going
to do about all this?

"Young people are young people," said another council
member mildly. "Sometimes they do quarrel. Our Great Spirits
are surely aware of this tendency. They created us this way. They
won't be offended by an occasional slip." The man paused to let
his words sink in. "I say this incident is not important enough,
neither to warrant the Town Council's involvement, nor to ruin
our benevolent deities' enjoyment of the ceremonies held in their
honor. I suggest we leave it to our honorable Clans Council and its
consideration, to settle the matter between the two young men
and their families to their satisfaction."

That went well with the foreboding circle of leading women
who stood behind the squatting elders, their faces dire, their
hands crossed over their chests or their hips. Oh, yes, Clans
Mothers did not like the Town Council stepping on their
authority. If the fight had not occurred on the day of the
ceremony, in between the festivities, it would have been left to
their sole deliberation to resolve.

"I do not share your opinion as to the spiritual harmlessness of
this matter, brother," said the first man, his frown deepening.
"The young people should be able to hold a tighter grip on their
tempers. Otherwise, they will not turn into respectable members
of the community."

"I didn't say this incident was harmless, and I'm not
suggesting to look with forgiveness upon the loss of temper that
was displayed here earlier. All I say is that we should let our
clans' leaders solve this problem, to reprimand the guilty, to ensue
punishment if the punishment is due."

The Heron Clan's leading woman leaned forward, clearing her
throat in a polite manner, demanding attention. "Let us not forget
that the quarrel happened in the interval, between the stages of
the ceremonial game. No sacred procedures were defiled and no
rituals violated." She cleared her throat again. "I believe our clans
leaders can deal with this matter, which is their duty and
responsibility to do."

A clear message, even if politely spoken. Ganayeda hid his

grin, noticing the impassive expression not wavering, not lifting off his mother's exquisitely chiseled face. She had been watching the entire meeting with her eyes calm and unreadable and her mouth relaxed, not pressed or twisted, sincere and as pleasant and serene as always. As though the matter had nothing to do with her or hers, as though she hadn't rushed all over the town earlier, between the Wolf Clan's longhouse, interviewing their victims and witnesses, and Ganayeda's Heron people's dwelling, where the culprit was pacing the corridor in a long, impatient stride, as tense as an overstretched bowstring, and as incensed.

He shook his head, incensed all over again himself. The young hothead! Why couldn't Okwaho control his temper better? Or just behave reasonably for a change. No matter what Onenha had done, it was inappropriate to yell at her in this way, and in the middle of the festivities, to threaten her and accuse her of every crime possible. Of course her man came to her aid. Wouldn't Okwaho himself have done the same in his place? Wasn't he screaming at the girl because she dared to say something nasty to his woman?

It was difficult to hang onto his own temper when he had brought Okwaho to his longhouse as instructed, to await the summons; difficult not to flare at the young buck and make matters nothing but worse.

"You are incurable, you know that?" he had said as they made their way along the narrow alleys, the silence too heavy, wearing on his nerves. "Nothing but a stupid boy, not a respectable man."

Okwaho's grunt marred the peacefulness of the air, his teeth clenched too tightly to let more reasonable sounds seep through.

"Why run around yelling at people, threatening women? What did you expect to happen?"

A forcefully kicked stone was his answer. "That filthy skunk Onenha was being nasty to my woman."

"And what of that? Women are nasty to each other sometimes. It is none of our business to solve their bickering."

The shorter longhouse towered ahead, its symbol of a heron carved in bold lines, wonderfully detailed. He had always wondered why their Wolf Clan longhouse, the largest and most influential in the town, never invested in a better symbol upon its facade.

"It's not that, and you know it," growled Okwaho, halting in front of the entrance, legs wide apart, as though ready to resist an attempt to drag him in. "Kentika is a foreigner, not adopted and not even accepted yet. She can barely speak our tongue. She has no friends and no family. To pick on her was too nasty of that stinking skunk Onenha, and so like that filthy piece of excrement, too. I swear I will kill her if something happened to Kentika, if she doesn't come back before evening falls. I don't care what the councils would want to do to me for that!"

"You are taking it too far." Beckoning the young man to follow, Ganayeda dived into the dimness of the storage room, relieved to be in the relative privacy of his home, craving the opportunity it offered to rest. "It wasn't as though your girl was all innocence. She beat Onenha hard enough to leave marks. No matter what Onenha said or did, it doesn't excuse the violence, and you know it. Mother must be furious with her. No wonder the wild thing has run away. Not that it was a wise thing to do." Shrugging, he watched the stormy eyes, boring into him, burning with fire. "That's the truth, Brother. Face it, instead of lashing out, hurting people and ruining ceremonies."

"No, it's not!" Refusing to move, Okwaho stood in the middle of the corridor, in front of someone else's compartment, deserted now, as the entire longhouse was. "You don't understand any of it. You don't know what it is like, to be a foreigner. You have never faced this sort of challenge. But Mother should have known better. She should have helped Kentika, instead of being stern and demanding. She was a foreigner too, once upon a time. She came from the lands of the Crooked Tongues, for all the great and small spirits' sake! She should have more compassion and understanding than anyone. But she hasn't, has she? She forgot all about it. And all the rest of our people don't understand." The handsome face twisted, turning frightening, ugly. "I will not stay with our people if that's the best they can offer, carrying on about the Great Peacemaker, forgetting that he was a foreigner, too. And you are no better. All incensed with the Crooked Tongues now, ready to go and fight them, despite what Father is trying to do. All because of some pretty face. And you know what?" The narrowed eyes flashed, having an almost victorious spark to them. "Now this sweet little Gayeri will have to adjust, to be like Kentika is here, a despised foreigner. No help, no family, no friends. Think about that pretty fox getting picked at and teased, and maybe even hurt, eh? Nothing out of the ordinary, just silly women's bickering."

Concentrating on the words of the town and clans' leaders, their argument still on, still raging with utmost politeness, Ganayeda tried to forget the wave of rage that had consumed him, the urge to grab his brother and shake him hard. How dared he mention Gayeri, or make it sound as though all he cared about were lusty thoughts! Oh, but the stupid troublemaker understood nothing, with his flashes of temper and his little savage who could not even be trusted to stay in the town for less than ten dawns without getting into a huge pile of trouble. To compare the wild thing to Gayeri was outrageous, and it was wrong, unacceptable.

Glancing at Okwaho now, his face closed and lips tight, he remembered how they glared at each other, ready to do the unthinkable, to start another fight maybe, just as Jideah came in, with their oldest daughter and a few other women of the longhouse in tow.

"What are you quarreling about?" she asked tiredly, pushing a pile of bowls she held beneath the nearest bunk. "As though the previous fight was not enough." The ringed eyes rested on Okwaho, clouded with an open reproach. "Sit down, and stop yelling at the top of your voice. You disturb the harmony of our longhouse."

"I can leave if my presence is so disturbing," muttered Okwaho, eyeing his hostess darkly, as challenging and unyielding as before.

"You can't until the councils call you. So just sit down and behave," said Jideah, unimpressed. Crouching with difficulty, she fished some trays and a large pot from under the same lower shelf, signaling to her companions to receive the goods. "Bring it to the girls, will you? And you, little one," her hand patted her daughter's arm warmly. "Go and find your sister and keep an eye on her until I'm back. She will do mischief if not watched. Just like that uncle of hers."

Nodding at his daughter, answering her shy smile—unlike her outspoken sister, this one was already reaching the self-conscious age, turning even more close-mouthed than before—Ganayeda made himself comfortable by pulling one of the hides that served as a blanket over his shoulders. It was getting cold, and the neglected fire of their compartment gave no warmth.

"So what was that all about?" she asked, straightening up with an effort, her face breaking into a crooked sort of a smile. "You two yelling at each other, about to break into another fight over some 'sweet little Gayeri' this time. Who is this fox?"

His stomach constricting again at the unexpected mention of *her*, Ganayeda rolled his eyes.

"Oh, it's just the girl we didn't manage to save," he heard Okwaho saying hurriedly. "I fancied her for a little while. She *was* little and sweet."

Arched eyebrows were his answer. "That's not what you've been yelling at the top of your voice."

"But that's what I meant," insisted Okwaho, eyes wide open, all innocence.

"Oh, you!" Now it was Jideah's turn to roll her eyes. "Your girl is busy struggling against the entire town. And what do you do? Run out there, looking for pretty sights."

The young man's face lost the traces of its briefly gained mirth. "I'll find her, and I'll make them accept her," he grunted, his face taking the color of the storm cloud again.

"You can't do it, and you know it." Matter-of-fact, she went toward the fireplace, reaching the embers with a nearby stick, stirring them idly, making the sparks fly. "She needs the acceptance of our women, of her clan's members and those of the others. You men have no say in any of it. You just flatter yourself with the thought that you do."

"If I have no say in that, I'll take her away and leave this town!" Okwaho's eyes were shooting fire bolts, to Ganayeda's slight satisfaction. Jideah was renowned for the sharpness and mercilessness of her tongue, but the young buck deserved that.

"I've been telling him that," he observed mildly, unable to fight the temptation to goad the wild thing.

She shot him a thoughtful look. "Come to think of it, that girl has not been doing that badly, even with no questionable presence of her violent protector. She is not a bad little thing, even if wild and strange-looking. I came to like her myself."

They both were staring at her now, taken aback. Jideah admitting to liking anyone, let alone a foreign girl with no proper ways? A puzzling statement.

She grinned back at them, pleased with herself. "She is strange and terribly foreign. A true savage, yes." Her eyes mocked Okwaho's direful frown. "Nothing womanly about her, either. And yet," shaking her head, she squatted next to the fireplace stones, holding her palms above the flames, as though in need of feeding on their warmth. "In her own very wild way, she has been gathering the sympathy of quite a few people. Your mother championed her to the point of exaggerating." Another log went into the pit, catching fire fast, making it crack in a friendly manner. "We all know that Seketa is kind and good-hearted to a certain point, but she is the Clan Mother of an important, not to say presumptuous, longhouse, and we were immersed in the last days before the ceremony. She should have been too busy to pay special attention to the troublesome girl, but she wasn't. By the way she kept saving that wild thing from conflicts, one could have claimed that she liked her, and not only wished to have peace in the Wolf Clan's longhouse."

Okwaho was leaning forward, listening avidly, mouth slightly opened, devouring every word.

"But for the hatred of spiteful foxes like Onenha and some others, she might have avoided getting into much trouble."

"So it wasn't her fault?" asked Ganayeda, now curious too.

She gave him an impatient look, a look that he recognized. The subject of the 'sweet little Gayeri' was not about to be dropped harmlessly.

"How would I know? I wasn't there. But even if the wild girl did the things she is accused of, she had been provoked, most clearly at that. I told that to our Clan Mother now that she went to the meeting." The look bestowed on Okwaho was not devoid of slightly amused sympathy. "You did a good thing by scaring Onenha this way. You did it badly enough to land yourself into trouble, but your wild escapade might help that girl, might warn the spiteful foxes to keep away from her."

And now, watching the Heron Clan Mother talking to this noble gathering, he understood her timely interruption better. So Jideah had put in a good word? She must truly like Okwaho's girl, as she would never have done it for Okwaho, or Ganayeda's family's sake alone. She had many admirable traits, this woman of his—clever, high-tempered, spirited, attractive, even after so many summers of mutual living—but kindness was not one of them.

"I suggest we resume our festivities," the Head of the Town Council was saying. "And let our Clan Mothers take care of the problem that lies within their area of responsibility as it is."

As the elders began shifting, nodding in agreement, about to get up, the deep voice of Hegweh, the Beaver Clan's representative in the council, made everyone turn their heads. "And yet, if allowed, I would like to take advantage of this noble assembly in order to ask a question of our war leader, the War Chief of our entire nation."

He saw the heads turning to Father, who had been standing in the front rows of the observers, slightly behind the Clans Mothers, where other prominent people would gather when willing, or allowed, to listen to the deliberations of the Town Council. Tall and as impressive as always, his headdress rustling with one upright feather, his face clear of paint, broad and weathered, displaying no decorations or tattoos other than the arresting pattern of scars alone, the war leader did not shrink under so many eyes, but met the people's gazes as he always did, calmly and good-naturedly, with the right measure of firmness in it.

"What do you want to know, brother?" he asked in a measured voice, his eyes flickering with pronounced coldness, the mutual dislike of the two men going back quite a few summers.

"Well, I believe we are entitled to hear your opinion on the new developments with the Crooked Tongues, our enemy from across the Great Lake." Getting up as to not be outdone by his rival in the matter of height, suspected Ganayeda, suddenly perturbed, the man turned to the watching people, encircling them with a meaningful gaze. "Are we to be kept in the darkness about what is happening with our enemies?"

"No, brother, no one is to be kept in the darkness," answered the War Leader, unperturbed. "When the War Council of our town and then the entire nation will gather to discuss this matter, no people of ours will go about with no knowledge and no insight of the decision reached."

The Beaver man's frown could rival that of the evening sky in its gathering darkness.

"And yet, we can inquire, can ask for your personal opinion on the news from across the Great Sparkling Water, in the face of the enemies growing bold enough to attack our settlements, such as Lone Hill; in the face of their possible union, a dangerous development that should be taken care of with no delay."

In the ensuing silence, the War Chief's voice rang out, as tranquil as before. "You know the procedure, Beaver Clan's representative. Until the War Council of our nation meets either here or near Onondaga Town, there is no use in speculating, or sounding private, ill-informed opinions." A brief pause accompanied with slightly raised eyebrows. "As a representative of your longhouse and the member of our Town Council, you should know our laws and customs better than this."

The air hissed, bursting from the tall man's widening nostrils. "I know our laws and customs well, War Chief."

The pause that followed bore the explosive quality of a thundercloud, and the danger of it. What was the man up to? wondered Ganayeda, perturbed, appalled by such bad manners being displayed. Luckily, Father was not in the habit of losing his temper, able to handle even the most vicious of opposition with the firmness and composure of a person sure of his power and position.

"Well, then, we can return to our ceremonial duties." The War Leader nodded to the surrounding people, eyes brushing past his rival, lingering for a heartbeat, as though daring the man. "We will discuss the peace and war matters, our people, their neighbors beyond the Western and Eastern Doors, and the ones from across the Great Sparkling Water, in due time."

"And what about the matters of plotting, of outright betrayal?" The words of the Beaver man caught many in the process of getting up or turning to go. "Are those also matters that would have to await this or that gathering's approval?"

Another spell of silence ensued, as loaded as before.

"Yes, those should be reported and left to the consideration of our Great Council of Five Nations." This time, the War Leader's voice rang more stonily. "Why do you ask obvious questions, Representative?"

Other people were staring at the Beaver man, the members of the Town Council and the others, while he glanced around furtively, as though looking for someone particular in the crowd.

"Because I came to the knowledge of plotting, or betrayal being done under our very eyes," he said finally, with the old resolution to his voice. "Of people of power and influence, respectable people, who have been conversing with our enemies, contacting their leaders in clandestine ways, receiving and sending messages behind our backs."

"What are you saying, brother?" The Head of the Town Council rose to his feet by now too, frowning direfully as he did this. "Why do you talk in a strange way?"

"Ask him!"

All eyes followed the accusing finger, resting on the War Chief again. Puzzled, Ganayeda saw Father's face turning stonier by the moment, and yet it had twisted for a heartbeat, contorted imperceptibly. Like a momentary ripple on the water, gone before noticed. He held his breath.

"I have no knowledge of your claims or barely veiled accusations." Father's voice had a thundering quality to it now, like the growling of a distant storm. "I came to no such information as this."

"And you say you didn't receive messages from the enemy, from the leader of the Crooked Tongues himself? You say you didn't conspire with them?"

The glare of the War Chief should have pushed the man to the ground, had gazes the ability to strike.

"You accuse me of conspiring against my people, the people I have led and protected for more summers than you can count on the fingers of your hands, the people I cared and fought for since I was a youth of little years?"

He stepped forward, and the Beaver Clan's man swayed back, while others just froze, even the members of the Town Council, even the Clans Mothers.

The Warriors Leader noticed none of it. "Your envy and hatred know no bounds, man of the Beaver Clan, but this time, you have taken it too far. I will not be accused by you, or anyone else for that matter, of betraying my people, people entrusted into my responsibility, people to whose well-being and prosperity I have dedicated my entire life. You are a petty man of no achievements, and I will not tolerate unfounded accusations from someone like you!" Another forceful step brought him closer to the flinching man, made his rival lean backwards, as though pushed by a gust of wind. "You will take back your filthy words, or you will regret it dearly."

The man paused to draw a deep breath, and the silence that fell was too heavy, too encompassing, making it difficult to breathe.

"Brother ..." The hand of the Town Council's leader rested lightly on the old warrior's back, but it seemed to bring the enraged man to his senses instead of startling him. "Let us go back to the ceremonies. If you wish to bring this matter, this man's unfounded accusation to our consideration, you are invited to do so after the festivities are over. Come, let us finish this day with appropriate thanksgiving speeches and offerings rather than anger and bad feelings."

Ganayeda watched his father's tense shoulders, the clenched fists. As the War Chief shook his head, obviously trying to get rid of the rage, or at least the sharpest edge of it, his heart went out to him. But for the timely intervention of the town's leader, it might have turned violent, worse than in Okwaho's case. Oh, Mighty Spirits!

"I have a witness to prove what I say." The Beaver Clan's man licked his lips, his hands trembling in a visible manner. "He is not here now, but I will bring him to testify before our council decides to discuss this matter, before the foreign delegation will leave."

While the War Chief whirled back at his accuser, his face a terrible mask, with no more calmness or typical composure to it, there was stir in the crowd, where the foreigners stood alongside their hosts, at the front rows, the place of honor.

"And who is your witness? Who would agree to lie on your behalf? Why isn't he here now?"

Again, the Beaver man was backing away, probably doing so without even noticing. The Head of the Town Council kept very close to the enraged warrior. They were friends of many summers, Ganayeda remembered, drawing closer as well. What if Father attacked that man, like Okwaho had earlier? What if he killed him right there on the spot, as he surely felt was his right?

"You are lying and trying to shame me before this honorable assembly, before this entire town," roared the War Chief, causing his adversary to lean backwards again. "But you are shaming yourself, instead. Had you had any witness, any proof, they would have been here now; otherwise, why paint yourself in such light? Why make such a fool out of yourself? Why turn me into your enemy?" The large eyes were blazing, burning with a terrible fire. "You were envying my position for summers, spreading gossip and filth whenever you could. But now you have taken it too far. Such an accusation in front of everyone cannot be ignored, cannot remain unanswered. You will either prove your words, or you will pay for your lies. I will make sure of that, and I will not rest until it happens, until you are made sorry for your despicable falsehood."

Again, the Head of the Town Council was signaling the War Chief with his hand, trying to steer him away from the rest of the confrontation. The other people came to life as well. One approached the unfortunate accuser, motioning him to cease, even though the man just stood there now, his entire willpower spent on the attempt to stay still, not to retreat anymore as it seemed.

Noticing the absence of his brother, Ganayeda spotted the

young beast standing next to Father, his body tense, pose alert, ready to fight if need be. Ready to bring more violence and trouble into the unfortunate meeting, was his private semi-amused conclusion.

He made his way there now too, aware of the unnatural quietness, as no one dared to say a word as yet—such a vast crowd, so silent. It frayed on his nerves, and on the nerves of the surrounding people, he could see that most clearly. It made everyone tense and afraid.

His stomach twisting, he looked around, encountering puzzled, or sometimes averted, gazes. What a terrible way to finish an unfortunate day, the second day of the ceremonies, expressed almost every face he saw. Would the Great Spirits understand?

He found himself echoing the question.

Oh, but it had all gone downhill since the day they had encountered the Crooked Tongues, since the day he had met Gayeri. The stony fist was back, squeezing his insides. Would Father agree to send a large enough force to retaliate, to open a true full-scale war? It would go against his plans, surely. And what did this man mean by saying that Father might have been conversing with the enemy leader in a clandestine way?

No, never, not a man of Father's integrity. But openly, yes, if he had a chance to contact the enemy leaders, had they united leaders to address, Father would not hesitate to open the talks. He had never tried to conceal his beliefs in this matter.

Shrugging, he hastened his step in order to catch up with the elders, now drawing away, his thoughts in a jumble. No, he would not start doubting Father, never. The jealousy-eaten bastard Hegweh was nothing but a filthy liar. He must be!

CHAPTER 18

Picking her step along the twisting pathways that wound their way between and around tobacco plots, separated from the rest of the town by a bit of a clear space that was all incline, Seketa strained her eyes, her ears pricked, listening. Not a murmur disturbed the deepening dusk, no stirring, no rustling. The night was coming down, to envelop the earth.

Perturbed, she pushed on, her worry welling, overwhelming. Where could he possibly be?

The rites down there at the valley were about to begin, yet no one but the faith-keepers went out as yet. Did he sneak away all the same? Would he? There was no privacy for the War Chief anywhere in the town, with so many people eager to talk to him, to discuss various matters, to ask questions or give advice, or to just chat idly, his various friends and peers. The War Chief was not his own man, but after a day like this, even such a prominent leader might wish to get away from watchful eyes and readily speaking tongues.

Yet, where to?

The dark mass of the fence was already upon her, when her ears picked up a sound. The crack of a branch, a rustling, as though someone threw a stone gently, made it roll into the greenery of the bushes.

"I see you managed to get away, too." His voice rang quietly, warm and unconcerned, his warrior's senses probably apprising him already about the nature of the approaching company. "I would expect them to keep you busy well into the night."

"Them? It's your son's trouble that kept me busier than I was supposed to be," she said lightly, heading toward the voice. From closer up, she saw his figure, squatting on an old stump, semi-hidden between the thick vegetation and among the broad leaves. "Such a nice day, turning into such an aggravating mess."

He grunted something in response.

Picking her way between the rustling plants, careful not to step on or smother any of them, she knelt beside him, greatly relieved. He looked calm, straight-backed and not sad, not desolate. Even his grunt held the usual calmness. The previous loss of temper did not seem to have left a lasting effect, neither on townsfolk nor on him.

"How is Okwaho?" he asked, moving thoughtfully, making a space for her to squat beside him. "Will the young hothead have to pay long and hard for his crimes?"

"No, he won't." She suppressed a smile. "He should have, if you ask me. But he got away lightly, like he always has. That boy has an easy life."

"Not that easy," he said grimly. "He went through much back in the Flint People's and their enemies' lands. He has matured through this span of seasons, hardened, grown wiser—one can see that, even if he still didn't find the opportunity to talk about any of it." His chuckle caressed the darkness. "He still has some things to learn, though. How to keep a hold on that temper of his, for one."

"His father had spectacular outbursts of temper back in his days."

His laughter was music to her ears. No, he was not going to take Hegweh's accusations hard. There was nothing to it, nothing but the jealousy of a petty man against a great leader. And yet … Oh, Mighty Spirits, why did she keep thinking that this alleged witness did exist?

"What compensation have the clans agreed on?"

She forced her thoughts back into safer channels.

"It didn't come to the gathering of the Clans Council at all. Everyone agreed that with both youths belonging to our longhouse, even if Onenha's man is not a Wolf Clan's member, it should be left to me, our longhouse's Clan Mother, to decide on proper procedures." She shrugged. "You see, Sgawah is the Beaver Clan's man, yes, but even if he takes his time to recover, the burden of taking care of him will fall on us, not on them. We will have to relieve our girl of her regular duties while caring for him. The Beaver Clan will not suffer. So they agreed not to demand compensation, unless he does not recover well. And if so, his family would be only correct if they complained and insisted on justice."

"Oh, he will recover." Her husband's voice rang with regular firmness, the voice of the leader, the reassurance in it welcome. "I visited that youth earlier, before the accursed meeting. He is a good boy; I always liked him. Well, he doesn't look like a person whose head has been cracked. He lost his senses because Okwaho's kick hit him in his temple, sharply at that. Now, a bit lower, and he might have cracked his jaw. That would have resulted in much damage to the poor boy." A silent shrug. "And to Okwaho as well."

Shaking her head, she reached for the nearest tobacco leaf, tracing its unevenness with her finger. "If you think that your son was unduly worried, you would be mistaken. That boy ran off and away from the town the moment the general meeting was over. So he doesn't even know what compensation he'll be made to pay."

"Why did he?"

"His girl, she is still missing, and he worries himself sick." She sighed. "With a good reason, I suppose. I should have kept a better eye on her."

His palm was warm on her shoulder, encouraging. "Let him handle his unruly treasure. She is his responsibility." His grip tightened in a welcome way. "He'll find her. If anyone can, it's him." A chuckle. "That boy has the senses of a forest creature. Something large and canine, with magnificent silvery fur, eh?"

She laughed softly. "You gave him his name."

"That I did."

She remembered Okwaho being born, a difficult delivery, such a large baby, stuck in her stubbornly, determined to go out in his way, not endangering his mother's life but not making it easy for her, either. Well, he had remained stubborn and unruly, as a baby, a toddler, a child, a youth, and now a man, always set on his own course of action, normally charming and easygoing, but not when provoked—then, the most spectacular stubbornness and temper would come out.

"Why can't he control his temper better?" she asked, frustrated with him on that score, as always.

The dusk seemed to lose some of its softness.

"Why, indeed?" he said quietly, with no more liveliness to his voice. "Why do we lose our tempers sometimes, in most embarrassing manners at that?"

Her hand went for his quickly, taking hold of it, pressing. "Because sometimes people manage to get under our skins; because there are always those who try hard to do that." He didn't attempt to take his hand away, and she turned to him, studying the outline of his face, closed and tight-lipped, but still noble, so prominent and attractive. "The greater person you are, the more there are those who would wish to see you going tumbling down."

She could feel his shrug. "I shouldn't have lost my temper the way I did. I behaved no better than Okwaho, and I can't even plead his circumstances or his young age."

"That despicable man accused you of terrible things. The circumstances were worse than those of Okwaho."

"Of betrayal!" he breathed. "How dared he? Me, who has served our people for so many summers, who has brought the Great Peacemaker to our lands and helped him to be heard and listened to." The air hissed, drawn forcefully through his clenched teeth. "I'm trusted by all our people, by our entire union of Five Nations. The members of the Great Council listen to me and ask for my advice; the War Chiefs of Flint People and Mountain People and the others consult me and trust my suggestions. Our Town Council and other prominent people don't think my ideas are so bad, but this worm, this ugly nonentity of the Beaver Clan allows himself to come up with such accusations, and in front of the entire town. How dare he?"

She wanted to hug him, to press him tight and hide him from

all this pain. He didn't deserve it, not this accusation!

"I know that my ideas concerning the Crooked Tongues are not always welcomed." His voice dropped and now was ringing gruffly, low and strained. "I know they would rather forget all about the possibility of peace with those nations. I know that even you would rather have me forget all about it." Now it was his turn to press her arm, to insist on not letting it go, as she was struggling to break free, if for no other reason than in order to turn and face him, to let her protests or arguments come out more eloquently. "I know your thoughts and concerns regarding this matter, and I respect them, Wife. I do prize your opinions. Like the rest of the town, I do not make the mistake of dismissing your advice, lightly or otherwise." The obvious smile in his voice made her unvoiced protests lessen. "And yet, I know that I'm right about it, and I do not do it because of the Peacemaker. I know he is gone. I had a hard time accepting this thought for long summers, but now I do. And yet ..." His sigh was light, barely heard. "And yet, I do want to make the last possible attempt." Suddenly, his voice dropped to a mere whisper. "There might be some cooperation this time, a measure of collaboration, a mutual effort coming from the other side of the Great Lake now that they are united. It may not work, but I want to give it a chance."

She caught her breath, understanding too well, wishing she didn't. Then there *was* a witness, there was. He did converse with the enemy, and just as his sons were busy fighting those same people. The thought of Ganayeda's face, pale with exhaustion, his dark, stormy eyes, the wounds upon his ribs and his shoulder, made her stomach constrict with anger, the anger that died as quickly, almost before it was born. Hadn't she trusted him her entire life? Didn't all people of his lands?

"Who?" she asked quietly, barely hearing her own whisper.

He was silent for a long time, not mistaking her question and not trying to avoid it by pretending misunderstanding.

"Hainteroh."

It came as a breath of air, not even a familiar word at first. But maybe, yes, a little, the forgotten past, her childhood, the town upon the windy bay, her family, her people; the neighboring longhouse of the Porcupine Clan, and the boy, a friend, to laugh and tease and grow up together; and then later on, the serious youth, in love with her, picking fights with the foreign boy, now her husband of endless summers. And then, and then … Seasons later, after she did the unspeakable by running away, by crossing the Great Lake in search of him, the man she loved, oh much later, this same Hainteroh, reappearing again, with the Crooked Tongues delegation, an escorting warrior, yet nothing but an angry enemy, causing so much trouble by his jealousy. The Peacemaker almost died because of him, and her husband too, but still he forgave, being such a great man, he forgave and didn't demand this youth's death. Because of his silly cousin, who had been in love with this same Crooked Tongues harbinger of trouble, but mostly because through his old-time rival he had seen the way to save the Peacemaker. Oh, what terrible days those were!

Beside herself, she pulled away, turning to face him, peering through the deepening darkness, desperate to see his features, to read what his eyes held.

"It can't be!"

He motioned her to keep quiet, a forceful gesture.

"I know it's strange and not easy to accept," he was saying, his voice quiet, calm, caressing, not strained or angered anymore. "But he seems to be quite a prominent leader there, in that hastily concocted union of theirs. So between the two of us, we may have a chance of making it work."

She still stared at him, speechless.

"It wasn't easy to establish this communication, you see. He was the one to initiate it, actually. Well, of course he was. It wasn't difficult to find me, while I couldn't possibly know what became of him. Or Two Rivers …" Even with the lesser ability to see, she could feel his mood darkening. "I still don't know what happened to him. Only that he is not around, but that the union of his vision, or some of it, came to exist, with our mutual friend heavily involved, an influential person these days, a leader, a prominent one."

Gathering her senses, she tried to make her mind work. "Are

you certain he is willing to work toward the goal that you are trying to achieve? He wasn't for peace before. If anything, he made so much trouble, trying to ruin it all ..."

"That was before the Peacemaker," he said softly, his confidence not to be shattered, not anymore. "But he must have spent enough time in this wonderful man's company to fall under his spell. All of us who have known him did, so why not your former admirer?"

The mischievous note in his voice was unmistakable. She felt the urge to sink her elbow into his ribs.

"Don't remind me of that. I never forgave him the trouble he brought along while visiting our lands. If you had died, I would have killed him with my own hands." His arms tightening around her made her feel better. "What became of your cousin, do you know that?"

He shook his head, still holding her tightly, as happy as she was inside his embrace, or so she hoped.

"The way we send messages, one can't communicate more than a few encouraging words, the confirmation of the promise to work to the same end." His chuckle was soft, floating in the strengthening wind. "Regretfully, it prevents any gossip in reaching me from the other side." A light shrug. "But I do hope that she is with him and as happy as we are."

"Me too," she said, remembering the exquisitely pretty, light-headed thing she had come to know very briefly during those long-forgotten, turbulent days.

Then the awareness of the reality came back, and she tensed, her sense of well-being disappearing.

"So there is a witness," she whispered, leaning so close her lips brushed against his ear. "How do we deal with that?"

"We'll see," he said quietly, as composed as before, but the easy warmth his entire being had radiated was gone. "If he appears, I'll deal with it, whoever it is. Someone from among the foreign delegation, the filthy rat has said. Well, I suppose my messenger did not keep his mouth as closed as he should have." This time, she could see him strengthening his head, holding it proudly, unafraid. "I have nothing to hide from our people, nothing to be ashamed of. The possible peace with the Crooked Tongues I have been advocating and pushing since before I was even a War Chief, quite a few tens of summers and more. There is nothing new about it. Well, if it wasn't called a betrayal before, then it won't be named as such now, even though a few more frowns than usual would appear." Another shrug. "We'll deal with it."

She was trying to think clearly. "I would take it straight to Onondaga Town and the prominent people there, even the Head of the Great Council. He would receive you, would listen to what you have to say in that matter. Bring it up before him, including that last message you received from the other side. Be open about it, enlist his help, or at least his good will." She paused, pushing away the flattering fringes that managed to escape her tight braid. "Don't let our town be involved, not after what happened. Let them find all of it out after it's been aired in the Great Council. This way, witness or not, your actions won't look as though you are alone in it and acting against your people's interest."

He was pressing her tight again, his smile radiating through every pore of his skin. "You are a wise woman, Seketa. The wisest and the kindest. And the most beautiful, too. There is no luckier man than me in the entire world of the Right-Handed Twin's creation."

She nestled into his embrace. "I wish you had no further duties tonight."

His smile again warmed the darkness. "This won't be a long affair this time. With the mood this town plunged into, the gathering in the valley will not be like that of the day before. A few quick speeches, two official dances, and we will be done with this unfortunate day."

CHAPTER 19

To get rid of the stupid shirt that tied her wrists behind her back in a sloppy manner turned into a real possibility as the darkness fell. The man who had been left to watch her was busy pacing back and forth, tapping an anxious, impatient rhythm with his feet, too preoccupied to pay her light wriggling any attention.

She had been careful not to do it when he was glancing at her, a rare occurrence, usually accompanied with a puzzled shake of his head, or even an occasionally derisive snort. Unable to fight the temptation, her nerves as taut, as on edge as his must have been, she would stare back, refusing to succumb to her fear. The Long Tails man told him not to hurt her, and it didn't seem as though in this particular quarters his words were in a habit of being overlooked.

"Why look?" she had asked him the last time, when the staring contest lasted for too long for even her peace of mind. "Expect I lay an egg?"

He snorted loudly, his forehead creasing with an intricate pattern, the puzzled expression making him look silly.

"You are something." It came out as a grunt. "I never understand, no understand why he wants to take you."

"Take me where?" She tried to disregard the chilling surge that ran down her stomach, attempting to freeze it.

He just shrugged, turning away and resuming his pacing.

"No one take me," she insisted, suddenly too frightened to go back to her squirming, her ties about to come off. "He just keep, keep here, until testify. You know, back in town, the War Chief. He no want me to interfere. Because I listened."

As if it was important to explain all this to him. His raised eyebrows told her how silly she was.

"He wants take, take you home, wild girl," he said after a while, his back still toward her, peering into the deepening dusk. "He fancy you. Why, I no understand, but he does. Clear, you see? One see clear that he fancy. So," another light shrug, "you go our lands. But I don't care. I live another town, not his town. So no see you around."

"He can't take me," she protested, aghast. "I belong man, man here, married, live with man. He can't steal. You no war. You can't take women."

"No war now." Coming closer, he knelt beside her, causing her to press into the tree trunk she had rubbed her tied wrists against earlier. There was no disturbing expression to his eyes, but she didn't want to have any of these people close, not after what he said. "No war now, but if he does, does other plan, then yes, yes war. Eh?" His gaze measured her, clearly wondering. "You foreigner, that's clear, but you must understand some things."

She shut her eyes against the probing intensity of his stare, unwilling to listen, unwilling to understand. Oh, but she did overhear enough to know that the Long Tails man was willing to endanger his life and those of his peers, his entire delegation for that matter—many of them unsuspecting, she surmised—to get the War Chief off his path of making peace with the Crooked Tongues. Even by violent means. Didn't he say it to that dreadful man from the town? And what if ...

She thought about the deepening darkness. It was evening already, past the ceremonial activities, past the thanksgiving speeches with their fragrant tobacco smoke and other offerings. No testifying could be done now, could it? They said the town council was gathering, but not now, in the darkness. Surely they didn't gather in the evenings like that, on the days of the ceremony. Even though Okwaho had done something, something terrible to warrant that. *Oh, Benevolent Glooskap, please keep him safe!*

"We need run maybe, eh?" The vibrating voice reached her, coming from too close a proximity. He was still kneeling, still staring at her! She could feel the warmth his body radiated, the waves of anxiety coming from it. He wasn't as calm or indifferent as he pretended to be. He was worried and in a need to talk. The realization made her feel safer, somehow. "Need to be ready. They chase maybe, and he leave like that, say nothing. What do I do with you?"

Encouraged further, she gathered enough courage to open her eyes and face him. "You untie. First, untie, then see." His frown was deepening, but she paid it no attention, the spark of hope too tempting not to cling to. "If need run what do with me tied, eh? Can't run this way."

In the gathering darkness, it was difficult to see his expression, but she could feel his hesitation, his indecision coming out like sunrays, almost perceptible.

"The Long Tails man, he be angry if you not manage, if have to leave without me."

"The Long Tails man?" Suddenly, he sprang to his feet. "We are all Long Tails men, girl, and he say keep an eye, keep safe, not let go." He was towering above her, nearly spitting with rage. "He leave here, guard you. How stupid! No come back, no tell what is happening. And it's your fault. You make him think wrong, not clear. You make all the trouble." As suddenly, he was back squatting, leaning forward, his face thrust so close she could see every pore of it, every speckle, every bead of sweat.

Terrified, she coiled into a ball out of instinct, her limbs reacting on their own, her pressed legs straightening with every bit of force they could muster, shooting upward and into his chest, pushing him away, to hurl into the next tree and crash against it quite strongly, making a strange squeaky sound.

Swaying, she tried to leap to her feet, losing her balance as she did so, her hands pulling hard, yanking at the ties, desperate to break free, to be ready for his attack, the retaliation that would be forthcoming. Her panicked mind kept yelling at her, her racing heart reinforcing the warning. It was thundering in her ears, the only sound to penetrate the raging waves of fear.

Loosely tied, the silly shirt came off quite readily, despite the strange way she was half-lying on her side, half-sitting, and as she sensed him nearing, it was easier to roll away, to avoid his grabbing hands, to kick at his legs, instead.

He didn't waver this time, but as his moccasin neared her with ardor, she didn't try to avoid the kick, catching it with both hands, yanking hard. In a heartbeat, he was beside her, landing with a resounding thud, the muddy earth splashing everywhere.

Scrambling to her feet with the aid of every limb possible, she caught a glimpse of his bow, lying temptingly unattended, not far away, offering help. She didn't try to think any of it through. One leap and the desired weapon was in her hands, to swing at him as though it were a spear while he came after her, more throwing himself forward than leaping, as panicked as she was. The realization that gave more power to her movements.

The sharp edge of the bow slashing over his face, it struck him hard enough to make him waver, to grope his way blindly as he tried to reach her despite her attack, his hands claws, one eye blinking, a crimson spot gathering above it, spilling over, gushing out of the gaping cut.

This time she had enough presence of mind not to ruin a good weapon by more mindless pounding. One strike over his head was enough to make him fall back, to squirm in the mud, spluttering and shouting unintelligible things.

Welcoming the momentary break, she looked around, then, spotting the abandoned quiver, she dashed for it madly, as though all the bad creatures, or even Malsum himself, were after her. Just to get away from here!

The touch of the decorated leather gave her more power. Not knowing what to do next, she didn't spend a heartbeat on looking at her fallen enemy, but broke into a mad run, straight into the darkness, chancing a bad fall with the breakneck speed she raced at, but unable to slow down, her fear making her run even faster.

Back to the town and Okwaho, and safety and normal people, those who did not plot against great leaders, who did not wish to shoot at them or just discredit them before their own countryfolk, did not try to kidnap women from the places they visited in a peaceful manner. What terrible people they were, with that Long Tails man being the worst, making friends with her only to use her against the War Chief, or kidnap her if she didn't cooperate.

The drums were pouring to her left, a calm, monotonous sound. The festivities, oh, yes, how could she forget about those? They must be still celebrating, the second day of the ceremony. How many days were they to go about it, thanking their spirits and deities?

The moon was shining more brightly, as full as on the night before, wonderfully round. She slowed her step, then hesitated. It would be safer to hide in the town, of course. To put as much distance as possible between herself and the man she had hurt. The double palisade fence was a reassuring measure of safety.

However, back in town she might get into more trouble, with Onenha, Ehnida, and the other filthy foxes she had forgotten all about through her afternoon's misadventures. Was it not wiser to look for Okwaho's mother, to try to talk to her, and maybe explain, to let her know about the plotting foreigners? Oh, yes! Having brought the influential woman news about her husband and the danger he might be in, she, Kentika, might be forgiven some of her crimes.

Still deep in thought, she began treading her way toward the valley, careful to make no sound. There must be a way to make it right again. Okwaho's mother was a reasonable woman. She would understand, and she would know what to do.

Did the Long Tails man testify already? Was the War Chief in trouble on account of that clandestine meeting of his?

The darkness dispersed, together with the thinning vegetation. From her new vantage point, she could see the fire and the people around it, some walking, some standing, some fiddling with the clouds of smoke—the faith-keepers? There were no dances as far as she could see, and no offerings of food. No happy commotion like yesterday. On the contrary, the current ceremony looked like a solemn gathering of the elders and other prominent people in their colorful attire. The rest of the town was not around at all.

In the generous moonlight, she found it easy to recognize the Clans Mothers, an eminent group that had formed half a circle around the fire, notable and foreboding, watching the procedures, their dresses as beautifully embroidered as on the day before.

Even from such a distance, it was easy to sense their foreboding mood.

The men around the fire were moving slowly, measurably. She could see the War Chief's figure, easy to pick out, even though the man's attire did not differ from the rest of his peers, his headdress as low and round as those of his fellow dignitaries, displaying a thin line of colorful plumage as opposed to an unpainted, upright feather belonging to other leaders. He was standing near the fire, watching it, his legs wide apart, hands crossed on his chest, an arresting view, impossible to miss.

How easy it might be for a good shooter, she thought suddenly, a shaft of ice piercing her chest, making it hurt. Standing where she was, pointing his bow. One single arrow and the prominent leader would be no more. Was that what the Long Tails man was planning?

Involuntarily, her eyes scanned the surrounding trees, her senses trying to reach out, to feel the darkness. It was bright enough to see that part of the valley, but not the rustling foliage all around her. Was someone coming?

There were sounds, yes, the woods murmuring and creaking, whispering their mysterious night tales. No invaders, not as far as she could judge, but how could she be sure? That man she had wounded back by the brook, could he not gather his senses and rush into a hot chase? If so, he would be very near now. Oh, Mighty Glooskap!

Clenching her teeth against their clattering, she tried to listen, her hands clutched so tightly around the bow and the quiver of arrows, she could not feel it anymore, her eyes wandering with no purpose, not registering what they saw. To listen to her senses was more important. What was that creaking still far, far away? Was it someone progressing in a hurry?

The opposite hill was lit as brightly as the valley below, the protruding cliff upon it of the same height as she was, hiding in a shadow. For a heartbeat, her eyes tried to penetrate the darkness, then another suspicious sound took her mind away. She needed to get away from here!

Stepping on carefully, determined not to let the panic get the better of her, not this time, she traced her way down the hill, two steps, then five more. The valley was still visible, the flickering fire making the figures around it stand out. The War Chief was speaking now, extending his hands in an obvious manner, addressing the sky spirits. She could hear the hum of his voice overcoming the fading drumming.

As though answering his words, or maybe eager to participate, to receive the gratitude it deserved, the moon made an effort to break free from the surrounding clouds, shining with new power, brighter than before. The world came alive in the silvery light, the valley, the people, the surrounding woods, even the shadowed shelf of the opposite hill.

Incredulous, she stared at it, the crouching figure on its edge looking barely alive, just a part of the scenery, like another cluster of bushes, or a rock, but different, grim and menacing, meaning death.

Her heart stopped, then threw itself wildly against her chest, in a terrified manner. As she struggled not to fall, she saw the figure moving lightly, imperceptibly, the silhouette of the stretched bow shifting, seeking a better angle. In such generous light, it would not miss its target, she knew; it could not.

Her own bow came to life at once, acting in complete disregard to her will. Outside herself, she watched it coming up firmly, deliberately, the decorated quiver slipping down, to fall onto the ground, discarded, having yielded the much-needed arrow already, to fit into the bowstring perfectly, belonging there. The previous heartbeat was not yet over—or maybe it was just that her heart had slowed its pounding, intending to stop for good—when the man on the opposite shelf jerked to life, looking up sharply, moving with his entire body, he and his bow.

Facing her? She couldn't tell.

The recoil of the released string made her waver, catching her by surprise. But of course it did. All those actions, they weren't her doing. She wasn't responsible for any of it.

Clutching the sturdy bow, she tried to understand what happened, the hiss of the flying arrow not surprising, familiar from the days of her village, but not the push that it brought along. It forced her to fight for balance, as she watched the crouching figure on the other side losing its solidness, waving its arms as it was hurled back, to disappear in the dark mass of the bushes behind it.

Compromising on the battle for the upright position by leaning against the nearby tree, she didn't dare to let her highly prized weapon go, even though one of her arms had lost some of its power, the upper part of it on fire, hurting with every passing moment. Trembling, she tried to see what was wrong with it, but her ears kept insisting, kept trying to steal her attention. Someone was coming up her hill, someone who must have followed her footsteps. Oh, Benevolent Spirits!

In desperation, she glanced back toward the valley, still brightly lit, still full of voices and rolling drums. The ceremony proceeded, undisturbed. They were not about to acknowledge her contribution or to help her out in their turn. Even the opposite hill was now lifeless, with no one to crouch upon the protruding rock. If it was the Long Tails man, he would not capture her and keep her unharmed, not anymore.

Clenching her teeth against their wild knocking, she slipped along the supportive roughness of the trunk, her bow thrust forward, dancing in her hands. With no arrow, it was a useless thing unless she proposed to fight with it using it as a spear or a club, like she had against her captor before.

A futile hope. The remnants of her strength were seeping away, with not enough left to withstand the attack of an angry toddler, let alone the enraged owner of the stolen weapon.

Oh, Mighty Glooskap, oh, benevolent creator of everything good!

The man was already there, treading on the shrubs carelessly, breaking many of them as he ran.

"Oh, Mighty Spirits!" he exclaimed, and the sound of his voice made everything right again, the fear and pain fading away.

Trembling, she clung to his arms, as they groped her forcefully, pulling her to her feet. Even though it hurt terribly, the pressure of one of his hands upon her harmed arm, she welcomed even this, clinging to him in force, wishing to curse the bow that got in their way.

"I can't believe I found you," he was murmuring, talking in a breathless rush. "What were you thinking running away like that? And why is..." His grip shifted, moved up toward her shoulder, bringing relief. "Are you hurt?"

He was pushing her away from his chest, probably in order to see better, but she wasn't ready to leave the safety of his embrace, not yet.

"I no, no hurt," she muttered, pressing back stubbornly, with enough force to make him give up. "I'm good."

"You are bleeding!" His hand was sliding back down, probing around the place where the fire was the worst. "What happened?"

Again, he moved her away gently, even if forcefully this time, his eyes narrow, straining to examine her in the moonlight that was already dimming again. His leg kicked her bow away with little ceremony. "Where did you get this toy?"

But as she swayed, his lightness disappeared as quickly as it came.

"Kentika, you are not well. Tell me what happened!"

Clenching her teeth against their annoying clattering, she motioned toward the valley and the opposite hill. "Th-there... the man, was man, t-try to shoot..." She could feel his body tensing, leaning toward the indicated direction, pulling her along, not ready to let her go. "Th-the man, there, on rock, m-man with bow..."

"Where is he?" he asked curtly, clearly seeing the advantage of the pointed position as opposed to the progressing ceremony down below.

"Gone... shoot... I shoot..."

Again, he was staring at her, holding her at arm's length. "With this bow? Why?"

"He try shoot... War Chief..."

"What?" This time his voice exploded in an outright exclamation, and she wondered if the people in the valley had heard him shouting. "Tell me what's going on!"

But the strain was getting the better of her, and the trembling that had attacked her before was nothing compared to the outright shaking that made it impossible to think lucidly, let alone to talk in a reasonable way, or even stand on her own.

Back in the safety of his arms, she tried to fight the choking sensation, but the tears were gushing out in an unstoppable flow, washing over her face and his chest, rendering her useless, but also cleansing away the last day's horrors, she knew. As long as he held her close, it was all right to cry, all right to break and sob and make stupid noises, or smear the pureness of his decorated shirt. He would not laugh or get angry, and he would not leave her alone anymore.

CHAPTER 20

"So, you'll have something to do to keep you busy through the Cold Moons."

Stretching, Ganayeda did not fight the wideness of his grin, tired after the Water Drum Dance, but feeling better than he had in quite a few days. At least the smile came more easily now, not as forced as it had been since returning to High Springs to find nothing but trouble.

Well, now, two days later, with the foreigners' delegation departing at long last, in quite a hasty way, and the general tension in the town's authorities dropping to its natural level, with no one trying to accuse Father of treachery anymore, he finally felt as though he could relax and take care of himself, his physical state and the turmoil his mind had been in.

His fury with the Crooked Tongues did not lessen, but even so, knowing that he would be joining the impending raid, no matter how displeased it might make Father, he felt that he could wait with a measure of patience for it to happen, not burning to rush to the other side and save Gayeri no matter what the consequences. After all, what was this girl to him? Nothing but a passing acquaintance, a pretty face, a wonderfully warm smile, the openly adoring eyes.

The rage and frustration were back, to be pushed away quickly. He would go to the other side, and he would try to find her and rescue her, returning her to her village and her people, but she would have to be patient about it. He could not do the impossible.

"Oh, well, don't smirk about it." Okwaho's voice penetrated

the rising wave of turmoil, taking the edge off it, in the most timely manner. "I'll prepare that silly club in less than half a moon."

"Half a moon, Little Brother?" To use the detested epithet helped. He watched the brief storm cloud darkening the young, handsome face, making the good-natured smugness disappear, if only for a heartbeat. "If you think you can get away with a barely polished stick, think again. Sgawah may have forgiven you, may have made his peace with you and not only publicly, but trust Mother to make sure you will still pay the price, and to its fullest." Beaming into the deepening frown, he fought the urge to use the resented way of address again. Little brother, indeed. "She hopes it will teach you a lesson, will make you behave reasonably next time, like a mature man should." Another smirk. "I wish her well in her hopes for you. She is such a rational person, but even the most realistic people among us can succumb to illusions or a measure of wishful thinking, can't they?"

However, Okwaho regained his composure faster than in his pre-warrior days.

"Oh, yes, Mother would never let me get away with half a club done," he said, laughing, eyes on the breaking circle of dancers they had just left themselves. "But I'll still make it in half a moon, all polished and pretty, easy to handle and with a good weighting tip to balance the top. That'll be enough. I won't be spending my treasures of flint on Sgawah, forgiveness or not." The large eyes sparkled, challenging. "Half a moon, Brother. What would you bet against this claim?"

Now it was Ganayeda's turn to lose the more beaming quality of his smile. The annoying skunk. How was he now to get away from the challenge without losing some of his priciest possessions, or a measure of his dignity, instead? There was no way out of it, and he could not even curse his brother beneath his breath. The young buck hadn't started it. He had.

"My spear against that pretty javelin you brought from the lands of the rising sun." Would that make the troublemaker back away from his challenge?

"That's not an even bet," protested Okwaho, waving both

hands. "My new spear is ten times better than your old stick with a flint tip."

Oh, yes, it was going to work! He didn't dare to believe his luck as yet. "Oh, so now we are not so sure?"

"Yes, we are sure, we are. Half a moon and that club is ready, good enough to pass Mother's and Sgawah's judgment. But we can't bet unequal things. Add something to that old spear." The young man pursed his lips, his pointed eyebrows almost meeting each other across the wideness of his creased forehead. "Either that, or bet that embroidered, prettily decorated quiver of yours. I'll put my Flint People's spear against it. How about that?"

"Nothing that belongs to my bow will be going into this bet!"

But the smugness was back, pouring out of the glittering eyes. "So, we aren't as sure ourselves now, are we?"

Oh, but he could have killed the annoying pusher. "I might agree in order to see you toiling day and night, with no pause to eat or relieve yourself. Because that's what you'll have to do to win that bet. And that's what you *will* do, you annoying piece of meat. I know you too well."

"Oh, what a foresight, Brother. You amaze me with your ability to see the future." Okwaho's beam was all happiness. "So the spear and the quiver against my javelin?"

"No, only the quiver. Take it or leave it."

"Done!" The young man began turning away, still smirking. "I wanted that quiver of yours since I was little. It'll be nice to have that thing."

"When I am the new owner of your javelin, I'll put it to great use." Glancing at the commotion to their left, with women now busy arranging clusters of mats around the boiling pots, he sniffed the air, enjoying the wonderful aroma. "Wait, I need to talk to you."

"What? Now?" Okwaho's elaborately made and decorated warriors' lock swung as the young man halted, balancing his weight on one foot, the other still hesitating in the air, poised to charge in the direction of the delicious smell. "Later, man, later. I'm hungry."

"The food will wait. Come."

"Where to?"

"Over there." Indicating the sacred fire, now abandoned save for the faith-keepers, Ganayeda rolled his eyes. "It won't take long, and your woman will make sure to save you a plate full of the best of it."

The young man's frown cleared at once, replaced by the typical mischievous twinkle. "Kentika? I wouldn't bet on that, not even the smallest shell from your quiver's decorations, the one that is about to peel off."

Against his will, Ganayeda laughed. "Actually, you can bet something more valuable than that. Not only will she save you that plate of the steamiest stew with plenty of meat, but she'll serve you this thing in the most proper of ways, like a good woman should. How about that? Want to bet that javelin now?"

The suspicious scrutiny of the narrowed eyes was his answer. "What do you know?"

"Nothing." Nearing the pleasantly dry, firmer ground that was flattened by many feet dancing around it for the entire morning, he headed on, pleased to see that the young man was following, even if with little enthusiasm. "I saw her in the company of my wife several times through this morning. Under Jideah's supervision, your wild girl can do nothing but well."

"Yes, I saw them too. I keep a close eye on her. I will continue to do that for the time being. With all those filthy foxes, of our longhouse and some of the others, one needs to be on guard." An angry snort marred the crisp high morning air. "Rotten skunks, each and every one of them!"

"Your fault, according to Jideah."

"Mine? How is it my fault?" Okwaho halted so abruptly, his feet made a screeching sound.

"You've been fooling around in your earlier days, haven't you? Well, that would account for some of the bad feelings. Women have good memories, Brother. Didn't you know that?"

"What does fooling around have to do with any of it?" the young man cried out, still staring at Ganayeda, refusing to move.

With the food commotion and even the sacred fire safely behind them, with voices of people reaching them dimly, floating in the crisp warmth, Ganayeda halted as well, glancing at the open space, pleased to see no vegetation to suggest eavesdropping ears.

"Don't try to look more naive than you are, wild buck. You know very well what I mean, and you know that it's true, too. Your woman is paying for your mischief. Live with that!" He eyed the furious face with a measure of satisfaction, wondering why he felt the need to put the wild thing in his place time after time. Because this brother of his never knew his place? Probably. "Anyway, that's not what I wanted to talk to you about."

"I'll keep a close eye on her, make sure no one gets to needle her or make her upset," Okwaho was saying, his glare rivaling the worst of the thunderstorms. "I don't care what you think, or what thoughts some silly foxes might have been cherishing. I made Kentika my woman, and that is that. They have no say in it and no right to be angry about it. I won't let them make her feel bad anymore!"

"You can't prevent any of it, either. But," bringing his hand up to stop the heated protest, Ganayeda hurried on, "that's what female friendships are for. So leave it to her and the others, those who like her, to solve. Jideah and Mother, for starters. They like her well enough for what she is. Which is a wonder, when it comes to my wife, at least. I don't know why, but she seems to take a true fancy to your girl. Therefore all will be well, and you will get away lightly again, like you always do." More forming protests. He held his palm up. "Forget the women. Tell me what happened last night."

The handsome face clouded all at once. "What do you mean?"

Ganayeda rolled his eyes. "I mean you rushing off to look for your girl straightaway from the mess of the Town Council, gone for the entire evening and half a night. Back briefly in order to drag Father from the rest of the ceremonial activities, both of you gone for the remaining half of that same night." He eyed the blankness of the dark eyes, the stubbornly pressed mouth. "The foreign delegation is gone in an indecent hurry. Your woman is back but sporting a suspicious-looking cut on her arm. Shall I go on?"

The air burst loudly through the widening nostrils, as Okwaho's eyes turned as narrow as two slits. "What are you trying to get at?"

"You know what I'm trying to get at. I want to hear what happened and how it's all connected to Father and what happened at the council meeting."

The handsome face was turning stonier with every passing heartbeat. Ganayeda just grinned.

"The food is getting cold," he commented. "All this tasty stew and the cornballs…" He shrugged. "You know me, Little Brother. Just spill it out, and I'll leave you in peace. After all, I deserve to know what is happening. As much as you do. I want to protect Father and to stand by his side. I'll do it better if I know what happened with the foreigners, what the real trouble was. Why did they leave in a hurry? How were they connected to the filthy accusations of that lowlife Hegweh?"

"Ask Father."

"I will. But I want to hear you first." He sighed. "Unless Father asked you specifically to keep it a secret from me, you should tell me. I'm entitled to know."

The young face was a mirror of indecision. "I'd rather Father talked to you about it. Of course he wouldn't ask me to keep any secrets from you. It's just," the wide forehead creased direfully, "it's just that I stumbled upon some of it by mistake. It wasn't even me but Kentika. You see, she happened to be in some wrong places, to hear things she should not. She saved Father's life yesterday!" The proud spark made the large eyes shine. "Don't look so taken aback. She did this. Ask Father. This girl has more to her than just strange ways and an accented talk."

"How did Father's life come to be in danger in the first place?"

"How else if not by the accursed lowlife Hegweh and some filthy foreigner who didn't know how else to solve his problems than by attempting to shoot at the great leader, and in the middle of the ceremony, too!"

"They tried to do that?" Taken completely by surprise, Ganayeda found himself staring, aghast. "It can't be."

"Yes, I know. They are true lowlifes, the most rotten pieces of human beings." Eyes as dark as the moonless night and as deep, Okwaho drew a loud breath. "Just think about it. I can understand some filthy foreigner going for such low means—Long Tails People must be desperate beggars—but an Onondaga man, a person of our town, a respectable member of the Town Council. Impossible to grasp!"

Yes, reflected Ganayeda, sharing his brother's indignant wonder, his dismayed astonishment at the face of such blatant treachery and low means. But was it true what his girl said? Had she been exaggerating, maybe, misunderstanding much of what she happened to overhear?

"I take it that Father took her warning seriously," he said, trying to show none of his doubt. "It was good of her to do that."

"Her warning?" This time Okwaho laughed, not a light-hearted laughter, but not a gloomy sound, either. "She didn't dare to go to him, and anyway, it was all more complicated. She had her own troubles to face by then. You have to know her to understand that to ask for help or to try to make people listen is not her way of doing things." The large eyes sparkled again, with more pride than before. "She just shot the man who was trying to shoot at Father last night. That's her way of doing things."

"She what?" Again, he found himself staring like a silly boy. "You must be joking."

"I'm not. She can shoot fairly well. I let her practice on our way here. She has a natural gift for handling that bow." The smugness was again radiating from every pore of the broad face, where the paint didn't smear too badly. "Good eye, strong arms, nice coordination between the two. Not your way of shooting all your arrows at once and straight to their targets, not yet, but she has time to learn, hasn't she?"

"Stop making jokes about it!" To stare his brother down didn't work, so he scowled at him, instead. The thought that it actually almost happened, that some lowlife was trying to shoot Father, and under their very noses, hurt almost physically, like the cut in his side, like the thought of Gayeri in the hands of the enemy. "What did Father do about it?"

"Well, there was nothing to do but to hasten the foreigners on

their way, before some of it leaked out and made their stay here
dangerous for them." The young man shrugged. "As for Hegweh,
well, there is no way to prove his involvement. Only Kentika
heard him, and Father doesn't want to have a scandal around it,
especially not now." A gaze that sneaked back toward the feasting
people held untypical thoughtfulness, unfamiliar depth. "Father
will take care of that lowlife. In his own way and his own time.
Trust him to do that."

"Did the Long Tails identify their man? Did they take his body
along?"

A blank gaze was his answer.

"The killer your woman shot, what was done with his body?"

"Oh, that." The young face lost some of its high-flying
confidence. "She didn't kill him, if you mean that. There was no
body. By the time I reached the place where that lowlife
crouched—a great vantage point, I must admit, right there on that
hill," a noncommittal wave indicated the northern slope of the
valley, to the left of the sacred fire. "By the time I got there, the
lowlife had evidently crawled away, leaving a nice trail of blood
behind him. I would have followed and finished the nasty rat off,
but she was in bad shape too, bleeding and crying, and I wanted
to find Father right away." The light shrug held a measure of
defiance, a bit of clear evasiveness. "So no body for you to
desecrate."

"Didn't Father send people to check that hill?"

"No, he didn't. I'm telling you, he didn't want to inform
anyone. There was no need to make a public scandal out of this
thing. Not when he is about to go to Onondaga Town with some
of the issues involved."

"With a scout and a warrior of your caliber, there was no need
to involve anyone. I can't believe you didn't go after the lowlife."
He exhaled loudly. "Not when your girl needed help, but later, at
night, or maybe with dawn. If that rat was wounded badly
enough, you could have caught up with him with no trouble."

The handsome face was closing again, turning to stone, rapidly
at that. "What is done is done."

That was a puzzling reaction. Taken aback, he stared into the defiance of the clouded gaze, knowing that some answers would not be forthcoming.

"There is more to it than you are telling me, Brother." Shrugging, he let the matter rest. For the time being. Until he talked to Father. "Oh well, let us get back to our food before they eat everything worth sinking our teeth into."

The relief that swept over the familiar face was so obvious, he wanted to laugh. Oh, but the young buck still had much to learn, how to control his facial expression being only part of the art of subtlety.

"One last thing." Turning away, he didn't let his gaze wander. "That witness Hegweh threatened to bring, was this the same foreigner?"

Again, his brother's face was a study of blankness. He wanted to laugh.

"Thank you. I wanted to know that."

"Who said there was a witness?" Okwaho cried out, grabbing his hand forcefully, blocking his way with his sudden stop. "I said nothing about that. Father would never betray our people, never do something shabby. You know it as well as I do. How can you think there was a witness to something that never happened?"

Ganayeda freed his arm in a sharp movement, resuming his walk.

"You have much growing up to do yet, Little Brother, much to learn, much to understand." He glanced at Okwaho, who didn't move, standing where he was, bursting with indignation. "I never said Father would do something shabby. He, of all people, has my highest respect and admiration, in addition to the love as a son. But he is a politician, Okwaho. He does things to promote his ends, things that all leaders are forced to do sometimes." The valley spread ahead, a celebration of colors and smells. "He is desperate to make us live at peace with the Crooked Tongues. He would do much to achieve this goal, clandestine meetings and messages being only one of them." Hastening his step, he shrugged. "I don't accuse him of shabby dealings, of not having our people's best interests at heart. I know he is the greatest leader our people could have had. I admire everything he did and does.

But frankly, I'm not with him in his Crooked Tongues mission of peace, not anymore. I will join the first warriors' party that will head across the Great Lake, and I will keep doing this, whether he likes it or not. I have made up my mind. Our Great League is better without these people and with their status set firmly, with no obscurity to it. Not anymore."

"Because of what happened near Lone Hill?" The young man was walking by his side as briskly now, his presence calm, surprisingly thoughtful.

"Yes, because of what happened near Lone Hill." Ganayeda grinned without mirth. "It caused my awakening. It made me see the reality as it is, without the endless admiration to our father clouding my eyes. People make mistakes, even the greatest among them. There will be no peace with the Crooked Tongues, Brother. There can be none."

"Will you go against Father's policies? Will you oppose him in front of everyone?"

"I hope it won't come to that." The clouds of tobacco smoke and the drums were upon them, and the clamor of hundreds of people farther away, eating and talking, happy, content.

Suddenly, he was sorry to lose the briefly gained privacy. Okwaho was proving too good of a company, a worthwhile companion, maybe a partner.

"I hope it won't come to a confrontation, but Father will have to accept that I'm a man on my own, not the promising firstborn to follow in his footsteps. Maybe you will do this for him, the way you seem to be open-minded, fascinated with all sorts of foreigners; the way you have managed to stop that fighting, making even your leaders listen, something your girl was boasting to my wife and our mother about. You've grown into a worthwhile man, Brother, and I'm glad to see that. But, that sets me free, doesn't it? Leaves me to walk my own path."

He held his breath, listening to his own words pouring out in such a free manner, with no forethought and no consideration, he who had always thought everything through. It was good, liberating. It made him feel light and delightfully free, as though a huge weight, one he hadn't even realized he was bearing, had fallen off his shoulders.

Oh, but it was good to do what he wanted, to go with his true desires. A liberation, indeed.

She watched them coming back, walking side by side, two impressively tall, imposing figures, standing out in any crowd, their decorated hair swaying with the breeze.

Where did they go, and why? she wondered, noticing with a measure of satisfaction that while his brother might have been taller and broader, dressed in a strikingly beautiful shirt and decorated leggings, displaying his higher status of a prominent hunter by many armbands and a necklace of bear claws, Okwaho was still much better looking, his shirtless torso glistening in the sun, oiled for the ceremony, his muscled chest on full display, not hidden under cloths or decorations. Oh, but wasn't he the handsomest of them all?

"Not a bad sight, eh?" Her companion's voice made Kentika jump, jerking her back to the sunlit reality of the celebration and the gushing river of feasting people, everyone either seated or strolling around, talking all at once, holding bowls of thick stew or plates of cornballs the women of the Beaver and Deer Clans, responsible for the feast this time, were plucking out of boiling pots. "They are a spectacular pair, those brothers, aren't they?"

"Yes, they good, look good." Smiling shyly, Kentika shifted the bowl she held, balancing it in one hand, the other one resting, the cut in its upper part still hurting, making it sting. "But they come eat now, yes? Good look or not, I no keep more. I eat his food."

Her companion burst into a healthy fit of laughter. "You would do that, I know you would." Balancing her own plate neatly, with no visible effort, even though she again looked very pale, having vomited not very long ago, helped and tended to by Kentika alone, unwilling to let the girls of her longhouse see her in such a state, Jideah shook her head. "We do need to take care of these men of ours, girl, no matter how careless they appear sometimes, how indifferent to the most trivial matters. Like food. They think it gets to their plates all by itself, warm and tasty. They accept this fact of life and pay no attention to it. And annoying as it is, that's what makes them mellow and nice, easily manageable. Try letting him go hungry for one day, try missing that morning or evening or ceremonial meal of his, and you have an irritable baby on your hands, but a baby with the strength of wild bear and no usefulness to it whatsoever. Do you see what I mean? It's easy to hold them in check, to make them behave and do what you want, to provide your compartment, your longhouse, you and your children with everything you need. It demands little from you, just a bit of consideration to his mealtimes, nothing more. Do you understand what I'm saying?"

"Yes, oh yes!"

She didn't manage to catch every word, but the general gist was clear, and enlightening, as efficient as this woman's company was. Safe and pleasant, and oh-so very enriching. No preaching on the proper behavior, like her mother and aunts always did, demanding things she didn't understand, providing no explanation to their demands; no kindly reserved words of wisdom like Okwaho's mother, the woman being so patient and well meaning but not truly warm, not truly friendly. None of this. With Jideah it was all practical advice and gossipy observations that never threatened to turn boring or unwelcome. She was so very chatty, this woman, but in an entertaining way, kind and well meaning, even if in her own spicy, sometimes hurtfully honest manner. It was safe with her and under her protection. No filthy fox seemed to be seeking to anger Jideah, chancing the fall under the lashing of her tongue, not even older women.

"Until the glorious heroes bother to reach us, how about you run behind those trees and fetch my little one. She and her sister should be playing there, with other children."

Not excited by the prospect of leaving just as Okwaho was coming back again, Kentika tried to make the best out of her facial expression. She owed this woman much, the plate in her hand for Okwaho to enjoy being only one thing.

"After men eat we feed children, yes?"

"Yes."

Getting up, she willed her tiredness away. And her impatience. Oh, but how she craved to stay alone with him, to wander somewhere, preferably far, to leave the clamor of the festivities behind. Or at least to run back to the abandoned settlement, curl around herself, and fall asleep for the duration of half a moon or more. Didn't she deserve that after the terrible adventures of the previous day and night?

A group of women from the Heron longhouse, or so it seemed, passed her, approaching her companion, their gazes not unkind. As she went away, she could hear them bursting into a breathless rush, evidently having something of importance to relate.

She didn't pause to listen. The troubles of the Heron Clan were none of her business. Although they might become one day, she reflected, her stomach tickling with excitement. If she decided to apply for this clan's consideration in case they didn't mind adopting new members. With the powerful Jideah's willingness to throw her considerable influence behind her, she had a fair chance at being accepted and treated well.

Unwilling to pass through the worst of the commotion, she turned to her left, circumventing the long arrangement of mats, with many men squatting comfortably, picking at the remnants of their plates, enjoying their after-meal time. By the fires with boiling pots, the clamor was growing again, among the women solely now. It was indeed a good time for Jideah's daughters to be fetched.

"The Great Feather Dance will begin shortly," she heard someone saying, talking in a resounding, authoritative voice. "The faith-keepers should begin getting ready."

That started a movement among the sitting men.

"The Old Woman's Dance will be the last," some were arguing.

"No, the Bean Dance. Three Sisters will be honored before it ends."

Recognizing the speakers of the Wolf Clan's longhouse, Kentika hastened her step. No matter how readily she had been forgiven—with their Clan Mother's active protection how could they not?—the people of this dwelling still made her skin prickle.

The Clan Mother!

Involuntarily, she sought the tall, graceful figure among the crowding women, remembering the dead of the night and them all, gray with fatigue, talking in whispers, huddling outside, near the fence, not in a hurry to enter the town, not until the story—her story—was digested, repeated for details, asked over and over, even the smallest parts of it. Okwaho was talking for her, of course, holding her close, supporting her, as by this time she was weak with exhaustion, barely able to stand at all. Still, her tale had better been told with no eavesdropping ears, not even as a remote possibility.

Shivering, she remembered that moment, that terrible moment when the moon had come out again, illuminating the valley and the killer crouching upon the distant shelf, his bow pointing at the officiating War Chief, unerring. Oh, what a terrible moment it was. And the next few to follow. How did she manage to shoot the man, and from such a distance? Was it her, or were the local spirits empowering her, making her do the right thing? Making her stop the shooting, yet not by killing the man who had been kind to her in his own off-hand, sometimes teasingly light, sometimes matter-of-fact way. The Long Tails man was not all bad.

She had told Okwaho that too, while crying in his arms and letting him check her for more wounds. She didn't remember getting cut in her upper arm too, even though, by that time, it truly hurt. The arrow he had found not far away, obviously the weapon that was responsible for her bleeding, puzzled her as much as it puzzled him. Until he heard the entire story, that is. Then it was back on their feet, rushing madly, trying to reach the opposite hill without crossing the valley and the people busy celebrating there.

That would not do, he had muttered, reassured that her wound was not bleeding seriously enough to make her weak or dizzy. He didn't wish to leave her alone upon that hill again, not even for a short while, and she didn't want to be left. If it meant running more of the nightly countryside, trailing after him this time, then that was that. She could manage.

Oh, but it was tiring, and daunting, this additional climb and the search. What if they found nothing? What if she dreamed that shooter up, having seen barely anything, with the view of him leaping at her out of the darkness? What if, in that moment, her mind had begun to wander from the terrible adventures of the previous day?

Well, reaching the accursed shelf helped. The moon was shining brighter again, disclosing many footsteps, many signs of someone wandering it, changing positions. By that time, Okwaho was as tense as an overstretched bowstring, and as taut.

"Here is where he fell," he whispered excitedly. "Your arrow threw him back quite a few paces. He was tossed like a cornhusk doll!"

The moon attempted again to hide behind the clouds, but he knelt closer, like a wolf on the trail of prints, feeling the earth more than seeing it, eager to find his prey. Or her prey, for that matter.

When he found the bloodied arrow behind the bushes, she had to press her lips tight in order not to groan. The sense of pride at proving her right once again, at the good shot she managed, at the prevented killing, all those refused to reappear. Instead, the stony fist was there, squeezing her stomach. All she could think of was the Long Tails man's strong, pleasantly handsome face twisted with pain, trying to pull the arrow out, trying to crawl away, maybe dying, maybe just hurt.

"Please, Okwaho."

Her whisper barely disturbed the darkness, but he looked up, abandoning the examination of the arrow.

"What?"

His frown was deep, not truly visible, but she knew his expressions by heart.

"No go after man, no chase. Please!"

"What?" This time it came as an open surprise.

She felt her feet tickling, like before a high jump.

"The Long Tails man, he was good, kind, to me. He wounded, maybe dead, maybe to die. We leave alone, not kill, please."

Another loaded silence.

"He kidnapped you!"

"He no kidnap, I told, remember? I spy, he no choice. Others want harm, kill, he say no. I..." She swallowed, her own words ringing in her ears weakly, with no strength to them, and no logic. "He wounded, either dead, or get away, never come back. Never mess here, politics. Not anymore."

Again, the silence. He was studying the arrow, not seeing it, of that she was sure, his shoulders as rigid as the rocky surface they stood upon, silhouetted clearly by the renewed moon. With her head reeling and no more strength to her limbs, it felt better to slide down, to curl around herself and close her eyes.

Even now, in the sunlit reality of the celebration and with the trouble safely over, she shuddered, remembering the all-encompassing exhaustion, the desperation, the feeling of giving up. But for his presence, the strength of his arms, the warmth of his spirit, she would have broken again, or maybe fainted, or cried, or let her mind go blank. It was all too much, everything and everyone. Everything but him.

Shaking her head to get rid of the unsettling memories, she hurried on, eager to reach her destination and get back, to spend some time with him before he went to participate in other dances. The men had taken their time eating, but he had spent most of it talking to his brother.

"Here you are."

By one of the fires, among the most respectable members whose food was clearly served first, Okwaho's mother was smiling, gesturing for her to wait. Fascinated, Kentika watched the spectacular woman making her way through the crowds, even the bowl balanced in her hand looking elegant, as if a part of her festive attire. Her dress was a celebration of purple with its multitude of decorative shells, with a matching band holding her flowing hair in place. No stern pair of braids for such an occasion. The woman intended to dance, that much was obvious.

"Haven't you received your share of food? You must be starving."

The doe-like eyes gazed at her, reserved as always, but friendly, warmer than they ever were. Kentika felt her smile coming out on its own, without the need to be forced.

"I hungry, yes, but go, go fetch girls. Jideah's girls."

"Oh, the little ones? Let me come with you." Falling into her step, steering their way with polite decisiveness, the woman took the lead, in a natural manner. "Where is Jideah?"

"Oh, there, back there. She keep food, for the men. Both our men."

"But she sends you to run around and keep an eye on her girls, even though you are wounded and exhausted." That came out as a less friendly statement. "How is your arm?" The smile was back, reaching the warm eyes.

"Good. No hurt. Well, yes hurt, but little."

The gentle palm was soft on her healthy shoulder, caressing it like the breath of a breeze. "You should rest and let us take care of you. I didn't do a good job of it before, but I will make sure you are taken care of now, feeling at home, truly at home."

Kentika's chest was tightening, constricting in a way that didn't let her say anything in response.

"I don't believe I happened to tell you in person, just the two of us, how grateful I am," the woman went on, her voice no more than a murmur, now that they walked the incline, away from the clamor. "It is not only personal, you see? My husband's life is so very important, to many people, many towns and nations. He has much work to do yet before it is his time to leave it to the others to manage. He is one of our greatest founders, the man without whom the Great Peace might not have been born at all. He brought the Peacemaker to these lands, and he was the one to enable the magnificent vision of this legendary person to blossom into what it became." A sigh. "I can't believe one despicable foreigner and one misguided vile local man wanted him dead!"

"Maybe they not, maybe they didn't..." She wanted to caress the woman's arm in her turn, but dared not. Grateful and dismayed into too much frankness she might be, her current companion still was highly dignified, the leading woman of this town. To do something as intimate touching felt wrong. "Maybe I wrong, maybe that man no shoot War Chief. Maybe he was just, just watching."

"I doubt that." Collecting her senses with an admirable swiftness, the woman bestowed another of her wonderful smiles on Kentika. "You are an exceptional girl. My son was wise to recognize the quality of your spirit. I'm glad he did." The warmth the eyes radiated intensified. "And I'm glad that you chose to follow him here. It wasn't easy, and we still have some work ahead of us, but I promise you full support from now on, a true aid and friendship."

And then, Okwaho's voice caught up with them, his magnificently wide shoulders casting a shadow upon their trail.

"Can I have my wife back, Mother?" he called out, nearing them as they paused, their smiles blossoming.

"Don't you want to eat in peace with your peers, oh, glorious warrior?" asked Kentika's companion, her laughter trilling teasingly, like that of a young girl.

"No, I don't." He beamed back at her, perfectly at ease, his bare chest glittering, its muscles bulging, a magnificent view. She fought the urge to jump into his arms right there, in front of his mother. "I want to enjoy the company of my woman in peace. Can I?" There was a mockingly pleading tone to his words. "Our clan is not responsible for today's ceremonies, and she can't be that irreplaceable, anyway."

"She is irreplaceable enough, but you can have her, you spoiled man. I'll fetch the girls myself," she added, turning back to Kentika, taking her completely by surprise with the mischievousness of her wink. "Go away, you two youngsters. Before anyone notices."

His free arm was already steering her around, the other clutching the plate full of cornballs and the juiciest of meat, still steaming, not the bowl of stew she was saving for him.

"Let her go back and eat first." His mother's voice reached them, vibrating with mirth. "The poor girl is starving."

"We'll share what I have," he said, without turning back.

Falling into his step easily, her tiredness gone with no trace, she breathed the fresh, smoke-free air with enjoyment, feeling lighter then she had in days, since before arriving in this town.

"Where get this? This plate, it's not what I keep for you."

He chuckled. "Yours was cold."

"It take you long, too long, not my fault," she protested, pleased to notice that they didn't proceed uphill but turned deeper into the woods, following an invisible trail only he seemed to see.

"Yes. My nosy brother was trying to fish about the happenings of the last night."

Aghast, she stopped dead in her tracks. "But you no tell, right? No tell what happen?"

"Some of it, yes, I did." His shrug made the plate he carried jump. "He is my brother, our father's son. He is entitled to know."

"But not me, not about me—"

"Don't fret. Nothing you did makes you look bad."

"But…" Hastening her step, she rushed to catch up with him as he didn't stop or slow his pace. "Your father say no tell. He say take care in his time. No make trouble in town. People panic, ruin ceremony, ruin peace talk."

His laughter was light, rolling in the dimness of the grove. "Maybe you don't talk too well as yet, but you certainly understand it all perfectly." Scanning the solidness of the shrugs with his gaze, he chuckled. "Like I said once upon a time, you'll make a great Clan Mother."

"Like your mother?" she asked, absurdly pleased.

"Oh, yes." Beckoning her to follow, he dived into what looked like a solid line of bushes and trees. A short waddling through the prickly corridor, and the prettiest brook she had ever seen was upon them, trickling invitingly in the sunlit celebration of colors, carrying reddish and yellow and orange leaves.

"Oh, Okwaho!"

She didn't dwell on the beauty of this clearing, only on the secluded nature of it. His arms were already taking hold of her shoulders, careful not to brush against the cut upon one of them, his plate miraculously gone.

As a parched traveler starving for a gulp of fresh water, having stumbled upon the clearest of springs, she threw herself against him, heedless of everything, her wound or the possible location of their food no longer mattering in the least, craving his warmth, his touch, the vitality of his love expressed in so many wonderful ways that her senses could not cope with all of them at once.

"You," he was murmuring, his hands busy, but lips still free, brushing against her face, exploring, eager and yet lingering, "I missed you. Missed how you feel. All this energy…"

By then, his murmuring grew inaudible, but she didn't mind, loving what his lips were doing instead, melting against his touch, knowing what he meant about missing the feel of it. Oh, but she had missed the feel of him as much, probably more.

Spent, they lay on the damp ground, their limbs still entwined, breaths caught, hearts racing. The wind was tearing at the treetops, showering the earth and the lovers upon it with colorful beauty, their rustling coverage wonderful, festive enough to celebrate their reunion.

"No, no go, not yet," she whispered, when he shifted, only to make them both more comfortable she discovered, greatly relieved. "I miss, miss feel, like you say. Don't want to go."

He grunted contentedly. "They'll manage without us."

"No go until dark?"

"Maybe until the dawn."

"Yes!" The loudness of her exclamation made them both jump, to laugh wildly and cuddle anew.

"Not eager at all, aren't we?" he said, pressing her tight, hands beginning to wander again.

She busied herself with explorations of her own.

"It was hard for you, wasn't it?" he asked, pausing all of a sudden, raising himself up on his elbow, studying her.

She shrugged.

"I shouldn't have left you so soon."

"Your mother, she wonderful. Kind, very good, beautiful person. She help. Try help. I'm no good women's work, you know. No use. No help. But she try. Give other work." Her peacefulness gone, she looked away, remembering, the first day of the ceremony, and the other days. Oh, how alone she felt then, how useless! But for his mother, and his brother's wife… "Jideah is nice, too. She kind, no talk bad."

"Which is a wonder," he murmured, his frown deep. "She is

not the kindest person around the town." Then his arms pressed her again, making the bad feeling go away. "I will stay around this time. Somehow. Even though ..."

She knew what he was thinking about. In her lands, this was the time for the hunters to go out in force, in large groups, shooting deer and moose, as many species as they could get, smoking the meat, getting ready for the Cold Moons. It couldn't be that different in these lands. He wouldn't be allowed to loiter around his longhouse, making his newly acquired bride feel good and protected. The town authorities would never settle for this.

"Unless," he was saying, as though following her pattern of thoughts. "Unless I'm not around to make me go hunting. Not in the town. Not in High Springs at all."

Now it was her turn to half rise, to peer at him closely, trying to understand.

"What do you think?" He beamed at her, the old mischief back, so delightfully familiar, spilling out of his eyes. "If I'm not around to make me go hunting, then there is nothing they can do about it, can they?"

"I... where... Where you be, where if not around?"

"A journey," he said gravely, his mocking sincerity making her wish to hit him, in no hurtful way. "Spiritual journey maybe, eh? After an entire span of seasons away, after turning into a true warrior one needs to call upon certain places, maybe honor some distant relatives with a visit, eh? In Onondaga Town, or upon the shores of the Great Sparkling Water, or maybe some other places. How would you like to visit all those?"

Her breath caught, she stared at him, afraid to believe it just yet, afraid that she might have understood him wrong.

"No? You wouldn't like that?" His eyes were sparkling with laughter. "Oh, well, it was just an idea."

She hit him with her free elbow. "You no joke? You say we can go, go journey? Like on the way here?" She heard her voice changing, vibrating in a silly way. "You tell honest; you no tease?"

His grin was turning wider with each one of her words. "We don't have to, if you don't want to." Bringing his elbow up against a possible attack, he burst out laughing. "Yes, yes, I no tease. Stop trying to kill me."

"We go away, like journey, journey here."

"Better," he said, catching her free arm, to make sure he was safe, she surmised. "Better because we would value our journey more, would use our brief freedom more wisely." A wink. "To practice shooting, eh, and to fool around, and make more love than on our way here, much more of this pastime you seem to like so much."

"You like too," she protested, struggling against his grip, trying to hold her laughter back. It was trying to erupt, in a wild shriek maybe, to shatter these valleys and hills. Oh, but to journey again, all those wonderful days with him and him alone, no people, no chores, no frowns and demands, just them and the woods, and the sky and the happiness, this all-encompassing elation at being free, truly free.

"We won't have much time," he was muttering, again busy with his hands and lips, having done too much talking to his taste, she knew. "Can't have the Cold Moons catching us out there. But at least half a moon, eh? Maybe ten, twenty dawns. If we are lucky." Helping her climb on top of him, he measured her with his gaze, which was turning deeper, losing its teasing quality. "And if it'll turn out shorter, there are more journeys, more traveling ahead, more running away on our part. After the Cold Moons. We have so much time ahead of us, don't we? Because our true journey has only started."

Making herself comfortable on top of him, she let her desires guide her, tell her what to do, her heart making strange leaps inside her chest, ready to explode with too much happiness. Oh, yes, he was right, wasn't he? Their true journey was only beginning.

"I love, love so much," she said gruffly, unable to control the trembling of her voice. "You are everything, wonderful, the best."

"Better than some stinking foreigner?" he asked, laughing, guiding her with his hands, evidently ready for the new bout of pleasure. Yet something was lurking in the depth of his eyes.

"What?"

"The stinky foreigner," he repeated, his eyes clouding with a frown. "The disgusting piece of rotten meat whom you were ready to shoot but not to kill. Did you fancy him? I bet he was happy to kidnap you when he managed to put his filthy hands on you out there and eavesdropping. He must have fancied you for real."

"I..." The ridiculousness of his accusation made her wish to laugh wildly. "You silly. Speak silly things."

"Am I?" His eyes refused to leave hers, and as she bent to kiss him, his lips remained pressed.

"You silly, so silly."

Instead of growing angry with such unfounded suspicion, or maybe offended, even frightened, she felt the most pleasant glow spreading inside her stomach, a warm, glorious feeling. It took her a heartbeat to understand, but when she did, her confidence spread like a mighty cloak, to wrap around her and make her feel powerful, like the prettiest of women. Could it be that he was jealous, jealous of someone paying attention to her, wishing to go to such lengths as kidnapping her even? Could he value her love so much?

"You talk silly things," she repeated, tossing her head in a manner that made her feel mighty and beautiful. "And if you no stop, I no make love. I go home, back longhouse. Leave and no lovemaking, eh?"

The staring contest lasted for only a heartbeat, as he caught her with both arms, rolling over her easily, despite her struggling to remain on top. Pinning her with his limbs, he stared her down with the most penetrating of gazes, before the reluctant smile dawned, reflecting her own, probably.

"You are mine, woman. Remember that. You are mine forever, and I will not let anyone take you away from me. Don't you ever forget that."

His lips were parting hers forcefully, like back near her village, when she refused to go with him before he admitted his love to her. Back then, she felt childish and silly, but now, oh, now, she knew how wonderful it could be, not fighting the thrilling sensation, the satisfaction of her smile well hidden. All those girls back in High Springs may have fancied him, may have hated her for taking him away from them, but she was a woman too, and not as unattractive as she used to think she was. Men may have wished to make love to her too, to kidnap her even. He knew it now, and she knew it, and the knowledge of it gave her a power like she had never known before.

"I love you," she whispered, giving in to the wonderful sensation. "I want you, only you. Fancy only you. You are mine too. Don't forget, ever."

And then the words disappeared, together with the coldness of the wild and the dimness of the clouded sky, melting in the blissful warmth and the all-powerful sense of belonging. Oh, but they did belong together, two people, turned into one.

AUTHOR'S AFTERWORD

The confederacy of the Five Iroquois Nations was an outstanding political body, an intricate democracy that the world was yet to see anywhere around the globe for quite a few centuries to come. The intricate set of laws that reached for every aspect of life, the complicated system of checks and balances that made sure no nation or individual people gained more power than the others, the direct and indirect involvement of people from every status and stance of the society, the equality of genders, all this and more manifested itself in the creation of the Great Peacemaker who came to these lands maybe as far as eight centuries ago, crossing Lake Ontario, leaving his original people, the Wyandot nations, or Crooked Tongues, as they were referred by the dwellers of the other side. Known to us in many great details, the Great League of the Iroquois keeps drawing the historians' attention.

But what about the other side?

Much less known, the Wyandot People seemed to be divided into four nations, organized in an alliance as well, maybe not as one political body, a confederation with mutual set of laws and closer ties, but like any other alliance, an organization that was designed to meet economical, trading, and probably military needs. It is assumed that this alliance was formed later, much later, maybe as far as the 15th century, but with no concrete evidence pointing either way, it is difficult to determine.

What we seem to know for certain was the fact that both sides of the Great Lake did not get along, even though their ways of life were strikingly similar, even the languages they spoke belonging to the same linguistic group, mutually intelligible, if not fully.

And yet, temporary peace agreements might have been reached over the centuries of co-existence, and this is the possibility I wanted to explore in this and the following novels.

What happened next is presented in the third book of the People of the Longhouse Series, "**Troubled Waters**."

The story continues with

TROUBLED
WATERS

People of the Longhouse, Book 3

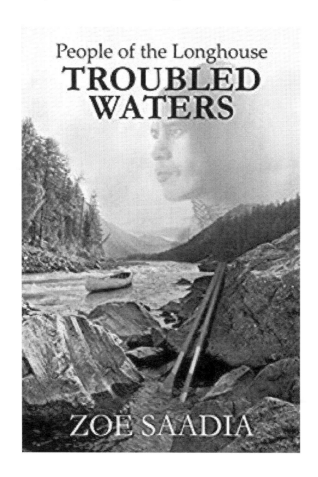

CHAPTER 1

In the lands of the Crooked Tongues

A gust of wind came unexpectedly, sweeping dry leaves that dotted the muddy ground. After the brief spell of rain on the day before, the alleys between the longhouses were slippery, making it difficult to walk.

"Watch it!"

The edges of the folded blanket fluttered, threatening to make the bowl it hosted topple over, spilling its precious contents.

"There is nothing to save there." Catching the woven vessel with one hand, Ogteah grinned, shielding his private treasure with his free palm. If the bowl held less than ten seeds, the pile before him boasted three times that amount. "It can roll away, as far as I'm concerned."

"And so will the pile of your precious winnings," said Seeta, one of his fellow players, grinning, covering his own small collection of seeds, pitiful earnings compared to Ogteah's. "If it goes scattering, maybe you won't look so smug anymore."

Ogteah raised his eyebrows, picking up the throwing stones with pretended indifference.

"Nothing in this pitiful village will make me look humble." His fingers caressed the polished chips, enjoying their touch, feeling them out. Oh, but these stones were on his side. He could feel their warmth. Not the accumulated heat of the hands that held them before, but their own delicately flowing life forces. The stones wished him well. "But I'll enjoy watching you running out of your seeds."

Seeta's raised eyebrows threatened to meet the shaved parts of his hair, right above his forehead. The third player frowned, but said nothing. His eyes were on Ogteah's hands that shook the chips gently, unhurriedly. He listened to their whispering as well. Not yet, they told him; in a little while. He grinned, not in a hurry himself. It was a good feeling.

"*Kahon-ta!*"

Not a single stone rolled outside the folded blanket, spreading around in a neat fashion, as though prearranged. Sporting their black, painted sides, they lay there reflecting the sunlight, with only one unpainted chip still wavering on the edge of the blanket, hesitating. But for this uncooperative one, he would have won twenty seeds, achieving the ultimate throw. Only eight painted chips gave a man the greatest win of the game.

"Guess I won't be collecting what is left right away."

Concealing his disappointment as well as he could, Ogteah reached for the basket. A result of all sides of the same color apart from one, gave him the right to pick four seeds out of the rapidly emptying basket. Still, it was nothing compared to twenty, not to mention the brief fame a lucky throw would give him.

"What? Won't we have the pleasure of hearing you ranting and raving about the unfairness of that stubborn stone, which teased you and promised, but did not fall like its fellow stones did?" Apparently, Seeta was seeing through him quite neatly. Ogteah answered with raised eyebrows of his own.

"Just throw it already." Yeandawa, the third player, did not see the funny side of it. His pile of seeds was so small he could have covered it with one finger. "It takes you moons between each throw, even without you two talking in between."

Shrugging, Ogteah concentrated on the stones, refusing to take offense. None of these people were malicious or hostile. He had lived in this town for some time by now, after arriving here with a group of hunters during the Cold Moons. The snow blizzards came unexpectedly, and then one thing led to another, and here he was, almost three moons later, still enjoying the hospitality of Arontaen, a fairly large settlement upon the Beautiful Lake's shores, where the People of the Cord lived, the enemies of his people once upon a time, but not anymore.

The thought of his people and his hometown made him frown, and he tossed the stones without due preparation, getting three painted as opposed to four unpainted sides. A bad throw that not only left him collecting no additional seeds, but also made him pass his turn to the player on his left, the one who eagerly waited for just that opportunity.

Ogteah shrugged. It was stupid of him to let the past interfere, even merely in his thoughts. Apparently, that was enough to make the good spirits turn their faces away from him.

Pressing his lips, he tried to banish the memories, the busy sprawling town not far away from the windswept bay, two days of sailing from the Great Sparkling Water. The town of his childhood, his youth; a frustrating place. Why was it always so cold, so uptight, so closed and reserved, intolerant of any lightness, any transgression, full of secrets? It stood there between the hills, as though daring the wind and the cold, itself devoid of any warmth, impeccable, not accepting any behavior that was less than perfect. Wary of him.

Well, he had come a long way since the summers of his childhood, a breezy, easygoing boy with not enough strength to resist their will, yet not about to comply, to live up to their expectations. Father's in particular.

He stifled a grunt. By now, Father would be disappointed if he did not disappoint him on this or that matter. The man must have gotten used to it, the bitter reality of his eldest son turning out to be a lightweight, a person with no purpose and no will to do anything of significance. There were enough determined people all around, those who cared, those who wanted to excel, ambitious hunters and warriors, purposeful leaders, bent on changing things, people who made everything work. Just like Father himself, always away, always busy, working hard to create the alliance between the nations of their colder side of the Great Lake.

Towns and villages used to war with each other; the elders never tired talking about it. Instead of fighting the common enemy from across the Great Sparkling Water, they used to raid each other's settlements. It all happened not long ago, before he, Ogteah, was born, and after that, too. His own People of the Bear and the People of the Cord, among whom he now resided, not to mention the Rock People and the Deer ones, they all used to fight and make temporary peace and then break it and fight again; all the while raiding the other side of the Great Lake, but only occasionally, the lands where the real enemy lived.

Now, the other side was populated by true savages, fierce and cruel, sometimes with snakes twisting in their hair, and the terrible feasts on human flesh reported in hushed whispers. The real enemy, who were also divided, and oh, what feats of cruelty they were reaching while fighting everyone and everything. Too terrible to mention, the storytellers were saying. The wild beasts that they were.

Well, wild beasts or not, a short time before he, Ogteah, was born, a prophet came to the vile enemy, a Great Peacemaker, a messenger sent by the Benevolent Spirits to deliver the message of peace. Astonishingly, the beasts listened. The fighting stopped. The other side of the Great Lake calmed down, united in an unbreakable union. Or so they claimed. And people listened. And shivered, and felt threatened. If the enemy was strong before, now it may grow invincible.

What sort of union was it? People didn't know for sure, while those who did kept quiet, thoughtful, sharing nothing, but working hard to unite their own four nations, people of their side of the Lake.

There was no need to fight among each other, Father would always say, when willing to talk privately—a rare occasion. Brother-nations as theirs should live in peace, working together. Just like the people from the other side did.

While most of his countryfolk would call the other side names, the more derogatory the better, Father never did this. He didn't like the enemy any more than anyone else, of that Ogteah was sure. Yet, although brave and fierce, an outstanding hunter and a fearless leader, Father never joined the warriors parties sailing across the Great Lake. Not one single raid.

And worse yet, he made it clear that he didn't wish his eldest son to engage in such warfare. Raid other places, the man would say. Anywhere you want, to the far west and to the east. But not the other side of the Great Sparkling Water, never that. And as much as Ogteah wanted to know why, he never found enough courage to ask straight out. Father was just not that sort of a person, to have a light conversation with. Even his wife, the mother of his other children, Ogteah's three half-siblings, never dared to question the man or to bring the troublesome subjects up. Instead, she would give her stepson dark looks, hinting that it all had to do with him, somehow.

How?

He never dared to ask that either, although he knew the woman might have been right on that. His gut feeling said so.

Maybe if he had known his mother, or at least who she was, to what town, clan, or nation she belonged. The frustration was back, the dull pain in his chest, too familiar, a constant part of his life. Who was the woman who gave him his life? Where did she come from, or where did she go?

She might have been dead, of course, must have been, probably, and yet, even dead people left a print, a memory, a family history, relatives to question, a clan to belong to and enjoy. But not his mother. It was as though she never existed at all, as though Father just had found him, Ogteah, somewhere and brought him home.

Maybe that was really the case. Stranger things happened sometimes, all sorts of mysterious happenings, according to the storytellers. But this was real life, not a story or legend, and he was no prophet. If anything, the complete opposite was true. He was nothing but a lazy good-for-nothing, prone to imprudence and reckless deeds, striving to arrive nowhere, no promising future in store for him.

Such an opposite to Father, but he had given up on the hope of pleasing the man so long ago, he didn't remember if he had ever tried. It was easier to do whatever he liked, to get by with carelessness and the certain amount of charm he knew he possessed in abundance. People used to shrug and forgive him a multitude of his small transgressions, elders and Clan Mothers alike, and later on, girls and women whom he tended to fool around with. Somehow, where others would get scolded or reprimanded, he was let off with rolled eyes and a dismissive wave of a hand. Not a particularly flattering state of affairs, he knew, but a comfortable one. People didn't expect great things from him, but he didn't expect anything of the sort from himself, either. Life was pleasantly light, and why would he complain if its demands were minimal, but its pleasures great?

"Did you fall asleep?"

The laughter of his companions brought Ogteah back to the present, in time to catch the throwing chips that were thrust into his hands in quite an unceremonious manner.

He rubbed his eyes with the back of his hand. "I think I did, yes. My mind went away for a while." Eyeing the basket, he exhaled loudly, counting the beans. "It is still full. I can't believe it. Why don't I just collect them into my pile and be done with it? It's a waste of time to have you throwing those stones."

"Just shut up and play." Seeta's elbow made it toward his ribs, but he paid it no attention, trusting his reactions to block the blow at the last moment. He was always good at that.

The rustling of the wooden chips calmed his nerves, making the memories go away, back into the dark corners where they belonged. The approval of his countryfolk didn't matter. His life was good as it was, especially when living so far away, quite a few days of sail from the uptight town and the disapproval of its dwellers.

Since Yahounk threw him from her longhouse, hysterical and in tears, the entire town had decided that he was no good, even those who used to smile and say that the youth just needed time to find his path. Well, close to thirty summers since being brought to this world, he was no youth, and the brief attempt at taking responsibility toward a woman and a mother of his child, proved what his father always suspected, that he *was* a lightweight, not a worthy person.

"It's good to be here," he muttered, coming out of his reverie a fraction of a heartbeat too late not to say it aloud.

Putting his attention back to the chips, he forced himself to concentrate. Why were the stupid memories attacking him this morning?

"Good, eh?" Yeandawa, another of his fellow players, grinned widely, taunting. "Oh, yes, our people know how to live. Unlike your snotty Bear People, all upright and thinking that they know it all because they raid some fierce savages from across their Great Lake, and those raid them back." The man snorted, beaming. "Some achievement!"

"It's not like that at all." Shrugging, Ogteah tried to put his attention back to the stones. "And they are not snotty." He chuckled. "Just uptight."

They laughed loudly.

"Judging by you, they are anything but." Seeta leaned forward, expecting the throw. "All they care about are games and betting, and some hunting when they get hungry. Nothing more."

"What else is there to care about?" Sensing the right moment, Ogteah opened his palms in one elegant movement, letting their contents out rather than throwing, following them with his gaze. The polished chips spread neatly, arranging themselves in a pretty pattern upon the frame of the blanket, not rolling out, their unpainted sides facing the sky. *All of them the same.*

They exhaled loudly. "What luck!"

He shrugged, pleased but not exalted. All unpainted sides allowed him to collect ten beans, while the painted ones would see him picking twenty. Not that the basket held that much by now.

"I told you I'd better just pour them all into my pile." He tossed one of the beans in the air, then caught it easily. "But you didn't listen. Cord People aren't that good at that, eh? At listening?"

"Would you listen to that one?" A grin and a frown were fighting each other over Yeandawa's atypically broad face. "Careful with your tongue before you are being kicked away, straight back to that snotty town of your uptight Bears."

"I'm careful." Contemplating the pretty picture the unpainted chips presented, not in a hurry to pick them up again, Ogteah grinned, unconcerned. "I'm not going back. Cord People are bearable, all things considering. A violent lot, and lousy at throwing games, but otherwise, they are fine."

This time the elbow managed to reach his ribs. "Watch it."

He just shrugged. It would have made him laugh if someone had told him that he would live so far away, among the people whose numerous villages and towns spread all around, so far to the north that before the unification process had started, his own countryfolk rarely came in contact with those dwellers. No one bothered to travel as far as that Beautiful Lake, not to mention all the way to the Freshwater Sea, neither to raid nor to visit. He didn't happen to see the huge water basin himself as yet, but according to the rumors, it was endless, like the Great Sparkling Water, or maybe even larger. Just to think of it! So far from home. A bliss.

"We will see more of your ugly southern faces in the following days, I predict," said Yeandawa, who was usually a good company but not this morning, being grim and atypically quiet.

"Why?"

"They are going to hold that meeting out there in Ossossane, at the new moon."

"I know that," said Seeta tersely, as though afraid to be caught lacking in knowledge of the local affairs. "Everyone knows that they are going to meet here. That haughty town thinks itself most important, entitled to hold all our meetings there. As though no other settlement can handle such a gathering."

"What sort of gathering is it going to be?" asked Ogteah, perturbed. A major event would have Father involved, traveling to these lands. And then, it would be difficult to avoid the meeting. Unless Father wished to keep clear of such an encounter himself. A possibility, of course. The prominent man might be inclined to save himself the embarrassment. None of the locals knew whose son Ogteah was.

"A serious gathering, both our nations, represented to this or that degree." The young man chuckled, and the shadows cleared from his eyes. "And they hope to get the stubborn Deer People to join this time. Quarrelsome beasts that they are. I hear that the leader of your countryfolk insisted." A glance shot at Ogteah had a provocative quality to it. "He pestered them for long moons, traveling their towns last summer. I'm sure they were tempted to just capture and execute him, make him run on the carpet of glowing embers. If for no other reason, than to make him shut up."

"I wish they had done just that." Choking on his laughter, Yeandawa barely managed not to overturn their bowl of beans, now empty but for three seeds. "We would have to join the furious Bears in their quest for revenge. And I say, I can use the diversion a good raid can provide."

Faking laughter, Ogteah made sure his expression was still one of a mild interest mixed with light boredom. Who was that insistent leader of his people but Father?

"They can't execute our people. We are not at war."

"But there is no official agreement with the annoying Deer, either. And I say, to raid their silly villages should be a pleasure. Deer People are such a nuisance." The youth's handsome face twisted, losing much of its good humor all of a sudden. "People like that leader from your lands are robbing us of the right to become good warriors."

"He wants to unite us; he wants us to be strong." Against his will, he felt the need to defend Father's actions. There was no doubting the fact that Father was a great man. "We used to war on each other, your people and mine too, but isn't it better to be like we are now, friends and brothers, instead of enemies?"

"Oh, this might be good for you." Yeandawa's eyes clouded, lost some of their friendliness. "You don't care about your name as a warrior. You don't care what they say about you."

"What do they say about me?" Straightening up, Ogteah glared at the man across the folded square, not liking to be challenged in this way. He may not care much about his good name, but not to this extent.

"All sorts of things." His companion was not about to back up either. "They barely know you here in Arontaen, and they barely care, not enough to gossip, but it's obvious that you left wherever you lived before for a reason, and that you are not eager to make a great name for yourself over here as well."

"What I am eager to do is not of your filthy interest, and neither is what they say about me, either here or back at home."

The next heartbeat of glaring saw Yeandawa shifting, as though about to get up, his eyes flashing darkly. Ogteah made sure no obstacles were around to prevent him from springing to his feet or evading a possible first blow in any other way.

"Stop bickering, both of you." Seeta did not bother to change his position, or even to look up for that matter. "You are worse than the people you were gossiping about. Speaking of wars and peace agreements." He motioned toward the bowl. "Go on, clean that thing. Whose turn was it, anyway?"

Ogteah unclenched his fist, watching the chips slipping out. "I don't need all this touchiness," he muttered, receiving yet another dark glare.

"Then go on, toss the stones, you passionate player."

For a while they proceeded in silence, none getting worthwhile results.

"Speaking of ill-luck!" Seeta's muttered exclamation came together with the determined footsteps of quite a few pairs of feet.

"What are you doing here, young men? Aren't you supposed to be out, clearing the fields?"

The elderly women Ogteah recognized as the dwellers of the Beaver Clan longhouse that was situated on the other side of the sprawling town, away from the longhouse he resided at, glowered at them, their hands on their hips. Even though those were Yeandawa's family members, having no authority to yell at the men of the other clans, Ogteah and Seeta lowered their gazes.

"I… I didn't know that we were expected at the fields today," muttered Yeandawa, ill at ease.

Frowning more direfully than a thunder cloud, the leading woman just stared at them, stern, uncompromising.

The young man got to his feet. *Later*, his grim expression told them, as he rolled his eyes, turning away, careful to conceal the gesture from the enraged matron.

They grinned back, as careful not to be too obvious about it, the eyes of the authoritative woman still upon them, relaying her displeasure.

"You should be in your clans' fields too," she tossed, turning away with such abruptness that her tightly braided hair swayed.

Her entourage, one older woman and three young girls, lingered for another heartbeat, their curiosity unconcealed. Well, the three of them did, as one of the girls stood at some distance from her companions, studying her undecorated moccasins, instead, tapping an impatient refrain with one of them.

Ogteah narrowed his eyes. There was a strange air of wariness coming from this one, a curious indifference, unusual in such a young girl. Those were always interested in men, weren't they? And also in gossip, an incident of someone caught slacking on his duties being a good exhibition to enjoy and tell every detail to one's peers.

Well, not this one. This girl seemed to be eager to keep as far away as she could.

He eyed her with curiosity. Even though dressed very off-handedly, in an outfit that barely fit, more of a blanket sewn so as not to fall apart than a dress, the girl was obviously very pretty, tall and clearly well built, with all the right curves. Of what he could see about her face—very little, the way she looked down and away—seemed to be a promising sight, the gentle curve of a cheek, the delicately high brow, the severely braided hair thick and shiny in the high morning sun. Her gait had unconscious elegance, a tempting sway, as she walked away, slim and delightfully pliant, her gaze still immersed in what was happening on the ground.

"Poor brother," muttered Seeta, watching the women drawing away, his voice trembling with mirth. "What an unfortunate encounter. My heart bleeds for you."

"You'll be put in the fields as fast," grunted Yeandawa, picking his bets with a certain haste he seemed to be wishing to conceal. "We'll set another game when the sun will be heading for its resting place."

"If they won't find it necessary to send us on more errands and tasks." Frowning, Ogteah scooped the beans up with both hands, his thoughts still on the girl. "I bet there is nothing urgent in the

Beaver Clan's fields this time. Nothing but the inability of its Clan Mothers to see a man doing nothing for one single morning."

"Well, it's not like you've been made to work hard on the day before, or even the one before that." Seeta's rolling laughter seemed to be trying to reach the departing women, unwisely at that. "There is much work to be done in the fields now, young man," he went on, imitating a clan mother's way of talking quite well. "You have to put the needs of the community before your personal wants."

"Shut up." Laughing in spite of himself, Ogteah poured the beans into the bowl, placing the stones alongside, reverently at that. "I may have been lazing around, but Yeandawa wasn't. He just came back with the hunting party last night. He has been working with enough zeal, contributing to the community," in his turn, he pitched his voice high, "doing his duties, lazy male that he is."

"Yes, the foreigner is right. I was busy and working, unlike you two."

"The foreigner, eh? Watch your tongue, young buck. They will want you out there, clearing the fields with your limbs functioning, unbroken."

"How did they stand you in your Bear People's towns?" Not attempting to help with the game's accessories, Seeta bent to pick up his own bets, leaving Ogteah's untouched. "Your Clan Mothers must have been livid."

"They were, sometimes, yes." Collecting his own belongings, a complicated birds' trap he had won in another game a moon or so earlier, or maybe when first arriving here, and a handful of arrowheads, Ogteah shrugged. "They are not too bad, my people. Just too demanding."

"It's no different here." Yeandawa shook his head impatiently, clearly eager to go but still lingering, waiting for them to keep him company on their way back to his side of the town. "And to think that foreigners like you are flooding our towns now, readying for that great gathering your Bear People's leader is eager to thrust upon us. So strange." Yawning showily, the young man made a face. "Although they say, they were prepared to listen to a Bear

People's man once upon a time, many summers ago." The gaze
shot at Ogteah held a fair measure of baiting mischief. "They say
he was quite a man, a mysterious person. They listened to him out
there in Ossossane. He had quite a following, my father says,
there and in some other settlements." His elbow made its way
toward Ogteah's side again. "Maybe we were sent another Bear
man to organize us better, eh? A prophet, a hardened veteran of
throwing games and other ways of betting."

"Oh, yes, you should listen to me. I keep telling you all that."
Stretching, Ogteah moved to catch more of the soft morning sun
upon his skin. It was still too cold, too early into Awakening
Season, to ignore such opportunity. "That man, that prophet, he
could not have come from among my people. Otherwise, they
would have known all about him, what clan he came from, what
town, what family. But no one knows a thing, just that he was a
man with the ability to see beyond the obvious, a man of vision.
Nothing more."

He shrugged, embarrassed by his own agitation. Why should
he care? Just because Father grew edgy when these events were
mentioned didn't mean he had to care about any of it. A
mysterious prophet from somewhere around his lands? No, it
didn't seem to be something of significance, not where he, Ogteah,
was concerned.

"Well, yes, he did not belong anywhere. Of course, he didn't."
Seeta waved his hand in the air, as though pushing an accusation
away. "Do you imagine a messenger of the spirits beyond our
understanding belonging to a town, answerable to his Clan
Mothers? Having a nagging wife maybe, eh?" The tall youth was
trembling with laughter. "That would be the most hilarious thing
to watch. A prophet yelled at by an angry fox."

"Yes, he was a Bear People man," insisted Yeandawa,
hastening his step. "My father traveled there at the time, with
some others who were involved. It happened thirty summers ago,
before any of us had been born. That man, he claimed to be the
messenger of the Great Spirits, but Father says they had their
doubts." He shrugged. "He made them listen, that man. He spoke
well. And he had the strangest following, a mix of everything,

Bear People and our people. But no Deer and no Rock. Oh, and women. Imagine that!" The young man's grin was wide, pleased with their undivided attention. "Women traveling with men, instead of staying at home, minding their own business. Foreigners with dreadful accents."

"What? Women?"

Yeandawa's spiked-up patch of hair jumped with his vigorous nod.

"Captive savages?"

"Maybe. He didn't elaborate on that." He frowned. "Or maybe he did, once. He said one foreign fox was mighty pretty."

This time, they nearly gasped.

"The messenger of the Great Spirits was dragging pretty foxes along?"

"So it seems." The young man's eyes glittered. "Look who is listening avidly, all ears. The wild foreigner, our own today's prophet."

Ogteah shook his head to get rid of the strange feeling. Why was he curious about any of that?

"You tell wild stories. I bet you are making it all up."

"That's how much you know, Southerner." Tossing a fishing spear in the air, one of the bet possessions, Yeandawa snorted. "Don't they teach you anything, tell you stories of the past out there on the shores of your Sparkling Water?"

Seeta's chuckle drifted in the breeze.

"They teach us many things, too many if you ask me." Picking up a stone, Ogteah tossed it toward the nearest pile of roots, to conceal his agitation mainly. Why did they have to bring any of it up? "We do know about this person, this messenger. Not much, but we have heard of him. I wish they would leave us alone, to live in peace, without their politics."

"Well, they are trying to achieve that, the peace. That's what our alliance is supposed to bring us."

"Not to be strong enough to strike the enemy, the true enemy?"

"That too, yes." Yeandawa rolled his eyes.

"For one who was eager to go and fight Deer People only a few heartbeats ago, you get mighty peaceful all of a sudden, Warrior.

Make up your mind."

"My mind is made up, you annoying piece of rotten meat—"

"Not again, you two." Now it was Seeta's turn to roll his eyes. "Just kill each other already, and be done with it. I'm tired of you two bickering over nothing." His shrug was a fleeting affair. "Peace among our people is not a bad thing; we all agree on that, don't we? No need to beat the juices out of each other over how to put it."

"We aren't." Yeandawa shrugged, back in good humor, his chuckle rolling down the alley, attracting the attention of passersby. "But for that precious peace with our neighbors, we would be missing out on some throwing games. Instead, we would be watching our guest running a gauntlet along the carpet of glowing embers. An interesting sight. Maybe we shouldn't have made peace with the Bear People after all."

Ogteah shook his head, not offended any more than his companions were. Since he had arrived here, they had spent much time together, the three of them.

"Unless you are the one doing the test of the fire in one of our towns. Not a bad sight as far as I can envision."

But now it was Seeta's turn to snort. "You are the one pestering Arontaen. No one has seen us nearing your people's towns to tempt them into thinking silly thoughts."

"Some of us have more courage than others, apparently."

"Oh yes, player of throwing games, keep flattering yourself." Measuring the angle of the sun, Yeandawa suppressed a yawn. "I'll make sure to let them in Ossossane know about your desires to reopen some wars, Seeta. If they talk of making peace with the savages, like that Bear People leader thinks we should, we'll make sure they reopen the war against the Bears. At least that. Which should make you happy, enable you to go after our player and take all the things he has won from you so far."

"He may try!" The struggle to push the thoughts of Father away was turning more difficult. "Why do you say that the Bear People's leader wants to make peace with the savages?"

"Because that's what they say he wishes to do." A contemplating gaze of the young man lingered. "Do you know that man, that leader of your people?"

"Maybe."

"Personally?"

Ogteah just shrugged. "Forget it. I can't stand any of it, this gathering you are so eager to attend more than anything. They'll be talking and talking, all those flowery speeches our leaders are so eager to deliver on every occasion, with or without provocation from anyone. They just love listening to themselves."

"He *knows* that leader," commented Seeta, pleased with himself. "Our mysterious guest knows that man, and he is incensed with him, too. Interesting development." The suggestive gaze was upon Ogteah, glittering with mischief again. "Did you run away from your lands because of that man? Is he after you? Will we have to hide you for as long as the Bear People are here and around?"

"No, you won't. Keep that unruly imagination of yours in check. You'll make a good storyteller one day. A good turn for this town."

"Why don't you tell us your story, foreigner, eh?" Nearing the first of the Beaver Clan's longhouses served to cause Yeandawa lower his voice. "Put that one out of his misery. He is bursting with curiosity."

"You are as curious," cried out Seeta, indignant.

"Not as bad as you are. You will be engineering his meeting with that annoying leader the moment you can. I know how your mind works."

The sight of elderly women pouring out of the nearest longhouse's entrance made them hasten their step.

"Who was this young fox among the crones who came to ruin our morning?" asked Ogteah, his thoughts drifting into more pleasant directions. "The one who was dressed badly."

Yeandawa frowned. "What are you talking about?"

"The women who came to fetch you, there was that girl who stood apart, not as nicely dressed as the others."

"Oh, that one." The young man made a face. "She is a foreigner, a savage, or so they say. From across your Sparkling Water, maybe. They don't know for sure."

"How so?"

"I don't know. They found her somewhere there in the woods. In a bad condition. Starved, hurt, nearly dead, they say. I wasn't around at the time. We were busy hunting. It was near the Cold Moons."

"I don't remember anything of the sort," said Seeta. "No savages from that stupid lake of theirs get as far as here."

"Well, they say she is from that far away." Yeandawa shrugged, indifferent. "I never managed to talk to her, though. No one has. She is the most unfriendly thing, doesn't like men, won't talk to any. Our women keep her away. Yosaha protects here as though she is a wolf mother with a cub, as though someone talking to her will do any harm."

Seeta's eyes lit. "Now you made me curious. I may be detouring by your fields sometime this afternoon."

"Don't bother. You won't get to her."

"We'll see."

This time, it was Ogteah's turn to stick his elbow into his companion's ribs. "Someone here evidently needs a wider hunting ground."

But Seeta just sighed. "They are pressing me into making up my mind. Eager to have me settled, you see?"

"The Clan Mother?"

"Not only. My father is anxious and my mother, and the elders of our longhouse. It is as though they got tired of me living in there, selfish people that they are."

"I can understand that." Smirking, Yeandawa turned toward the gaping entrance of the facade. "Enjoy your day, you lazy pieces of meat. Try not to get caught by your own Clan Mothers. Even you, mysterious foreigner."

"I won't. The fearsome matrons have no interest in me. I'm not important enough to warrant their attention."

"You are a strange bird, you know that?" Shifting his possessions into a more comfortable grip, Seeta shook his head. "I always wondered what made you run away from your town and your people." A side glance of the man was piercing, lacking its usual twinkle. "You aren't that young, eh. Were they nagging on you to settle as well? They must have."

Ogteah tried not to let his mood deteriorate once again. "They gave up on me long before that." Hastening his step, he headed toward the alley between the two nearest longhouses. "My town is not missing me, trust me on that."

"But are they looking for you? Are you guilty of some crime you are trying to hide?" His steps wide, Seeta caught up with him easily, not about to give up on the questioning.

"No, nothing like that. They breathed with relief, when I left. Especially my father's family. And one other longhouse, for sure. But no, they are not after me, eager for my blood, if that's what you've been thinking."

"I didn't think that," protested the young man. "I was just curious."

"Well, don't strain your head too much; it may begin to ache." Kicking a round stone out of his way, Ogteah shrugged. "And anyway, women can grow intolerable when you move to live in their compartment, especially if you make them heavy with child. Then you find out what the word 'hag' means. So my advice to you is to enjoy your freedom as long as you can."

"Oh, so you ran away from *that* sort of thing. I see." Seeta's voice peaked with excitement. "Mysterious man from the south. How did we not think of that?"

"Well, don't go around, spreading rumors. I don't need your respectable Clans Mothers frowning at me more than they already do. They'd throw me out if they knew."

"That they would. Well, I'll be off now. Want to hear more about that impending journey to Ossossane. There is no chance I'm missing out on that. They can't make some of us stay, as though we are not as important as some others." A measuring gaze brushed past him, lingering for a heartbeat. "Why don't you come, too? Plenty of your countryfolk will be around that snotty town for sure. The uptight, pushy types that they are, the Bear People will not miss the opportunity to try to lead this gathering."

Ogteah felt like shoving his companion into the muddy puddle they were passing by. "Not for me. You will bring them enough trouble all by yourself."

ABOUT THE AUTHOR

Zoe Saadia is the author of several novels on pre-Columbian Americas. From the architects of the Aztec Empire to the founders of the Iroquois Great League, from the towering pyramids of Tenochtitlan to the longhouses of the Great Lakes, her novels bring long-forgotten history, cultures and people to life, tracing pivotal events that brought about the greatness of North and Mesoamerica.

To learn more about Zoe Saadia and her work, please visit
www.zoesaadia.com

57378962R00201

Made in the USA
Middletown, DE
30 July 2019